"You married her after you kidnapped her?"

Molly bit her lower lip. "But that'll be making no sense."

"Sense? There's no sense here at all." Dirk leaned over her shoulder, his eyes glittering dangerously. "Enough of your lies. *You're* the woman I married, and I think this has all been part of your plan."

"Married?" Molly remembered Ida's comments. Then she searched deeper for the few words she'd overheard between the monster and the . . . *Jesus, Mary, and Joseph.* Ida had mentioned a reverend. All the blood rushed from her face and the flesh around her mouth tingled. Maybe she could manage a bit of a swoon after all. "What have you done?" Her words were barely more than a strangled whisper. "Mother Mary, save us all." She tried again to free her arms, but he held her with very little effort.

"Too late for both of us." The monster's expression softened some, and he licked his lips.

The movement of his tongue sweeping across his full lower lip drew Molly's attention like a candle drew a moth. A queer sensation oozed through her and an odd fluttering commenced in her belly. Low in her belly.

Heat pooled and eddied through her, and she studied his changing expression and the softening of his lips. There was something about the man's mouth. She swallowed hard, reminding herself he was dangerous and was holding her against her will. The man was responsible for Lady Elizabeth's fate.

Dark and dangerous—that was Dirk Ballinger.

Pinnacle and Zebra Books by Deb Stover

Shades of Rose

A Willing Spirit

Some Like It Hotter

Almost an Angel

Another Dawn

Stolen Wishes

A Matter of Trust

A Moment in Time

No Place for a Lady

Published by Kensington Publishing Corp.

NO PLACE FOR A LADY

Deb Stover

ZEBRA BOOKS
Kensington Publishing Corp.
http://www.zebrabooks.com

ZEBRA BOOKS are published by

Kensington Publishing Corp.
850 Third Avenue
New York, NY 10022

All Kensington titles, imprints and distributed lines are available at special quantity discounts for bulk purchases for sales promotion, premiums, fund-raising, educational or institutional use.

Special book excerpts or customized printings can also be created to fit specific needs. For details, write or phone the office of the Kensington Special Sales Manager: Kensington Publishing Corp., 850 Third Avenue, New York, NY 10022. Attn. Special Sales Department. Phone: 1-800-221-2647.

Zebra and the Z logo Reg. U.S. Pat. & TM Off.

First Printing: November 2001
10 9 8 7 6 5 4 3 2 1

Printed in the United States of America

For Dave—my hero since 1976 and forever. . . .

One

London, 1888

A pity Scotland Yard frowned on the practice of strangling one's employer. Molly Riordan couldn't count the number of times she'd struggled against that urge during her eleven years in Lady Elizabeth Summersby's service.

Like today . . .

Lady Elizabeth pressed the back of her hand to her forehead and closed her eyes. "I'm ruined. How could this have happened to *me?*"

Molly gave the sash at her mistress's expanding waistline an extra tug and censored the colorful description she desperately wanted to offer. She could just imagine the horrified expression on the woman's face at hearing her carnal act described in intricate detail.

"The deed's done, my lady," she said quietly. "You'll be married soon." After all, Lady Elizabeth's behavior had been imprudent, at best.

"Don't remind me," Lady Elizabeth said with a delicate shudder. "Well, at least he's rich." She walked away just as Molly finished tying the sash, then turned sideways to view herself in the mirror. "I really didn't think the one time could—would . . ."

"Oh, sometimes it takes only once." Molly gave a dramatic sigh. "You know about the new girl Cook hired, don't you?"

Lady Elizabeth furrowed her usually flawless brow and shot Molly a scathing glare. "Are you suggesting I'm anything like that common—like *her?*"

No, young Annie might be foolish, but at least she *has a heart.* Molly chewed the inside of her cheek. She couldn't place her position at risk, no matter how sweet the truth might taste tripping off her tongue.

"No, my lady." Molly forced a solemn expression— no easy task, considering her true feelings. "Young Annie claimed the bloke never even got it all the way in, and look what happened to—"

"Enough!" Openly horrified, Lady Elizabeth glowered at Molly, then turned her attention back to her rather pale reflection in the mirror. She studied her profile again, patting her abdomen and tilting her head to the side in a thoughtful manner.

Swallowing her grin, Molly placed the silver brush and comb set back on the dressing table and stepped nearer. What had Lady Elizabeth expected? She'd been easily persuaded to enter the rogue's carriage during the party. Of course, duty required Molly remain nearby in the event her mistress needed her for anything. And as compensation for her staunch allegiance, she'd overheard every sound from inside the carriage. She would never forget the way Lady Elizabeth had giggled and carried on while the big American had his way with her.

"It's too big. It won't fit," Lady Elizabeth had cried.

"Yeah, it's fair size, darlin', but we'll make it fit," the American had boasted while Molly remained secreted behind the carriage, stifling her laughter and shock.

She resisted the urge to laugh aloud now as Lady Elizabeth's feeble complaints flashed through her mind anew. Whenever she resented her mistress's imperious air, Molly could summon her memories of that night and feel justice had been served, but only because Lady Elizabeth had been so willing. Had Molly detected any indication the American was forcing Lady Elizabeth into the carriage, her reaction would have been far different, despite her personal dislike for the woman.

No matter how much Lady Elizabeth deserved her fate, Molly couldn't prevent far more than a twinge of remorse. She hadn't been reared to think ill of people, and on occasion she even suspected Lady Elizabeth could be and, perhaps, even *wanted* to be a nice person. Alas, if indeed she had attempted this, Lady Elizabeth had failed. Miserably.

Well, Molly had been true to her upbringing toward everyone she'd ever known, except this one person. If Gram had known Lady Elizabeth, surely even she could forgive Molly this one trespass.

She missed her Gram something fierce. If the old woman had lived a while longer, Molly could have completed her education. She'd be a governess now, rather than a lady's maid. Her training, her proper speech, her personal preferences all pointed in that direction, but again fate had intervened.

Lady Elizabeth's voice intruded on Molly's memories. "The man didn't even have the decency to marry me here."

"It is a great distance, but he sent enough funds for first-class passage, my lady." Molly shrugged, wondering if the American realized what sort of wife he was acquiring for one night's dalliance. Somehow, that seemed unlikely. "Even his lordship seems satisfied Mr. Ballinger is an honorable man."

"Yes, I know. Since Father's lost his money—ah, but never mind that." The woman deftly changed the subject as if every servant in the place didn't already know about his lordship's financial ruin. "I'll never drink champagne again." Lady Elizabeth wrinkled her face in disgust. "A dreadfully dangerous potion. Oh, and the worst part of all . . ."

"Aye, my lady?" Molly forced her expression to remain passive.

"I . . . I can't remember what he looks like."

Feigning shock, Molly covered her mouth again and opened her eyes as wide as possible. "You really don't remember?"

"Oh, I remember . . . *some* things." Lady Elizabeth's face flushed crimson. "It was a costume ball, if you remember, Molly. Everyone was masked."

"Aye, that's true enough." Molly vividly remembered the tall American, with his wavy black hair and a tan leather mask surrounding eyes as green as any she'd ever seen—like the hills of Ireland she so dearly missed. "I don't recall seeing him without his mask either, now that I think of it, my lady."

"He took it off later, but it was dark." Lady Elizabeth reddened even more. "Oh, do tell me, Molly. Does the . . . the child show yet?"

Lady Elizabeth's anxious query made Molly grin again. Taking a deep breath to bring her wicked thoughts under control, she walked over to stand directly behind her mistress, making a great show of inspecting her ladyship's profile in the mirror. "Aye, my lady, I fear it does, but only a trifle."

"Oh, I am truly ruined. Does it really?"

At Molly's solemn nod, Lady Elizabeth gasped. A

truly priceless moment. Guilt prodded Molly, but she forcibly quelled it. All the years of verbal abuse she'd taken from this selfish noblewoman were almost worth the sheer agony she saw flashing through Lady Elizabeth's eyes now. Almost. No, she refused to feel guilty now.

Then why did she?

"You'll be married soon," Molly said simply, battling between guilt and resentment. "What does it matter that the babe will come a few months early?"

"Months, not weeks." Lady Elizabeth turned to stare at her own reflection. "How will I ever explain it?"

"No one here need ever know about the date of the baby's birth, my lady," Molly said quietly, more concerned with the stigma to the child than to Lady Elizabeth.

"But the Americans will know." Lady Elizabeth rolled her eyes and sighed again.

Molly couldn't resist watching her employer's panic-stricken expression in the mirror. As always, Lady Elizabeth's hair was neatly pinned at the nape, while a few tendrils artfully brushed her cheekbones. If one didn't know better, one might believe Lady Elizabeth had conspired for her brown eyes and hair to match. She was beautiful . . . and she knew it.

If only Molly could be as beautiful. Since shortly after her fourteenth birthday, she had served as Lady Elizabeth's personal maid. Eleven years—each and every one pure torture.

'Tis wrong to take pleasure in another's misfortune. Her dear departed Gram's words haunted Molly, layering guilt upon unwanted guilt.

Molly caught a glimpse of herself in the mirror over the bride's shoulder, jarring her back to the present. The contrast between Lady Elizabeth's soft coloring and Molly's raven dark hair and bright blue eyes was startling in such close proximity. She stared for several moments, wondering if she could be beautiful, too.

Stunned by her discovery, Molly smiled, unable to draw her gaze from the mirror before it was too late.

"What are you smirking at, girl?" Lady Elizabeth asked sharply. "Do you find this tragedy amusing?"

"No, my lady," Molly lied, lowering her guilty gaze in an attempt to conceal her true feelings.

"I'd advise you to remember where we're going, Molly Riordan, if you know what's good for you." Lady Elizabeth turned slowly and lifted her chin a notch to glower at her maid, who stood a few inches taller than her mistress. "America," she whispered with a shudder. "We'll probably be scalped before we even reach Mr. Ballinger's ranch. Imagine, *me* living on a . . . a *cattle* ranch. With cows, Molly. *Cows.*"

Which you'll bear a remarkable resemblance to in no time at all. Molly's lips twitched.

Still, their impending journey sounded thrilling, and the thought of seeing America made her toes literally curl in anticipation. This promised to be quite an adventure.

Especially watching her ladyship adjust to being a rancher's wife in the wilds of Colorado.

Of course, Molly had her own selfish reason for wanting to go. Was Da still there? The last letter she'd received had arrived shortly before her grandmother's death. Since entering Lady Elizabeth's service, Molly had received no word at all from Niall Riordan. She didn't even know if he was still alive. But soon she'd have the chance to search for him herself.

Colorado. Just the name of their destination made Molly's blood thrum through her body. She couldn't wait. Was this how her da had felt before embarking on his journey to America? Finally, something exciting was going to happen to Molly Riordan.

And, no doubt, to Lady Elizabeth Summersby.

Molly stared out the coach window, watching the vast, unchanging prairie. It was similar to the ocean they'd recently crossed, where the ship had been surrounded by a perpetual expanse of water.

Here the coach was their ship and the blowing grasses were the rippling waves—a never-ending sea of grass. Everything about this place was so large, so brutal, it made Molly feel vulnerable and filled with reverence.

Of course, Lady Elizabeth was anything but reverent.

"I've never seen so much dirt in my entire life." Lady Elizabeth daintily pressed a lace handkerchief to her nose and leaned back against the seat. "Why on earth couldn't we have taken the train *all* the way?"

"The train doesn't *go* this way. Remember?" How many times would they have to repeat this discussion?

"Well . . ." Lady Elizabeth sniffed and seemed at a total loss for words.

If only she could remain so.

"Mr. Ballinger shouldn't live in such a godforsaken place, then."

Short silence, but sweet. If Molly couldn't have Lady Elizabeth's silence, she'd have her own a while longer. Besides, despite the bumpy ride, she preferred the coach to the train. It wasn't as crowded, nor was it filled with tobacco smoke and soot as the train had been. In fact, only one other passenger shared the dirty coach with them.

The conveyance lurched as it struck another deep

rut. Accustomed by now to being thrown about, Molly braced her feet and gripped the edge of her inadequately padded seat. Lady Elizabeth landed at Molly's feet with an indelicate thud and a screech of dismay. The woman didn't even have enough sense to keep herself on her throne. Shaking her head in resignation, Molly assisted her mistress back to her seat, hoping Lady Elizabeth's clumsiness wouldn't harm the unborn child.

The gentleman sitting across from them obviously knew better than to offer assistance again. His last attempt at such gallantry had been met with one of Lady Elizabeth's brutal tongue-lashings. Now he merely shook his head and looked out the window.

In truth, Lady Elizabeth looked ghastly. Though her belly was now swollen with child, her face was gaunt and drawn. A wave of genuine and persistent compassion swept through Molly. This truly was a bothersome situation for a woman in Lady Elizabeth's condition, and perhaps even dangerous to the babe. As much as Molly wanted to hate Lady Elizabeth, she couldn't. *'Tis a weakness and a curse.*

"This is dreadful. I want to go home." Lady Elizabeth covered her face and wept, certainly not for the first time during their long journey.

"It shouldn't be much longer now, my lady," Molly assured her mistress.

Lady Elizabeth sniffled and nodded, dabbed her eyes with the white handkerchief, then brought it away smudged with dirt. When she glanced back up at Molly, muddy streaks marked the paths of her tears. "I hate this place. I hate all of this." She clenched her jaw and her eyes glittered with bitterness and resentment. "And why didn't Mr. Ballinger come to meet me, or *at least* send a private coach?"

Molly didn't bother to answer. She knew the safest course would be to let Lady Elizabeth vent as long as necessary.

"But most of all," Lady Elizabeth said, a fist clenched in her lap, "I hate that . . . that *man* for doing this to me."

Molly checked her words. She'd been about to remind Lady Elizabeth that Mr. Ballinger hadn't been the only willing participant that night in the carriage. *So much for compassion, Molly.*

"Molly, promise me . . ." A strange desperation entered Lady Elizabeth's voice.

"What is it, my lady?"

Lady Elizabeth gripped Molly's hand and whispered, "If anything happens to me, you'll raise my baby."

Molly wanted to dismiss the woman's plea as foolishness, but something in Lady Elizabeth's expression stayed her. Again, she was struck with the suspicion that this woman was really a decent person deep inside.

Very deep.

"Promise me, Molly. Please?"

"I . . . I promise."

The coach rumbled to a stop before a small square building. Their respites from the constant bouncing were infrequent but precious.

"Water stop only," the driver called. "No services."

Lady Elizabeth started to speak, but clamped her mouth closed and stared straight ahead. Knowing she'd be subjected to another of her employer's tirades if she remained in the coach, Molly studied the driver's kindly, bearded face as he opened the door.

"Might I at least stretch my legs, Mr. Slim?" she asked politely.

Though the tall Irishman had introduced himself as simply Slim, Molly had elected to add "Mister" in deference to his maturity. So far, he hadn't objected. In fact, he'd said Molly's accent reminded him of home. He wore a full beard, and extensive scarring on the left side of his face gave him an almost frightening appearance, though his blue eyes reflected a man with a warm heart.

"Aye." The man nodded and pushed his hat back on his head, dragging his gloved hand across his sweaty brow. "I'll be fetchin' water from yonder creek. You're welcome to tag along, but don't be wanderin' off, 'cuz I haven't the time to come lookin'."

"Of course." Molly should ask her mistress's permission first, but she climbed down from the coach without looking back. A brief respite from Lady Elizabeth now would fortify Molly for the miles to come. She needed that. Desperately. And something about this wild country made Molly crave freedom.

The driver walked quickly, carrying an empty pail in each hand. "I'll only be takin' water to the horses here. There's still enough in the barrel for the rest of us."

Sensing a reply wasn't expected, Molly maintained her silence and marveled at the abundance of small creatures scurrying about. Tiny birds perched on tall blades of grass, singing, and a multitude of insects hopped, crawled, or flew out of her path as she tried to keep up with Mr. Slim.

A stand of trees broke the monotony of the prairie, making Molly draw a deep breath of appreciation. *Blessed shade.* She quickened her pace, passing Mr. Slim in her haste to see and smell water. She'd already learned trees meant water in this savage land.

She saw the sparkle beyond and rushed down the rocky bank, bending to scoop a handful of cool refreshment to her mouth. It tasted clean and cold against her parched lips, easing the dryness in her throat.

"Ah, I reckon now you're seein' why I don't mind fetchin' water at every stop." Mr. Slim chuckled as he imitated her actions, then removed his hat and dipped water into it, dumping it over his head.

Molly smiled at the man and splashed her face, though she wished she could dump an entire hat filled with water over her head, too. Still, even a little was refreshing.

"The barrels are fine when there be nothin' else, but it tastes foul after a bit."

"It does that." Molly rubbed the back of her neck with damp fingers, trying not to moan with pleasure. She looked across the creek and sighed.

Da, are you near? She'd come so far—would she find her da? Was he still alive? Could this kindly, scarred old man know him? There would be no harm in the asking.

Swallowing the lump in her throat, she looked at him. The driver was Irish. Maybe . . . "Mr. Slim, I'm searching for an Irishman. Maybe in your travels you might have met him?"

"Would it be your husband, lass?"

"No. I'm searching for my da."

At her words, he looked up sharply and Molly studied the man's expression, surprised to find an odd glitter in his gentle eyes. "What be your surname, lass?" he asked quietly.

Of course, the stage driver only knew her given name, since the tickets were purchased for Lady Elizabeth and her servant. "Riordan. Have you heard the name, sir?"

He looked down again, and the cords on the side of

his neck tightened. " 'Tis sorry, I am, lass. So very sorry."

Why did she have the feeling he was lying? A strange tingling at the nape of her neck told her so. "As am I," she finally said.

"So ye be searchin' for your da?"

"Aye, but many years have passed since I last heard from him, and I haven't even a likeness of him to show you."

Mr. Slim didn't look at her as he spoke. "Where was he when ye last heard from him?"

"In the mountains seeking his fortune." Molly looked toward the dark smudge on the horizon—the Rocky Mountains. "His last letter came from a place called Serendipity."

Mr. Slim scratched his bearded chin and gazed up at the sky. "Serendipity." After a moment, he shook his head. "I've heard tell of the place, but I fear I can't help ye, lass."

Molly released the breath she'd been holding.

Mr. Slim waded into the stream to dip his pails in deeper water. "That duchess grates on a man."

Sensing Mr. Slim wanted to change the subject, Molly laughed as she straightened, smoothing her skirts. "Aye, Lady Elizabeth can be trying."

A twinkle appeared in his eyes as he waded to the bank with his buckets in tow. "I sure wouldn't want to be triggerin' that one's temper."

"A wise decision." Molly resisted the urge to vent her own frustrations about Lady Elizabeth. That would be inappropriate and, obviously, unnecessary. Guilt crowded her again as she recalled her mistress's discomfort. "Before you tend the horses, could I please have a dipper of fresh water for Lady Elizabeth?"

"Ye be a good girl, Molly Riordan." A wistful expression entered his eyes and he sighed. After a moment, he seemed to shake himself. "Aye, fetch your mistress a dipper." He flashed her a gap-toothed smile. "We'd best be gettin' ba—"

A sharp crack sounded from the direction of the coach.

Mr. Slim froze. The expression on the man's face made Molly's blood turn as icy as the stream. Bewildered by the driver's reaction and her own, she started up the slope.

A woman screamed.

Lady Elizabeth.

Molly's feet felt like lead as she rushed toward the embankment. Mr. Slim yanked her behind a tree, but she peered around it toward the coach.

"Road agents. Highwaymen." Mr. Slim spoke from behind her, his voice quiet and filled with dread. " 'Tis nothin' to do but wait, lass. And pray."

"Wait?" A loud roar began in Molly's ears and she swallowed the lump in her throat. "But we can't just let them—"

"If we rush up there now like fools, we're both good as dead."

Molly met Mr. Slim's gaze; the man was serious. Deadly serious. "But . . ." Her mouth went dry and her heart faltered a beat as she searched for a response. A noble one. The right one.

What would Gram have done?

Another scream rent the air and Molly peered beyond the tree again. She saw the stagecoach, surrounded by strangers. Some of the highwaymen had dismounted and were on foot.

With Lady Elizabeth.

Determination slashed through her, stubborn and Irish. Somehow, she knew what Gram would've done.

Molly thrust out her hand. "I ask you for your weapon, Mr. Slim."

His eyes flashed with surprise, then something resembling pity. She refused to be pitied. "Your weapon, Mr. Slim?" she repeated, louder this time.

"By the saints, lass, but ye remind me of—" He looked away for a few seconds, then faced her with a stern expression. "Hush, or they'll be hearin' ye." Sweat trickled down his face and he shook his head. More gently, he added, "Are ye wantin' to get us both killed, lass?"

She pointed toward the coach. Whistles and shouts from the highwaymen punctuated her statement. "You're letting *them* be killed."

Mr. Slim's eyes narrowed and he shook his head. "No, lass," he repeated, his emphatic tone leaving no room for doubt or argument. "If ye go up there, ye'll be dead, too." Mr. Slim's faded blue eyes glistened. "Yer . . . yer da would want me to protect ye."

He held her gaze, and she saw something in the depths of his eyes that compelled her to remain frozen. He had claimed he didn't know Niall Riordan, yet that had been a lie. She knew that with a certainty that left no doubt. Why?

More shouts sounded and unshed tears burned Molly's eyes as she looked back toward the coach. She would question Mr. Slim again later. Right now, a part of her wanted to rush toward the horrible highwaymen and demand they leave them alone. Yet another, more sane part realized that would do none of them any good. In her heart, she knew Mr. Slim was right.

Mother Mary, help us.

"Get down."

The driver's curt words stunned Molly, but not nearly

so much as the sound of his full pails spilling across the ground, or his rough hand pushing her downward.

"Stay down," he said, pushing her shoulder harder.

Molly dropped to her knees, her cheek pressed against the rough bark of the nearest tree. The berm shielded them from the highwaymen, but by the same token prevented her from seeing the coach as well. She considered rising again, but Mr. Slim's hand remained firmly on her shoulder.

"I have to go up there, but ye stay," he said.

Words froze in Molly's throat as she faced the man who had saved her life. "But—"

"Stay here for your da."

Two

Mr. Slim crawled on his belly, then straightened and darted behind a tree. Molly's heart thundered in her ears. Then she realized the sound she heard wasn't her heart at all. It was something terrifying, growing louder and louder with each thud of her heart.

Hoofbeats.

The highwaymen were riding toward them. Why? They couldn't have seen or heard them from such a great distance. The drumming sounded like hundreds of riders, though Molly knew it was only four, as she'd counted the horses earlier when she looked. Ever onward they came, galloping across the prairie.

Toward them.

"Hold up, boys," a man called.

Molly heard the horses' snorting, their hooves pawing the earth. A few clods of dirt shifted and fell around her.

They were close. Too close.

"Any sign of the driver?" a man asked.

"Chances are he skedaddled when the shootin' started," another man answered.

Molly's gaze sought Mr. Slim, where he stood flattened against a tree, his weapon aimed toward the highwaymen. She knew without reservation that wisdom rather than fear had prevented him from rushing into the fracas to save Lady Elizabeth. Suddenly, Molly re-alized how lucky she was, and muttered a silent prayer of thanks.

If only Lady Elizabeth—

"Unhand me, you filthy—"

"I've already heard enough out of you for one day, woman."

Molly eased herself upward a little until she could count four men on horseback. The nearest one had Lady Elizabeth perched in the saddle in front of him, his arms wrapped tightly around her.

The expression in Lady Elizabeth's eyes was any-thing but passive. Molly's employer was very much alive and in one of her famous snits. *Thank you.*

"I demand you release me at once."

The highwayman chuckled and reached down be-tween himself and Lady Elizabeth. The woman's squeal left no doubt that he'd pinched her. Under other cir-cumstances, Molly might have been amused. Instead, regret sliced through her. She never should have taken pleasure in Lady Elizabeth's misfortune.

Still laughing, the highwayman turned his horse to-ward the bank, gazing out across the stream. Molly inched lower, though for some reason, she couldn't drag her gaze from the man. Sunlight through the trees flashed off the ebony curls that protruded from around the bandanna covering his face. A pair of emerald green eyes sparkled in the dappled sunlight.

"I repeat, I—"

He dealt another pinch to Lady Elizabeth's backside.

"My . . . husband will be outraged when he learns of your abuse."

The highwayman chuckled and shook his head. "Oh, I'm real scared."

"As well you should be." Lady Elizabeth's voice rose to a screech. "Dirk Ballinger will—"

The highwayman grabbed a handful of Lady Elizabeth's collar and jerked her around to face him. "What'd you say?" he demanded, his voice harsh, ominous.

"Let her go," Mr. Slim said as he stepped from behind the tree, his gun aimed at the highwayman's chest. Unfortunately, Lady Elizabeth was between him and the bandit. "Let her go."

"Do yourself a favor and stay out of this, old man." The highwayman chuckled, then he narrowed his gaze. "You try to shoot me, you'll hit her."

Mr. Slim's gun never wavered, but Molly saw his Adam's apple work in his throat. What a brave soul. Her eyes stung and she wished she had a weapon, too.

Then she remembered the expression in his faded eyes when he'd said, *Stay here for your da.* She held her breath, waiting. And praying.

"Don't be a fool. Killin' ain't my way, old man."

One of the other men turned his weapon on Mr. Slim. His movement was so smooth, so practiced, it was almost imperceptible.

But Molly saw. And knew. She brought her knuckles to her mouth and bit down hard. Two guns exploded almost simultaneously. She blinked and focused on the driver's form on the ground, blood staining the front of his shirt. No one else appeared to have been hurt, but Lady Elizabeth was now silent, her eyes wide as she stared at the slain man.

"I told you I didn't want any bloodshed," the leader said, his voice shaking with rage. "Now you've gone and done it, Desperado."

"I recognized the old coot," the man who'd pulled the trigger said, still brandishing his weapon, though not aiming it at anyone in particular. "Couldn't take a chance he might recognize me."

The leader stared at Mr. Slim with genuine regret— not that it would undo the heinous crime. "Shit." With a sigh, he grabbed Lady Elizabeth again and jerked her around to face him. "Now what did you say?"

"I . . . I said my husband will—"

"His *name*."

Molly's guilt magnified, though she silently wished they would all leave so she could help the driver. *Just tell him.*

"Dirk Ballinger."

Two of the other highwaymen whistled low. The one holding Lady Elizabeth released her collar and looked around at his companions. "Well, how about that, boys?"

Laughter without a trace of humor drifted through the group. Sinister and nervous, the sound faded within a few moments.

"Yessirree." The highwayman nudged his horse until it turned away from the bank and back toward the coach. "We got us a real important hostage here, boys. Let's ride."

Hostage? Perhaps that meant they didn't intend to harm Lady Elizabeth. A shudder rippled through Molly and she clenched her fingers into the soft earth. *Leave, leave, leave.* She had to help the man who had saved her life and who knew her da.

The riders finally disappeared in the sea of grass and Molly scrambled over the bank and crawled to Mr. Slim. Tears streamed down her face as she recognized the copious amount of blood spilling from his wound. She opened his shirt to expose his injury, then yanked up her skirt and tore a strip of fabric from her petticoat, pressing it to the gaping hole in his chest.

"Live," she whispered. "By the saints, please live."

He groaned and his eyes fluttered open. "No, lass."

"You . . ."

"Help me . . . to the coach," he whispered, lifting his head and pushing up onto his elbow. "Someone will . . . find us there."

"Don't move," she said, noting the way his bleeding increased when he tried to rise. "Please."

"Must." He rose bit by bit, leaning heavily on her arm for support. "Get . . . me gun."

Molly bent down and retrieved his heavy pistol with one hand, keeping her other wrapped around his waist. Blood seeped around the scrap of fabric and covered them both. Once she had him settled in the coach, she would stop the bleeding.

Let him live. She would worry about Lady Elizabeth later. *Please, just let him live.*

"Other . . . passenger," he whispered, his voice strained as they staggered across the prairie.

His simple words slammed into her and she stumbled, almost falling. She looked toward the coach and saw the man lying face up alongside the coach.

"Saints preserve us," she muttered, and would've crossed herself but for the gun in her hand. Her throat worked, but no more words passed her lips. A single bullet hole marred the man's forehead, obscenely neat considering it had snatched away his life.

Her legs stiff and her body weary, Molly forced herself to practically carry Mr. Slim the last few yards. The horses were gone, and she had no idea where to go for help. With another mighty lurch, the driver landed inside the coach on the floor. Molly climbed in after him, placing the gun on the seat.

She squirmed out of her petticoat. There was almost as much blood on her dress as on Mr. Slim now. With shaking hands, she rended the cotton in two, then folded one large square and pressed it to the injured man's chest.

"There, now," she said with mock cheerfulness, "we'll have that bleeding stopped in no time."

"No, lass," he said, coughing weakly. "The heathen had to kill me, because I know his name. He . . . took something from me. No matter. 'Tis time to meet my Maker."

"Don't be silly." She bit the inside of her cheek, knowing the man spoke the truth—he would not recover. "We'll pray together."

"Tell me . . ."

"What?" She leaned closer. His voice was much weaker now.

"How . . . you came . . . to be here, lass."

His Molly had come to find him. Niall Riordan stared up at his daughter's lovely face. She was the image of his dear, sweet Alanna, who'd been gone from this world since Molly was but a babe.

"The horses are gone," she said. "That's why it's so quiet."

"Aye." He blinked, hoping to keep his vision clear enough to enable him to watch Molly's face until the very end. He'd hungered for the sight of her, and here she was at last.

To watch him die.

What a cruel world, to take his life with his lovely daughter at his side. He coughed again, trying to ignore the powerful burning in his chest. The metallic tinge of his own blood filled his mouth now, and he knew it was only a matter of time before he'd be joining his beloved.

He should tell Molly the truth. She had a right to know. She continued to tirelessly tend his wound, though it would be for naught.

"Tell me," he repeated. "How . . . why . . . you're here, lass."

"Shhh, rest."

"Give a . . . dyin' man his wish," he teased, managing a weak smile. "Please?"

Solemnly, she nodded and told a tale of scandal. He listened intently to the story of Lady Elizabeth's indiscretion with the wealthy rancher, and how neither Ballinger nor the woman could identify the other. A plan formed in Niall's mind and spread to his heart with sweet certainty.

His beautiful Molly had just given him the means to accomplish what he'd been unable to do himself. When he'd come to America, it had been to seek his fortune, so he could raise Molly the way she deserved. He wouldn't be here with her now, but she would be safe and never have to worry about money. His plan would work, too, for surely she would see the wisdom of it after he was gone.

Aye, his plan would work, but only if help came while he still had enough breath to plant the seeds.

Helplessly, Molly watched Mr. Slim's life ebb away. She had to help him. She had to do *something*.

"Jesus, please show me the way," she murmured. The words no sooner left her lips than a shuffling sound came from outside the coach. She glanced up to find one of the stage horses grazing a few feet from the dead man. God must've led it back to her.

She tried not to look at the dead man again, and forced her attention back to the horse. "I must go for help." She eased Mr. Slim's head from her lap and onto the floor. He was barely conscious now, but his eyes opened briefly. "Lie still and I'll bring help."

"No, stay." His voice was so weak now, she barely heard him.

"You need a doctor." Her voice broke, but determination drove her to climb from the coach. *So much blood.* Her hands and arms were streaked with it, and her skirt was completely soaked. It didn't matter. Getting help mattered. She approached the horse slowly and caught the harness, stroking the animal's head and neck.

"I'll wager you're unaccustomed to being ridden," she said gently, remembering someone telling her that horses were also spooked by the smell of blood and death. She would do her best to soothe the beast with words. "That makes us even, as I'm unaccustomed to riding."

The horse seemed gentle and didn't balk when she led it closer to the stage. Molly put her foot on the step and boosted herself onto the beast's back. The horse's flesh quivered and its muscles bunched beneath her.

Then everything happened at once. The animal reared so high she feared it would go all the way over and crush her. Instead, it came down hard on its front legs and bucked, throwing her clear of the coach and flying hooves. Her head struck a rock and her body slammed into the ground. Pain exploded between her temples and throughout her body.

She blinked and her head rolled toward the coach. Its dark shape loomed in the distance, but she couldn't move. She lifted her arm toward the vehicle and Mr. Slim.

Now she couldn't help any of them—Lady Elizabeth, Mr. Slim, or even herself. She wasn't far from the coach, but it seemed a hundred miles to her.

The highwaymen had been thorough with their pillaging and killing. Then she remembered Lady Elizabeth. *Kidnapping, as well.*

Molly blinked, trying to focus on the object hanging haphazardly from the top of the coach. Her head pounded and her vision blurred, then cleared momentarily. "Lady Elizabeth's trunk," she murmured.

She frowned, trying to summon the strength to stand, but the sound of approaching horses jerked her to more urgent matters. "The highwaymen?" she whispered.

Mr. Slim didn't answer, if he'd heard her at all. "Don't die," she said, but he still didn't answer. She swallowed hard, but the tightening in her throat refused to ease.

The sound of approaching riders grew louder, and she could feel the earth rumble beneath her throbbing head. She blinked again as horses circled the stage, pausing to paw the ground.

"Damnation," someone said.

"Slim's inside, but he's bad hurt. That man is dead, and there's a woman over yonder," another man said.

She tried to focus, but her eyes refused to cooperate. Darkness pressed down on her, though she could still hear clearly.

"Well, now we know why Slim was late bringin' in the stage."

"Slim, I thought you was a goner for sure." This man's voice was closer and gentle. "Don't you die, old man."

No, don't die.

"Ain't . . . dead . . . yet."

He's alive. Molly tried to lift her head, but the pain burst behind her eyes and she fell back.

"Easy, miss." A hand touched her shoulder. "Lie still until we get the stage hitched up. What's your name?"

Molly tried to speak, but her mouth wouldn't obey her mind, and an incoherent groan came from her throat. Her vision cleared somewhat and she saw three men. One was at the stage door working on Mr. Slim, and another had his hand on her shoulder.

The third one stood above them. He wore a silver star pinned to a leather vest, the image of illustrations she'd seen in Penny Dreadfuls. The peculiar-looking, yellow-haired man was too late to help them.

"Lovejoy . . . Gang. They took . . . a woman," Mr. Slim whispered, his voice thick and his breath rattling. "This one's . . . maid."

Stunned, Molly struggled to speak. By the saints, why would he tell such a lie? *No, they took Lady Elizabeth,* she screamed silently.

Another man approached them. Tall, lean, and broad-shouldered, he wore a pale blue shirt and a brown leather vest with a matching hat. She squinted, focusing on his face. Green eyes.

Familiar green eyes.

She remembered those eyes surrounded by a mask, months ago at Lady Elizabeth's costume ball. Black hair curled about his collar and she realized another shocking truth. A wave of dizziness swept through her as she stared at him, recalling the events of the past few hours.

This was the second—no, the *third* time in her life she'd seen eyes this particular emerald shade. *Jesus, Mary, and Joseph.* What kind of hideous game was this man playing?

"Well, I guess this makes you Lady Elizabeth," he said in a slow drawl, his thumbs looped through his belt. "We'd best get you home where Doc can get a look at you."

"Lord, look at all that blood," another man said, shaking his head. "It didn't all come from her head wound, Mr. Ballinger."

"No, I suspect not."

Ballinger? Molly had to tell him about Lady Elizabeth, but her parched throat worked silently.

Dirk Ballinger pushed his hat back farther on his head and stooped beside her. There was something lethal about the man's carriage, his casual air, his purpose. . . .

What *was* his purpose? Molly narrowed her eyes and met Mr. Ballinger's gaze. A sinister game was unfolding around her—she felt it. Somehow, she had to solve this mystery in order to save Lady Elizabeth.

Dirk Ballinger's expression remained intense as he studied her, almost as if he were delving into her mind for the truth. Of course, he had to know Mr. Slim was lying. For some heinous reason, he'd kidnapped Lady Elizabeth, and now he was trapped by his own lie.

As was she.

Three

The Lovejoy Gang. Those words set Dirk Ballinger's gut on fire and his teeth on edge. The driver might as well have said the devil himself had kidnapped Lady Elizabeth's maid.

The truth was, Dirk didn't know Lovejoy well enough to guess what the outlaw might do with the woman. Would he rape her and leave her dead in the wilderness?

No. Remembering the short time he'd spent with the man last year, Dirk shook his head. Of course, that didn't mean the rest of the gang wouldn't have their way with her, then sell her to one of the seedier madams in Denver. Neither option was acceptable.

"Men, hitch that horse to the stage," Sheriff Templeton ordered.

"Too late for Slim," the deputy said with a sigh. "Damn shame. Hell, I don't even know his real name."

Clyde Yeager approached Dirk, a grim expression on his gnarled features. As his foreman and best friend, Clyde was the only man alive—besides Lovejoy himself—who knew why Ray Lovejoy's name was the last one Dirk wanted to hear. Not even the family lawyer knew the entire truth.

And Dirk intended to keep it that way.

"We're ready, boss," Clyde said quietly. "You want me to—"

"No. I'll do it." Dirk released a sigh as he knelt beside the woman who would become his bride. He stared at her blood-soaked skirts. If she lived long enough.

He slipped one arm under her knees and the other behind her head, trying not to jostle her too much. There was no way to avoid getting blood on his own clothes. *So be it.* Her bright blue eyes fluttered open, and something akin to terror flashed across her face when she saw him.

Of course, she didn't know who he was yet. She might even believe he was one of the bastards who'd kidnapped her maid and left her here to die.

"It's all right. I'm Dirk Ballinger—your betrothed," he said gently, his face burning with both embarrassment and rage at the man who'd done this to him.

Who'd done this to them all.

None of it was Lady Elizabeth's fault. Well, perhaps back in England she could've resisted temptation a bit more, but Dirk was absolutely certain she'd been thoroughly seduced.

She moaned as he lifted her into his arms, then her inky lashes swept downward and she lost consciousness again. It was for the best. She wouldn't feel the pain of being moved this way.

She was tall for a woman, and her almost black hair against her fair skin was unusual and appealing. In fact, he suspected that once she recovered from this nightmare and regained some color in her cheeks, she would be quite beautiful.

For some reason, he'd expected a short, pudgy woman with plain features—not a tall, striking one. It didn't make sense that such an attractive woman would surrender to a visiting American's charms when she could have had her pick of eligible British noblemen.

"It's a little late to wonder why, Ballinger," he muttered to himself.

He turned toward the stage, Clyde keeping stride alongside him. His foreman held the door open while Dirk climbed carefully inside with his burden.

The other passenger and the driver were stretched out, a worn saddle blanket tossed over their lifeless faces. The sight reminded Dirk of the horrible crimes that had been committed today. "Damn." In comparison, this carnage made what Lovejoy had done to him seem minor.

Drying blood coated the coach floor, making his boots stick as he tried to ignore the sickly stench of blood and death. Gritting his teeth, he settled in the remaining seat with his bride-to-be cradled in his lap, hoping his efforts weren't doing even more damage to her battered body.

His gaze dropped to her belly and his breath caught. He'd almost forgotten about the child. Lady Elizabeth's blood-soaked skirts clung tenaciously to her alarmingly slender form. Where she should've been round . . .

He looked up and met Clyde's clouded expression. "It don't look good, boss," the man said, shaking his head. "She's lost a lot of blood."

Dirk swallowed hard and nodded. "Ride and tell Doc and the preacher to meet us at the ranch," he said, trying not to think about the fate of the child. "And tell Johnny to drive this thing. *Now.*"

Clyde closed the coach door, leaving Dirk alone with the dead and dying. Was the child dead, too? Would Lady Elizabeth also die at the hands of—

He bit the inside of his cheek and forcibly quelled the thought. The irony of the entire, sordid mess was

something only he and Clyde could possibly understand. And his housekeeper, the incredible Ida Jensen.
She'd come to work at the ranch shortly after Edward
Ballinger lost his sight. She'd been there for Dirk
through his adolescence and had helped him grow into
a man when his own father had lost interest.

Following receipt of the letter from Lady Elizabeth's
father, Dirk had been left no choice but to tell Mrs.
Jensen everything. Besides, she'd been present the day
Edward Ballinger's sin had come calling.

"A day from hell and then some," he whispered on
a sigh of regret.

A familiar face appeared at the window. "Ballinger,
we gotta take these men to the undertaker," Templeton
said. "Since town is on the way to your ranch, I figured
we could take the woman to the doctor's office, then
head for the undertaker."

Dirk drew a deep breath and pinned the sheriff with
his gaze. He had general disrespect and little use for
Kevin Templeton, and this time the lawman pushed too
far. Of course, Templeton couldn't have any way of
knowing why it was so important for Dirk to take Lady
Elizabeth directly to the ranch.

"The living come before the dead, Templeton," he
said quietly, but in a tone that could not be mistaken.
"Johnny takes his orders from me, and the doc is meeting us at the ranch. Understood?"

Templeton glanced at the woman in Dirk's lap and
released a ragged sigh. "Yes, sir," the lawman said, a
muscle clenching in his jaw before he turned and strode
away.

Throwing his weight around didn't set well with
Dirk. As owner of the biggest spread in this part of
Colorado, he was by default the most powerful man in
the region. His father had never hesitated to let every

living soul know it, too. However, Dirk could count the occasions he'd used his influence to his advantage on the fingers of one hand.

And he didn't like it—not one bit. It left a bitter taste in his mouth. But this time it was necessary. Transporting Lady Elizabeth to the ranch was crucial. Dirk spared the dead an apologetic glance. Later would suit the deceased just as well as sooner, and he'd already sent word for the doctor to meet them at the ranch. He couldn't take the risk that they might miss him in town.

The coach lurched away from the grisly scene after what seemed like an eternity, and Dirk adjusted his grip on his future bride, settling her weight more fully in his lap to cushion the ride.

"Live," he said quietly, gazing into her pale but serene features. He couldn't very well fulfill his mission if she died before the wedding. Besides, she sure as hell didn't deserve this. He glanced at the dead driver and the other passenger again. No one did.

"Ray, you've gone too far this time." Dirk sighed and gritted his teeth as his pulse thundered in his temples.

Dusty air blew through the coach, far preferable to the stench of blood and death. Riding in the bloody conveyance was like a journey through every man's worst nightmare. Dirk would much rather ride alongside on Cloud, but he couldn't leave Lady Elizabeth unattended. Her condition was too uncertain.

And he didn't know the origin of all this blasted blood. Her head wound wasn't serious enough to have produced such a copious amount. Bile rose in his throat, and he wished for a doctor or midwife who could examine her and confirm his fears. Either way, he would soon know the truth.

Dirk gazed out the window, focusing on the changing scenery. The coach slowed, as the lone horse was unaccustomed to pulling it without an entire team. The climb grew more steep and they passed through a narrow canyon where water trickled down the walls to the creek below.

The Ballinger Ranch began at this canyon, and the sight of his own land strengthened Dirk's resolve that he was doing the right thing. The only thing.

His father had been an honorable man, except for one terrible transgression. Dirk was determined to right that wrong, even though very few people actually knew about Edward Ballinger's most serious mistake. That didn't matter. Dirk knew, and that knowledge had destroyed his memory of the man he'd called father.

Lady Elizabeth groaned and twitched in his arms. She settled again after a moment, and he watched the steady rise and fall of her chest. If her head injury didn't have any lingering effects, it could prove a blessing now by keeping her unconscious and unaware that she might have lost the child.

He drew a steadying breath, releasing it very slowly. Even if the child was dead, Dirk would still marry her. He'd given his word to do the right thing, and do it he would.

Assured that Lady Elizabeth was still very much alive, Dirk turned his attention back to the passing landscape. Cattle and rocky outcroppings dotted the land, still green from the spring thaw even in July. Another month, and the grass would turn brown and the creek would slow. Soon afterward, his men would cull the stock they would drive to market, then the snows would come again.

The continuous cycle of the ranch comforted Dirk. No matter what happened, no matter what his father had done, the land remained unchanged. Untouched. Unsoiled.

He lifted his gaze to the distant peaks that were never completely free of snow. The Ballinger Ranch occupied most of three counties in northern Colorado, butting up against Estes Park on the south and the lofty peaks of the Rockies on the west. The northern edge of the ranch stretched almost to Wyoming.

Dirk had grown up proud of this ranch and proud of the man who'd carved it from the wilderness. Now that pride drove him to do anything necessary to right past wrongs. His destiny had been decided years ago by the man who'd sired him.

Unfortunately, Edward Ballinger had died without making retribution for his sins, and Dirk hadn't learned of his father's fall from grace until after the old man's death. Dirk couldn't change the past, but he could sure as hell ensure that past sins were never repeated in the name of Ballinger.

He gazed down at Lady Elizabeth's still form, his resolve strengthening. She was the key to redemption. "Live," he commanded again.

The sins of his father were *his* cross to bear.

Molly struggled against the heavy cloak of darkness, frightened and helpless. She didn't like being helpless. She'd taken care of herself for most of her life, and now she couldn't. She was dependent upon strangers.

And that was the most terrifying thing of all.

She saw images in the darkness and felt herself being moved again—carried slowly but persistently upward. Her head swirled and she opened her eyes to find the same green gaze peering at her again.

Dirk Ballinger. Where's Lady Elizabeth?

Molly tried to pull herself away, but stabbing pain shot through her head and she ceased her struggle, closing her eyes against the agony and rising nausea. What would this monster do with her? What had he already done with Lady Elizabeth? And *why?* He could have simply refused to marry her. Had he used the marriage as a ruse to lure Lady Elizabeth here so he could kill her?

The pain and fog grew more intense as she felt herself being lowered onto softness. Her aching head protested as she tried again to open her eyes.

She heard voices—a woman and that man, Dirk Ballinger. Then another man joined them and she tried to focus on their words, but their voices were too faint to understand. *Why are they whispering?* She caught only a word here and there, but not enough to determine her fate.

A cool cloth touched her head and she opened her eyes to gaze up at a snowy-haired woman with a kind face. "There, dear," she said gently. "I'm Ida Jensen, and I'll take care of you. The doctor will be along soon. Then we'll get you cleaned up. I don't want to move you any more until he's examined you."

Examined her? Yes, her head. Someone needed to check her head. At least the woman wasn't whispering now, so Molly could hear and grasp her words. She knew instantly that Mrs. Jensen would take care of her. Like many women in Molly's family, this one was a caregiver. Somewhat soothed, she allowed her eyes to drift closed again.

The men continued to whisper near the door, too far away for Molly to hear anything but meaningless murmurs. Molly strained to hear their words and turned her head from one side to the other in frustration.

"Don't move so, dear," Mrs. Jensen said quietly, replacing the cloth with a cooler one. "Dirk, I think you should leave until the doc—"

"Is she awake?"

Dirk Ballinger's voice sliced through the fog. She wanted to answer him, to scream at him, to demand explanations, but thought better of it. She would pretend, for now, that she couldn't hear or speak. The longer she could convince them she was being held prisoner by her own battered body, the more time she would have to devise a plan.

"She's drifting in and out, sir," the woman said, her tone clipped and edged with open disapproval.

Did Mrs. Jensen know that her employer was a kidnapper and a murderer? Would she protect Molly from this man's unknown intentions? And would she help Molly find Lady Elizabeth?

"I can't let her die before . . ."

His words ended on a inaudible murmur as he walked away. Molly groaned again, denying herself the pleasure of voicing her true feelings, though she did reopen her eyes. Pain exploded in her head and she rolled onto her side.

"She *is* awake," Mr. Ballinger said. "Reverend?"

Reverend? Am I dying?

"She's in pain, sir," Mrs. Jensen argued.

"Give her some of that laudanum Doc left for Lance after that fall last month," Mr. Ballinger said.

Molly didn't want the medication, but she swallowed obediently when the spoon was pressed through her lips. To argue would reveal that she was actually quite alert. The bittersweet syrup went down hard and she coughed, which sent bursts of pain through her skull. Groaning for real now, she clutched her head as the men continued to speak in hushed tones.

The drug ebbed through her veins and made the

room spin. She closed her eyes, and her body felt heavy and useless. The pain in her head eased and she felt as if she were floating.

She tried to focus, but the two men were nothing but dark blurs across the room now. Mrs. Jensen bent closer and bathed Molly's face with another cool cloth.

"The fool won't listen to me," Mrs. Jensen said with a sigh. "He doesn't have to do this. None of it is his fault. Heaven save us all."

The men moved closer to the bed, exchanging more words Molly heard, though they didn't make sense to her drugged mind. She could tell from his tone that the other man—the reverend?—was speaking to her, and she tried to respond. She sounded drunk even to her own ears.

Only faint whispers and unintelligible words left her parched throat and she growled in frustration. She would have to wait until the drug wore off before she'd be of any use to herself or Lady Elizabeth.

After a while, the strange man leaned closer to Molly and asked, "Do you understand what just happened here, madam?"

Aye, she understood that Dirk Ballinger and his highwaymen had kidnapped Lady Elizabeth and murdered Mr. Slim. She managed a slight nod and the man straightened.

"Very well," he said, then turned to face Mr. Ballinger again. "It's done, Dirk. I hope you're satisfied."

What was done? Molly drew a deep breath and winced. Her eyes closed again. She had to get well to help Lady Elizabeth. She'd thought ill of the woman, and now she was being punished by not being able to help her.

She heard the door open and the men exchanged more whispered words, then Mrs. Jensen spoke to Mr.

Ballinger in angry tones. Well, at least she could hear *that,* though not clearly enough. Molly strained to listen more carefully, tried to understand, but to no avail. If only they'd stop their cursed whispering.

Her lethargy intensified and her limbs felt so heavy she thought something was on top of her. Blackness swirled around her and she must have slept, though she had no idea for how long.

A soft knock sounded at the door, startling her back to consciousness. Heavy footfalls told Molly that Mr. Ballinger had opened the door. How much time had passed? That laudanum was dangerous. She needed to keep her wits about her.

Another man entered the room. From the sound of his low voice, Molly sensed he was asking questions which Mr. Ballinger and Mrs. Jensen answered.

"Dr. Stein," Mrs. Jensen said as they approached the bed, where she removed the cloth from Molly's forehead, "I'm certain all this blood couldn't have come from this wound."

It's Mr. Slim's blood, spilled because he tried to save Lady Elizabeth. If only Molly could risk saying the words to make them understand.

"I see." The doctor leaned closer, opened each of Molly's eyes, and felt her neck and shoulders. "I agree with your assessment, Mrs. Jensen," he said, straightening. "Once the laudanum wears off, she should be fine." He shifted away and reverted to whispering again. Even so, Molly realized he was speaking to Mr. Ballinger now.

"I'll be just outside the door," Mr. Ballinger said from right beside her, then she heard him leave the room.

"Now, dear," Mrs. Jensen said, moving Molly's legs as she spoke, "Dr. Stein has to examine you. I'll be right here. This is one of the things us womenfolk have to endure because of Eve's foolishness."

What nonsense was this? A moment later, Molly felt the doctor probing her abdomen. She slapped at his hands, but Mrs. Jensen held her fast and the probing continued.

"My . . . head," Molly said clearly, her face flaming with heat at the violation. By the saints, why were they probing her abdomen instead of her head?

"She spoke," Mrs. Jensen said, giving Molly's hands a squeeze. "Will she be all right, doctor?"

"Certainly. The head injury isn't serious." He pulled Molly's skirts down around her and placed his hand on Mrs. Jensen's shoulder.

Molly's vision cleared and she saw that Dr. Stein was a small man with a silver beard. In fact, he resembled a billy goat wearing spectacles. She kept her breathing steady, willing her eyes to remain open and her vision to keep improving.

No more laudanum for Molly Riordan.

The only way she could help Lady Elizabeth would be to regain her wits and keep them. Dr. Stein removed another wretched brown bottle from his bag and gave it to Mrs. Jensen with instructions to give it to the patient for pain and nerves.

Not likely.

He said little else about Molly's condition, then left the room, where Molly heard him speaking to Mr. Ballinger in hushed tones.

"Ah, child," Mrs. Jensen said, "it's a sad, sad day."

What did she mean? Was Lady Elizabeth dead?

The door opened and Molly looked at Dirk Ballinger again, seeing him clearly for the first time since she'd opened her eyes at the stage. His gaze locked with hers and she saw confusion and pity cross his features. He certainly didn't look like a murderer or kidnapper now.

"Dr. Stein says you're going to be just fine," he said, approaching the bed. "Does she know?" He glanced at Mrs. Jensen, who shook her head.

"Know . . . what?" Molly asked, licking her parched lips and trying to push herself into a sitting position. "Lady . . ."

Mrs. Jensen placed a firm hand on Molly's shoulder and pressed her back to the soft featherbed. "Don't try to get up yet, dear." Once Molly settled again, the older woman faced Mr. Ballinger. "I'll need some warm water to bathe her. Will you stay while I fetch it, sir?"

"Only if you'll stop this 'sir' nonsense."

Mrs. Jensen grinned at him and he nodded. Molly wanted to beg Mrs. Jensen not to leave her alone with the man. All she managed was a "no" that went unheeded.

"I'll be back in a bit and we'll get you cleaned up," Mrs. Jensen said. Before Molly could protest, the woman was gone, closing the door behind her.

Molly might be nothing but a lady's maid, but it was still improper for Mr. Ballinger to remain above floors with her unchaperoned. Still, she wasn't in any condition to argue about propriety or anything else at the moment. Besides, he knew where Lady Elizabeth was and Molly would have the truth.

"I'm sorry," he said, sitting on the edge of her bed.

Sorry, are you? Molly bit the inside of her cheek to silence the words she ached to voice.

His expression was gentle and distant. Deceptive. "Dr. Stein says there is no child," he said hurriedly. "You must have lost it when—"

"What?" Molly blinked and tried to rise again, managing to prop herself against the headboard. Her head swam and her belly lurched. She dropped her hand to her middle and grimaced.

"Are you in pain?" Mr. Ballinger asked, reaching for the brown bottle the doctor had left.

"Aye, but I'll be having no more of that," she said carefully, forcing each syllable past her lips. She wanted no more medication that might dull her wits. "My head aches, but that will pass."

He straightened, the brown bottle clutched in his fist. His eyes widened and he looked at her as if she'd grown two heads.

Molly's hand went to the lump on the side of her head. From the size of the thing, she practically *had* grown another head. Her face was probably swollen and discolored, too.

"Your accent." He made a strange sound in the back of his throat and shook his head. "You sound . . . *Irish.*"

"Aye." Molly frowned, but the movement tugged at her scalp and sent pain spiraling through her skull. She clutched her head and said, "I am Irish."

"Forgive me." Mr. Ballinger sighed and folded his arms across his belt. "I expected you to be very, *very* English."

"Well, you expected wrong." Feeling stronger, she straightened even more, glancing down at her blood-soaked clothing. She looked like she'd been in a massacre. Tears stung her eyes. In a way, she had been. "Mr. Slim?"

"Who?" Mr. Ballinger asked, his voice deceptively gentle.

She watched his expression very closely, wondering how far he would carry this ruse. "The driver?" *The man you and your filthy highwaymen murdered.*

A muscle bunched in Mr. Ballinger's square jaw and his green eyes flashed with anger. "Dead."

"You bloody murderer," she whispered.

"I'm sorry, but I didn't hear you." Mr. Ballinger clenched his fists in his lap and narrowed his eyes.

Had he heard her? She couldn't be certain if his reaction was from guilt or confusion. "Nothing." Molly bit her lower lip, reminding herself she was alone here and at this man's mercy. Or lack thereof. Spouting accusations was foolish, to be sure, though she was feeling stronger with every beat of her heart. Except for a bit of wooziness and a throb in her head, she felt well enough to learn the truth now.

"What was it you said about a . . . a child?" Had he meant Lady Elizabeth's babe?

His babe?

"Dr. Stein is gone, and I'm sure he could explain this better than I." Mr. Ballinger tilted his head to one side and rubbed his chin with his thumb. "It seems impossible, but I should ask him if your injury might cause you to speak with an accent."

"What foolish nonsense." Molly glanced at the door, wishing Mrs. Jensen would return. She was anxious to rid herself of her bloody clothing and to begin her search for Lady Elizabeth. "I sound Irish because I am Irish. It's as simple as that. And what was it you said about a child?" Was he deliberately changing the subject?

A shock of dark hair fell across his forehead, giving him a boyish air as he leaned forward. "Your baby," he said gently. "Dr. Stein said there is no child. You must've lost the baby when—"

"What?" Molly's belly roiled and she clutched it again, gulping air and trying to steady herself. "You mean Lady Elizabeth's babe?"

"But you're . . ." He stopped himself and shook his head as if to clear it, then raked his long fingers through his unruly curls. "It must be the head injury. Dr. Stein did say there could be some temporary lapses of memory."

"My memory is just fine." Molly kept her voice steady, forbidding herself from ranting at the man. He didn't seem dangerous now, and Mrs. Jensen would undoubtedly return any moment. Molly waited until Mr. Ballinger looked at her again. Then she pinned him with her gaze.

"What is it?" he asked, leaning closer. "Are you sure you don't want the med—"

"I'm ready to hear what you've done with Lady Elizabeth."

The woman was insane. Either that, or the blow to her head had addled her brain. She was obviously suffering from far more than the memory lapse Dr. Stein had warned him about. Pity the physician had needed to leave so quickly for another case. He'd offered very little explanation about the lost child or anything else. When Dirk had questioned him about Lady Elizabeth's pregnancy, Doc had looked at him as if he'd lost his mind.

Maybe he had.

"There is no child," Doc had said, shaking his head.

Dirk stiffened, reminding himself of his bride's delicate condition. *"You* are Lady Elizabeth," he said gently, hoping to bring her to her senses with simple truth.

"I most certainly—" She stopped in mid sentence and pressed her hands to her flushed cheeks. "Mr. Slim. By the saints, I'm remembering now. He told you . . ."

"Of course, he told us who you are," Dirk said, forcing a smile that probably more closely resembled a grimace. "Maybe you should rest now. Ida will have you bathed and fed soon."

"Don't be patronizing *me,* Mr. Ballinger," she snapped, her perplexing Irish brogue growing thicker with her ire. "I *saw* you."

Dirk frowned, wondering what the hell she was ranting about now. "Saw me where?"

"At . . . at the masquerade ball," she said, her voice barely more than a whisper. Her lower lip trembled slightly, though she kept her accusing gaze locked on his. "And . . . and back there. Don't you be denying what I saw with my own two eyes."

He gnashed his teeth, remembering the correspondence from Lady Elizabeth's father. He'd stated that Lady Elizabeth couldn't physically identify her masked lover, but that she vividly recalled his name. "Your father said he—we—were masked."

"Aye, but I saw your eyes."

Those damned, incriminating Ballinger eyes. *Ray, you've gone too far.*

Dirk closed those eyes for a moment and drew a steadying breath, then faced her again. Except for the purple bruise that had spread to her forehead, she was lovely, especially with fire sparking in her blue, blue eyes. He traced the long, slender column of her throat with his gaze, lingering at the swell of her bosom. And her body was long and lean, with curves in all the right places.

Damn. What am I doing? He shook his head, then forced his gaze back to hers. What difference did it make that she wasn't homely? *None.* He'd done the honorable thing and would live by his decision.

"Back to practical matters . . ."

"Faith! Do you deny you and your highwaymen killed two men and kidnapped Lady Elizabeth?"

Damn you, Ray Lovejoy. Dirk shot to his feet, slamming the brown bottle of laudanum to the nightstand. "I've never committed a crime in my life. How dare you—"

"I dare because it's the bloody truth."

She was completely alert now, sitting at attention, her hair mussed and wild around her oval face, the veins in her throat distended in her rage.

She was magnificent.

"Elizabeth," he began, taking a step toward the bed. "May I call you Elizabeth?"

The expression on her face was one of total incredulity. "You may call me anything you like, Mr. Ballinger," she said, jutting out her chin and folding her arms across her waist, "but I'll not be answering to anything but my own name."

The head injury had definitely taken its toll. First of all, she thought she was Irish. Secondly, she believed he was Ray Lovejoy. The latter was far more disturbing than the former.

"Where the devil is Ida?" He strode to the door and swung it open, shouting for his housekeeper. She called up the stairs, saying the boys were on their way up with the bath water.

Clenching and unclenching his fists, Dirk returned to Lady Elizabeth's side, willing himself to hold his temper in check. "You're not well," he said, focusing on one of the ridiculous flowers on the wallpaper rather than on her face.

"No, I'm not a bit well," she said.

And he knew she was winding up for another of her accusing tirades.

"And since you're not well," he said quickly as she drew in enough air to allow her to rant and rave at length, "we'll delay discussing this, uh, situation further until you are."

"I'll be begging your pardon, Mr. Ballinger, but you'll not be telling Molly Riordan what to do." She swung her legs around and pushed to her feet, clutching her head a moment later as she slumped back to the bed.

He reached for her, but she shrugged him off. "Molly Riordan?" Did people suffering from head injuries create such detailed imaginary identities? *Unlikely.* Besides, Dr. Stein had assured Dirk her head injury was minor and she was suffering more from shock than anything else. Of course, he'd also said there was no child, which meant she'd miscarried. But Dirk didn't have time to analyze anything at the moment. "Call yourself whatever you wish, but Ida and the boys are on their way up here now with water for your bath."

"Good." Lady Elizabeth glanced down at her skirts. "I'm beyond ready to part with . . . this." She looked up again, a lone tear streaming down her cheek. "You did this, but I'll be learning the why of it. And I'll be finding Lady Elizabeth, too. Mark my words."

"You are—" A knock sounded at the door and Dirk abandoned further argument with the beautiful but demented Lady Elizabeth. "Come in."

Ida Jensen shuffled in with a pail of steaming water in each hand, followed by three of his wranglers. One wheeled the copper tub in front of him and the other two carried pails of steaming water. They filled the tub quietly, but Dirk caught their curious glances at Lady Elizabeth. He'd have to make some kind of official announcement soon.

"Dr. Stein didn't say you couldn't have a tub bath," Ida said, shooing the three men out the door, "so I thought it might make you feel better."

"Aye, it would at that."

Ida stared at Lady Elizabeth. "You sound Irish."

"So it seems," Dirk said, shrugging at Ida's questioning gaze.

"I put some broth on to warm," Ida continued, laying out soap and other items. "I'll fetch it up once it's ready."

"I'll bring it myself," Dirk said, eager for an excuse to leave the room. "And I'll send up your trunk."

"My trunk?" Lady Elizabeth frowned. "I remember now. The highwaymen took my things, but not—"

"Never mind that." Dirk held up a hand to stop her before she spouted more nonsense in front of Ida. "I'll leave you to your privacy now. Ida, I'll be visiting Lance if you need me."

"He'll like that," the older woman said, bending to test the temperature of the steaming water.

Dirk reached for the door handle, ignoring the sputtering noises Lady Elizabeth made from the bed. Just as he was about to escape with what remained of his hide, Ida's voice made him freeze.

"Do you need my help with your bath, Mrs. Ballinger?"

Damn. Dirk allowed his head to rest against the edge of the door as the silence ticked by. Then he pushed away and turned to face his bride. Her eyes blazed with rage, and roses had bloomed in her cheeks, contrasting brilliantly with her blue, blue eyes.

She lifted one arm and pointed at him. "I'd marry the devil himself before I'd marry the likes of him."

Ida gasped, and Dirk did the only thing a gentleman could do under these circumstances.

He escaped.

Four

The door closed firmly behind Dirk Ballinger, leaving Molly struggling for breath. Her throat squeezed and her head throbbed. She forced the image of the man's face from her mind and turned to confront the obviously confused Mrs. Jensen.

"I'll be begging your pardon, Mrs. Jensen," she said quietly, "but I'm not *Mrs.* Anyone." Molly drew a deep breath and held it for a soothing second before releasing it very slowly. "Lady Elizabeth will become Mrs. Ballinger . . . once we find her."

"But . . ." Mrs. Jensen held a cloth and a cake of soap in her hands, her expression one of total befuddlement. "I don't understand." She shook her head. "You're Lady Eliz—"

Molly pressed her hands over her ears. "Stop," she pleaded. "I'll not be hearing any more nonsense." She eased her hands away from her ears, studying the older woman's changing face.

My head is all mushy from that bloody drug they fed me. Molly needed to think clearly. She had to. Lady Elizabeth's life depended on it . . . and maybe Molly's, too. *Think, Molly.*

Worry etched itself across Mrs. Jensen's wrinkled brow. "As you wish, Mrs. Ba—"

Molly shook her head and pressed her palms to her

ears again. "No," she said, her voice catching as she struggled against rising panic. She had to proceed carefully, because she needed help in searching for Lady Elizabeth. "I'll be pleased if you'll call me Molly."

"Very well . . . Molly, and please call me Ida." Mrs. Jensen busied herself with the bathing items. "Will you need my assistance . . . ma'am?"

"I've been bathing myself most of my life, and I'm not ready to stop yet." As Molly released the buttons of her stained bodice, a wave of dizziness gripped her. Was it the laudanum or her injury? Or both? She swayed and grabbed the bedpost to steady herself.

Ida slipped her arm around Molly's waist. "Just the same, I'm staying until I have you safely back in bed, young lady."

Molly met the older woman's gaze. That mysterious silent communication women often shared during times of crisis stretched like an invisible thread now between Molly and Ida. Perhaps Ida would be a friend. With Lady Elizabeth, Molly had been an employee. A mere servant.

That's still true, Molly Riordan. Don't you be forgetting it, either.

Even so, Molly knew she'd found a friend in Ida. The woman could prove invaluable once Molly recovered and began her search. "Thank you."

The woman nodded and helped Molly out of her soiled clothing and into the tub. Molly released a ragged sigh as she lowered her aching body into the warm water. Every tortured muscle relaxed as she leaned back against the sloping edge of the copper tub.

Ida busied herself collecting Molly's discarded clothing. "I'm afraid these stains will never come out."

"No doubt. The fabric's not even fit for the rag bin."

Molly peered at the woman from the corner of her eye. "Except maybe my drawers . . . ?"

Ida held that item out in front of her, a puzzled expression on her face. Her eyes widened and her cheeks turned crimson, then she cleared her throat and balled up Molly's undergarments with the other soiled clothing. The older woman didn't meet Molly's gaze as she dropped the bundled clothing near the door.

"Mr. Ballinger had your trunk put in the adjoining dressing room," Ida said, her voice sounding strained. "I'll fetch you some clean clothes and be right back." She hesitated a moment and gave Molly a stern look. "Don't you dare try to get out by yourself."

"I promise." Molly poured a pitcher of water over her head and soaped herself thoroughly. After several rinses, she felt clean at last. The water cooled and she suppressed a shiver. She could wash away the blood from today's nightmare, but never the memory. Closing her eyes, she swallowed the lump in her throat and vowed again to right these terrible wrongs. There was nothing she could do for poor Mr. Slim or the murdered passenger, but Lady Elizabeth might still be alive.

Dear Jesus, please help me find her and make things right again.

"Here we are," Ida said, bustling into the room with various articles of clothing.

"Those don't belong to me," Molly said, recognizing Lady Elizabeth's favorite blue silk dressing gown. How many times had she herself assisted Lady Elizabeth from her bath and into that very garment? Fear and worry returned like a lump of coal to Molly's belly.

"You're just confused right now, dear," Ida said gently, placing the clothing over the back of a chair. "I'll change these sheets, then help you dress. I'm sure Mr. Ballinger will be up with your broth anytime now."

She would have to convince Ida of her true identity later. Right now, she needed to be clothed. The last thing Molly wanted was to be naked and vulnerable when that monster returned. She bit her lower lip, forcing herself to remember that the highwaymen had taken her satchel and left Lady Elizabeth's heavier trunk. She needed clothes, though a silk dressing gown seemed frivolous. For now it would do. Later, she would find something more practical among her employer's wardrobe—something to wear during her search.

A few moments later, Molly was warm and dry . . . and encased in silk that slid like liquid against her skin. The soft blue shimmered in the sunlight that spilled generously through the open window. No wonder Lady Elizabeth always liked silk against her skin. Guilt pressed down on Molly again as she lowered herself into a chair.

She sat there safe and dressed in Lady Elizabeth's clothes, while she had no idea what fate might have befallen her employer. Her throat burned and filled with unshed tears. Blinking them back, she met Ida's solemn expression.

"Are you ready for that broth now, Mrs.—er, Molly."

Molly tilted her head to one side. "Why do you call me Mrs. Ballinger?" she asked with surprising calm. "Even if I were Lady Elizabeth—which I'm not—she hasn't yet married Mr. Ballinger."

Ida's cheeks pinkened and she cleared her throat. "I told him to wait until you were better." She sighed and clicked her tongue in open disapproval. "You don't remember, then?"

"I'm not remembering much of anything since the highwaymen attacked the stage." A shudder rippled through Molly.

"It isn't my place, child. Dirk will have to tell you."

Ida pressed her lips together in a thin line, busying herself with gathering the bathing items. "Will you be all right in that chair for a while, or would you rather climb back into bed?"

Molly lifted her chin a notch, determined to remain upright and less vulnerable when she next confronted Dirk Ballinger. The beast didn't deserve a name. She would think of him from now on as the monster. *Aye, that fits.* "I'll be waiting right where I am, and I'll be just fine. The dizziness seems to have passed now. Thank you for your help, Ida."

"You're very welcome, child." A worried look crossed the woman's face and she released a weary sigh, then wheeled the tub into the hallway and retrieved the other items. She returned once more for the soiled clothing, looking down at the bundle with a frown. "I'll check on you later," she said, then left, closing the door with a click.

A soft knock sounded on the door a few minutes later. "Come in," Molly called, though it seemed strange to invite someone into a room she had no right to occupy, let alone claim as her own.

The door opened and a young man entered, carrying a tray laden with dishes. His head bent over his task and he chewed his lower lip as he balanced the tray, obviously uncertain of his ability to deliver it without spilling its contents.

Molly watched as he bent his knees and slid the tray onto a small table, then straightened and released a breath in a loud whoosh. A low chuckle sounded from the doorway.

The monster stood there, smiling at the young man. "See? What'd I tell you, Lance?" he asked, still smiling.

Molly allowed her gaze to barely skim Dirk Ballin-

ger. The man was far too handsome, and she hated the
way her belly fluttered and her face heated whenever
he looked at her. By the saints, Molly Riordan had more
sense than to let a pretty face turn her head.

Pretty or not, Dirk Ballinger had the eyes of a killer.

Reminded of his role in the day's events, she turned
her attention back to Lance. He was grinning now, obviously proud of his accomplishment. Molly studied
his features for a moment, noting his odd-shaped eyes
and ears, and the slack look of his mouth and jaw. She'd
known a boy like him once back in Ireland, before
Gram's death. Gram had said he was special, though
Molly never knew him well enough to understand why
this was so. The only thing she remembered clearly
was that the boy had been a bit slower than most. From
what she'd seen of Lance, it seemed he shared that trait.

Her gaze darted back to the monster. Watching the
man encourage Lance was incongruous with the
beastly image she remembered so well. She would
never forget the hard glint in those green eyes above
the outlaw mask. Back in England, then again at the
stage, all she'd seen above his mask had been those
eyes. Those unforgettable eyes.

Now, here he stood smiling and encouraging this
special young man. Molly shook her head, more confused than ever.

"Thank you, Dirk," Lance said with an obvious lisp.

"Come, Lance," the monster said, approaching the
boy and patting him on the back. "Let me introduce
you to . . ." An expression of momentary confusion
crossed the man's face. Then he chuckled low. "I'll let
her introduce herself. It'll be safer that way for all of
us."

Molly glowered in his direction, but she held her
tongue for now. Young Lance didn't deserve the words

itching to cross her lips, though the monster would hear them, and more, once they were alone again.

A question flickered across the man's face as he led Lance toward Molly. As much as she wanted to pretend she didn't understand it, Molly couldn't do that. The man had trapped her by placing Lance between them.

Molly would restrain herself. For now.

"This is Lance Jensen," the monster said, his hand still resting protectively on the boy's shoulder. He stood a head and a half taller than Lance, and there was something almost pleading in his expression.

Disconcerted, Molly dragged her gaze from his and extended her hand to Lance. "I'm Molly Riordan, and it's pleased I am to meet you, Lance Jensen," she said. Lance gazed at her proffered hand for a few awkward moments, then took it and continued to stare. Still holding her hand, he finally met her gaze and a huge smile parted his lips. A moment later, he lifted her hand to his lips and kissed it.

He seemed as surprised by the action as Molly. He stared at her with his mouth agape for a few startled moments, then dropped her hand and ran out the door.

"Well, I'll be," the monster said, chuckling.

Molly recovered from her shock and turned her attention back to the monster. "Son of Ida?" she asked.

"Yes." The monster glanced at the tray, pointing to the covered dishes. "There's broth and tea."

Aye, and it smells like a bit of heaven. Silently, Molly pushed herself to her feet, vowing to regain her strength as soon as possible. She took a few steps toward the tray table, but the swimming sensation returned to her head and she swayed into something warm and solid.

The monster.

His arms went about her shoulders to prevent her fall, and she looked up sharply. He perused her with an intensity that stunned her. Questions and something indefinable mingled in the depths of his green eyes, holding her captive for a few startling moments.

His grip was solid and warm; his breath smelled of mint. The dizziness passed and she pushed herself away from his warmth. "I'll be doing this on my own," she said, proceeding toward the nourishment unassisted, though she sensed his presence right behind her. He was so close, in fact, she still felt the heat of him.

Steady, Molly. She drew a deep breath as she reached the chair next to the table and lowered herself into it.

"I could've brought the tray to you," the monster said.

Molly's cheeks warmed, but she didn't look at him. "I'll refresh myself with this, then I'll be having answers to my questions, Mr. Ballinger."

At least a minute of silence ticked by as Molly poured tea and milk into a cup, then added sugar. She didn't offer to pour for him, nor did he ask, though there were two blue china cups with matching saucers on the tray.

"Very well," the monster finally said.

The sound of a chair being dragged across the room prompted Molly to glance at him. He settled himself across the table from her and poured himself a cup of tea, then pushed the broth toward her.

"Eat up," he said, leaning toward her. His nostrils flared slightly and his eyes darkened to emerald. "You're going to need your strength before I'm finished with you."

Dirk appreciated her small gasp. It was about time he regained the upper hand with this crazy woman. Avoiding her gaze, he sipped the tea. "Awful stuff."

He cringed and placed the cup back on the tray. "Can't imagine why anyone would rather have tea than coffee."

He folded his arms across his torso and leaned back in the chair, propping his ankle on the opposite knee. Well, at least he'd managed to silence the woman. Lady Elizabeth Summersby—rather, Ballinger—had one hell of a lot of explaining to do. After Ida had shared her discovery with Dirk, he'd been angry and confused. Now he was more than that.

He was vengeful.

Dirk had no room in his life for liars. He slid a glance in her direction, watching her spoon the broth with trembling fingers. "Is it still warm?" he asked, enjoying the sound of her spoon hitting the tray. "My apologies. I didn't mean to startle you."

Her cheeks reddened and she retrieved the utensil, though she didn't look at him. "Aye."

At least she was consistent with her damned accent. Dirk watched every movement, admiring her poise. She had to know he was staring, yet she spooned every drop of broth between her lips with impressive precision.

He watched the spoon slide from her mouth, followed by the tip of her tongue. She licked a drop of golden liquid from the glistening ripeness of her lower lip. A flash of fire plundered his body, so unexpected and powerful he nearly groaned aloud.

He grew hard so fast he would've passed out if he'd been standing. But he *never* reacted this way. Never. He was always in control, never drawn in the wrong direction at the wrong time. Or to the wrong woman.

Until now.

The shock of his sudden arousal made it all the more potent, and he carefully steadied his breathing as he continued to watch her every movement. The spoon went repeatedly to her mouth, past her ruby lips, and he imagined the broth sliding over the smoothness of her tongue. Then he followed the long slender column of her throat as she swallowed. Damp tendrils of black hair curled around her face and clung to her neck. When completely dry, her hair would shine and curl wildly if unconfined.

She reached for her tea and he watched the fall of silk across her breast. Her nipple stood out proud and prominent against the fabric. Good Lord, was the woman naked beneath the shimmery blue dressing gown?

His ability to breathe became downright questionable as Dirk struggled against the onslaught of bewildering yet undeniable lust. He was hornier than a bull at first frost.

And the object of his lust was a liar and, perhaps, worse. Was she in cahoots with Lovejoy? Had this entire sordid series of events been a carefully calculated deception of the gullible and laughably honorable Dirk Ballinger?

Anger dampened his carnal thoughts and Dirk drew a steadying breath, crossing his hands in front of the prominent bulge at the front of his trousers. He might find the woman attractive—who wouldn't?—but that didn't mitigate the fact that she'd deceived him into . . .

"Damn." A sinking sensation pressed down on him. *I'm married to the woman.*

He met her gaze and fury obliterated every shred of lust. Good. Anger would help him get to the truth. Lust would only distract him.

She placed her cup on the tray and folded her hands in her lap, her vivid blue eyes intent as she cleared her throat. "I'm feeling much stronger now," she said steadily, her gaze unwavering. "Now I'll be having the truth, Mr. Ballinger."

Fury whipped through him. His booted foot hit the floor with a loud thud, then he leaned toward her. "That makes two of us, *Mrs.* Ballinger."

She stiffened, obviously taken aback by his words. Blinking rapidly, she appeared flustered, then drew a deep breath that thrust her voluptuous breasts toward him. Deliberately, no doubt. Well, it wouldn't work this time. He wouldn't allow it.

"Don't bother trying that game with me," he said.

"Game?" She shook her head and her expression seemed sincere. Then anger flashed through her eyes and the woman he'd dealt with earlier returned with a vengeance.

"Drop the ruse, lady. Come clean now, and maybe I won't involve the law."

"I beg your pardon," she said, stiffening. Her voice grew louder with each syllable. "I'm not understanding your nonsense at all. If anyone has been playing a game or ruse here, it would be you with your masks and highwaymen and *seduction of innocents.*"

Dirk studied her for a moment, then put his hands together and applauded. "Brava, my dear."

She glowered.

"Excellent performance." He rose, towering over her. He needed to hear the truth. Violence didn't suit him, but frightening her might be his only hope. He reached down and grabbed her wrists, jerking her to her feet. She struggled against him, and he wrapped his arms around her arms and body like a vise. "Now *I'll* have the truth," he whispered.

She tilted her head back to meet his gaze. Daggers practically flew from her eyes. The woman was in an impressive temper.

"The truth," he repeated, leaning closer.

She stood before him, her eyes blazing with outrage, her nostrils flaring with indignation. She was trapped. Vulnerable. He couldn't help noticing her lush breasts molding against his chest, and his gaze dipped to the generous curves showing above the neckline of her dressing gown.

Incredible.

Until she sank her sharp little teeth into his shoulder.

"Yeow!"

Molly couldn't prevent her smirk of victory as she wrenched herself free and moved so the tray table was strategically between herself and the now thoroughly outraged monster.

With one hand clutching his injured shoulder, he lunged for her with the other. The table tipped, sending the tray and its entire contents crashing to the floor. China splintered and the silver tea service provided a metallic percussion.

"You little she-devil," he said, maneuvering himself around the mess on the floor. "Why, I ought to—"

An urgent knocking sounded at the door. Molly crossed herself, giving silent thanks for the interruption. The monster had murder in his eyes, and this time *she* was his intended victim.

"Go away," he barked.

"Sir, is everything all right?" Ida called through the door. "I heard a crash."

Molly heard the doorknob rattle and realized the monster had locked it without her knowledge. She darted a glance at the door to the dressing room, noting it stood slightly ajar. If she could make her way there, she could slam and bolt the door from the other side.

"Go away, Ida," the monster said more calmly, dragging ragged breaths as he continued to stalk Molly. "This is between me and my . . . wife."

Molly resisted the urge to correct him. His attention was diverted at the moment, and she intended to keep it that way. She inched around the upset tray, stepping gingerly over fractured cups and saucers.

"Very well, sir," Ida said.

If only the woman would keep talking a bit longer. Molly knew the monster's attention would revert to her now, so she did the only intelligent thing a woman in her situation could do.

She bolted.

The monster's arm encircled her waist and hauled her back against the unyielding wall of his chest. His hot breath scorched the back of her neck, and the pressure of his arm against her abdomen made it impossible to completely fill her lungs.

"I'll have the truth now, even if I have to tie and gag you," he said.

"I . . . I can't breathe." Pity she wasn't the type to faint easily. Now would certainly be an opportune moment for such strategy. Lady Elizabeth would've done so, and with style.

Amazingly, he loosened his hold just enough to allow her to draw a deep breath. "Release me," she said, hoping.

"No." A menacing chuckle filled her ears as he dragged her toward the looking glass in the corner. He pivoted until she faced the mirror with him towering over her from behind. "I want to see your face. I want to watch your eyes when you lie to me again."

"I never lie."

He tightened his hold again. "The hell you don't."

"Please . . . let me breathe." His arm about her waist

forced her bosom into prominence against the fragile silk of Lady Elizabeth's dressing gown. Why, it was positively indecent.

He eased his grip again, just enough to enable her to breathe. Molly shifted slightly, testing whether or not she might free herself. Defeated, she released a long sigh. "I never lie," she repeated. "Why do you believe I've lied when *you're* the one who led the highwaymen and kidnapped Lady Elizabeth?" She met his reflected gaze.

His eyes were hard. His expression was hard. Everything about him was hard. *Faith.*

"I *never* lie," he repeated, his lips barely moving. "If neither of us has lied, then we have a serious problem here."

"Aye, I'll be granting you that." Of course, Molly knew he'd lied, though the expression in his eyes argued the opposite. "All I know is that Lady Elizabeth is missing, and I must find her."

"And all I know is I married the woman who *claimed* to be carrying my child."

Molly's cheeks warmed at his plain talk. "Lady Elizabeth is missing. She *is* carrying your babe," she repeated, searching his eyes for any clue to his motives or the truth. "How could you have married her when she isn't here? Unless . . ."

"Unless what?"

"You married her after you kidnapped her?" Molly bit her lower lip. "But that'll be making no sense."

"Sense? There's no sense here at all." He leaned over her shoulder, his eyes glittering dangerously. "Enough of your lies. *You're* the woman I married, and I think this has all been part of your plan."

"Married?" Molly remembered Ida's comments. Then she searched deeper for the few words she'd overheard between the monster and the . . . *Jesus, Mary, and Joseph.* Ida had mentioned a reverend. All the blood rushed from her face and the flesh around her mouth tingled. Maybe she could manage a bit of a swoon after all. "What have you done?" Her words were barely more than a strangled whisper. "Mother Mary, save us all." She tried again to free her arms, but he held her with very little effort.

"Too late for both of us." The monster's expression softened some, and he licked his lips.

The movement of his tongue sweeping across his full lower lip drew Molly's attention like a candle drew a moth. A queer sensation oozed through her, and an odd fluttering commenced in her belly. Low in her belly.

Heat pooled and eddied through her as she studied his changing expression and the softening of his lips. There was something about the man's mouth. She swallowed hard, reminding herself he was dangerous and holding her against her will. The man was responsible for Lady Elizabeth's fate.

Dark and dangerous—that was Dirk Ballinger.

Yet he wasn't. Not really. *Jesus help me, but he doesn't seem like a monster.*

But instead of the logic for which she prayed, a wickedness stole through her, a burning need to touch and be touched. Was this the core of it all? she wondered. Was this the feeling that prompted women to fall at men's feet? Was this why Lady Elizabeth had followed this dangerous man into the coach so many months ago?

By the saints, was Molly Riordan becoming a wanton? "Jesus, Mary, and Joseph."

"They aren't here," the monster whispered just before his tongue traced the whorls of her ear.

Molly melted. If not for the steel band of his arm, she'd be nothing but a puddle at his feet. Something very strange commenced inside her. She'd never felt this way before, so lost, so out of control.

So . . . needful.

A sane, logical corner of her mind told her she could use this to her advantage. If he dropped his guard enough, she could break away. *Aye, that's it, Molly.*

He drew breath against the flesh he'd just dampened, sending a quiver through her that had nothing to do with the temperature of the room. He nibbled the lobe of her ear, kissing his way down the side of her neck to the curve of her shoulder, where the dressing gown left her tender flesh exposed. Vulnerable.

He moaned, pressing himself against her from behind. The large bulge at the front of his trousers rubbed intimately against her buttocks, making her feel hot and empty and hungry.

Aye, hungry. He made her hungry for something she couldn't begin to comprehend, something she'd never experienced before. He traced the top of her shoulder with his tongue, shoving the silk down her arm, baring more of her to his will.

"Sweet," he murmured, nuzzling her.

Molly stared at their reflection, awed by the sight of this strong and handsome man having his way with her. Oh, and what a way he had! A sigh slipped from between her lips and she leaned back against him, her head resting against his shoulder as he tantalized and teased her with his lips.

The man's mouth should be outlawed.

He eased his hand around and inside her open robe, drawing her gaze back to their reflection. Her breath came in short, rapid bursts as he cupped the weight of her breast in his warm hand, his thumb brushing against the taut, aching tip. An odd sound drifted from her—part groan, part moan. All thoughts of escape fled as he massaged her bare flesh, creating a maddening need within her.

He was the devil. He was an angel. No, a wizard. *Aye.* Whatever he was, he wielded his magic well, for Molly was lost.

"God, what are you doing to me?" he murmured, parting her robe until her bare breasts spilled forth.

Molly's gaze riveted to the image of this man's hands on her nakedness. Her breasts swelled before her eyes, filling his hands with a bounty she'd never noticed before. Their peaks were large and erect, thrusting forth as if in search of something.

He brushed both tips with his thumbs as he continued to kiss her neck and shoulder. Spasms of powerful need gripped Molly. He rotated the long, hard ridge below his belt against her in a rhythm that beckoned her.

It was like a primitive dance between a man and woman. She recalled having heard someone refer to coupling as the mating dance. Was this it? This raging hunger deep inside her? All she knew was that the profound emptiness within her had to be filled.

"Sweet," he said again, turning her until she faced him. He cupped her chin in his hand, lowering his mouth toward hers.

His breath fanned her face and Molly tilted her head back to receive his kiss. At last she would have his mouth on hers. His lips had been driving her mad, and now she would be knowing the why of it.

His hands tightened on her shoulders and he suddenly straightened. "Shit."

Molly heard his curse as if from a fog. "What?"

"Is this how you work?"

"What?" She stiffened as his fingers dug into her shoulder. *You're a fool, Molly.* She'd wasted her opportunity to escape. He'd placed some kind of spell on her. "Let me go." A woozy sensation reminded her that wretched drug still lingered in her blood. Had that made her succumb to him so easily? "Let me go," she repeated, sounding as confused as she felt.

A nasty sneer spread across his face. "That's not what you said a few minutes ago, Jezebel."

Molly clenched her fist, struggling against the urge to slap him. He'd bested her this time because of her ignorance about matters of the flesh. She wouldn't succumb so easily next time. Her gaze rested on his mouth again.

No matter what he'd be about with that mouth of his.

"Tell me the truth now," he said.

She pulled her robe together and tied it securely, suddenly embarrassed by her nakedness. No man had ever seen her naked body before. Why did it have to be this one? "The truth about what?"

He took a step back from her and pulled a white garment from inside his shirt.

"What?" Molly stared at the familiar fabric Ida had taken away earlier. "My . . . my drawers. What the devil are you doing with my drawers?"

He thrust them toward her. "I want the truth about *these*."

Five

A red haze filled Dirk's mind and clouded his vision. This witch had deceived him into marriage, and now she was trying to lure him into consummating the biggest mistake of his life.

"A gentleman shouldn't be handling a lady's . . . undergarment," she said, blushing, "but seeing as you're not a gentleman . . ."

"That is irrelevant." He leaned closer. "Tell me."

"Just what is it you're wanting to know about my drawers?" she asked, tilting her chin at a haughty angle. "I stitched them myself of muslin, and you'll see there's nary a thread of lace to be—"

"You know exactly what I want to know." He closed his eyes and drew a ragged breath, then opened them to find her inching her way around him. "Stay put or I swear I'll tie you to that bed."

"Begging your pardon, *Mr.* Ballinger," she said, tossing her head so her raven locks swung seductively over one shoulder, "but I haven't any notion what it is you're wanting to *know* about my drawers."

He barked a derisive laugh and shook his head. "I have to hand it to you."

"What?"

"You're damned good."

"Good?"

Dirk held the crumpled fabric in front of him again. "There's no *blood*."

Her brow furrowed and an expression of total bewilderment crossed her face. "You're mad," she whispered, her lower lip trembling. "There was far too much blood spilled today. Now you'll be wanting more?"

He leaned closer, wondering if her head injury really had affected her memory. No, this was all part of her ruse. It had to be. "When Dr. Stein told me there was no baby, I thought you'd miscarried." He held the pristine fabric right under her nose. "I'm not totally ignorant of such matters. Women *bleed* when they miscarry." He lowered his voice to a ragged whisper, watching her changing expression. "Even noblewomen, *Lady* Elizabeth."

Her eyes widened in horror and her cheeks flamed crimson. "I . . . I . . ."

"You *what?*" He threw the garment aside and gripped both her shoulders, forcing her to face him.

"You're mad."

"You said that already."

A lone tear trickled down her cheek and dropped onto his wrist. The sight of the sparkling droplet against his tanned skin gave him pause. She wasn't the weepy type, though maybe this was also part of her detestable game. He couldn't let her fool him again.

"On the contrary, madam," he said. "I'm quite sane. What, pray tell, is your excuse?"

She drew a deep breath and tilted her head back to meet his gaze. "Very well, if you insist on humiliating me this way."

"I do."

"As I told you earlier, I am *not* Lady Elizabeth."

"So you claim."

"I'm not." She closed her eyes for a few seconds,

then met his gaze with an impressive and surprising steadiness. "I'm Molly—"

"I've heard enough. The driver wouldn't have told us you are Lady Elizabeth if you aren't." He released her and marched toward the door. "I'm locking you in this room until you're ready to tell me the truth," he said, deciding even as the words left his mouth. "You won't leave here until—"

"By the saints, I *told* you the truth! Mr. Slim was bleeding to death. He must not have been thinking straight when he told you who I was." She hurried toward him, her eyes flashing angrily. "You and your highwaymen kidnapped Lady Elizabeth. I'm Molly Riordan, her lady's maid. You *know* where she is."

My God, she's telling the truth. He'd been denying it to himself since the moment he first heard her Irish accent. The driver had misled them or was confused or something. Dr. Stein had said there was no baby because this was the wrong woman.

Oh, God. The real Lady Elizabeth, the baby . . .

Dirk dragged in a shaky breath as realization slammed into him with all the force of a bucking mustang. He swallowed hard and continued to stare at Molly's blue eyes.

Her *sincere* blue eyes.

"Damnation." He dropped the fabric still clenched in his fist and raked his fingers through his hair. "I don't understand this," he said, mentally sorting through the scene back at the stage. "Why did the driver tell us you're Lady Elizabeth? And he specifically said the outlaws took *your* maid."

"The man is dead and we have no way to know the why of his false words. What matters now is Lady Elizabeth." Her eyes flashed again, and she set her mouth in a hard line. "What have you done with her?"

"Lovejoy, damn your soul to eternity." He punched his fist into his palm and gritted his teeth, trying to sort it all through. "You're Lady Elizabeth's maid," he repeated, shaking his head in total confusion. "The driver was dying. He must've been confused."

"What have you done with Lady Elizabeth?" the woman repeated, placing a clenched fist on each hip.

Damn, she was beautiful. Remembering how her breasts had felt filling his hands earlier, he lowered his gaze to where her nipples jutted against the silk of her robe. His mouth went dry and he drew a deep breath, forcing his thoughts away from her delectable body and back to the problems at hand.

Somehow, Dirk had to convince her he wasn't an outlaw without letting her believe a different man was the father of Lady Elizabeth's child. That would destroy everything.

He *would not* allow another child with a drop of Ballinger blood to be raised a bastard. No matter what it took, he had to enlist Molly Riordan's trust and assistance.

He had no choice but to tell her the truth—at least part of it.

"It's a long story." He sighed and pointed to the chairs near the overturned tray table. "Sit and I'll try to explain."

She glowered at him. "I'll not be sitting with the likes of you until you tell me what you've done with Lady Elizabeth."

"I'm *trying* to explain it to you." He looked heavenward, then back at her. "You are the most stubborn woman I've ever met."

"Aye, that I am." She didn't budge.

"Fine. Stand and listen." He closed his eyes, then reopened them to find her still standing, still glowering, still breathtaking. Forcing his gaze not to linger on her mouth or the long column of her throat—and certainly not lower—he sighed. "I am not the outlaw who attacked the stage today."

"Ha! I saw you with my own two—"

"No, you saw someone else."

"But your eyes are the same," she said, though he saw uncertainty flicker in her eyes. "The same green."

He nodded. "The same color, but not the same eyes. And if you'd seen the outlaw's entire face, you'd know for certain. The resemblance stops there." Dirk tried to ignore the burning bile rising to his throat. "The outlaw who attacked the stage is Ray Lovejoy. Not me."

"But . . ." Her brow furrowed and she shook her head. "Why should I be believing you? Of course, you would deny your crimes."

"I've never committed a crime." It was a miracle his teeth didn't shatter, as hard as he clenched his jaw. "The man who attacked the stage . . ."

"Aye?"

"He's my half brother." Dirk spat the words, reliving all the hell he'd endured since the day he'd first laid eyes on his only living relative. "Ray Lovejoy is my dear, departed father's bastard."

She stared at him for several moments. "How am I to know this Ray Lovejoy isn't someone you made up to protect yourself?"

She tilted her head at an angle, drawing his gaze to her incredibly long neck again. Dirk bit the inside of his cheek, forcing his attention to her words and not her appearance.

"Trust me, Lovejoy is quite real," he said. "And he's been the bane of my life since I first learned of his existence."

She appeared thoughtful for several moments, then

said, "Whether your story is true or not really makes little difference." She drew a deep breath and exhaled in a loud whoosh. "You must help me find Lady Elizabeth. The baby . . ."

The baby. Dirk swayed and closed his eyes. When Lady Elizabeth's father had accused him of impregnating his daughter, Dirk had seen it as an opportunity to make amends for his father's sin. Ray was a criminal because of his upbringing, not because of bad blood. If Ray had been raised at the ranch with family, he wouldn't be a criminal. Dirk believed that emphatically. Instead, Ray had been raised by his mother—a notorious madam—in a Denver parlor house.

Dirk couldn't change the past, but he could sure as hell make sure it didn't repeat itself. Lady Elizabeth's child *would* be a Ballinger, raised at the ranch with all the benefits legitimacy provided, both legally and socially.

Like a fool, Dirk had insisted the minister perform the ceremony, even while his "bride" was only semiconscious and drugged with laudanum.

"Damn." He looked at Molly. "I married the wrong woman."

All the air rushed out of Molly's lungs. "I'm married to no one."

"I'm afraid Reverend Adams would disagree," the monster said, his voice gentle now.

"Even if this Reverend Adams claims to have performed a ceremony, it can't be binding." She tried to think it all through as she spoke. "I'm not Lady Elizabeth."

"And he used her name." The monster rubbed his chin and stared at the floor as he spoke. "Ida witnessed the ceremony."

"The only proper wedding is in church with a priest

and communion." Molly lifted one shoulder and shook her head. "Besides, the reverend wouldn't have used my name."

"No, because I believed . . ." He shook his head and looked up at the ceiling, then met her gaze. "We have to find Lady Elizabeth, then we'll worry about what's legal." His gaze fell to her bosom. "Or not."

Heat spiraled through Molly as his gaze lingered on her. She wouldn't be forgetting the spell he'd cast on her earlier, but she couldn't let it happen again. Her gaze rested on his full lips, slightly parted and softer than they'd been during his tirade. More like the lips that had caressed her neck and shoulder earlier.

Something deep inside her clenched around unbearable emptiness, and she brought her knuckles to her mouth and bit down to steady herself. She had to be keeping her wits about her now. Lady Elizabeth was in danger.

Easy now, Molly. Dirk Ballinger isn't the man for you. Besides, she still wasn't convinced about this half brother business. Until she saw both men in one place at the same time, she couldn't be sure. The monster might very well be both the highwayman *and* the man who'd wooed her into a blubbering idiot a short time ago.

Either way, he was dangerous.

"Aye, we must be after Lady Elizabeth." Her words obviously startled him, drawing his gaze from her bosom to her face. Relief and disappointment melded within her, but she allowed herself to recognize only the former. To dwell on the latter would be dangerous and foolish.

Molly Riordan was nobody's fool.

She made a mental note to ask Ida about this Ray Lovejoy. If the man really existed, the housekeeper should know.

Mr. Ballinger raked those long, slender fingers of his through his wild mane as he paced. After a moment, he paused and faced her again. "Do you remember hearing any conversations between the outlaws?"

Molly shook her head, then caught herself remembering the terrifying minutes by the creek just before Mr. Slim had been shot. "Aye, you—or this Lovejoy person—had Lady Elizabeth."

"And you heard what was said?"

"Aye." Molly closed her eyes, forcing herself to relive the nightmare. Her heart thundered and her throat constricted. "Lady Elizabeth told them she was already married to you."

"Already mar—" He punched his palm with his fist again. "That's it. And Ray believed her."

"Or you pretended to."

He shook his head and held her with his gaze. "You still don't believe me?"

"I . . . I'm not sure," she said, her voice somewhat shaky. "Part of me is wanting to believe you, but until I see this Lovejoy and you together, how can I know?"

A muscle twitched in the monster's jaw and he made a sound of utter disgust. "You may never see the two of us together in one place."

"Then I may never be sure." Molly kept her gaze on his face, waiting for his temper to flare again.

Instead he remained calm.

"That's your problem, then," he said, his voice quiet but adamant. "I know the truth, and I know we have to find Lady Elizabeth before he . . ."

"Before what?" An icy chill shot through Molly and she shivered. "Will he be after harming her, then?"

The monster resumed his pacing. "Ray may see her as a means to an end. If he believes she's my wife, I suspect he'll have ransom in mind."

"Then he might not harm her," Molly reasoned. "Not if he's after collecting that ransom."

He paused and looked at her. "I wish I could be sure of that."

"But . . ." Molly ticked off the weeks remaining in Lady Elizabeth's pregnancy. "Surely he wouldn't be harming a woman so near her time."

"How . . . near?" Surprisingly, the monster's face reddened.

"You don't remember the when of it, then?" Her own cheeks burned as she recalled the sounds coming from inside the rogue's carriage that night.

"Not . . . precisely." He cleared his throat and looked beyond her at something she suspected only he could see.

"The babe should be born in September." She studied him curiously, willing him to look at her again so she could see his eyes. Most souls showed their truthfulness—or lack thereof—in their eyes. Gram had taught Molly that, and she believed it. But this man was proving himself unreadable. When he didn't meet her gaze, she added, "I wouldn't wonder if the birthing comes sooner, though."

He rewarded her by looking directly at her, his expression surprised, if not wary. "Why?"

Discussing the details of childbearing with a man was unseemly and totally foreign to Molly, but in this case, it was necessary. She squared her shoulders and held his gaze. "Lady Elizabeth was—is—quite round already." She shrugged, watching him for any sign that he might remember the exact date of his tryst with the Lady in question. Finding none, she added, "Perhaps her time will come early."

His eyes widened and his mouth gaped. "Early?" His voice sounded strained.

Molly nodded. "All I know is that we must find her soon." *If you don't already know where she is.*

"Yes, of course." He commenced pacing again. "Then we'll worry about the legalities of our, er, marriage."

"There was no church, so there is no marriage." Molly straightened, swallowing the lump in her throat. His gaze raked her, making the clenching in her belly return. No man had ever turned her all quivery before, and all this one had to do was look at her to send her heart thundering away and her innards dancing a jig.

"Hmm, I wonder." He rubbed his chin, creating a rasping sound in the quiet room. "I'll ask my attorney to look into it while I'm searching for Lady Elizabeth."

"Aye, you do that," Molly said, trying not to look at his mouth. She licked her lips, remembering how close he'd come to kissing her with that mouth. His gaze followed her movement and she gasped, fearing he might have read her thoughts.

"I . . . I'll get the sheriff to form a posse." His voice was hoarse. Intense. His gaze never left her face as he spoke. "You stay here, and I'll send word after I find Lady Elizabeth."

His words penetrated the fog enshrouding Molly's brain. "I'll not be staying here or anywhere you say," she said, lifting her chin. "I *will* be going along to find Lady Elizabeth."

"You *can't*," he said steadily, his expression unreadable. "I've no doubt Ray is holed up in the high country, and that's no place for a lady."

Molly drew a deep breath. "Well, then, it's settled. With me being a lady's *maid*, there's absolutely no reason for me not to go."

Besides, she couldn't trust the man. If he was lying about the highwayman's identity, Molly had to stay close until he led her to Lady Elizabeth. Then she could tell the law what she knew.

He stood there staring at her, his eyes narrowed, one corner of his devastating mouth lifted in a crooked smile. "You are *not* going."

Remembering the way he'd blushed and stuttered when they discussed Lady Elizabeth's condition, Molly knew what she had to do. She looked him straight in the eye and said, "Lady Elizabeth will need me if the babe comes early." She lifted a brow. "Unless you're experienced at birthing ba—"

"No," he said miserably.

Neither was she, but he didn't need to know that. "Then it's settled. I'll be going."

He didn't answer and Molly looked down, hoping he wouldn't see her lie in her eyes. Right or wrong, she had to see Lady Elizabeth legally wed.

She cast him another wary glance. Heaven help her, but he didn't look so much like a monster now. He was handsome, his eyes intense as he stared at her. He stood a full head taller, and his wild dark hair grazed his collar in back with glistening waves. His nose was narrow and straight, his jaw square and strong. His shoulders were broad, and Molly couldn't help remembering how he'd held her against his well-muscled chest, how he'd kissed her neck and shoulder.

How he'd touched her.

But he could be a kidnapper and murderer.

Then again, he might not be. *Jesus, Mary, and Joseph, but he looks like neither a killer nor a monster.*

Her insides coiled into a spring of anticipation as she studied him. Then her gaze came to his mouth again, and he moistened his lips with his tongue. A shiver skittered down her spine and her breath caught.

By the saints, she wanted to feel the man's touch

again. Her fears had been well founded, for Molly Riordan *had* truly become a wanton. She crossed herself and muttered a prayer of salvation.

"Very well. You may accompany me," he said finally, "as long as you remember that *I* am in charge."

Molly laughed quietly, knowing she would do anything necessary to find Lady Elizabeth. Besides, she had no money or influence here. She knew no one. There was no one to help her find Lady Elizabeth except the very man who might have kidnapped her in the first place. Resigned, she swallowed the lump in her throat and nodded.

"I'll send a man to town for the sheriff." He reached for the door handle, then arched a brow in her direction. "You seem to be feeling better now. Amazing recovery."

"Aye." She inclined her head slightly. "That I am, now that the wretched medicine has worn off. Strong enough to begin the search for Lady Elizabeth."

His smile faded and the intense expression returned. His gaze drifted slowly down her neck to her bodice, searing her as it passed, making her breasts ache.

He closed his eyes for a moment, and when he reopened them his expression made him appear as tortured as she felt. His Adam's apple worked in his throat.

Then he did something amazing. He smiled. A full smile. The action transformed him from a charismatic monster to a devastatingly handsome man. A man whose touch could reduce her to the consistency of bread pudding.

Easy, Molly. She forced her breathing to slow and her flushed body to cool. Finding Lady Elizabeth was most important, and that was Molly's quest. Her duty.

She couldn't allow her unreasonable attraction to this man to interfere again. No matter what, she had to keep

her thoughts from such matters, even if he proved his
innocence in the kidnapping and killing. It wouldn't
really matter in the end.

Because he wasn't hers to want.

Dirk's blood thrummed through his body as he stood
there smiling like an idiot at a woman he barely knew.
A woman who was his wife. Maybe. He burned to take
her into his arms, to kiss her senseless, to consummate
their marriage. Legal or not.

Damn.

He'd set out on a mission to ensure no Ballinger
came into this world illegitimately, and he would
damned well see that mission through. Somehow, he
had to find Lady Elizabeth, have his marriage to her
maid dissolved, and marry the right woman before her
child was born.

But first he had to find his bastard half brother.

That thought cooled Dirk's blood and stifled his
arousal. Thank God. He had to think clearly, and that
meant keeping his thoughts off the impudent organ between his thighs.

Enough. He smiled at Molly Riordan again, enjoying
the transformation in her eyes. She was downright enchanting and, right now, that was dangerous as hell.

For all he knew, she could be in cahoots with Ray.
His throat tightened and sweat beaded his brow. Where
had that thought come from? More importantly, could
it be true? He drew several ragged breaths, struggling
against the raging battle between common sense and
his powerful physical response to this woman.

The truth was, he had no way of knowing. In fact,
now that he thought about it, had Ray known that Dirk's

intended bride was on that stage? Had something far more sinister than mere coincidence been at work here?

If so, that meant Ray had an accomplice. Someone on the inside had to have slipped the outlaw information. But who? The only people who knew about Lady Elizabeth's child and engagement to Dirk were Clyde and Ida.

And Molly Riordan.

He had to get away from her long enough to think clearly. "I'll leave you to rest now," he said, turning the door handle while continuing to meet her gaze. She was too damned beautiful. "Ida will be up again to check on you." He needed to make every effort to make sure he was alone with Molly as little as possible.

"Don't be thinking of leaving without me now." She arched one dark fine dark brow. "I'll be after finding Lady Elizabeth on my own, if necessary."

"Understood." *If you really want to find her at all.* Frowning, he opened the door. "I have to make arrangements before the trail gets cold."

"I'll prepare myself."

And he knew she would. He stepped into the hall and pulled the door shut behind him, shaking his head to clear his thoughts. The sight of Lance standing in the corner near the top of the staircase surprised him.

"Lance," he said, approaching the younger man. "How long have you been standing there?"

Lance seemed startled as he dragged his gaze away from the door to Molly's chamber. Remembering the way the younger man had kissed Molly's hand and fled, Dirk smiled to himself. He understood Lance's affliction entirely too well.

"She's pretty," Lance said, blinking.

"Yes, she is." *Beautiful.* Dirk commanded himself to maintain a solemn expression.

"You're married." Lance frowned, then met Dirk's gaze. "Ma told me so."

How the hell did Dirk respond to that? He wasn't sure of anything at the moment, but if Ida had told Lance he and Molly were married, then that was that until they located the real Lady Elizabeth. In fact . . .

Dirk glanced back over his shoulder, a plan forming in the shadows of his mind. Maybe he could beat old Ray at his own game. Maybe. It might also be a means of keeping his eye on Molly until he was certain of her guilt or innocence.

"Yes, we were married this afternoon," Dirk confirmed, convincing himself his words were true—at least, literally.

"She . . . was hurt." Lance lifted his gaze to Dirk's. "Bad?"

"No, she's better now." In fact, she seemed to have made a remarkable recovery. Too much so. Dirk stroked his chin with his thumb and forefinger, anchoring himself in the rasping sound of his whiskers against work-roughened fingers. "Much, much better."

"Good." Lance turned and started down the stairs. "I want her to stay better."

"Of course." Dirk followed Lance down the wide staircase to the main hall of the massive ranch house. Beamed ceilings two stories tall crowned the room, while paintings of landscapes and one huge portrait of Edward Ballinger occupied most of the opposite wall. His father's gaze seemed as fierce in oil as it had in life. Dirk clenched his fists and his gut roiled.

"Lance, will you tell Clyde I need to see him in the study?"

"Yes." Lance headed for the door as quickly as his short, chubby legs would carry him.

After the door closed, Dirk went to his father's study.

No matter how much time had passed since the old man's death, Dirk still thought of this masculine room as his father's study rather than his own. He poured himself three fingers of bourbon and an equal amount in another glass for Clyde.

Could he trust Clyde? The man had worked for Edward Ballinger since before Dirk's birth. His father had trusted him. Then again, had the old man really trusted anyone?

Including his own son?

Doubt and frustration picked at him. His father had been a man with secrets, and Dirk was paying the price for those secrets now. Not only Dirk. The stage driver and a male passenger were dead because of Edward Ballinger's sin.

And Dirk had kept the horrible secret. He was no less guilty than his half brother. It was Dirk's duty to demand and deliver retribution.

Resolve settled in his gut and he released a ragged sigh. He couldn't trust anyone until he learned whether or not Lady Elizabeth's kidnapping had been a deliberate and carefully planned ploy. He sure as hell wouldn't put it past Ray.

He'd made the mistake of underestimating his father's bastard once. He wouldn't make that mistake again.

Dirk stared out the window at the lengthening shadows of dusk. The sun sank slowly behind the mountains, bathing the valley in purples and grays. Mist rose slowly from the pond beyond a rocky outcropping.

The land never failed to soothe Dirk. He took a sip of bourbon, savoring the warmth as it spread through his limbs. A knock sounded on the heavy door behind him, and he called, "Come in."

"Lance said you wanted to see me, boss," Clyde said.

Dirk turned and handed his foreman the shot glass he'd already filled. "Drink. You're going to need it."

Clyde arched a woolly brow, then downed the bourbon in one smooth gulp. "I'm listenin'." He set the glass on the desk.

Dirk walked around the desk and sat in the leather chair he'd seen his father use like a throne. "Have a seat."

Clyde slumped into the chair on the far side of the desk and steepled his fingers beneath his chin. "You got somethin' cookin' in that mind of yours. A plan?"

Dirk nodded, deciding to keep his bride's identity to himself for now. Unless, of course, Clyde already knew. "We're going after Lovejoy."

"You think the maid is still alive?" Clyde leaned back in his chair and let his hands fall to his lap. "She might wish she was dead by the time the Lovejoy Gang's through with her."

Clyde hadn't faltered in his belief that the woman upstairs was Lady Elizabeth. Dirk was being paranoid. *Could* he trust Clyde?

Maybe the whole kidnapping had been pure coincidence. Molly had seemed convinced the kidnapper was surprised when Lady Elizabeth mentioned Dirk's name.

If it had been coincidence, did Ray realize the identity of the woman and her unborn child? Clenching his teeth, Dirk wondered if he was the only one who realized the irony of the entire situation. Maybe if Ray recognized the woman, he wouldn't harm her. Then again, maybe that would make things worse for her.

"We're going to find her." Dirk cleared his throat. "And this time, Ray's going to pay."

"Kin or no?"

Fire churned in Dirk's gut. "Kin or no." He exhaled and raked his fingers through his hair. "I can't stand by and let him kill innocent people if it's within my power to stop him."

"What about the law?"

"It's on our side. Remember?"

"How's the missus?"

The missus. "Much improved." Dirk knew the unasked question on Clyde's mind, and he leaned forward, deciding to use the same words Doc Stein had used. "There's no baby."

Clyde sighed and shook his head. "All the more reason to give Lovejoy what he deserves."

Dirk rose, hoping he was doing the right thing in keeping his bride's identity his secret. For now.

"Ride into town and tell Templeton we're forming a posse." Dirk inclined his head toward his foreman and friend. "With or without his cooperation."

Clyde rose, chuckling. "Whooee, but you're startin' to sound like the old man."

Dirk stiffened even as he recognized the truth. Rather than denying it, he shrugged and met his foreman's gaze. "I suppose it's about time."

"I'll ride like the devil hisself is on my tail," Clyde said, pivoting on his heel and swaggering out the door.

Dirk returned to the window to stare at the darkening land. He lifted his gaze to the mountain range that rimmed the western edge of the ranch his father had carved from the wilderness.

Sometimes he hated his father.

And sometimes he didn't.

Six

Molly spent the evening rummaging through Lady Elizabeth's trunk until she found some less frivolous clothing. Muttering a prayer that Lady Elizabeth would understand and forgive her maid's pilfering of her personal belongings, Molly chose the three plainest dresses in the collection, the requisite undergarments, and one sturdy nightgown. All were too short.

She immediately changed from the luxurious blue silk robe to the flannel nightgown, feeling less guilty and infinitely more . . . conservative. Safer. If Dirk Ballinger returned this evening, he wouldn't see the outline of her unfettered bosom through *this* heavy fabric.

Heat rose to her cheeks as she placed the silk robe back in the trunk and closed the lid. Armed with the bare necessities, Molly returned through the adjoining door to the bedchamber she'd been assigned, hoping it wasn't also intended for Lady Elizabeth.

Though it wasn't her fault Mr. Slim had told them she was Lady Elizabeth, she couldn't prevent guilt from pressing down on her. A staunch Catholic upbringing did that to a girl. Sighing, she crossed herself again as she hung the dresses neatly on hooks inside the wardrobe standing in the corner. She folded the clean drawers and stockings and placed them on a shelf, then busied herself cleaning the drops of dried blood from her own shoes. Lady Elizabeth's fancy slippers would hardly do, and Molly knew they would be too large for her own slender feet.

Since Ida had taken all of Molly's bloody clothing, the act of removing the final evidence of today's massacre from her sturdy shoes strengthened her resolve. She *would* find Lady Elizabeth and set things right. As she placed her clean shoes beside the door, she remembered the feel of that man's lips on her bare shoulder.

Her hand went to her shoulder and she rubbed it through the soft flannel. A lump formed in her throat and she swallowed hard. Guilt settled heavily in her heart, even as she remembered the thrilling way her flesh had tingled beneath the man's seductive lips and hands.

"Enough of that, Molly girl," she whispered, summoning Gram's most no-nonsense tone. Her response had been caused by the laudanum. What else could it have been?

Molly turned to the mirror and used Lady Elizabeth's brush to wrestle her wild curls into one long braid. Satisfied that she appeared far less wanton now than she had with her hair wild and free and her bosom displayed through the delicate silk, she stared at her reflection.

Why had he touched her? Why had he kissed her neck and shoulder? A tingling sensation started in the side of her neck and crept down her shoulder, resurrecting the odd, hungry feelings all over again. Molly's breasts swelled and ached, her womanly core clenching around some imagined need she couldn't begin to comprehend. He had made her aware of her own unspeakable physical needs, and he hadn't seemed at all like a monster in the doing of it, either.

Liquid fire suffused her cheeks and she turned away from her reflection and climbed into bed. The air had cooled considerably since the sun had set, so she pulled the quilt up to her chin.

And stared at the ceiling.

The lamp still burned on the nightstand, and Molly feared she would never get to sleep this night. Too much had happened. She'd witnessed murder, kidnapping, been married—in a manner of speaking—and discovered the beguiling awakening of physical desire.

All in one day.

No wonder she couldn't sleep. Sitting upright, she flung the quilt back, then swung her legs over the side of the high bed. She should be exhausted, but she wasn't.

Ida hadn't returned to let Molly know what time Mr. Ballinger planned to leave. Would he attempt to leave without her? The niggling thought tormented her until she rose and glanced at her reflection again. Confident she was modestly covered despite the fact she wore nightclothes, Molly went to the door and opened it just a bit.

She peered through the crack, noting the lamps burning along the wall between her and the staircase. Drawing a deep breath, she opened the door and crept into the blessedly vacant hallway, then tiptoed down the stairs.

The house was massive and silent. Deadly silent. Many lights burned, so she knew someone was awake. Surely they doused the lamps at bedtime even in this savage land.

She needed to make certain the monster wasn't planning to leave without her. Determinedly, she walked through the great entry hall, pausing to stare up at the paintings. One at the end bore a remarkable resemblance to Lady Elizabeth's future husband. Those eyes again, she realized.

Deciding the older figure must've been Dirk Ballinger's da, Molly listened at several doorways for any sounds coming from within the numerous rooms.

She heard nothing. Her stomach rumbled audibly, reminding her that all she'd eaten today was broth. There was no reason for her to continue her fast, as the only lingering effect from her injury was an ugly bruise. Otherwise, she felt fine and was suddenly famished. After all, she would need her strength to search for Lady Elizabeth. And perhaps she might find Ida in the kitchen and learn something more about the mysterious Dirk Ballinger and the even more mysterious Ray Lovejoy.

Guessing that the kitchen would be toward the back of the house, she pushed through a swinging door and found the spacious room with a gigantic table in its center. She paused to brush her fingertips across it. Tiny crevices marred the surface, and the wood's grain showed through the finish. She actually liked it that way.

Her gaze swept the quiet room, where a lamp had been left burning on a sideboard. That probably meant Ida would return before turning in for the night. Molly opened the pie safe in the corner and found a basket of rolls. She took two and poured herself a cup of water from the pitcher. After pulling one of the heavy, ladder-backed chairs out from the table, she glanced around warily before sitting for her repast.

She felt like a thief, though that was ridiculous, of course. She hadn't asked to be brought here and wed to a man under another's name, after all. A sigh drifted between her lips and she shook her head, then tore into the first roll with the glee her empty stomach demanded.

The roll was crusty on the outside and yeasty on the inside and had an odd but familiar flavor. She'd tasted it before and liked it. Another bite reminded her of the biscuits she'd eaten in Independence. Ah, the rolls were sourdough. That explained their unique flavor.

She washed the roll down with a sip of water, marveling at how clean and pure it tasted. From what she'd seen of Colorado so far, she could understand why Da had been drawn here.

And stayed.

What she couldn't understand was why he would leave his only child waiting for him year after year. Molly took a bite of the second roll and tried to summon her da's face. After so many years, she could scarcely remember his features. She had his eyes— hadn't her mother told her so often enough? She remembered his thick, curly hair, too. Alas, by now his black hair could be white, or he could even be bald. If she found him, how would she ever recognize him?

Then again, perhaps he would recognize her. Except for the eyes, she looked exactly like her mother. Surely Niall Riordan would remember the woman who'd borne his child and who'd waited for him until the day she died.

Tears clogged Molly's throat and burned her eyes. She reached for the cup to wash away her tears, but her sorrow remained. "Ah, Da, where are you?"

The expression she'd seen on Mr. Slim's face flooded Molly's mind. *Wait here for your da,* he'd said. She gazed heavenward and said a quick prayer for Mr. Slim's soul, wishing she knew his real name. What had the old man known of Niall Riordan, and why —*oh, why?*—had he told Dirk Ballinger that *she* was Lady Elizabeth?

The dear man had no way of knowing how much trouble he'd caused with his tall tale. Remembering how Dirk Ballinger had touched her, Molly wondered how much more trouble she might find before this nightmare ended and Lady Elizabeth was safely wed to the father of her babe.

Molly's future lay elsewhere. She had to find her da—her only family since Gram had died. All Molly had was her position as Lady Elizabeth's maid.

Cold dread settled in Molly's heart. What if Lady Elizabeth was dead? *No, not that.* She crossed herself quickly and squeezed her eyes shut for a moment. But what if no one ever found her? Molly would have to seek a position elsewhere in this foreign land.

But where? She bit her lower lip, a plan forming in her mind. Once Lady Elizabeth was properly wed, Molly would be free to leave or stay as she chose. And if the worst happened and her employer was never found, then Molly would also be free, but without a choice.

Aye, she would have to go to Serendipity. That was the town from which her father's last few letters had come. That was also where Gram had written to inform Niall Riordan of his wife's passing. That long ago letter had gone unanswered.

Those traitorous tears gathered again, but she blinked them away and drew a deep breath. Squaring her shoulders, she finished the last bit of roll and downed her water. She felt stronger now.

She rose and took her cup to the basin, where she washed and dried it, then returned it to the cupboard where she'd found it. She leaned against the sideboard,

chewing her lower lip. How long should she wait for
Ida? Molly still wasn't a bit sleepy.

Perhaps she'd look around a bit more. She opened
the kitchen door and emerged into the foyer again. The
house remained eerily quiet as she padded on bare feet
across the gleaming wood floor.

One door stood slightly ajar, light spilling through
the opening in a golden rectangle against the dark floor.
Had that door been open earlier? She didn't think so.
Silently, she traversed the wide room and paused outside the door to listen. The sound of shuffling papers,
perhaps the turning pages of a book, reached her ears.

She leaned toward the opening, listening intently. Finally, she peered around the door's edge and into the
room. A figure sat in a chair near the desk with a large
book spread across his lap.

The room was long and narrow with a high ceiling,
and the walls were lined floor to ceiling with books.
Beautiful leather-bound bindings stared back at her,
and Molly's breath caught. She dearly loved reading.
Perhaps she'd borrow one.

She returned her attention to the man in the chair.
With his back partially to her, Molly couldn't be sure
of his identity, though she *was* certain he wasn't Dirk
Ballinger. This man was slight of build, much shorter
than her host, and his hair was several shades lighter.
Squinting, Molly watched him tilt his head ever so
slightly, angling it so she saw a pair of spectacles
perched on his nose.

Ah, he would be the young man who'd brought her
tea and broth. Lance? Aye, that was the name. He'd
kissed her hand and looked at her as if he worshipped
her. Molly smiled to herself, then knocked softly.

The boy—barely a man, really—started and rose
abruptly, dumping the large book to the floor with a

crash. He stood frozen, staring at her, his mouth forming a perfect circle.

Sensing the lad was too stunned by her sudden appearance to speak, Molly said, "I'm sorry I startled
you."

He continued to stare, though he did finally close
his mouth.

"I was wondering if your mother would be about."
Molly waited for Lance to respond. He didn't. "Is Ida
your mother?"

He nodded and cleared his throat. "Yes."

Determined to put Lance at ease, Molly pointed at
the book. "What were you reading?"

"Cattle." Lance stooped and gathered the huge book,
holding the cover toward her.

"Aye, I see." It appeared to be a book on the various
breeds. "You're interested in cows then?"

"Cattle. Not cows." Lance smiled, appearing years
younger. "Ma should be in the kitchen."

"I was just there and didn't—"

"I'm surprised to see you up and about," a deep
male voice said from directly behind Molly.

Startled, she swallowed her gasp and pressed the heel
of her hand to her breastbone. "Jesus, Mary, and
Joseph," she whispered, turning to confirm the intruder's identity.

He towered over her. She looked up at the squareness
of his jaw, the corded muscles in his neck. His eyes
twinkled as lamplight flickered in their green depths.

Heat oozed through her as his gaze drifted to her
bodice, then back to her face. He arched an eyebrow
and one corner of his generous mouth turned downward. Why, the devil was actually mocking her choice
of clothing.

Lifting her chin a notch, Molly met his stare. "Is it your habit, then, to sneak up on folks, Mr. Ballinger?"

"Dirk," Lance corrected, drawing Molly's gaze back over her shoulder.

"It's my house," the monster said, and Molly turned back to face him.

"Aye, that it is, Mr. Ballinger."

"Dirk," Lance repeated.

The monster shrugged. "I'm afraid she doesn't like me very much, Lance." Mischief danced in his eyes.

"I beg your pardon?" Molly said, her voice barely more than a whisper. "Considering all that transpired today, you can hardly be blaming me."

"But . . . you're married," Lance said, and Molly darted a startled glance over her shoulder.

She would dispel that misconception once and for all. "Oh, but I'm afraid there's—"

"That's right, Lance," Mr. Ballinger said, taking Molly's hand and forcing her attention back to him. "And a man's bride shouldn't be wandering around in her nightclothes." His gaze raked her. "Such as they are."

"But . . . but . . ." Sputtering, Molly had no choice but to allow the brute to half-lead, half-drag her from the library and up the stairs. "I was looking for Ida," she argued.

"Ida went to check on you and found you missing," he said, not looking at her as he hauled her up the stairs by the hand. "For some reason, I had the strangest notion you might have run away."

"Run away?" Molly struggled for breath as he opened her bedroom door and pulled her in after him, then kicked the door shut. "And where would I . . . be running?" Breathing heavily, she watched wavy lines stretch before her and clutched her chest. "There's no air."

"It's the altitude." He pulled her toward the bed. "You'll get used to it. Sit."

"Altitude?" Molly sank gratefully down on the edge of the bed, her breathing and vision slowly returning to normal. "Your ranch would be in the mountains, then?"

"That's right, you slept the whole trip here."

"I wouldn't be calling that sleep exactly." Molly suddenly felt very vulnerable here alone with Mr. Ballinger, and she clutched the neckline of the demure nightgown closer. "I could see the mountains in the distance when the stage stopped for water," she said quietly, remembering those few moments with Mr. Slim down by the creek.

"You're well into the foothills here," Mr. Ballinger said, pacing beside her bed. "The Ballinger Ranch stretches from the plains to Long's Peak, then north to Wyoming."

"It would be a big ranch, then?"

He chuckled and flashed her a boyish grin. "Yes, it's fair size."

Molly had a sudden memory of the night Lady Elizabeth had accompanied this man into his carriage and the words they'd exchanged. Heat rose to her face and her breath caught.

"It's too big. It won't fit," Lady Elizabeth had argued.

"It's fair size, darlin', but we'll make it fit," the rogue had boasted.

There was something about his voice. A chill replaced the heat and she shivered, lifting her gaze to meet Dirk Ballinger's. He stood a few feet away, staring at her as if he were a beast of prey and she his next meal.

Never mind that, Molly. She drew a blessedly deep breath, hoping she would become accustomed to the altitude very soon. She folded her hands demurely in her lap, wishing she had something besides bare skin on beneath the nightgown, and that he weren't so close or nearly so handsome.

Aye, she had to admit it to herself. The monster was a handsome devil. And why was he lingering here? It was most unseemly. Of course, she reminded herself, this wouldn't be the first time they'd been alone together.

"When do we leave to begin our search for Lady Elizabeth?" she asked steadily, trying to avoid his probing gaze and her own improper thoughts.

"Tomorrow." He continued to stare.

Molly's cheeks warmed and she glanced down at her hands folded in her lap. "Very well," she said. "I'll be ready."

"I'm sure you will be." He released a heavy sigh. "Damnation, woman, but the high country is rough, and if you have trouble breathing here, just wait until we reach the mining camps. You'll be fainting all over the place."

"I never . . ." Molly hesitated, recalling that she had been unconscious earlier. Of course, it had taken a blow to her head to render her thus. "I can take care of myself."

"Do you ride?"

She looked up and licked her lips, unable to summon a lie. "No, but I learn quickly." A knot formed in her belly as she remembered what had happened when she'd mounted the stage horse. She touched the tender bruise at her temple in remembrance. "I'll learn."

"It's no place for a lady," he said again.

"And I told you I'm a lady's *maid*." Molly met his gaze and narrowed her eyes. "May I remind you Lady Elizabeth is up there somewhere, swollen with your babe?" The blunt talk made her cheeks burn, but the words had to be said.

The man's eyes darkened and a muscle clenched in his jaw. He placed a hand on each hip and looked heavenward, muttering something under his breath.

"We leave tomorrow," he said, meeting her gaze again. "We travel light."

"I have nothing but a few borrowed items from Lady Elizabeth's trunk."

"Good." He raked his fingers through his curls. "There's something else."

Trepidation wound its way through Molly like a serpent uncoiling to strike. "What?"

His expression became rather sheepish and he shrugged. "Folks believe we're married."

"Then we'll be after correcting them, of course."

"It . . . isn't that simple." He commenced his pacing again, then paused and did the unthinkable.

He took her hand.

Hell, now what? Dirk stood there like a fool, staring at the woman's tiny hand swallowed by his larger one. His mouth went dry, and he dropped her hand. Why had he touched her in the first place? Touching her was dangerous.

She was dangerous. Tempting.

"And why wouldn't telling the truth be a simple thing, Mr. Ballinger?" she asked, barging into his libidinous thoughts.

Her blue eyes were blazing again. The woman had a way about her. *Enough of that crap.*

He sighed, swallowing the lump in his throat. "It's like this," he began, scrambling for words. "Like I said, folks believe we're married. You heard Lance, and he learned about it from his ma. And the wranglers who brought your bath water have probably told every soul on the place *and* in town by now."

"Aye, but they'll soon know the truth of it," Molly said.

He shook his head, watching her eyes narrow and suspicion enter her expression. "It isn't that simple."

"You said that already," she argued, wielding the same words he'd used earlier. "And, for the life of me, I still can't fathom *why* it isn't simple."

How could he make her understand? He was still sorting through it all himself. Having to explain his half-cocked plan to someone else was downright impossible.

And what if she *was* in cahoots with Ray? If only he could be sure. For all he knew, Molly and Ray had hooked up over in England, too.

That thought made his gut burn, and he stared long and hard at her. Molly was beautiful, but Ray would've been more interested in a woman with a title. Even so, Dirk had no way of being certain. He only had only one choice—the hardest one.

He had to trust her.

Clenching his teeth, he grabbed a chair and dragged it over beside her bed. Straddling it, he faced her at eye level now. "All right. It's like this." He cleared his throat. "I can't help wondering if Ray Lovejoy *knew* my . . . fiancée was on that stage."

She shook her head, and he found himself wishing her braid would come loose so he could run his fingers through those luxurious raven strands again. His breath caught and a bolt of lightning struck right between his legs. His position straddling the chair suddenly seemed one hell of a lot less comfortable, but at least it would conceal his predicament.

The memory of them standing before the mirror flooded him, and he gripped the rails of the chair so tightly his knuckles turned white. He couldn't breathe. He didn't dare. His palms itched from the remembered weight of her lush breasts filling them.

Oh, God.

"You were saying, Mr. Ballinger?" she urged, startling him back to the present.

He dragged his hands over his face and released a long, slow breath, willing himself to pull rein on his cock and his thoughts. "I think it's best to let folks keep thinking you're Lady Elizabeth, and . . ."

Her eyes widened and she shook her head, loosening a few strands from her braid. "But I'm *not.*"

"I know that—at least now I do." He remembered the scene back at the stage and winced, then the memory of the driver's words jarred him. "Why did the driver want us to believe you were Lady Elizabeth? Was he just confused?"

"He knew my real name *and* Lady Elizabeth's." Molly sighed and her eyes glittered dangerously. "Down by the creek . . . we had a conversation about my da."

The last thing he could bear right now were her tears. Damn, but this had already been a long and grueling day. They both needed sleep.

"Your father?"

"Aye." Molly sniffled and stiffened, as if willing herself back under control.

The woman had an impressive amount of grit. Admiration bloomed and grew within Dirk, followed closely by a rasher of respect.

Unless this was all part of a wicked game.

No. He was shying at every little thing. Time for Dirk to reclaim his Ballinger balls.

He *had* to trust Molly.

"What about your father? Did you know the driver before?" Dirk forced his voice to remain passive, though a niggling voice in the back of his mind wondered briefly if the driver had been part of Lovejoy's scheme, too.

The man is dead, fool. Guilt punched Dirk in the gut.

"No, though Mr. Slim was an Irishman." A sad smile parted her lips. "I thought he might have met my da." She sighed.

"Had he?"

She shook her head. "He said not." A strange expression clouded her eyes.

"You didn't believe him." It seemed Dirk wasn't the only one filled with suspicion around here. "Why?"

"He said something . . ."

"What?"

She tilted her head to one side and stared beyond him at something he suspected only she could see. "When he went to confront the highwaymen . . ." Her voice broke and she cleared her throat. "He . . . he said . . ."

"Said what?" Dirk wasn't sure if this was leading to anything useful, but he sensed her need to talk. "What did he say, Molly?"

She met his gaze at the sound of her given name, then she nodded, as if somehow reassured. "He said, 'Stay here for your da.' " A tear slipped from the corner of her eye and she swiped it away. "Then, later, as he lay dying, he begged me to tell how I came to be in America."

This woman had lived through a nightmare today, and Dirk had compounded it all by mistrusting her. "What did you tell him?"

"The truth, of course." She lifted her chin and squared her shoulders. "Molly Riordan always tells the truth."

What you know of it, anyway.

"I'm afraid I told him about . . ." Her cheeks flushed and she lowered her lashes. "I told him about Lady Elizabeth's . . . transgression."

Dirk smiled. "Of course. Lady Elizabeth's transgression, as you call it, is the reason you're here."

Molly nodded vigorously, then surprised him by crossing herself. "And Mr. Slim—may he rest in peace—will never tell anyone about . . . that."

Hope eased through Dirk. Molly was—he hoped—too open and sincere to have formed a liaison with Ray. "I'm sorry about what happened to you today. To all of you."

She looked up, narrowing her eyes. "Are you, now?"

"Yes, of course." He shook his head. "No one should have to endure what you and the others on that stage did today."

"Why, Mr. Ballinger, you're sounding as if you actually mean that."

He chuckled quietly. "Of course I mean it."

She bit her lower lip and nodded. "Then I'll listen to the rest of it."

"The rest of it?" He held his hands out, palms up, totally baffled.

"Your confession."

"My *what?*" He rose, towering over her. She didn't even blink, let alone cringe.

"Your confession, of course." She slid to her feet and tilted her head back, meeting his gaze steadily. "I'm still not convinced you and Ray Lovejoy aren't one and the same."

"Damnation, wo—"

"And I'll thank you not to be swearing in my presence, Mr. Ballinger."

Dirk clenched and unclenched his fists, then his teeth. For several moments, it was all he could do not to roar until the rafters trembled. Lord knew it wouldn't be the first time this house had endured a Ballinger's rage.

She folded her arms across her waist, unwittingly thrusting her breasts toward him. Of course, that wretched flannel concealed the details, but his memory was more than able to provide them. "I'm still waiting to hear why it isn't a simple matter to set things right with Ida and the others." She maintained a bland expression, though her eyes sparked like a dry thunderstorm across the mountains.

"I'm trying . . . to explain."

"And I'm listening."

He sighed again and forced himself to meet and hold her gaze. If he was going to trust her, he needed to see her eyes. "It's like this."

"Aye?"

Dirk reminded himself that this woman wasn't responsible for his father's sins or Ray Lovejoy's bad seed. If she was telling him the truth—and for some crazy reason, he wanted to believe her—then she was very much a victim. As was he.

But Ballingers weren't allowed to be victims.

"It's like this," he repeated, planning it all as he spoke. "Ray Lovejoy has tormented me and half the state of Colorado for months. He's a menace."

"Aye." Her voice fell to a whisper and her eyes softened. "I know that better than anyone."

"Yes, I know." Dirk sighed and raked his fingers through his hair. "In case he knew somehow that Lady Elizabeth would be on that stage . . ."

"Go on," she urged, her interest obvious.

"I want him to believe he grabbed the wrong woman."

Molly swayed slightly and her breath came out in a soft whoosh. "Why? If you're right, then Lady Elizabeth would be valuable to him."

Dirk alone knew that Ray was likely to determine his captive's identity on his own as her belly grew. "If Ray believes the real Lady Elizabeth reached the ranch and married me," he said, sorting the details through in his own mind as he spoke, "then his plans will be foiled."

"As I was saying, won't that put Lady Elizabeth in harm's way?" Molly's brow wrinkled as she tried to follow his logic.

"I think Lovejoy really wants something else."

She shook her head, more hair falling out of her braid to curl about her face. "It's confused I am."

"I know, but will you trust me when I say I want Lady Elizabeth returned safely as much, or more, than you do?"

Unwavering, Molly met his gaze. "There is the babe," she said quietly.

Was that the beginnings of trust he saw in her eyes? Did she finally believe he wasn't an outlaw? "And that baby is the reason you're both here."

"I still don't understand how it will help for the outlaw to believe I'm Lady Elizabeth." She worked her lower lip with her teeth, obviously deep in thought.

"But I agree that Ray Lovejoy must be stopped, not rewarded."

The thirst for justice and retribution seeped through Dirk's veins, reinforcing his decision. "Believe me, I intend to give Ray Lovejoy exactly what's coming to him."

"And to rescue Lady Elizabeth?"

Dirk bit the inside of his cheek as he nodded. "And to make sure her child is raised a Ballinger."

Molly stared at him for several seconds. "All right, then, I'll pretend to be Lady Elizabeth for as long as I believe it might help." Her cheeks reddened and she looked away briefly. "With obvious exceptions, of course."

"As you wish." Dirk lifted one corner of his mouth, wishing suddenly that things could be different. He was a man doomed to duty. Doomed, period.

Unfortunately, Molly Riordan intrigued him and he wanted to know her better. His gaze drifted along the creamy column of her throat to the ridiculous ruffle at her collar. Oh, yes, he wanted to know her better.

Much better.

Seven

Molly slept fitfully, drifting between nightmares of blood and murder and darkly erotic images of herself in Dirk Ballinger's arms. She awoke with a start, drenched in perspiration and trembling with a powerful need. The yearning billowed through her as awareness took root and grew. She sat upright in bed and gasped the thin mountain air.

She wanted Dirk Ballinger to . . . *do* things to her. It was wrong, of course. A sin. Regardless of what others believed, they were *not* married. Besides, Dirk was destined to wed the mother of his child.

"Enough of this, Molly Riordan," she whispered fiercely, swinging her feet to the floor and stretching. The floor was chilly beneath her feet and she shivered. Good. The chill should help take her mind off heated flesh and a man's forbidden touch.

She hoped.

Banishing thoughts of stolen kisses and improper caresses, Molly considered last night's conversation with Dirk Ballinger again. She was now convinced he was not the monster she'd feared. Relief grew with every breath. That meant Ray Lovejoy was actually another person. A highwayman. A murderer. A kidnapper.

And he has Lady Elizabeth.

Suppressing a shiver, Molly padded over to the win-

dow and pushed aside the delicate lace curtains to peer
out at the morning. The sun was just peeking above
the horizon. Rocks and small hills gave way to the vast
prairie stretching toward the dawn. She looked to the
north and saw part of a mountain range curving around
the ranch, almost as if to hold and protect it. To the
south, a similar smudge where the dark earth met the
lightening sky made her realize the ranch was nestled
against the mountains. She was eager to see what lay
on the opposite side of the house.

Then she remembered that today they would leave
to go in search of Lady Elizabeth. Molly hurried to the
wardrobe and pulled on her clothing, lacing her sturdy
shoes and brushing her hair. She replaited it and se-
cured it in several places with scraps of ribbon she'd
found in Lady Elizabeth's trunk. Eventually, she would
purchase new ribbon from her meager savings, but for
now she couldn't venture into the high country with
her hair blowing free.

Besides . . . she remembered the way Dirk had
touched her hair. Heat swelled within her and her
cheeks flamed. A pulsing commenced in her womanly
core and her breath quickened. *Concentrate.* She swallowed the lump in her throat and checked to ensure the
ribbons were secure. Her hair would remain confined
today, a temptation to no one.

She froze, staring at her reflection. Taking a step
closer to the mirror, Molly studied her image. What
about her could possibly tempt a man? Especially a
man like Dirk Ballinger? After all, he'd seduced Lady
Elizabeth, one of the most beautiful women Molly had
ever seen.

Molly was but a maid. She had no business wanting
such a man.

Oh, but want him she did.

And the wanting of a thing can't make it so, Molly girl, Gram had always said.

She drew a deep breath and sighed, watching her warm breath fog the mirror. However, it didn't last long. Back in England and Ireland, windows and mirrors were often coated with moisture. Here the air was so dry it practically crackled.

In fact, Molly's lips were red and chapped, and her skin felt tight and dry. All part of the "high, dry" weather Mr. Slim had warned them about. He'd said many people came to the mountains to take the cure the air allegedly offered.

A smile curved her lips. "What air?" Though she had to admit she was feeling much stronger today, and the swelling at her temple was all but gone. The bruise would take longer to fade, but she was adequately recovered from her ordeal. Enough to go in search of her employer.

As images from yesterday burst to the forefront of her mind again, her lower lip trembled. Aye, physically she was much better, but inside . . . she would carry those horrifying memories with her for the rest of her days.

A soft knock at the door startled Molly, and she crossed the room to the door, eager to begin the search for Lady Elizabeth. She swung open the paneled door to find Ida there. The older woman gave Molly a tentative smile.

"Good morning, Mrs. Ballinger," she said.

"Good morning." Remembering her promise to pretend to be Mrs. Ballinger for a while, Molly resisted the urge to correct Ida. She was, in essence, a borrowed bride—in name only, of course.

"You look much more pert this morning, I see."

"Aye, that I am."

"Your husband thought you might want to join him downstairs for a proper breakfast." Ida's cheeks pinkened.

Did the woman wonder why the newlyweds hadn't shared a bed last night? The thought brought a flash of liquid fire to Molly's face as well. "Aye, I should like to break my fast at table." She couldn't quite bring herself to say "with my husband."

Ida nodded and turned to leave, but Molly reached out to touch her sleeve. The woman waited patiently for Molly to explain her action.

"I, uh, would like to visit the necessary before . . ."

The woman dimpled and gave a knowing nod. "Through the kitchen and out the back door." She turned again toward the stairs. "I'll tell Dirk you'll be along shortly."

"Thank you."

Molly hurried down the stairs, hoping to avoid her host for as long as possible. Realizing and accepting that he wasn't a highwayman made her feel quite awkward about facing him again. After all, it had only taken a bit of laudanum and a few caresses from a man she'd believed a monster to render her a wanton. What power could he wield against her now as an honorable man?

The possibilities stole Molly's breath. She paused at the kitchen door, remembering the thin mountain air. After a moment, she proceeded through the room, where a plethora of wonderful aromas assaulted her senses. Aye, she was ravenous this morning.

A dark-skinned woman stirring a pot at the stove smiled at Molly, saying something that sounded like Spanish. At a loss, Molly smiled and nodded, and the woman returned the gesture with a partially toothless grin.

Molly continued through the kitchen and emerged

into a wide room filled with pails and tools, then stepped out the back door. "Jesus, Mary, and Joseph," she whispered, standing on the stoop, her mouth agape.

Nothing could have prepared her for her first close look at the majestic Rocky Mountains. The air was clear and cool, the morning sun setting the towering peaks ablaze. Not a single cloud marred the brilliant blue sky, which stretched high and wide above the mountains, where flashes of white graced the highest places.

Only God could have painted such breathtaking beauty. Molly giggled to herself, remembering how often this mountain air had stolen her breath. *Breathtaking, indeed.*

The tops of the mountains were in full sun now, though the earth was still cloaked in shadows. She watched as the sunlight drifted down the side of the mountain, bathing it in pinks and yellows.

Remembering her mission, she proceeded to the necessary, then stopped to stare again on her way back to the house. She'd never imagined . . .

Enough light shone down now to allow her to make out more details. The mountains were rugged and multidimensional—not smooth as they'd first appeared. Water trickled through a crevice, disappearing into the mountainside, only to reappear again much lower, and numerous pines grew in patches. Where they were dense, the slopes appeared almost black.

It's no place for a lady, Dirk had said.

A shiver raced through Molly, but not from fear. From excitement. Anticipation. The thought of venturing into what Dirk had called the high country made her almost giddy.

And her da could be up there somewhere. The lure and challenge of the mountains humbled Molly. Perhaps she was more like her da than she'd realized. He also must have been lured by the Rocky Mountains' siren song.

Renewing her vow to find Lady Elizabeth *and* her da, Molly swung around and headed toward the house. A figure stood in the open doorway, watching her.

"There's nothing more beautiful," Dirk said, his voice rich and deep.

"Aye, the mountains are incredible." She looked over her shoulder and saw a large bird. "Would that be an eagle?"

"Hawk." He cleared his throat, drawing her attention back to him. "What makes you think I meant the mountains?"

One corner of his mouth curved and he seemed gentler, somehow, in the light of this new day. Molly noted the direction of his gaze and awareness spiked through her. He couldn't have meant she was beautiful. *Foolish girl.* Deciding to ignore his bewildering remark, she asked, "Will we see eagles in the high country?"

He nodded, his gaze continuing to drift over her. "Possibly."

Her cheeks warmed, and she struggled to maintain her decorum. She absolutely must not let him see how he affected her. Not again. To do so would make her vulnerable, and she couldn't afford that. There was too much at stake.

"What time will we be leaving?" she asked, wanting to direct the conversation back toward Lady Elizabeth—his rightful and future bride. "When no one woke me this morning, I thought . . ."

He arched a brow and grinned. "You thought I'd left without you?" He chuckled low. "I gave you my word." His eyes narrowed. "And you gave me yours."

Molly didn't miss his message. "Aye, so I did." She

stepped through the door he held open for her. Without looking at him, she said, "You didn't answer my question. What time will we be leaving?"

"I'm not sure."

Molly paused and he walked past her. "But last night you were very sure it would be early."

He stopped and turned to face her. "Sheriff Templeton sent word late last night—he already has a posse on Lovejoy's trail."

"Then . . . Lady Elizabeth could be returned anytime?"

Dirk rubbed his chin, appearing thoughtful. "We could have word soon, anyway."

His unspoken meaning made her sway. "Lady Elizabeth is alive," she said quietly. "I'm sure of it."

He held Molly's gaze for several moments, his green eyes darkening to a mossy shade. "I hope you're right." Silence stretched between them. "I sent word we would wait until noon. If we don't hear by then, we're heading out."

Molly nodded. "I'll be ready."

"After breakfast, we'll pick out a mount for you and see if you can ride."

Molly suppressed a shiver, determined not to let him see her fear. He was tall and strong and very sure of himself. He probably feared nothing—no man. However, he didn't need to know that beneath the stubborn set of her chin and her false bravado, she was terrified.

Even in the kitchen, this man didn't appear out of place. This ranch suited him. Of course, he'd grown up here. It was his home.

A home.

Molly hadn't thought of home in years—the small farm in Ireland she'd given up to work for Lady Elizabeth in England. After Gram's death, Molly'd had no choice but to seek employment, though that had meant leaving their isle.

"Ida said something about buckwheat cakes," he said, pushing open the swinging door. "I can almost taste them."

Nodding, she preceded him through the door and waited, not certain where in the massive house they would dine. He stopped beside her, and she felt his gaze on her again.

Looking up at him, she caught her breath. His expression was intense, but a slight smile curved his lips—the same lips that had caressed her so tenderly yesterday.

He held his arm crooked at the elbow, obviously expecting her to take it. "Breakfast is waiting, Mrs. Ballinger," he said, his voice deep and his tone filled with patience.

And something more.

Molly swallowed once, hard, then looped her arm through his. Heat radiated through his shirt and penetrated the fabric of her dress. His arm was solid and his muscles well defined. He led her to a door just to the right of the kitchen.

Two men rose as they entered. One was young Lance, who ducked his head and grinned. The other was a stranger—older than Dirk and much harder on the eyes. His skin appeared tough and leathery, and his silver hair was cropped short, unlike Dirk's unruly mane. He sported a handlebar mustache, clutched his hat in his fist, and wore a string tie. She'd seen the unusual western attire once during their journey. Certainly no gentleman in England or Ireland owned such a tie. He appeared almost as uncomfortable as Molly felt.

"This is my ranch foreman, Clyde Yeager," Dirk said, indicating the older man.

"Howdy do, Mrs. Ballinger." Mr. Yeager shook the hand she offered. "You're looking better this mornin'."

"Have we met, Mr. Yeager?" Molly nodded, forcing herself not to cringe at being addressed as Dirk's wife.

"Clyde was with me yesterday when we found the stage," Dirk explained.

"Ah, that would be why I don't remember." Molly turned to Lance. "Good morning, Lance," she said to the younger man, who responded with another bashful grin.

Dirk pulled out a chair for her at one end of the table, then took his seat at the head. The dark-skinned woman returned and proceeded to serve hotcakes. Another, younger one ladled thick, warm syrup over them.

Molly's mouth watered as Ida held a silver dish filled with slices of ham. She only took one piece, though she felt as if she could eat much more. From what Molly had seen of America, she was convinced they ate very well.

The younger girl poured coffee without asking and Molly smiled at her. She was attractive and had the look of innocence about her.

"Mrs. Ballinger, this is Rosa," Ida said, indicating the older woman she'd seen in the kitchen. "She's our cook." The woman bobbed her head and smiled again, though this time she didn't speak. "And this is her daughter Elena."

"It is a pleasure to meet you, *señora,*" Elena said in careful English. "Welcome to Colorado."

"Thank you, Elena," Molly said, smiling. "The food smells wonderful."

Still grinning, Rosa nodded and followed Ida from the room. Elena placed a pitcher of cream and a bowl of sugar on the table, smiling at Lance, who blushed again.

Molly watched the expression in Elena's eyes. She didn't gaze upon Lance with pity. In fact, the girl looked at Lance with the eyes of a girl who was smitten. Smiling to herself, Molly glanced across the table to find Dirk staring at her, a knowing smile on his handsome face.

Molly's face warmed as she laced her coffee heavily with cream and sugar. She'd grown to tolerate coffee prepared this way, though she still preferred tea.

The men ate in silence, giving Molly the opportunity to savor her breakfast. The cakes were light and soaked up the delicious syrup, and the ham added just the right touch of saltiness. By the time she finished her serving, her strength had returned. She now felt ready to face the day.

"Mrs. Ballinger," Clyde said, clearing his throat, "I want you to know we're gonna do everything possible to bring your maid back safe and sound."

Molly's breath caught and she clutched her napkin with both hands. "Thank you, Mr. Yeager."

She met the older man's gaze and found him staring at her with a curious expression. "Beggin' your pardon, ma'am," he said, "but I can't help noticin' that you sound Irish."

Molly felt Dirk's gaze on her as she searched for the answer. "Aye, so I do." She gave a nervous laugh. "I spent much of my childhood in Ireland." That was certainly true. "My family owned property there." Also true. "My . . . my governess tried to break me of the accent, but I'm quite hopeless." A lie, most probably *not* the first or last one she might tell before this charade ended.

Mr. Yeager seemed to accept her explanation, for he merely grunted and nodded and returned his attention to his breakfast.

So much for Molly Riordan never lying . . . She held her breath for a few moments and said a silent prayer of forgiveness.

Thou shalt not bear false witness.

She felt Dirk's stare and looked up to meet his gaze. The expression in his eyes was one of suspicion. Surprised, Molly continued to stare at him. Hadn't she played the role he'd asked her to portray? Had she said something wrong?

Dirk Ballinger was a complex and confusing man. Unfortunately, he was also an attractive one. Recalling her physical response to him yesterday, she reached for her coffee and swallowed it with difficulty. The man would drive her mad yet with his shifting moods and suspicions—not to mention her own illogical desires.

If anyone should be suspicious, it was Molly. The man had wielded his gift for seduction against her yesterday with shocking results. And now he'd asked her to pretend to be his wife. *Jesus, Mary, and Joseph.* Her heart pressed upward against her throat as she remembered what had happened between them, and what she'd almost allowed herself to forget.

No matter how tempting the man might be, she had to remember she wasn't the only woman who'd fallen victim to his charm.

And the other one was carrying his child.

Dirk couldn't keep his mind or his eyes from straying to his alleged bride. He swallowed a bite of buckwheat cake, but it lodged halfway down his throat. After washing it down with tepid coffee, he drew several deep breaths.

Molly Riordan was not his wife. His gaze drifted to the high neckline of her borrowed dress, noting how the fabric strained across her voluptuous breasts. That told him something about Lady Elizabeth, sight unseen. Furthermore, the fabric hung in folds at Molly's waist.

His gut twisted as he remembered why Lady Elizabeth's waist would be thicker. *Damnation.* Reminded of his mission, his vow, and the identity of his promised bride, Dirk stiffened. He had to keep his mind, his eyes, and his hands off Molly Riordan. She would play a role—nothing more, nothing less. *In name only,* she'd said.

More's the pity. He exhaled very slowly and met her gaze. Her brow furrowed and her lips pressed together in flagrant disapproval. Why the devil was she angry with him now? He hadn't touched her again, though he'd certainly thought about touching her. A lot.

Lance said something, jerking Dirk back to the breakfast table and away from libidinous thoughts of his fiancée's maid. "I'm sorry, Lance," he said. "What did you say?"

Lance heaved a sigh. "I said she can ride Sadie."

Ride? Oh, yes. Molly needed a horse. "Sadie belongs to you, Lance." Dirk studied the younger man, noting the way he blushed and the way his gaze kept drifting to Molly. The kid was outright enslaved by her beauty.

Well, God help him, so was Dirk.

"She can borrow Sadie." Lance looked down at his plate. "I don't mind."

"Lance?" Dirk waited for the boy to meet his gaze. "Thank you. Sadie is the gentlest mount at the ranch."

"Durned near dead, if'n you ask me," Clyde muttered, earning a scowl from Lance. "Sorry, kid."

"I'm not a kid," Lance said, his eyes blazing.

"Not a kid at all," Molly said, earning a bashful grin

from the young man in question. "A man, and a generous one at that. Thank you, Lance."

A pang of unreasonable jealousy pierced through Dirk and he bit the inside of his cheek. Jealous of Lance? *Pitiful, Ballinger. Just pitiful.* He definitely had to regain control of himself.

So Lance was sweet on Molly? Dirk sure as hell couldn't blame him, but—unfortunately—he could empathize.

"Templeton said he'd send word by noon," Clyde said, bringing the topic of conversation right back to where it should've been all along.

Dirk nodded, contemplating the search for the Lovejoy Gang. "I figure Ray's holed up near one of the mining camps."

Nodding, Clyde refilled his coffee and took a sip. "I don't reckon he's as far from here as we'd like."

"But that's good," Molly said. She met Dirk's gaze. "Isn't it?"

"For now, I suppose." Dirk hoped he didn't accidentally refer to Ray's hostage as Lady Elizabeth. Of course, Molly was even more likely to make such an error, and he could hardly blame her. He had the distinct feeling she blamed herself for the fate that had befallen her employer. That was ridiculous, though. If Ray had set out specifically to kidnap Lady Elizabeth, there wouldn't have been any way for Molly or the stage driver to prevent it. He met and held her gaze, hoping to reassure her, yet not wanting to instill her with false hope either. "We'll find her." *One way or the other.*

Molly nodded, her cheeks growing pinker as her lashes lowered. The hankering he had for her slammed into him again, even more powerful now than yesterday.

Tugging at his collar, he cleared his throat and reached for his coffee again.

What the devil had happened to the days when the only thing Dirk Ballinger hankered over was a piece of pie? Not that he hadn't wanted a woman before—and acted on it—but this was different. Unsettling.

Frustrating as hell.

"You wantin' me to go along?" Clyde asked, redirecting Dirk's wayward thoughts again.

Thank God one of them had a lick of sense. He cast a sidelong glance at his foreman, hoping his trust in the man wasn't misplaced. "I need you here to run things," he said, knowing part of him wanted to make damned sure Clyde Yeager was nowhere near Ray Lovejoy until this hostage situation was resolved.

"Fair enough, boss." Clyde inclined his head toward Lance. "Lance here'll gimme a hand."

Lance beamed at Clyde and nodded, reminding Dirk that the younger man always had a way of reading people. After all, Lance had never remained in the same room with Edward any longer than necessary. *Damned fine judge of character.* If Lance still trusted Clyde, then Dirk could, too.

Couldn't he?

"Good. Then I won't have to worry while we're gone." *The hell I won't.* Dirk pushed away from the table and rose, meeting Molly's questioning gaze. "Are you ready to go meet Sadie?"

Molly bit her lower lip and nodded. Dirk stepped behind her chair and pulled it back as she stood. Clyde and Lance pushed to their feet as she did.

Clyde chuckled and said, "I ain't seen or had such good manners in these parts since old Evans brought that English lady calling on your old man."

"Isabella Bird." Dirk grinned, trying not to notice

the enchanting floral scent of Molly's hair. His throat tightened and his heart pressed upward against it as he spoke. "I was only twelve, but I remember thinking how strange she was."

Clyde looked at Molly with admiration and respect—no hint of subterfuge. Dirk told himself again how foolish he was to suspect the old man of betrayal. And Molly? He wanted to believe her. Clenching his teeth, Dirk turned his attention back to Clyde's words.

"Mrs. Ballinger passed on when this one was still wet behind the ears," Clyde continued. "All Dirk here had was me and his ornery old man."

"And me," Ida said as she strolled into the room.

A strange expression came over Clyde, and Dirk glanced from the ranch foreman to his housekeeper. The old cuss had a twinkle in his eye Dirk had never seen before. He had been so preoccupied with the problem of his half brother that he hadn't been paying much attention to matters at home. And Ida appeared downright smitten.

Well, I'll be damned.

"Lance, will you please introduce me to Sadie?" Molly asked, and the boy blushed and nodded.

Had Molly invited Lance along as a chaperon? A sigh drifted between Dirk's lips. Maybe that was for the best.

Her breast barely brushed against his arm as she turned, releasing an inferno in Dirk's blood that aimed straight for his crotch. Yes, having Lance along was definitely for the best.

No maybe about it.

Ray thought the posse had their trail once, but he led his gang and their hostage through a shallow stream for several miles, exiting in the high country near their hideout. That posse could search in a hundred different directions and not come anywhere near finding them.

He'd fooled them again, and he knew it. Grinning, he shifted his weight in his saddle and glanced at the woman. At least the horse they'd stolen near Estes Park had moved her farther away from him. He'd have gone deaf by now if she'd remained in his lap any longer.

The woman was *still* caterwauling. She'd been at it since they left the road behind and headed into the mountains. Yet she hadn't said another word since claiming to be Dirk Ballinger's wife.

Hell, he hadn't even heard about Dirk's marriage. Of course, it wasn't as if he and Dirk were on speaking terms. Bile rose in Ray's throat. Did that make her his sister-in-law? Half sister-in-law? Could a bastard be an anything-in-law?

No . . . just an outlaw.

He gnashed his teeth, convincing himself he didn't give a damn.

And hating himself because he did.

She looked like hell now. Her brown hair was matted to her face where it had stuck in her sweat, tears, and snot. She sure didn't seem so highfalutin now. Strangely, that knowledge didn't make Ray feel any better about the whole mess.

No matter how irritating the bitch was—and he'd have preferred a bed full of rattlers over another moment of her wailing—that didn't change the evidence he'd missed back at the stage. She'd felt a little round when he'd first hauled her into his lap, and he liked his women with some flesh on their bones.

But not breeding.

"Shit." He wiped his sweaty palm on his shirtfront and gave the signal for the boys to dismount.

He swung his leg over the horse's rump and dropped to the ground, dreading having to deal with her again, but he wasn't fool enough to pass up this prime opportunity. Dirk's wife would be worth some serious ransom. She glowered at him and fell silent for a blessed moment, then puckered up her mouth and spit in his face.

Wiping spittle from his cheek, he released a wheezing chuckle. He resisted the urge to haul her to the ground and slap her around a little. After all, he didn't want to damage the merchandise.

Ah, hell, Lovejoy. The truth was that he'd never hit a woman in his life, and he wasn't about to start now.

He'd lost all desire to woo the bitch the minute he'd heard the exalted Ballinger name on her lips.

A name that should've been his.

He fought back the memories surging to the surface—his mother's stories about his powerful sire and how she'd planned to make him pay one day for planting his seed and walking away. Ray clamped his jaw shut and untied his hostage's hands, holding the bridle with one hand to steady the nervous horse. It was too high-strung to suit him, but it seemed just right for the fancy Mrs. Ballinger and her uppity accent.

When she didn't make any move to dismount, he grabbed her under the arms and dragged her from the saddle. Kicking and screaming, of course. Her long nails caught his face near his eye and drew blood.

"Why, I oughta . . ."

"What?" she asked, breathing hard in the mountain air.

"So you remembered how to talk?" He chuckled low—menacingly, he hoped. "That's real fine. We're gonna get some grub, then you're gonna write a nice little letter to your loving husband."

She swallowed so hard he heard it.

"Don't you *want* Ballinger to save you from big bad me?" he taunted, suddenly wary.

"Oh, I'm dizzy." She drew a shaky breath and swayed.

Ray caught her before she fell. "You ain't used to the altitude." A nagging voice in the back of his mind wondered if bringing her up so high so fast would hurt her baby.

His half brother's child.

"Danged if I don't got me two hostages," he muttered, shoving his illogical guilt to the back of his mind. "Old Dirk oughta be willing to pay double for you."

She shook her head as if to clear it, staring at him as if seeing him for the first time. Her eyes widened, and she swayed again. "Do you always . . ."

"Do I always what?"

"Your beard." She sighed and cleared her throat. "Never mind." Straightening, she drew a deep breath and lifted her chin a notch. "What are you going to do with me?"

"I done told you." Ray chuckled again, though he couldn't shake the eerie sensation of the hairs on the back of his neck standing on end. The way she'd looked at him earlier . . . his brother's wife was a bigger pain in Ray's ass than he'd expected. "You're gonna write your husband a letter."

She narrowed her eyes, but he dragged her through the trees to the hidden entrance. The boys had it open, so he hauled his hostage inside and shoved her into a chair. She sat gasping for air, her swollen belly rising and falling, reminding Ray of her condition.

"A letter?" she finally asked, resting her hand over her belly. "Why?"

"Desperado's gonna deliver it to the ranch, so I can

tell the high 'n mighty Dirk Ballinger how much it's gonna cost him to get his wife and kid back."

"Ransom?"

He nodded, watching her shifting eyes. By God, he'd seen eyes like hers on gunfighters just before they pulled the trigger. There was one hell of a lot more to this little English hellion than he'd first realized.

The prickly feeling on the back of his neck intensified as he stood staring down at Dirk's wife. When Ray had first heard her accent, he'd been reminded of the trip he'd taken last year with the payoff his brother had given him.

And now he couldn't shake the notion that he should remember something more. "I reckon you could call it ransom," he said, wondering why his voice sounded so odd.

She licked her lips, and a downright sly expression glittered in her eyes. "How much ransom?"

Eight

Molly stared across the paddock at the huge, terrifying beast, her heart performing a respectable Irish jig. "She . . . doesn't look like a Sadie." Molly's voice sounded small and nervous even to her own ears. *More like a Satan than a Sadie.*

Dirk chuckled, but stopped abruptly when Molly glowered in his direction. "Sadie is the gentlest horse on the ranch," he said quietly, though his lips twitched as if the effort not to laugh was gargantuan.

"I'm not so sure the word 'gentle' can be applied to such a . . . a large creature." Molly swallowed hard and took a step closer, casting a furtive glance at Lance. "She's huge."

"Sadie will be nice," Lance said with conviction. "I found a sidesaddle."

At least *he* wasn't laughing. "Thank you, Lance."

"No sidesaddle." The sound of Dirk's voice startled her.

"Why not?" Molly turned her attention from the tall gray horse to her . . . her what? Certainly not her husband. "Don't women use sidesaddles in this country?"

"Most do." He stood there with his arms folded and a somber expression. "But where we're going, you'll need to ride astride."

"It's . . . it's unseemly," Molly said, though even

with her inexperience regarding horses, she understood his meaning. "You're saying it will be safer in a regular saddle?"

He nodded. "Lance, there's a small saddle at the back of the tack room that has a long enough cinch for Sadie's belly." He grinned at the younger man. "Used to be yours."

Lance blushed and shot Dirk a look of indignation that warmed Molly's heart. The lad obviously adored this horse *and* Dirk Ballinger. If such a gentle young man found something to love about Sadie, then she couldn't be all bad.

And neither could Dirk.

Molly watched Lance enter the barn on short, stocky legs, then returned her attention to Dirk. "I'm thinking that young man doesn't have a bit of meanness anywhere in his body."

"None."

"How old is he?"

"Older than he looks. Twenty-five or so." Dirk grinned when she met his gaze. "And he's mooning after you."

Molly's face warmed, but she couldn't deny Dirk's words. How could she have failed to notice the way Lance stared after her? She cast a sidelong glance at Dirk. The expression in his eyes was far more potent than the one Lance wore when he looked at her. A shiver skittered down her spine, and that perplexing and persistent emptiness returned to her womanly essence with a voraciousness that left her stunned.

"There's something . . ." His voice faltered and he cleared his throat. "Molly, I need to know something more about what happened yesterday."

She closed her eyes and drew a steadying breath,

then met Dirk's solemn gaze. "All right. What is it you're after knowing?"

Dirk gazed toward the mountains, sunlight glinting off the ebony hair curling beneath the brim of his hat. When he looked at her again, the sorrow in his green eyes revealed the significance of his request.

"I'm listening," Molly said quietly, studying him and liking what she saw. He was magnificent, especially outside with the rugged land serving as a backdrop to his strong features.

"Did Ray . . ." A muscle clenched in his jaw and he shoved his tan hat away from his eyes. "I need to know if Ray Lovejoy actually shot the men who died yesterday."

Molly blinked, surprised. She swallowed the lump in her throat, battling against the remembered image of the bullet slamming into Mr. Slim. "He didn't shoot the driver," she said, struggling to remember the crucial details. "In fact, he seemed angry that one of his men did it. I . . . I didn't see who shot the passenger, though."

"So it could've been Ray." Dirk's lips pressed together and he looked toward the mountains again. "At any rate, I know he's the leader of that bunch of cutthroats, so that makes him responsible enough."

Realization swept through Molly, along with her first inkling that Dirk Ballinger really didn't want to hate his half brother. It took a big heart to love unconditionally. Wasn't that what Gram had always said? But even Molly could see Dirk wasn't yet ready to face such feelings. And if Ray Lovejoy proved to be a killer, Dirk would never be able to love him—blood or no.

"Come on over here and meet Sadie," he said, obviously needing to change the subject. "You're going to be spending a lot of time with her."

And with you. Holding her breath, Molly dragged her gaze from the inspiring sight of Dirk Ballinger's profile. She'd never been so close to such a large and virile man before. *Until yesterday.* A heated flush washed over her body as she recalled the gentleness of his lips, the hunger of his touch.

"Sadie, meet Molly." Dirk stroked the side of the beast's head, and Sadie made a soft, friendly sound. He reached down and captured Molly's hand, bringing it to the horse's velvety muzzle. "There, that isn't so bad. Is it?"

He looked down at her, and Molly met his gaze. The feel of his strong hand over hers stole her breath. He guided her fingers to the side of Sadie's head, where he showed her how to stroke the horse.

"Talk to her," he said, his voice gentle. Compelling.

Molly drew a shaky breath. "Hello, Sadie. I'm pleased to meet you."

Though her words were for the horse, her eyes were for the man. He met and held Molly's gaze, his thumb sliding gently along the side of her hand and against her palm. With slow, circular motions, he massaged her tingling flesh, sending rivulets of pleasure up her arm and awakening the sleeping desire he'd introduced her to yesterday.

The breeze was warm, the sun hot, and her blood ablaze, but Molly shivered. This wanting was a powerful elixir—one she didn't understand. She only knew it was bigger than she or Dirk or even gigantic Sadie.

The horse snorted as if reading Molly's mind, jerking her gaze, if not her thoughts, back from danger. "She . . . seems friendly enough." Molly's voice sounded breathy and foreign, even to her.

"Hmm." Dirk moved closer, the warmth of his thigh

seeping through Molly's borrowed skirts. His breath tickled the fine hairs at the nape of her neck. "Friendly."

His voice rumbled through Molly, compounding her growing and perplexing need. Her skin tingled and her breasts swelled inside her already tight-fitting bodice. He dropped his hand from hers to her waist, holding Sadie's bridle with the other.

With his thumb, he gently massaged Molly's back, just beneath her ribs. Continuing to stroke the horse and trying to ignore the burning temptation to turn into his embrace, she bit her lower lip. Though reckless, she ached to seek more of what he'd shown her yesterday. *Aye, more.* From the corner of her eye, she watched him watching her. His mouth still beckoned her. She could almost feel his lips against her bare shoulder again, though they now stood fully clothed in the light of day.

"You're making me crazy," he whispered, tightening his hold on her waist.

Was he about to kiss her? Molly melted inside with the thought, watching him intently for any indication that she might finally feel his glorious mouth on hers. *Aye, just once, so I'll know.*

His breath fanned her face, feeding the flames that licked along her veins. Feverish moisture churned within her, making her more acutely aware of that private place that begged to be filled. He lowered his face toward hers so slowly Molly wanted to cry out in frustration.

Hurry. Kiss me and be done with it. Though, somehow, she sensed she would never be done with the urgent demands of the formidable passion she hadn't known existed until coming to this place.

And this man.

Closer he came. Her breath froze. Her blood boiled.

Her insides clenched and tightened. Anticipating. A thin film of perspiration coated her as she waited.

Dying a little with every beat of her heart, she lifted her chin a wee bit, angling her lips to receive his kiss. She would not deny him this once, for she could not.

Their breaths mingled first, then, miraculously, she felt the warm brush of his mouth against hers. A small whimper escaped her and he tugged her closer, slipping his hand around until his arm half encircled her.

The pressure of his lips grew, and she trembled in his embrace. The power and strength of him surrounded and inflamed her. With his tongue, he coaxed her lips apart, deepening the kiss with an intimacy she'd never even imagined. His hot, slick tongue mated with her mouth, coaxing her to give and to take and to want even more.

Somehow, her hands found their way to the back of his neck, her fingers entwined with the silken strands of hair curling about his collar. She pulled him closer, her limbs quaking as she clung to him.

A low, primal groan rumbled from deep inside him, into her mouth, spiking straight to the heart of her hunger. He tightened his hold on her and dropped the bridle, using both arms to hold her full against his long, hard body.

Even through the fullness of her skirt and petticoat, Molly noticed the hard bulge pressing against her. His glorious mouth continued to feast on her, inciting her already rampant desire. He slipped his hands lower, cupping her buttocks and pulling her slightly upward and against him, cradling his hardness against the hottest, most needy part of her.

Intimately.

The emptiness within her grew unbearable, and she suddenly knew precisely how to fill it. A shocking and stalwart urge to wrap her legs around him and pull him inside her made her moan.

That wanton, animalistic sound jarred her back to reality. *Faith, Molly Riordan, what are you doing?*

Shocked by her torrid response to his kiss, and even more by her powerful desire to continue, she pulled back. "Jesus, Mary, and Joseph," she whispered, pushing him away and escaping the tempting circle of his embrace.

She swayed and he reached for her arm, but she held up a hand to stay him. "Please," she murmured, "don't."

The pull toward him was palpable. Surrender would have been her easiest course. But Molly Riordan rarely chose the easy path.

She whirled around, turning her back on him and on her infuriating attraction to the man. After drawing several deep breaths, she turned to face him again, her shoulders squared, her determination firmly in place. She hoped.

Lance stood a few feet behind Dirk, appearing thoroughly shocked . . . and something more. Was that a sense of betrayal she saw on the lad's face? *He saw us.* Her guilt compounded, giving her the strength she needed to resist Dirk Ballinger—at least for now.

Then a movement beyond Lance distracted her. A tall man on a golden horse sat near the barn, staring. At this distance, his expression and identity were impossible to determine. Even so, a growing uneasiness filled her, almost as if she'd seen him before.

She lifted her hand to point and looked at Dirk as she did. A mistake. The intensity of his gaze distracted her. Wrestling with herself, she asked, "Who is that?"

"Who?" He turned to look toward the side of the barn where she continued to point.

But the stranger was gone.

* * *

Dirk couldn't deny that Molly had been visibly shaken by the man she thought she'd seen. There were nearly two dozen wranglers employed by the Ballinger Ranch. The rider could've been anyone.

Then why couldn't he shake his own sense of foreboding?

With a sigh, he stared out his office window, shoving thoughts of disappearing horsemen from his mind. He had real concerns about real people, namely his half brother and the Lovejoy Gang.

Under protest, Molly was upstairs with Ida, preparing for their journey into the mountains. At Dirk's insistence, Ida was providing "Mrs. Ballinger" with jeans and boots from some Lance had outgrown.

Molly's argument that wearing men's trousers was unseemly hadn't influenced Dirk's insistence at all. If she persisted with her insane plan to accompany him into the high country, then she would ride astride and dress accordingly. He wouldn't have any woman in his charge sliding off her prissy sidesaddle and falling into a canyon or off a cliff. After seeing her fear of gentle old Sadie, Dirk had grown even more determined.

He glanced at the mantel clock and scowled. Templeton had promised him a report by noon, and Dirk refused to wait a moment beyond that. The sheriff had exactly twenty-three minutes to fulfill his promise. After that, Dirk, Molly Riordan, and Jeremiah Zane would leave in search of Ray Lovejoy and his cohorts.

Dirk squinted into the bright, midday sun. As instructed, Zane led their saddled horses and a pack mule to the front of the house. Dirk glanced at the clock again. *Almost time.*

One part of him hoped Templeton would end this

nightmare for them all. Another, far more confused part of Dirk wanted the satisfaction of capturing the infamous Ray Lovejoy himself.

His own flesh and blood.

Lovejoy had become an obsession for Dirk, ever since that day over a year ago when his unknown half brother had shown up at his front door. Dirk had known at first glance that Ray was related somehow. Those Ballinger eyes—bright green and fringed with thick black lashes—were rare and distinct.

Ray had been cocky and smirking at first, then he'd become charming. The charming side had been infinitely more dangerous. Dirk had fooled himself into believing he'd seen something more behind the sarcasm and false charm.

A need to belong. Dirk had been mistaken, of course. Sadly mistaken.

Ray had asked for Edward. The old man had been dead for eight months by then, but Ray obviously hadn't heard the news. Or maybe he had. Maybe taking advantage of honorable, gullible Dirk Ballinger had been Ray's plan all along.

And he'd sure as hell succeeded.

Ray had put on one hell of a show for Dirk—feigning disappointment at hearing of their father's death and asking if his half brother would teach Ray about the father he'd never known. *Pure bull.* But Dirk had fallen for it. All of it.

Dirk clenched his fists, remembering how he'd actually felt *guilty* about inheriting the ranch when his half brother didn't even have their father's name. He'd offered to let Ray stay, hoping for the chance to get to know him better. He'd wanted to share part of Edward Ballinger's legacy. In fact, Dirk asked the family lawyer if there was some legal way to give Ray the family name.

Ray stayed at the ranch for three weeks, ingratiating himself to Lance and even the highly suspicious Clyde Yeager. And Dirk. With a burning in the pit of his stomach, Dirk remembered that last night.

Over after-dinner brandy, Dirk presented Ray with a letter the lawyer had drawn up, soliciting the court to give Ray the Ballinger name. Ray stared at the letter for several silent moments, but said nothing.

Dirk should have known when his half brother avoided meeting his gaze that all was not right. Even after he presented Ray with the bank draft for twenty-five thousand dollars.

The next morning, there was no sign of Ray Lovejoy. Dirk had tried to find him, but the trail only indicated a quick stop at the bank to cash the draft.

For six months, there'd been no word from or about Ray Lovejoy. However, when the letter arrived from Lord Summersby, insisting Dirk had left his daughter with child after his European tour, Dirk knew immediately how his half brother had spent the twenty-five thousand dollars.

Lovejoy had treated himself to a European vacation, pretending to be Dirk. How many women had the bastard seduced under Dirk's name? So far, he'd heard only of Lady Elizabeth, but only because she'd had the misfortune of conceiving Ray's child.

A child Dirk vowed would be raised a Ballinger.

"Damnation." He shoved his fingers through his hair and paced his father's study, cursing Edward Ballinger. His father's sin was being visited upon Dirk again and again. But that was about to end.

Upon his return to Colorado, Ray and the Lovejoy Gang had launched a crime spree covering half the state. Ray had obviously run out of money during his European sojourn.

Gritting his teeth, Dirk grabbed his hat and shoved it on his head. Lying and cheating Edward Ballinger's legitimate son was one thing, but stealing and kidnapping was another. One way or another, Ray Lovejoy had to be stopped.

And, by God, it was Dirk's duty to stop him.

Molly stared at her reflection in the mirror, her mouth agape. "I . . . I can't," she whispered.

Ida made a tsking sound and patted Molly on the shoulder. "There, there, child." Her smile was indulgent, almost motherly. "Where you're headed, you'll be thankful for the heavy fabric covering your legs. Ranchers' wives often wear dungarees and go on roundup."

Aye, but I'm not a rancher's wife. Molly swallowed. Gram had always been a practical woman, but the old woman would've been scandalized by the sight of her granddaughter in dungarees. "Jesus, Mary, and Joseph," Molly muttered, glancing heavenward. "I hope no one sees me like this."

"Your husband and Jeremiah Zane will see you."

My husband. Molly's cheeks warmed, and she avoided the older woman's gaze. She'd been embarrassed around Ida upon realizing the woman knew Molly couldn't have lost a child yesterday. Her promise to Dirk about pretending to be Lady Elizabeth prevented Molly from explaining.

Ida smiled. "You've married well," she said. "Dirk Ballinger is a fine man. He'll make you happy and take care of you."

Molly's cheeks burned, and she was thankful when

the older woman returned to packing the leather pouches Dirk had dubbed saddlebags. He had also informed her that she could take only what could be contained within those pouches. Her bedroll would be tied across the back of her saddle, and she would wear one of Lance's hats.

With the hat over her braided hair and one of Lady Elizabeth's shirtwaists tucked into the waistband, Molly looked like a lad. She furrowed her brow, staring at herself. Perhaps that was for the best. At least Dirk Ballinger wouldn't be finding her attractive now.

"We'd best get downstairs," Ida said, arresting Molly's thoughts before she could relive what had happened out by the barn.

The kiss.

Her cheeks burning, Molly bit her lower lip and collected the saddlebags. As she followed the older woman down the stairs, she glanced down and took comfort that at least she had her own sturdy shoes. Everything else she wore had been borrowed either from Lance or Lady Elizabeth.

Elena waited at the base of the stairs, a worried expression on her lovely face. "Mama has packed food for your journey," she said, wringing her hands. *"Señor* Ballinger is outside, waiting for you."

"Is Sheriff Templeton here?" Ida asked, glancing nervously over her shoulder at Molly. "If his posse was successful, Mr. and Mrs. Ballinger won't have to go."

"No, the sheriff isn't here yet." Elena gave a dramatic sigh. *"Señor* Ballinger waits for him."

If the sheriff had been successful, Lady Elizabeth would take her rightful place as Dirk's bride. A pang of regret shot through Molly, startling her. Wasn't that what she wanted? Aye, but then she would once again become a lady's *maid* instead of a lady.

The realization that she didn't wish to resume that role made her heart race and her palms perspire. Was that the only reason?

She couldn't lie to herself. Dirk's kiss had branded her. He was like the forbidden fruit Gram had mentioned. *Once tasted, its flavor makes a body be craving more and more.*

Oh, aye—more and more.

Ida took the wrapped bundle from Elena and proceeded toward the door. Molly followed her out into the bright sunshine, her gaze immediately seeking Dirk. He was pacing before the house, consulting his pocket watch more than once.

Remembering the stricken look on his face when he'd asked her if Ray had killed Mr. Slim, Molly's chest tightened and her throat clogged. *Please, Jesus, let his brother be a better man than we both fear.*

Another man stood a few feet away holding the reins of three saddled horses and a mule laden with supplies. Ida tied the bundle of food to the mule without hesitation. The older woman had obviously prepared for similar journeys many times before.

"Where the hell is he?" Dirk continued pacing until he saw Molly. Then he froze, his gaze locking with hers. His eyes glittered as he looked down the length of her, then back to her bosom.

He's remembering, too. Molly's heart fluttered and her cheeks warmed. She'd done more blushing since arriving at the ranch than she had in years. And judging from the way Dirk Ballinger's emerald green eyes smoldered when they beheld Molly, her face would be red more often than not.

He shook his head and shoved his hat back as if that action would bring his wayward thoughts under control. "Zane, I'd like you to meet Mol—Mrs. Ballinger," he said. "This is Jeremiah Zane. Nobody's better at tracking than Jeremiah. He's half Kiowa and seems to know things before they happen."

The gangly old man nodded and touched two fingers to the brim of his hat. "Ma'am." His mode of dress and accent resembled that of a cowboy rather than an Indian.

Molly took in his long silver hair and wrinkled skin. "I'm pleased to meet you, Mr. Zane."

"Just Jeremiah, ma'am."

His black eyes twinkled. Molly couldn't even begin to guess his age, but she suspected he was even older than Gram would have been if she were still alive. Molly had never been so close to an Indian before, though she'd seen a few at some of the train stations.

Her confidence about rescuing Lady Elizabeth grew. Dirk Ballinger was strong and determined, and the man he'd chosen as their guide appeared almost otherworldly. With their combined talents and strength, perhaps all truly would be well again.

"Riders coming," Jeremiah said without looking.

Molly stared in the direction Dirk stared, spotting a cloud of dust out on the prairie. How could Jeremiah have known without seeing?

Dirk tensed and looped his thumbs through his belt, drawing Molly's attention to the holster and pistols he now wore. An icy chill permeated her and her breath froze. She realized with a start that her fear wasn't for her own safety as much as for his. Instinct assured Molly he would protect her.

But who would protect him?

And what about Lady Elizabeth? She mustn't forget that her employer's life was in danger.

Dirk and Jeremiah both faced the approaching riders, and Molly stood near the porch while Ida examined the supplies tied to the mule. Someone touched her sleeve, and Molly turned to find Lance. He wore a solemn expression and held his fingers to his lips.

"What?" she whispered, sensing he wished to tell secrets.

He held his open hand out to her. A small silver pistol lay cradled in his palm. "It's loaded," he said. "Take it."

Molly shook her head. She'd never even touched a gun, let alone fired one. "I . . . I can't."

"Take it." He took her hand and placed the weapon in it, closing her fingers around it. "Please?"

Molly met Lance's gaze and saw raw emotion in his eyes. The lad was definitely smitten with her, and that knowledge humbled her. She couldn't refuse his gesture of kindness, though the thought of carrying a weapon made her wary. Even so, Dirk was armed, as was Jeremiah.

"Thank you," she whispered, shoving the small gun inside her saddlebags. "I'll return it to you safe and sound."

Lance stared at her for several moments, then spun around and ran up the steps and into the house.

Molly made a personal vow to do anything she could to redirect Lance's romantic interest toward Elena and away from her. After they brought Lady Elizabeth home.

The sound of hoofbeats grew closer, and Molly joined Dirk to watch the riders approach. There were three men on horseback. They slowed their approach as they neared the house.

"You're late," Dirk said, consulting his pocket watch again.

The man closest to them wore a shining star on his vest. "That we are," he said, swinging his leg over the horse's rump and dropping to the ground. He mopped sweat from his brow and approached Dirk. "The ~~bas~~ tards gave us the slip."

Dirk stared stonily into the distance. "We'll find them."

Something about the sheriff made Molly uneasy. The way he looked at her, for one thing, as if he knew her darkest secrets. Of course, Molly Riordan only had one secret—her identity.

She swallowed the lump in her throat as the men discussed the direction the Lovejoy Gang had taken, but her anxiety dragged her thoughts back to the man she'd seen by the barn earlier. Cold crept through Molly as she remembered the eerie feeling she'd had while the stranger watched her from beside the barn. She'd been unable to see him clearly, but his horse had been distinctive, gleaming like gold even from a distance.

"Where'd you lose the trail?" Dirk asked.

"South of the pass," the sheriff said. "Down West Creek a piece from Serendipity."

Serendipity? Molly's heart lurched, and she swung her gaze back to the sheriff. One corner of his mouth quirked upward, almost as if he was struggling not to smirk.

Had he known, somehow, that Molly's search for her da would lead her to Serendipity? But how could he? And, more importantly, why would it matter?

Then her gaze shifted to the lawman's beautiful golden horse.

Nine

In the past, trips into the high country had always been for pleasure. During his boyhood, Dirk and his father had traveled into the mountains to hunt. In later years, Dirk had gone with Clyde instead of his father, who'd lost his eyesight and all interest in anything and everything having to do with his son.

But this trip into the mountains was for anything *but* pleasure. Dirk had a serious mission to complete—a distasteful one.

The forest closed in around them as the horses picked their way up the trail toward West Creek. The trail followed a gentle grade here, though Dirk knew that wouldn't last. Once they crossed the creek, the trail would steepen until they came to West Creek Falls.

He smiled, suddenly eager to show Molly the falls. Under different circumstances, they might have shared a picnic there. Alone. With a sigh, he resigned himself to speculating about her reaction to her first look at the beautiful two-tiered waterfall flowing through a rocky hollow. In fact, if they made good time they'd probably camp there.

Old Jeremiah Zane rode several yards ahead with the mule. Molly and Sadie were directly ahead of Dirk, where he could keep an eye on her in case she ran into trouble. Despite her earlier reservations, however, Molly appeared to have a natural aptitude for horses.

Of course, Dirk had never met an Irishman without an affinity for horses and the willingness to brag about it. Why shouldn't an Irish *woman* share that gift? Except for the bragging. Dirk smiled at the thought of Molly being arrogant or boastful. *Unlikely as hell.*

His gaze traveled down her straight back to her slender waist, partially hidden by the bedroll tied to the saddle. Against his better judgment, he allowed his thoughts to drift back to how she'd looked standing in those form-fitting jeans with a frilly white shirt tucked in at the waist. Her breasts filled out the shirt nicely. *Very* nicely.

His male anatomy sprang to attention as memory provided the missing details. The way those jeans hugged her hips and buttocks had surprised Dirk. He'd had no idea Molly's curves below the waist were every bit as appealing as those above.

His cock gave an insistent throb as he remembered that kiss. *Damnation.* When he'd cupped her butt in his hands and hauled her up against him . . .

"Shit," he muttered to himself, mopping sweat from his brow with his bandanna.

Dirk shifted his weight in the saddle to accommodate his responsive body. He had to get his thoughts back to their quest. All he had to do was remember the numerous crimes Ray had committed against innocent people—and against Dirk—to cool his passion and restore his ability to concentrate.

Justice would be done. Templeton had wanted to deputize Dirk, but he'd refused. This job was too personal, and a badge wouldn't make any damned difference in the end. Dirk had what he needed to get the job done—a healthy thirst for vengeance and justice. In that order.

It wasn't the money he'd given Ray that made Dirk want to capture him. It wasn't even the knowledge that his half brother had bedded at least one woman using Dirk's name. The crimes he'd committed against others would have been enough to make Dirk want justice. The murders particularly demanded justice, though he still wasn't certain what role Ray had played in those. A niggling part of Dirk wanted to believe his half brother was incapable of murder.

The foolish part of him.

No, what galled Dirk most was the betrayal. Ray had taken Dirk's good faith gestures and flung them back in his face. Dirk had fallen for his false charm, and now innocent people were paying the price for Dirk's misplaced trust.

And he had to remember Lady Elizabeth. She carried Ray's child, a Ballinger by blood. The high and mighty Edward Ballinger's grandchild. Dirk gnashed his teeth, renewing his vow to see that child raised at the ranch with the Ballinger name, as Ray should've been. The only way Dirk knew to accomplish that was to marry the mother of the child—before she gave birth. If she was still alive . . .

The thought of marrying Lady Elizabeth dragged Dirk's thoughts back to Molly. A sigh drifted from him as realization made itself known with relentless certainty.

The prospect of being married to Molly Riordan would have been far preferable to marriage to the mysterious Lady Elizabeth. Not that Dirk had wanted to marry anyone just yet.

Still, the outspoken Molly had insulted him, called him a monster numerous times, threatened him with

all sorts of bodily harm . . . and set him on fire with
wanting her. He couldn't remember ever wanting a
woman as much. What a pity he'd never taste more
than a very potent appetizer.

Dirk was promised to the mother of his bastard half
brother's child.

A child who would *not* be raised a bastard.

They were going to Serendipity.

*Oh, Da, are you still there? Will you be remembering
your own daughter?* Molly prayed Niall Riordan was
still alive and that she would find him in Serendipity.

Aye, and once they arrived, she'd be giving him a
piece of her mind. Or two. She dearly hoped he had a
very good reason for not sending for her after her
mother died, though she couldn't think of one acceptable enough. Other than death.

Be alive, Da. Be alive.

Sighing, Molly clung to the pommel with both
hands, but not as tightly now as when they'd first left
the ranch. Sadie was living up to her reputation as gentle and slow. And didn't Molly appreciate both attrib-
utes more than she could say?

Furthermore, though she hated to admit it, having
one leg on either side of the horse lent her a modicum
of security she realized would have been absent with
a sidesaddle. Hence, the dungarees had proven their
worth.

Besides, weren't her buttocks and inner thighs already sore enough? Surely that would be worse without
the sturdy fabric between Molly and the saddle. Aye,
she could now understand why men appeared more
confident and limber when they moved—though she

suspected she would be anything but limber after her first day in the saddle.

The mountains were even more glorious up close than they had been from the ranch. She drew a deep breath of the cool mountain air, the scent of pine and freshness tingling her nose and enlivening her senses. If they had been walking, she would have run out of breath many times by now. Even riding, she was a bit short of wind, but Dirk had said she would grow accustomed to it.

Dirk. Thinking of him made her remember what she must try to forget. *Aye, too late, for I can never forget.* Reliving their forbidden kiss, she could actually feel the brush of his lips, the compelling hardness between his legs, and the texture of his fingers on her heated flesh.

She rotated her head and rolled her stiff shoulders, struggling against the persistent ache Dirk had triggered within her. There was no escaping the gnawing hunger now. The frustrating man had cursed her with his magic, making her want even more.

The thought of having more of what Dirk Ballinger had to offer reminded her how she'd lost control this morning. *No, Molly—enough of that.* She had to direct her thoughts to the problem before them. Her first priority had to be finding Lady Elizabeth and ensuring that the mother of Dirk's child took her rightful place as his wife.

A lump formed in Molly's throat at the thought of Dirk kissing Lady Elizabeth. But hadn't the man already done that . . . and a lot more? Summoning the memory of that night in England when Dirk had planted his seed, Molly's belly roiled and a perplexing heaviness gripped her heart.

She had no right to the man—none at all.

Then why did she want him so?

Jeremiah and the mule stopped ahead and he half turned in the saddle, waiting for them. "They came this way," he said without preamble.

Molly pulled steadily on the reins as Dirk had demonstrated, and Sadie rewarded her by stopping. Dirk halted his gray horse, appropriately called Cloud, beside Sadie.

"You see sign?" Dirk asked.

Molly wondered what that meant, but remained silent, waiting for the men to say more. Jeremiah made a grunting sound and pointed from where they'd come. "Horsehair on some trees back there." Then he pointed to a tree beside the trail. "And this was the same horse."

Noticing the reddish brown hair caught in the branches of a young tree, Molly shook her head. How in the world could the man be certain of that? How had he even *seen* the hair, for that matter? She furrowed her brow, but continued to listen.

Dirk nodded again. "So they came this way?"

"To the creek." Jeremiah pointed ahead of them now, through dense pines and the white-barked, quaking trees she'd never seen before reaching Colorado. Dirk had called them aspen trees.

"Templeton said he lost them at the creek." Dirk shoved his hat back farther on his head and mopped his brow. He looked up at the sky. "We'll make camp soon. We got a late start and Molly isn't used to traveling this way."

Her cheeks burned. "I can go farther."

Dirk gave her an indulgent smile that warmed her heart and lifted her spirits. Unreasonably so, Molly told herself.

"I think your Irish stubbornness can do anything you

set your mind to," he said, holding her gaze. "But see those dark clouds gathering over the summit?"

Molly nodded, watching lightning streak down to the earth several times. "Aye, is it going to storm?"

"Even if it doesn't rain, the lightning makes it too dangerous to continue now." He looked at the gathering storm, then back to her. "Besides, dark comes fast and relentless along the front range. Once we crest the summit, that won't be the case."

She inclined her head in feigned comprehension and acceptance of his explanation of dark, though she had no idea why that would be better once they "crested the summit."

"You gonna camp at the falls?" Jeremiah asked, facing forward now.

"I can't think of a better place." Dirk gave Molly a smile that stole her breath. "You're about to see one of the most beautiful places on earth."

"Ah, but have you seen Ireland?" she quipped, returning his smile. "There's not a green to match it." *Except maybe your eyes.* Her face flooded with liquid fire at the thought.

"So I've heard." His smile faded and that smoldering expression returned. "I've never been to Ireland, but I hope to see it one day."

She nodded, somehow relieved to learn he hadn't visited her homeland during his trip to England. Though it was silly, knowing that comforted her. An even more foolish part of her yearned to show him the verdant isle where she was born.

But, of course, that would never happen. If he journeyed abroad again, his wife would be at his side. Perhaps Lady Elizabeth would want to visit her father after the babe was born.

That annoying pang of jealousy shot through Molly

again and she tore her gaze away, feeling suddenly and illogically betrayed. *Molly Riordan, you are a fool.* If anyone had been betrayed, it was none other than Lady Elizabeth herself. By her own lady's maid. Renewed guilt pressed down on Molly and she sighed.

The sooner they found Lady Elizabeth, the sooner Molly could put her annoying attraction to Dirk behind her. *So let's be getting along with it now.* Relief filled her when Jeremiah moved again, and she nudged Sadie into a slow walk, feeling Dirk's gaze on her back. Jesus, Mary, and Joseph, but even the man's eyes held heat.

She heard the falls before she saw them, and the air felt cooler here. Molly inhaled the fragrance of water, relishing it after the dryness of this land. She would savor a soft day in Ireland about now, but the falls certainly held promise. Dirk called for her to stop, then dismounted and led both her horse and his toward the creek. Molly saw water glittering through the branches. Then she caught sight of the falls and held her breath.

Dirk glanced back over his shoulder once and flashed her a boyish grin that crawled into a tender spot in her heart she'd failed to protect. The realization made her bite her lower lip, and her heart fluttered a bit.

Wanting the man was annoying and inconvenient—naughty—but genuinely caring for him was dangerous. Risky.

But true.

Faith. She didn't need or want this. Not now, and certainly not with this man. He belonged to her mistress—her employer. He'd plowed Lady Elizabeth's field and planted his seed, as Gram would've said. Crude but so very true.

That knowledge sent a sharp stab of pain through her heart every time she remembered it.

Jeremiah dismounted and stood watching the falls.

Molly stared at the water pouring from the side of the mountain. It pooled high above them, then reappeared as twin falls that fed the creek.

Dirk appeared at her side, reaching up to assist her dismount. She'd been in this saddle for hours, and her backside was practically numb, her legs stiff and sore. She hesitated to let him touch her, but she was too eager to feel her weight on her own two feet to delay any longer.

He'd removed his leather gloves, but she still wore the pair Lance had loaned her. At least she would have that slight barrier between her hand and Dirk's. But her hand wasn't what he was after. Alas, he gripped her waist with both hands and lifted her to the ground.

Molly's knees quaked and one collapsed, requiring Dirk to maintain his grip on her even after she was safely on the ground. She made the mistake of meeting his probing gaze. The man practically made love to her with his eyes, and the pity of it was that her body responded with a glee that made her cheeks burn with shame.

"I can manage," she said, needing to break the tension—rather, the spell he'd cast over her.

He released her and stepped back. "I need to tend the horses."

Jeremiah rode his small black horse with only a blanket between him and the horse's back. Now he used the rough fabric to rub the horse's hide, while the animal nuzzled his long silver hair. "Hungry?" he asked his horse, laughing.

While Dirk unsaddled Cloud and Sadie, Molly tested her legs by approaching Jeremiah. He appeared even older now with his hat hanging down his back from a leather strap around his neck. "Your horse is very pretty," she said.

Jeremiah gave her a shy smile and nodded. "Mustang." He led the horse to the creek and gave her enough rein to drink from the clear water. After a few moments, he raised her head. "Not too fast, girl," he said.

Molly reached out a tentative hand and stroked the animal's side. Back on Gram's farm in Ireland, they'd raised sheep, goats, and some chickens. Horses were for the rich, but in this country everybody had a horse. "What's her name?"

"Midnight."

"It suits her."

Jeremiah allowed Midnight to drink again as Dirk joined them with Sadie and Cloud. Molly knew more about horses after today than she'd ever thought possible. She stretched the muscles of her back and rubbed her backside.

"Sore?" Dirk asked quietly.

She looked up and found him staring at her bosom. Glancing down, she realized that while stretching out her stiffness, she had inadvertently made her bosom more prominent. *There I go blushing again.* It seemed all she did around this man was blush and . . . and want.

"I'm going fishing." Jeremiah left his horse's reins hanging free. He pushed up his sleeves and sat on the creek bank to remove his boots. A moment later, he waded into the water.

"He doesn't use a fishing pole?"

Dirk lifted one shoulder. "He's never needed one."

Molly watched Jeremiah stand there very still, bent over with his hands cupped in the water. Waiting. Then, suddenly, he flung a fish onto the bank, its scales glistening in the waning sunlight.

Molly stared, incredulous, as another fish joined the

first. They both flopped about on the rock-strewn bank until they fell still and were joined by a third, even larger fish. "That's amazing."

"That's trout," Dirk corrected, chuckling when she scowled at his silliness. "I'd better start a fire."

Molly filled the tin coffeepot with water, upstream from the horses, and carried it to the small fire. Dirk had placed rocks in a circle around the fire, explaining that was to contain the flames. Due to the dryness, fires were a constant threat in the Rockies.

That reminded Molly that the storm had never reached them. She looked up to confirm that the clouds and lightning were now gone, and the sun had vanished behind the highest peak. The only light they had now came from the fire. The sky high above them gleamed silver for a while longer, then went dark as the sun sank farther.

"I told you darkness is relentless around here," Dirk said from her side.

Molly didn't object when he took the coffeepot from her and placed it over the fire beside where the scaled fish were propped on sticks. He stooped and removed the lid, poured coffee into the pot, then replaced the lid and straightened.

Jeremiah poked the largest fish with a pointed stick and said, "Almost done."

A few moments later, Molly sat on a boulder with a plate of tender trout and a handful of berries Jeremiah had picked. The coffee was far too strong and bitter without cream and sugar, so she opted for cool water instead. However, the fish and berries were delicious, and she was ravenous after the long afternoon.

After dinner, she knelt beside the creek and washed out their plates and the coffeepot. Dirk dried them and stored them with their supplies, then spread her bedroll near the fire, and his very near it.

Too near.

She swallowed the lump in her throat, reminding herself that they were in the wilderness with wild animals and untold dangers. Besides, they were not alone.

Thankfully.

Jeremiah placed all their food in a bundle and tied it with a rope, then tossed the free end over the limb of a tree and hoisted the items into the air. Bewildered, Molly stared as he tied the rope to the trunk of the tree to hold their supplies in midair.

"Why?" she finally asked.

"Bears." Jeremiah offered no additional explanation as he gathered his bedroll and headed toward the falls.

Molly shuddered. She'd never seen a bear, nor did she wish to now. "Where is he going?" she asked Dirk, staring at the departing Indian.

Dirk remained silent as Jeremiah disappeared behind a boulder the size of a small cottage near the base of the falls. Suspicion slithered through Molly and that lump returned to her throat with a vengeance.

She whirled around to face Dirk, her hands fisted at her hips. "Where is he going?" she repeated.

Dirk sighed and folded his arms, gazing down at her in the darkness. "He said he didn't want to intrude."

Suspicion slithered through her. "Intrude on *what?*"

"You'll need to undress before climbing into your bedroll," he said, obviously ignoring her question.

"Undress?" She gulped. "Out here?"

He lifted one shoulder, his dark silhouette in stark relief from the glow of the fire. "Suit yourself, but if the bears smell food on your clothes . . ."

She hesitated, trying to follow his thoughts. If a bear smelled food on her clothes . . . it might mistake her for its supper. *Oh!* "I understand." She pulled the only nightgown she'd brought along from her saddlebags. "Turn around."

She undressed and slipped on the nightgown faster than she ever had. "All right," she said, once the warm flannel had covered her. "You can turn around now."

"Now give me your clothes." He reached toward her.

"Why?"

He glanced up at the suspended bundle of food. "They're going up there, along with mine."

Molly gulped again. "You're . . . undressing, too?" She sounded childish even to herself.

Dirk gave a low chuckle and placed her clothes in the middle of a blanket he'd spread on the ground, then he started unbuttoning his shirt. "Watch if you want."

Molly spun around, her face blazing. The man was disconcerting, to say the least. He was, quite simply, driving her mad. By the time they found and rescued Lady Elizabeth, she would be a raving lunatic—all from an overabundance of wanting what she couldn't have.

She heard an odd noise and looked over her shoulder. He was hoisting the bundle containing their clothing high into the air where bears couldn't reach it.

Nor could she.

The fire had died down to nothing more than glowing red embers now. Dirk approached it and tossed a large log on, and flames licked up its sides almost immediately.

As the light of the fire grew, she noticed the way it glowed against his skin. All of it. On a gasp, she muttered, "Jesus, Mary, and Joseph." He wore a blanket wrapped around his waist.

And nothing more.

"Unlike you," he said, watching the fire and poking it with a long stick, "I don't have a nightshirt."

"You don't?" Her voice actually squeaked. *Pitiful, Molly.*

"I don't care for them, so I don't even own one." At her gasp, he chuckled low, but not unkindly. When she remained silent, he said, "That fat log ought to burn a good long while."

Molly continued to stare at the way firelight danced along the planes and angles of his magnificent chest. The muscles in his arms rippled whenever he moved. His abdomen was flat with ridges like a washboard. He was far too beautiful. Temptingly so . . .

"Better get some shut-eye." He straightened, jabbing the long stick into the earth next to a rock.

Her earlier suspicion returned, followed closely by something akin to panic. "What, exactly, did Jeremiah wish not to intrude upon?" she asked steadily, then held her breath as she awaited Dirk's answer.

He turned to face her, his expression solemn, his eyes glittering through the darkness.

"What?" she repeated, hating the breathy quality of her voice.

"Our honeymoon."

Molly's eyes grew so wide Dirk feared for a moment she might faint. She swayed, clutching at the demure ruffled collar of her nightgown. As if he could seduce her through all those yards of flannel.

Then again, he appreciated a challenge.

"Molly, our clothes are suspended up there for our safety," he said evenly, trying to ignore the enthusiastic pounding of blood through his veins, culminating between his legs. "And Jeremiah believes we're married. Remember?"

She nodded very slightly. "Aye, and didn't I agree to the ruse with certain restrictions?" Her voice was barely more than a nervous whisper.

He grinned. "Actually, you never defined those restrictions."

Her sharp intake of breath came as no surprise. "And are you trying to say you *need* them defined, Mr. Ballinger?"

Her voice was stronger now. His feisty Molly had returned. The more vigorously she argued with him, the more he wanted her. Crazy as it was, the woman's fiery temper and outspoken ways aroused him.

You're a sick, sick man, Dirk Ballinger. You should be ashamed.

His cock gave a belligerent throb.

Down, boy.

And if his anatomy had been able to speak, the response would've been something along the lines of, "The hell I will."

He was harder and hotter than a branding iron. Clearing his throat, he raked his fingers though his hair, careful to keep the blanket closed at his waist. If the moon had been full instead of a mere crescent, Molly would've had no difficulty seeing the tented fabric. Furthermore, it wouldn't have taken her long to determine the catalyst for that tent, either.

Against his better judgment, he remembered the way he'd felt with her cradled against his hardness during this morning's kiss. He'd never lost control like that with any woman before this perplexing Irish lady's maid. But there they'd been, standing out in the paddock in front of God and everybody. He'd lifted her up and against his erection simply because he'd wanted it.

Oh, he wanted so much more. He wanted to strip away the barrier of clothing and slide himself deep and hard into her warmth, to feel her close tightly around his throbbing shaft, to—

Oh, God. A guttural groan rumbled from his chest, drifting into the cooling night air.

She didn't speak, though she must've heard him. After the way he'd pressed himself against her this morning, she undoubtedly knew why he'd made the sound, too.

He wanted this woman. It was that simple.

And that complicated.

"You'd better get some sleep," he said, his voice hoarse and thick and sounding very, very strained. He sure as hell didn't have any questions about why he sounded strained, either.

"Aye," she whispered, her tongue slipping between her lips to moisten them, leaving a silken sheen behind.

Golden firelight danced in the moisture, making Dirk ache to kiss it away. And so damned much more. "Go to sleep, Molly." His words came out gruffer than he'd intended, but he needed to put some distance between them before he forgot she wasn't really his wife. That she was only pretending . . . with restrictions.

A shudder rippled through him and he groaned again. She spun around and rushed to her bedroll, climbing inside and pulling her blanket up to her chin.

Hide yourself well, Molly Riordan. I'm not to be trusted.

Dirk practically dragged his frustrated body to his own bedroll—less than two feet from Molly's—and slid inside. He knew sleep would elude him, for his body continued to ache and throb for the woman at his side. She was so close. So appealing.

So forbidden.

He bunched some blanket under his head for a pillow, gnashing his teeth the whole time. Maybe he'd doze off and take her in his dreams. That was the only way he'd ever have her, so why not?

He swallowed the lump in his throat, his cock giving another insistent throb. All he had to do was convince himself that sleep was his reward. Right?

He closed his eyes, listening to her breathing and knowing she was also awake. "The stars are pretty tonight," he said. "The moon is almost new, so it's dark enough to see them."

"Aye."

Her voice carried to him and his heart leaped at the sound. She was so close. *Stop it, Ballinger.* He bit the edge of his tongue in frustration, cursing to himself at the sharp sting of pain. Then again, maybe pain would ease the infernal ache between his legs.

No, it hadn't helped at all. He turned on his side, facing her. Torture. He'd hoped to be unable to see her at all.

Then why the devil didn't you turn on your other side? With a sigh, he stared at her through the darkness. All he could see was her dark hair, her pale face, and the dark blanket pulled up to her chin. Not much there to feed his thoughts.

But after touching her and kissing her, it didn't take much. He knew firsthand how responsive she could be. And, damnation, he wanted to feel her quiver and cling to him again. And again.

And again.

Enough of that. I'll dream about her, and that will be enough.

But sleep eluded him. He knew why, too, besides the obvious and insistent pulsating between his legs. He needed to fill in one missing detail before he could begin his dream. The only way to find out was to ask, since he hadn't thought to look at her clothing before hoisting it into the air.

"Molly?"

Several silent seconds ticked by, and he thought she'd fallen asleep. Just his luck when only she could answer his question.

"What?" she finally returned.

"Are you . . . wearing anything under your nightgown?"

She gasped and sputtered, then fell silent again.

"You aren't going to answer me?"

"No," she said. "Go to sleep."

"I will." He cleared his throat. "After you tell me."

She sighed and said, "No."

"No, what?" His heart leaped and his stomach pressed upward against it. "No, you aren't wearing anything or no, you aren't going to answer me?"

"Just . . . no."

"Does that mean I can make up my own answer?"

"You're naughty," she said, her voice husky and enticing.

"Yes, and I'd like to get a lot naughtier."

"No."

"So answer my question and I'll dream about you instead."

Her gasp filled the night and made him yearn to swallow it with a kiss she'd feel to her toes.

"Mr. Ballinger . . ."

"Dirk," he corrected, aching to reach out and touch her.

"Dirk," she whispered, her voice so quiet he barely heard her.

"Are you wearing anything under that prissy nightgown, Molly Riordan?"

More silence filled the night. Then an owl hooted from the trees towering over them. She wasn't going to answer him, and he was doomed to lie awake all night counting the damned stars . . . and wondering if her skin was bare beneath her nightgown.

Then her answer drifted to him on the night air, so sweet, so soft, he almost missed it.

"No."

Ten

Ida Jensen stared up at the portrait of Edward Ballinger, her eyes burning and her lower lip trembling. He looked so powerful, so infallible . . . so merciless.

However, he hadn't been infallible—he'd lost his eyesight and had eventually died, proving he'd never been anything but a mere mortal, after all. But he'd remained powerful and merciless even without his sight. In fact, his son was still suffering because of Edward Ballinger's sins even after the old man's death.

"It's a fine mess you've made of things," she whispered, shaking her head. "You did only one decent thing in your life, you know, and you didn't have the courage to see it through."

"Talking to ghosts, Ida?"

The deep baritone startled her and she whirled around, pressing the heel of her hand to her thundering heart. Clyde Yeager stood near the kitchen door, watching her.

She gave a nervous laugh and regained her ability to breathe. "Mr. Yeager, have mercy. You frightened ten years off my life."

He came toward her with his long-legged swagger, his hat clutched in his hands. "I sure hope not, ma'am," he said. "I'd like for you to live a good long while yet. I'm sorry for startlin' you."

Ida studied the man's sincere expression. She'd known for some time that he'd been watching her, but she'd argued with herself about his motives. The man couldn't be interested in her for any personal reasons. *Heavens.* The mere thought made her pulse race and her palms perspire.

"I forgive you, Mr. Yeager," she said, regaining her composure. "What brings you up to the house? Have you received word from Dirk? He said for us to watch for any news about Mrs. Ballinger's maid."

Clyde shook his head, tilting it at an angle. A warm smile curved his lips, accentuating the white lines in the tanned skin around his mouth. "I came to see you," he said. "Ma'am. If that's all right."

Ida's heart did that strange fluttery thing again—something she hadn't felt since first meeting her husband so many years ago. "Of course it's all right." Her voice sounded strange even to her own ears. "What can I do for you?"

His silver eyes twinkled and he cleared his throat, then he looked up at the portrait of Edward Ballinger. "I've been doin' some rememberin'," he said, still staring at the portrait. "When Edward first come to Colorado and hired me on as a wrangler."

Ida swallowed hard and watched Clyde's stoic expression as he stared at the painting. "You . . . were here then?" she asked, barely breathing.

Clyde chuckled and nodded, meeting her gaze. "Yep, and he weren't near as mean back then."

"I don't . . . that is, I didn't realize you'd been here that long." Ida furrowed her brow, watching Clyde carefully.

He cast her one of his charming lopsided grins, then pointed at Edward's portrait. "Well, ma'am, except for a few years durin' the war, I've been part of the Ballinger Ranch since it was nothin' more'n a cabin and a few scrawny longhorns."

"The war . . ." she echoed, trying to sort through all the implications of his words.

"The War of Northern Aggression—it was my duty, ma'am." His expression grew solemn. "I left as soon as I heard and joined my brother's company down in Texas in '63."

"I see."

"By the time the war ended, I was hankerin' for these mountains." He sighed and met her gaze, smiling again. "This land has a way of crawlin' into a man's soul, if you know what I mean, ma'am."

And a woman's. Ida nodded, not trusting herself to speak.

"I, uh, thought maybe you'd walk out with me this evenin'." He cleared his throat again and continued to hold her gaze. "The stars are durned near as . . . purty as you. Ma'am."

Shocked, Ida pressed her hand to her breastbone again, staring silently at the man who'd come calling. *Yes, calling.* That realization brought her back from the past to the present again. *Thank heavens.*

Who'd have believed any man would ever want to call on Ida Jensen again? Her cheeks warmed, and she struggled for a deep breath.

"I'm sorry if I've come at a bad time." He lowered his gaze and rotated his hat between his fingers. "I'll skedaddle on back to the bunk—"

"No, wait." Ida touched Clyde's muscular forearm, startled by his warmth and strength. She dropped her hand to her side when he turned toward her again. "I'll get my shawl and meet you on the front porch."

A shy smile curved Clyde's lips. "Yes, ma'am."

She watched him stride through the front door, a

wave of happiness flooding her. Never in her wildest dreams would she have pictured herself with a beau at this stage of her life.

She caught a glimpse of Edward Ballinger's portrait, and she pivoted to face the scowling patriarch again. "Amazing, isn't it?" Smiling and humming to herself, she dashed to her room just off the kitchen for her shawl.

A few moments later, she opened the front door and stepped into the cooling evening air. She drew a deep breath and saw Clyde leaning against the rail. He straightened and crooked his elbow.

Ida felt downright giddy as she looped her arm through his and they stepped off the porch together. A woman could do much worse—especially one whose bloom had long since begun to fade.

She glanced up at Clyde's profile as he looked down to meet her gaze. The only light was a faint sliver of moonlight and the lamplight shining through the ranch house windows. Heat pooled within her, and she had the sudden urge to grab the man and kiss him. But she decided to wait for him to do the kissing. At least the first time.

A smile curved her lips as she recognized the rebirth of long absent desire.

By heavens, you aren't done yet, old girl.

Molly stared up at the stars for what seemed like hours. She was totally exhausted after her first day of mountain travel, but with one little question, Dirk had ensured sleep would not come easily to her this night.

Are you wearing anything under that prissy night-gown, Molly Riordan?

And she'd actually answered the man. Shame and

guilt pressed down on her. If Gram had been watching from heaven, she had probably rolled over in her grave upon hearing her granddaughter's scandalous words. *Jesus, Mary, and Joseph.*

Drawing a deep breath, Molly turned onto her side, facing the forest. She'd lain awake listening to Dirk breathe until the steadiness and depth of his breathing assured her he was finally asleep.

And dreaming, no doubt.

Oh, I don't want to think about that.

When he'd asked her if she wore anything beneath her nightgown, she'd nearly swooned from both embarrassment . . . and something far less noble. The wanting would be the death of her yet, and it was wrong. Sinful. Wanton.

So why did *you answer the man, Molly Riordan?*

The why was easy enough. He'd cast some sort of lustful spell on her, of course. The man had a way about him. There was no sense denying it. She could easily see how and why Lady Elizabeth had succumbed to his charms.

However, the Dirk Ballinger Molly knew was very different from the masked man who'd wooed Lady Elizabeth into his carriage. This Dirk's behavior toward Molly was—or at least appeared to be—less rehearsed. More natural.

Aye, but isn't that because he's had more practice?

Her eyes burned and she squeezed them shut, trying to summon anything resembling anger or resentment. Unfortunately, her efforts proved futile.

Ah, if only she could hate him. But she couldn't. No amount of reasoning or remembering could convince her heart or her wanton urges that Dirk was anything less than the ideal man of her dreams.

Dreams? Bah. Are you listening to yourself, Molly

Riordan? She pressed her lips together tightly, growing angrier by the moment, but not at the man lying at her side. Her anger was directed at herself—rightfully so. *That will be enough of this nonsense. Go to sleep.*

Resurrecting memories of the green isle where she was born, Molly counted imaginary sheep leaping over the stone wall behind Gram's cottage. After more than a hundred woolly jumpers, sleep finally lowered its soothing hand.

And the emerald hills of Ireland promptly transformed into a pair of haunting green eyes.

He said nothing with words, though his smoldering expression mirrored the same forbidden thoughts plaguing her. Molly rose and stood before him. The decadent blue silk had replaced the flannel, and a gentle breeze molded it against her, revealing the shape of her legs, her hips, her breasts.

"I want you," he said, reaching for her.

Without hesitation, Molly took his hand, gasping as he pulled her into his embrace. The heat of his bare skin seared her through the silk, prompting her to gaze down between them. He wore only a blanket wrapped around his waist.

Unlike the crescent moon she'd watched before falling asleep, her dream moon was full and bright, bathing them in a silver cocoon. They were alone. So very, very alone.

Molly trembled in his arms and he massaged her back, his breathing growing ragged as he cradled her bottom in his large hands. He growled, sending a shudder rippling through him and into her.

She wanted to feel his lips on hers again. Now. Here. In the darkness. In the wilderness.

In her dreams.

Dreams were safe. In a dream she could be as wanton as she felt. No one could judge her dream but her. Surely even God would forgive dreams *about sin.*

Oh, aye, sin. Molly wanted to dream about sin and stolen kisses. She wanted to feel Dirk's heated flesh sliding against her own. She wanted him to touch her everywhere he'd touched her before. And more.

He pulled her even closer, brandishing the enticing bulge between his legs. Molly was curious about the male body, and she experienced a sudden and powerful urge to touch him there. Oh, but she couldn't. She mustn't.

Then his lips sought hers and she moaned, drinking in the taste and texture of him, savoring the thrilling heat that permeated every fiber of her. His kiss grew more demanding, harder, and she gave as much in return.

She couldn't get enough of him. She drew his tongue into her mouth, reveling in his explorations, and doing a bit of exploring of her own. Encircling his waist, she stroked the heated flesh of his bare back, wanting to delve beneath the blanket to feel his buttocks. He would be firm there, as he was everywhere.

He devoured her mouth, then trailed tiny kisses along her jaw and down the side of her neck. His warm lips lingered at the curve of her shoulder, where he traced wet circles with his tongue, then blew gently on her dampened flesh.

A shiver of molten need welled within her and

she moaned again. With his teeth, he nudged aside the silk until her entire shoulder was bare and silver in the moonlight. She watched his dark head against her pale flesh, wondering what madness he had planned for her next.

Her breasts swelled and ached, her nipples thrusting against the soft silk. As he kissed his way lower, she knew somehow what he sought. Trembling, she brought her hands to the back of his corded neck and twined her fingers through his silken curls. His unkempt hair gave him a roguish air that endeared him to her even more. His curls were so long they almost grazed his shoulders.

The urge to pull him against her pulsed through her, growing stronger by the moment. His tongue blazed a trail of fire across her shoulder, then inward. She felt him untie the sash at her waist and the silk robe slipped downward, trapped at her wrists, but revealing her nakedness.

He froze, pulling away ever so slightly to stare at her. Molly held her breath as his eyes gleamed silver in the moonlight, like a wolf perusing its prey.

Aye, willing prey.

"Perfect," he whispered, then dipped his head and brushed his warm, wet tongue against the taut peak of her breast.

She'd overheard Cook and Annie back at Lord Summersby's place speak about this—the suckling and licking. But their giggling explanations had done little to prepare Molly for this dream, let alone reality.

The contact was explosive and, oh, so very intimate. Sensation spiraled through her from that brief but powerful contact. Her back arched, thrusting her hips brazenly against his where the hot ridge of his manhood pulsed through the blanket encircling his waist. She gripped the back of his neck for support, clinging to him.

He sketched maddening circles with his tongue, then finally drew her nipple deeply into his mouth. Spasms ricocheted from her toes to her head, then centered deep in that hungry and relentless emptiness within her. Each tug of his hot mouth against her breast generated an enthusiastic response from her womanly core.

Gently, he lowered her to her bedroll, slipping the silk robe from her wrists. He hovered over her, devouring her with eyes she suspected missed nothing. Then his incredible mouth was on hers again, kissing her senseless as he cupped her breasts in his large hands.

He rose above her, his breathing ragged, then took her nipple into his mouth again. Molly's hips thrust upward and she rolled her head from side to side.

She was on fire with the wanting, the need, the fierce hunger. Inside her. She wanted him inside her. The emptiness grew unbearable as he took one, then the other of her breasts.

Frustration mounted and she emitted a low growl from deep in her throat. Continuing to suckle at her breast, he stroked the curve of her hip, then dipped his hand between her legs, cupping her. Her pelvis thrust against his hand, instinctively seeking fulfillment she didn't fully understand.

He stroked her damp flesh and the fire licked her blood, her soul, her heart.

She didn't know what would happen next. The frustration of not knowing how a man and woman dealt with these urges loomed before her even in her dream.

How would this madness end? How would she douse the flames he'd ignited within her?

A frustrated scream tore from her throat and Molly bolted upright. She clutched her nightgown at her throat, amazed to find herself still covered with flannel. Perspiration trickled down her face, into her eyes, and along the side of her neck to pool between her breasts. She shoved her hair back from her face and licked her salty lips.

A dream. It was nothing but a dream.

She drew several deep breaths and looked around. The fire still burned low, the embers glowing in the darkness. The air was chilly, the night quiet.

Her heartbeat slowed and her flesh cooled. She swallowed the lump in her throat and slid beneath her blanket again, hearing nothing but her own breathing in the silence.

She closed her eyes and rolled onto her side, but suspicion made her eyes pop open again almost immediately.

Dirk sat staring at her. She saw only his silhouette in the darkness, but she felt his gaze on her. Had he heard her? *Jesus, Mary, and Joseph, did he know?* And how had he managed to get so close?

Silently, he leaned on his elbow and peered down at her, his breath caressing her cheek. Feigning sleep now was pointless. He caressed her cheek with his palm, brushing the pad of his thumb along her jawline. He leaned closer and kissed her lips very softly, then straightened, withdrawing his hand.

"I think I'm jealous," he said, no trace of humor in his tone.

Molly held her breath, embarrassment washing over her.

Then he leaned close to her again, without touching her. "I want you to know," he whispered, "that I'd like nothing better than to finish that dream someday. For both of us."

Dirk awoke in the watery gray light just before dawn and felt the tent in his blanket before he saw it. After dreaming about Molly naked under all that flannel, he'd dreamed of having her naked *without* the flannel.

Then he'd suffered through her dream, amazed by how vocal she was. Would she be as vocal awake? God, but he wanted to solve that little mystery himself. Desperately. Listening to her moan and squirm had nearly driven him to seek methods of relief he hadn't utilized in well over a decade.

But he'd dreamed again instead, and now he was hard enough to drill for water—he sat up and winced—through granite. Keeping his blanket tucked around him, he stood and grabbed a stick to poke at the fire, then dropped a few small pieces of wood on it.

Once the fire was going well, he staggered toward the falls. That cold mountain stream would take care of his randy state in no time.

The icy sting felt like a billion needles against his bare skin. "Holy shit!" He'd seriously overestimated the water's temperature. He scrubbed his wet hair and stood in the water until his feet started tingling, then stepped out and rubbed himself dry with the rough wool blanket he'd left hanging on a branch.

Well, at least the water had taken care of his little

problem. In fact, after this he wondered if he'd ever get hard again. Hell, he'd frozen the Ballinger Family Jewels.

The sun was just climbing up the mountainside. He had started back toward the campfire and warmth when he saw her. Molly just stood there. Staring.

Then he noticed she was fully dressed. Suspicion sent his pulse into a full gallop. "How long . . . have you been standing there?" he asked, swallowing the lump in his throat.

She licked her lips—God, but it drove him mad when she did that—and blushed.

"Since, uh, you got up to tend the fire," she said, lowering her lashes.

Then she met his gaze with a hunger in her eyes that damned near sent him to his knees.

Alas, the Ballinger Family Jewels were far from frozen.

"You were . . . watching me?"

The pink in her cheeks transformed to crimson, and she bit her lower lip as she nodded.

"Now who's being naughty?" Trying to ignore his throbbing cock, Dirk arched his eyebrows. "Did you get a good peek?" He started to tug the blanket free.

"No. I mean, aye." The look she sent him was pleading, and her voice fell to a whisper. "Don't."

Chuckling, he headed toward the campfire again, resisting the urge to grab her and swing her into his arms. Zane came around a boulder at that moment, saving Dirk. And Molly.

"Good morning," Zane said, glancing at the bundles they'd hoisted into the trees last night. They were now on the ground.

"You did that?" Dirk asked Molly. "By yourself?"

Molly nodded, regaining her composure on her next breath. "I found the end of the rope."

Dirk watched her gird herself for battle. This was the Molly he loved best, though naked would've—

Whoa, Ballinger. Loved? Slow down there. Easy. He stumbled over a rock, then paused, gathering his wits.

"Dirk's woman is stronger than she looks," Zane said, gathering supplies for breakfast.

Dirk's woman. He'd like nothing better than to make that true. The realization jarred him to his senses—he hoped—and Dirk retrieved his clothes, then strolled into the woods to dress.

So Molly Riordan had watched him. Secretly. A wicked grin tugged at his lips as he pulled on his jeans and gingerly tucked his impudent organ inside. "Restrain yourself."

He might have been able to do that without too much difficulty . . . until he'd overheard Molly's dream. A cold sweat popped out all over him as he remembered her moans, her groans, the way she'd shoved her hips toward heaven.

Ah, yes, heaven.

"Damnation." He shoved his fingers through his hair. She wasn't really his wife. She was his fiancée's maid. And he knew without being told that Molly was a virgin, too.

The part of him that wanted to do the honorable thing and prevent another Ballinger bastard from coming into this world reared its ugly head just in time. *Yeah, perfect timing.* He couldn't seduce Molly, then marry Lady Elizabeth. That would make him no better than his old man.

Setting his jaw and his mind, Dirk finished dressing and stomped into his boots. A few minutes later, he walked into the clearing to the mingled aromas of boiling coffee and frying bacon.

Zane was obviously confident enough about where they were headed to take time for a real breakfast. Dirk trusted the ancient Indian, but the sooner they found Lady Elizabeth, the sooner he might stop yearning for Molly.

She stooped beside the fire, turning bacon over in the black frying pan. Lance's jeans molded to her backside, hugging every curve.

And she had plenty of curves.

She'd pulled her hair back in a ribbon without braiding it today. It curled riotously down her back. He itched to run his fingers through it and mess it up thoroughly.

"Did you read sign this morning?" he asked Zane, needing to focus on their mission.

The wrinkled old man nodded. "We will continue as we have been."

"Upstream?" Dirk knew the answer, but he needed to concentrate on his duty. Maybe talking about it would help keep his mind and his hands off Molly Riordan.

Zane grunted and flashed Dirk a toothless, knowing grin. *The old cuss knows exactly what I'm doing.*

However, even the mysterious Jeremiah Zane didn't know Dirk *couldn't* act on his desire. And even Zane didn't know Molly wasn't really Dirk's wife.

But someone else did. Whoever had leaked the information about Lady Elizabeth to the Lovejoy Gang had known Dirk Ballinger's intended bride was on that particular stage. Dirk gritted his teeth, reminding himself he still didn't have any proof that any of this had been deliberate. After all, it was still entirely possible the stage robbery had been nothing more than a random act with surprising consequences to all parties.

Molly rose and turned to face him. "How soon will we reach Serendipity?" she asked, her expression unreadable.

He lifted a shoulder. "We might not need to go all the way to Serendipity at all. Why?"

Her shoulders slumped and she glanced away, but not before he saw the look of disappointment in her eyes.

"Why?" he repeated, waiting until she looked up to meet his gaze again. "What's in Serendipity?"

She glanced nervously at Zane, then faced Dirk again. "Lady Elizabeth," she whispered. "Remember?"

Confused, he shook his head. "We don't know that for sure. All we know is they headed that way."

"Oh." She forced a smile, but her eyes still held that curious disappointment. "I see. I must have misunderstood."

Maybe she saw, but he sure as hell didn't. *You're turning into a suspicious man, Dirk.* First he'd suspected Clyde, then anyone else he could think of.

And now? He watched Molly return to the cooking. Though he still appreciated the way she filled out her jeans, he had a gut load of doubt to go along with his desire.

Molly Riordan, what's your secret?

Eleven

The Lovejoy Gang's hideout was nothing more than an abandoned silver mine. Ray figured no one would ever look for them there, and the overgrowth the entrance hid it from view. Only someone who knew exactly where to look could find it, and since the mine had been abandoned a few years ago, he was pretty confident of their safety.

What he wasn't confident of was their sanity.

"I'm hungry," Dirk's wife said for at least the hundredth time today.

"You're always hungry." Ray folded his dismal poker hand and shoved away from the overturned crate that doubled as a table.

"But all you have is hardtack and jerky." She gave a delicate shudder and hoisted her nose even higher. "Might I remind you I'm eating for two now?"

"*Only* two?" He scowled at the new cards Luther had dealt. With a snort of disgust, he tossed his cards facedown and stood, remembering to watch for the low beams. Old timbers supported the mine's ceiling, but he'd reinforced the worst of them. From the look of the main beam, it was time to do it again.

Desperado claimed the owner of the mine had tried to return once, but he had advised the old miner to never come back. Ray hated to consider how Desperado might have "advised" the man. After all, if not for Desperado, the Lovejoy Gang wouldn't have the reputation of being killers now.

Shit.

"When do you expect to hear from Mr. Ballinger?" the woman asked.

The woman's constant use of his brother's name jarred Ray. Every time he heard the name Ballinger, his gut twisted and he had to swallow the burning bile that invariably rose to his throat.

"Yeah, boss, when do you think we'll be hearin' from the high-n-mighty Dirk Ballinger?" Luther asked, rolling his rheumy eyes in the direction of their hostage. "Sure hope she's worth all the trouble."

"So do I. So do I." Ray shoved his fingers through his hair and paced the width of the mine, kicking the satchel containing the clothing Dirk's wife claimed belonged to her maid. Their captive had been unable to button a single dress around her growing belly, which had made her start that dad-blamed caterwauling all over again.

Now she wore one of Ray's shirts hanging over a skirt she'd managed to fasten above her belly. She looked downright pitiful, though there was something about her that nagged at him. She gave him that long, searching look again that made him squirm.

"I do wish you'd shave off that beard." She heaved a sigh and turned her attention back to the book they'd found in her maid's satchel. "I've read this four times already. Don't you have any—"

"Hush, woman." Ray's voice echoed off the cool stone walls. "Just. Hush."

Luther and old Teddy both stood and stretched, mumbling under their breath. A few moments later, they left through the entrance, shoving aside the branches that made this the perfect hideout.

"Cowards," Ray called after them.

"You got that right," Teddy yelled back.

"I'm hungry."

Her whine reached a new octave that went right through a man. Ray handed her a piece of jerky, struggling against the urge to throw it at her. "Jerky, hardtack, and an occasional fish are all we have until your darling husband comes through with the ransom."

"Are you certain my note was delivered?" She tore off a bite of jerky with straight little teeth and chewed.

"Yes, I'm sure the note was delivered." Ray mocked her, which he reckoned would just piss her off again. Lord knew the woman was pissed all the time anyway. "Desperado delivered it himself."

"I don't like that man," she said, shuddering.

"That makes two of us," Ray muttered just for himself.

"He killed those men." She paused long enough to sniffle delicately. Then she said, "I'm so tired of being stuck in this . . . this hole." She took a swig of water and started her infernal hiccuping again. "And I'm sick of being fat and ugly and—hic—poor."

"Poor?" Ray watched the way her brown eyes shifted between hiccups. "You're married to the rich and powerful Dirk Ballinger. How could you be poor?"

"Dear me, did I say poor?" She gave a nervous laugh that started the hiccups again. "How—hic—silly of me."

"Hmm." Ray tried not to remember that he could've stayed at the ranch, that he could've lived there in luxury with his half brother. Dirk had invited him to stay, after all.

But Ray hadn't been able to stay in the house his

father had built—the father who'd wanted nothing to
do with him. Bitterness oozed through Ray all over
again. Edward Ballinger had bedded a whore in Denver
and hadn't given a shit when she'd conceived his child.
Hell, Ray hadn't even known who his father was until
his mother was on her deathbed. She'd taken great pleasure in telling her only child he was the son of one of
the most powerful men in the state.

As if being the bastard son of someone wealthy and
powerful could have made a difference.

If Ray had never heard his father's name, he never
would have met his half brother, seen the fine house
his father had built, or known his father had died without ever meeting his bastard son. Ignorance would've
been better than what Ray had lived with since the last
time he'd seen Dirk.

Well, it was too damned late now. Ray had squan-
dered the money Dirk had given him. After all, it had
been his inheritance. The bastard son's share of the
Ballinger fortune.

The stupid *bastard son.*

And now what did he have to show for his inheritance?

Wanted posters in three states.

The die was cast, and he had to take his lumps. Once
he had money lining his pockets again, he'd head west
to a place where no one had ever heard of Ray Lovejoy . . . or Dirk Ballinger.

The part of all this that gnawed at his gut was the
fact that Dirk had offered him the one thing Ray had
once wanted with all his heart. A name. His *rightful*
name. And Ray had stupidly flung his heart's desire
right back in his half brother's face.

He shot the woman another sidelong glance. Why
the devil did she look so familiar? Right now her face

was puffy from crying and eating everything that held still long enough for her to sink her teeth into it. And her body was distorted to the point where it was a miracle she could even stand.

Not that she did that very often, either.

"What are you staring at?" She sniffled and hiccuped and wiped her nose with the back of her hand.

He paused in front of her and held her gaze. "Are you sure we've never met before?"

She made a delicate snorting sound. "Hardly." She waved a hand before her delicate nose. "I don't believe you'd even be *received* in my circles."

He grinned, wondering if he should tell her that he'd been to England and had attended balls and parties with royalty, and had even bedded a few—

Oh, shit. He looked at her more closely, trying to remember. No, he was imagining things. She was married to Dirk, and obviously many months with child.

Even so, a sinking feeling hit him right in the gut. "What's your name?" He tried to picture her without the belly or the puffiness in her face, but failed.

"Mrs. Dirk Bal—"

"No, not that." He swallowed and took a step closer. *"Your* name before you were married."

She lifted her chin a notch. "Elizabeth," she said. "Lady Elizabeth to the likes of you."

Oh, shit. It all came back to him in a rush. The dancing, the champagne.

The host's daughter.

Oh, shit, shit, shit.

But . . . she was married to Dirk. He looked at her swollen belly again, remembering the night in question and trying to understand how his memory and the facts could have become so distorted.

Think, Lovejoy. Lord Summersby's daughter had

been fairly easy to coerce into Ray's rented carriage during the costume ball. She'd worn a feathered mask and a Marie Antoinette costume that included a huge white wig and a pasted beauty mark . . . and a dangerously low-cut gown. He'd practically drooled all over her during their dance.

His gaze fell to her current melonlike breasts beneath one of his old shirts. No danger of his drooling over her now, but he had to know.

He'd dressed all in black with a cape and a leather mask. His fingers stroked the scraggly beard that now covered his face. She'd asked him earlier if he always wore the beard. Maybe he'd surprise her by shaving it and seeing if she remembered him.

Damn. Swallowing the lump in his throat, he pulled a stool over and sat facing her. He needed facts. "All right. *Lady* Elizabeth what?"

"I don't understand your question." She sighed and leaned back in her chair, making the wood groan in protest.

"Your name or title or whatever you call it." He bit the inside of his cheek to curb the words he wanted to fling at her.

She finished the jerky, taking her sweet time about answering him, then took a leisurely sip of water. "My father is Lord Summersby, which I'm sure means absolutely nothing to a crude American highwayman."

"Crude?" That's not what she'd called him the night of Lord Summersby's costume ball. Ray's gut roiled, and he thought for a minute he might lose what little he'd eaten today. He tightened his fists and ground his teeth together so hard they damned near shattered. "I need a drink," he muttered, lunging for the whiskey left with the scattered cards.

He upended the nearly empty bottle and drained it

in three pitiful swallows. Growing more agitated by the moment, he flung the empty container against the wall, taking little comfort in the explosive shattering of glass, or the glittering shards that littered the mine floor. Gasping and wheezing, he whirled around to face her again.

The woman narrowed her eyes, and her normally smooth brow furrowed. "What is *wrong* with you?"

Ray laughed, shaking his head at the irony of this latest mess. He was his own worst enemy. First Dirk . . . now Lady Elizabeth Summersby.

The more she stared at him, the harder he laughed. After several moments, he dried his eyes with the back of his hand and returned to the stool.

"You're not only detestable, you're insane." She pointed her dainty little nose in the air again. "How soon will my husband bring the ransom?"

A cold sweat popped out all over Ray and his gaze fell to her belly again. *Oh, God.* "When and where did you meet your . . . *husband?*"

"That's none of your—"

He rose swiftly, hovering over her. "Answer me." His voice was low but filled with menace. He'd never hit a woman before, but this one sorely tempted a man. Even so, he just planned to rattle her some. "Answer me *now.*"

"We met at a costume ball in England." Her cheeks turned fiery red and she looked down at her lap. "He swept me . . . off my feet."

An obscene sense of calm settled over Ray, and he resumed his seat before her. He had to think this through logically, and he had to be sure. Very, very sure.

"Lady Elizabeth Summersby," he said quietly, struggling to keep his tone as emotionless as possible.

"I . . . I hope you aren't planning to ask my father for ransom, too." She looked up then, and he saw a tear trickle from the corner of her eye.

This sure as hell wasn't the first tear he'd seen her shed, but this lone one made his chest tight and his breath scarce. *Get a rein on it, Lovejoy.* He needed the truth. He drew a deep breath and released it very slowly. "I want you to think before you answer," he said, clearing his throat again. *"When* did you marry Dirk Ballinger?"

"Why do you ask?" Her cheeks reddened even more and she looked down at her hands resting over her belly. "Why does it matter? It doesn't make any difference."

He leaned closer and lifted her chin with the tip of one finger, forcing her to meet his gaze. "Because, *Lady* Elizabeth, I need to know how much you might be worth to your . . . *husband."*

Her gasp filled the small enclosure and she snapped her head to the side, closing her eyes. "Why are you doing this?" She met his gaze again, her eyes blazing with fury now, rather than fear or embarrassment. *"Why?"*

"You're not answering my question." He arched a brow, but her only reply was another string of hiccups.

Should he tell her about his suspicions? No, not yet. He looked at her swollen belly again. "When is the baby supposed to come?" His voice softened and he held his breath, waiting for her answer, deciding that was more important than knowing when she'd married Dirk.

"September." She hiccuped again. "It's unseemly for you to even ask a lady such a question."

Now it's August. He silently counted the months since he'd wooed Lord Summersby's daughter. "September." He held his breath and faced the possible truth with a numb sensation around his lips.

Had he unknowingly bedded his half brother's wife?

Ray rose slowly, his legs weighing about a ton apiece. Grappling for a sense of reason and his breath, he leaned against the cool stone wall and pondered the possibilities.

The potential nightmare.

Was this woman carrying *his* child? He had to know the truth. He *had* to know.

He'd been born a bastard. The stigma of being a kid without a father had been a fact of life for him and others like him. Having grown up in Denver, he'd always stayed in the part of town where he knew other outcasts like himself.

Everything would've been fine if he'd stayed the hell away from the Ballinger Ranch. He could've worked in Denver and lived the lowly life society maintained a bastard like him should live.

But he'd had to push. He'd wanted to see his father's face. No, he'd wanted more than that.

He'd wanted a name.

He glanced back at Lady Elizabeth, who'd stood to stretch, her belly even more pronounced as she rubbed the small of her back.

His child? Or Dirk's?

What madness had thrown them together again?

And, more importantly, *why?*

Molly sensed the sudden change in Dirk. Between the time he'd walked into the trees to dress and returned to camp, he'd turned himself totally inward, and she didn't understand why. Through breakfast and packing their supplies to leave, he hadn't spoken more than a few words.

And none directly to her.

As he assisted her onto Sadie's back, he didn't meet her gaze or utter a word. He released her and moved away as if touching her was somehow distasteful.

Swallowing the lump in her throat, she settled herself in the saddle for another day's journey, deciding Dirk's withdrawal was for the best. Certainly safer.

The memory of last night's dream made her face burn, and she drew a shaky breath. Never in all her days had she experienced such a dream. Her ignorance about the physical relationship between men and women left her at a frustrating disadvantage, for even though she'd given herself permission to sin in her sleep, she hadn't quite achieved it.

Because she didn't know *how* to finish it. She could guess, of course. Having spent her childhood on a farm, she understood the basic physical activity, but not how it would feel, or why she should want it so much.

I am a wanton and utterly mad.

Opening her eyes to discover that Dirk had observed her dream had been shocking and humiliating. Even so, a wicked part of her had found it somewhat exciting, too.

His words came back to tempt and torment her. *I'd like nothing better than to finish that dream someday. For both of us.*

Remembering his words brought another heated flush to her face . . . and other more intimate regions. Wasn't it true that the only way she'd ever finish that dream would be if someone more experienced were to show her the way?

Someone like Dirk?

Aye, but it wasn't likely she'd find another man quite

like him. His half brother the highwayman had the same eyes, but Molly wasn't fool enough to believe Ray Lovejoy could possess even a fraction of Dirk's character.

Are you forgetting the night of the costume ball, Molly lass? Gram's voice flooded Molly's head and she released a long, slow sigh.

Aye, actually, she would like to forget. She'd even *tried* to forget. The thought of the man of her dreams making love to another woman left a foul taste on her tongue . . . and in her heart.

Well, haven't you gone and done it now, Molly Riordan? You've fallen in love with the rogue.

But that voice didn't belong to Gram. It belonged to Molly's heart and soul.

No, she couldn't love him. She had no right to feel anything at all toward the man beyond the respect due her employer's betrothed.

Reason didn't help. Molly squeezed her eyes shut a moment, confident Sadie would follow Jeremiah and the pack mule. The horse was definitely smarter than the rider.

I'll bet you wouldn't fall in love with a stallion promised to another mare. Irritated by her own silliness and inability to convince herself she hadn't fallen in love with Dirk Ballinger, Molly opened her eyes and looked at the stream they still followed.

Oblivious to Molly's problems, the crystal clear water chuckled its way over shiny stones and pebbles, growing still and deep in the various areas where beavers had built their dams. She watched a bird soar and dip in the cloudless sky, and wondered if birds had problems such as hers.

Did animals fall in love with the wrong animals? *Now you've gone daft, too.*

If only Gram were here now to offer guidance. Molly sighed, deciding she should pay more attention to the scenery and less to Dirk and her ludicrous attraction to the man. She would concentrate on her future. Once Lady Elizabeth was safe, Molly would be free to travel on to Serendipity and her da.

In fact, maybe Molly shouldn't return to the ranch at all. She could ask Jeremiah Zane to take her to Serendipity if their search fell short of there. It would be for the best if she put some distance between herself and Dirk Ballinger.

The man of her dreams . . .

We'll be having more than enough of that nonsense before now. She straightened and resigned herself to a future without Dirk. He belonged to another, and that was that.

However, despite her best efforts, she felt Dirk's gaze on her back. No matter how hard she struggled to control herself, the sad truth was he seemed as attracted to her as she was to him. That certainly didn't help matters.

Perhaps if she concentrated on the night of the costume ball and his rather vocal seduction of Lady Elizabeth, Molly could keep things in better perspective. Remembering that night, she heard the words the masked American guest and Lady Elizabeth had exchanged all over again.

Much giggling and groaning had followed, then a long stretch of annoying silence. She remembered hearing the rustle of clothing as they'd dressed, then more words she'd forgotten until now. He'd chuckled and Lady Elizabeth had grown angry.

"What was all that virgin bull you were tryin' to pass off, darlin'?"

"How dare you?"

Lady Elizabeth had emerged a moment later, her wig crooked and her pasted beauty mark missing. After pleading a sick headache, she'd ordered Molly to assist her preparations for bed.

Molly remembered obediently following her mistress, but she'd glanced back once from the porch. The man had stood there staring after them, lamplight glistening off his dark hair. It had been too dark to see his green eyes outside, but Molly had noticed them earlier during the ball. He'd stood there silently watching until Lady Elizabeth and Molly had disappeared into the house.

He'd looked right at her. Most aristocrats treated servants as if they were invisible, but she remembered feeling that Dirk Ballinger had stared too long and hard not to have remembered.

Then why had he insisted so firmly that Mr. Slim's words regarding Molly's identity had been true? It didn't make sense. He must have seen her that night, and Dirk Ballinger didn't strike her as a man with a poor memory.

Ah, but it didn't matter now. She shook her head, hoping to banish Dirk from her thoughts.

Was it true Lady Elizabeth wasn't a virgin before that fateful night? Molly bit her lower lip, realizing she'd never know the answer to that question. Furthermore, it was none of her business.

The facts were that Dirk Ballinger had wooed Lady Elizabeth into his carriage, had his way with her, then left her with child. Granted, he couldn't have known when he'd left England that Lady Elizabeth was carrying his baby, and he *had* offered to marry her immediately once he'd learned of the unborn child.

Again, Dirk Ballinger had proved himself an honorable man . . . in a way.

An honorable man who plagued her dreams and made her yearn for things proper young ladies—or ladies' maids, for that matter—should never even contemplate. Molly cleared her throat, realizing such propriety was impossible. She *was* proper—always had been before, anyway. Now that she considered it, she realized how foolish it was to believe no one ever cogitated on matters of the flesh.

She was just realizing this a bit late due to her lack of experience. If she'd gone on to finishing school rather than to work for Lady Elizabeth, doubtless she would have heard enough to make her curious about the intimacies between man and woman much earlier in life.

Instead, she'd had to experience it—part of it, rather—to believe it. And now she wanted more.

There you go again. Furious with herself, Molly muttered under her breath and adjusted herself in the saddle. She would put Dirk Ballinger out of her mind. She had no choice.

They would find Lady Elizabeth alive, then Molly would get on with the rest of her life.

And Dirk would marry the mother of his unborn child.

Dirk's mood darkened as they climbed the pass. The sooner this nightmare was over with, the better. If Lady Elizabeth was still alive, he would marry her, raise her child as his own, and no one would ever know otherwise.

Unless Ray had recognized her and figured it all out by now. Dirk sighed, forcing his attention farther up the trail. He dared not allow his gaze to linger on the rider directly in front of him. To do so would gain him nothing but misery.

Physical and emotional.

Molly Riordan was not his to want. Therefore, he wouldn't want her.

And I'm a liar.

He wanted her, but he couldn't and wouldn't have her.

The dense forest provided enough shade that Dirk didn't even need the hat he shoved farther back on his head. His gaze rested on Zane, who suddenly brought his horse to a halt and half turned, looking beyond Molly. Beyond Dirk.

The Indian had seen or heard something. Dirk's senses sprang to awareness as he watched the ancient tracker.

Finally, Zane inclined his head and said, "Rider coming."

Dirk didn't hear or see anyone, but if Zane said there was a rider coming, there was a rider coming. He turned to wait and watch. At least now he couldn't see Molly's slender back, nor would he see her lovely profile when she looked back over her shoulder, which he knew she would.

Far down the steep trail, Dirk saw a figure on a small horse making his way uphill. As the rider drew closer, it was clear that the horse had been ridden hard. The animal's coat was lathered and flecks of foam ringed its mouth.

The man lifted his hand in greeting. A few minutes later, he dismounted and led his exhausted horse the final few yards.

Dirk recognized the rider as Tex Arnold, one of his own wranglers—one who knew better than to ride a

horse this hard. He must've had a damned good reason
to ride his mustang into the ground this way.

Worry slithered through Dirk. The hairs on the back
of his neck stood on end and that infernal prickling
sensation tingled all over him. Arnold was bringing important information. And for some reason, Dirk didn't
want to hear it.

But he would. Duty, honor, responsibility—they all
reared their ugly Ballinger heads.

"What is it?" he asked once Arnold stopped in front
of them, breathing almost as hard as his horse.

"Got a letter for you, sir." Arnold pulled the envelope from his vest pocket and handed it to Dirk, then
removed his hat and mopped sweat from his brow.

"You might want to give your horse the same cour-
tesy," Dirk said.

"I'm aimin' to do just that." Tex didn't sound of-
fended. After all, a man took care of his horse. That
was just a part of being a man—and staying alive—in
this country.

While Tex unsaddled his horse and rubbed him down
with the saddle blanket, Dirk turned his full attention
to the letter. Molly guided Sadie alongside him and he
felt her gaze on him, but he didn't look at her.

The handwriting on the outside of the envelope was
unfamiliar. "Who gave this to you?" he asked the messenger.

"Miss Ida found it slid under the front door last
night." Arnold led his mustang to the creek, but only
let her drink for a second before pulling her back. He
absently stroked the animal's side, waiting before allowing her to dip her muzzle in the cool stream again.
"Clyde told me you needed to have it right away."

"Clyde did, huh?" Dirk hated mistrusting someone
he'd known all his life. Hell, Clyde Yeager had been

more of a father to Dirk than Edward Ballinger had. Dirk swallowed the lump in his throat and turned the envelope over, noticing the seal was unbroken. Of course, Clyde must have suspected it was about the hostage.

Enough stalling, Ballinger. Still, he had a bad feeling.

A very bad feeling.

Molly's knee brushed against Dirk's thigh, reminding him they were still mounted. "Give the horses a rest while I read this."

Zane must have sensed Dirk's mood, because he assisted Molly without being asked. Distracted, Dirk dismounted and walked upstream a ways before opening the envelope. The paper was limp from being stuffed in Arnold's pocket, but the letters were still clearly legible.

Dearest Dirk,

I am being held hostage somewhere in the mountains. Please give them what they want. I don't want our baby to be born this way. They say I will not be harmed, but I am frightened.

Your loving
Elizabeth

Dirk paused and reread the words several times. The words "this way" were underlined, and he knew exactly what she meant. On this subject, he and Lady Elizabeth were in complete agreement. Neither of them wanted her child to be born out of wedlock.

Her message didn't give him the information he needed. Where were they? How much ransom did Ray expect? When and where was it to be delivered? He glanced inside the envelope and upended it. Another smaller piece of paper fluttered to the ground. Dirk stooped to retrieve it, knowing before he read the words who had written them.

His brother. Half or full, still his brother. They had the same Ballinger blood pulsing through their veins. The same green eyes.

The second note was short, the printing obscenely neat, the message clear.

> *Dear Dirk.*
> *Send money. The same amount as last time should do. Go to Serendipity and wait for instructions. Your wife and baby are fine.*

The neat printing became bold and sloppy, and something was scribbled through.

> *If you ever want to see the kid, you'll do as you're told.*
>
> R.L.

Dirk barked a derisive laugh, barely resisting the urge to crumple the note in his fist. Foolish Ray didn't even realize that the child he'd threatened was his—not Dirk's.

"What is it?" Molly's quiet voice came from right beside him.

"A ransom note." Dirk sighed, passing her the first letter. "Do you recognize this as Lady Elizabeth's handwriting?"

Molly skimmed the words and nodded. "Aye, I believe this was written by Lady Elizabeth. This means she's alive." Her gaze fell to the other slip of paper. "And that one?"

Dirk closed his eyes and said, "From my half brother, of course."

She touched his arm, jarring Dirk from his dark mood. Then he met her gaze and remembered his earlier doubts about her motives. "This tells me Ray must have known my fiancée would be on the stage," he said, watching Molly's expression.

"It seems possible, but isn't it good to know she's still alive?" Her voice was calm, with no indication of guilt. "Does it really matter whether or not Ray knew she was on the stage?"

"Yeah, it's good to know she's still alive, and it doesn't really matter in the end whether or not Ray knew." He lifted his shoulder. "The result will be the same either way. I hand him twenty-five thousand dollars and he walks away."

Molly frowned. "And you get Lady Elizabeth and your child."

"There is that." Dirk looked away, fearing she might read the truth in his eyes. "But, God help me, I also want revenge." He looked at her again, knowing anger would help disguise any other emotions that might be lurking in his eyes. "And I want justice."

"I can understand that, but Lady Elizabeth and the babe are more important." She dropped her arm to her side. "How far is Serendipity?"

"We should reach town by tomorrow afternoon." He cocked a questioning brow at her. "Guess you're going to Serendipity after all."

She slid her gaze away, sending a sizzle of uneasiness through Dirk. For some reason, the thought of Molly betraying him was even worse than knowing Ray had done it. Molly Riordan wasn't of his blood, but she had sure as hell crawled inside him and set it ablaze.

She had some sort of power over him he didn't want her to have.

Oh, but he did want her in the very physical sense. That was probably most of his problem. Pure lust. He wouldn't let it be anything more, because the last thing he needed was to care about someone else who would betray him.

Don't lie to me, Molly. Whatever else you do, just don't lie.

Twelve

Ray listened patiently while old Teddy told him Desperado was waiting by the creek, then asked Luther to stay with their hostage while he took care of business. He buckled on his holster and made sure his pistol was loaded before sliding it into place.

The bottom line was, Ray didn't trust Desperado. Hell, he didn't even know who Desperado was, and he wished like hell he could go back and undo the day he'd invited the man to join the Lovejoy Gang—not that it was much of a gang.

Desperado was more violent than all of Ray's men combined. Until the mysterious man had joined them, they hadn't killed a single man.

Now there were at least two dead, and the entire Lovejoy Gang could end up at the end of a rope because of this lone trigger-happy man. Stealing was one thing, but killing was another. Ray wasn't a killer, and he hadn't wanted that reputation. Now he had it, whether he'd pulled the trigger or not.

Hell, all he'd wanted out of this was enough money for a fresh start. He sighed and gnashed his teeth, wondering how and when he'd turned into a fool. Seemed every decision he'd made since Ma's death had been the worst possible thing.

That was about to change. Resolve settled in his gut

and burned through him. Ray Lovejoy was finished being a fool. Now if he could just stay clear of the business end of a rope, he might manage to make something of the rest of his life.

He clenched and unclenched his fists as he approached the area where Desperado waited. Pausing beside the creek, Ray said, "It's about time you showed up."

Desperado and his fancy horse stepped from the shelter of several tall pines, and he flashed one of those smiles that never quite reached the man's eyes. "I'm here now, Lovejoy." Desperado held one hand out in front of him, examining his fingernails.

Ray suspected the only thing under Desperado's fingernails was other men's blood. He swallowed his anger and faced the man. "I told you I didn't want any bloodshed back there." His anger hummed just beneath the surface, threatening to overtake him at any moment. "There was no call for it. We had things under control without killing that passenger and the driver."

Desperado lifted one shoulder, a sneer marring his face. "I saw things different."

Ray drew a deep breath. He couldn't undo the damage—two men were dead and nothing would bring them back. But he wanted to make damned sure it didn't happen again. "This is *my* outfit. You do what I say while you work for me."

Desperado narrowed his eyes, but after a long pause, he nodded. "That's what I'm doing."

Ray resisted the urge to send the man on his way now. He needed information first. "Did you deliver the letter?"

"Done." Desperado examined the nails on his other hand.

"And?"

"I slid it under the front door of that fancy house, just like you said."

Ray shoved his fingers through his hair. "Did Ballinger get the message?"

The shoulder lifted again. "I didn't hang around to ask." He grinned again and arched a brow, his brassy yellow hair gleaming in the sunlight that filtered through the trees. "I'm sure he has the letter by now. After all, he lives there, doesn't he?"

"Yeah." Ray bit the inside of his cheek. He could've lived in that house. Hell, he'd been *invited*. Regret settled low in his gut, adding to what had been building for almost a year. "Yeah, it's definitely his house." His ranch. His life.

His name.

"What now . . . boss?"

Somehow, when Desperado called Ray "boss," it sounded like an insult. Ray stiffened, deciding now was as good a time as any. "I think it's time you moved on."

Desperado shook his head very slowly, his hooded whiskey-colored eyes glittering. "Not just yet, Lovejoy. I aim to have my share of that ransom first."

Ray wished like hell he had enough money to pay off the asshole and be done with him. But he didn't. He'd lived too damned well during his trip to Europe. Remembering the night of Lord Summersby's costume ball, his gut churned. Yes, he'd lived very well then and had nothing to show for it now.

Except a whiny, hungry, pregnant woman.

But that was another matter—one he would also deal with today. Right now he had to settle things with Desperado. "Fair enough, I reckon." He rested his fists on his hips and watched the man's shifting gaze. "You'll get your share as soon as it's delivered." Narrowing his eyes, he hoped the man wouldn't push this too far. "Then I don't ever want to see you again. Understood?"

That nasty smile returned to Desperado's face and he didn't seem at all surprised by Ray's demands. "As you say," he said, turning toward his horse. "I have somewhere to go, but I'll return at week's end to collect my share."

"Then you'll leave for good?"

Another insolent shrug was his only answer. Without another word, Desperado swung himself into the saddle and rode down the mountain.

A chill raced through Ray despite the warm sunshine. Letting Desperado into the gang had been a grievous mistake. It seemed Ray's life this past year had been filled with those.

But he couldn't do a damned thing to undo the past.

After living most of his adult life haphazardly, Ray was ready to settle down. He was tired of running. Once he had the rest of what he liked to think of as his inheritance, he'd head west and put Colorado and Dirk Ballinger behind him.

Sure you will, Lovejoy. Sure you will.

But he wasn't stupid enough to deny the truth—at least not to himself. No matter how far he traveled, he'd never be truly rid of Dirk Ballinger—his own flesh and blood—or the damned regret that tormented him. Well then, Ray would just have to learn to live with it.

Teddy appeared at his side, staring down the mountain. "I don't much trust that fella."

"That makes two of us." Ray sighed and rubbed his scraggly beard, then clapped the older man on the shoulder. "Teddy, old boy . . ."

"I don't much cotton to bein' called 'old' anything, greenhorn," the man said with mock fierceness.

Ray laughed. "Good enough."

"All right, whatcha want this time?" Teddy grinned, folding his arms across his middle. "You only cotton up to a man when you want somethin'."

"You know me too well."

"And don't you forget it." Teddy's gray eyes twinkled. "Just don't ask *me* to stay in there with that . . . princess, or whatever the hell she is."

Ray quirked an eyebrow. "She's pretty hard to take for very long."

"Oh, she's a lot worse'n that." Teddy shook his head. "Luther'll probably have her bound and gagged by the time you get back."

Ray chuckled, knowing Luther was as big a pussycat as his brother Teddy. "Sure he will."

"Don't say I didn't warn you."

"My money's on the woman."

Teddy wheezed a laugh and shook his head. "Darned if mine ain't, too."

Ray rubbed his beard again. "Mind if I borrow your razor?"

"I know'd you wanted somethin'." Teddy aimed his thumb toward a pail hanging from a branch near the mine entrance. "Help yourself."

"Thanks, ol—I mean, Teddy."

The old man shot a toothless grin in Ray's direction. "Remember what I told you last spring about me'n Luther headin' south before winter?"

Ray drew a deep breath. "I remember, and I'm plannin' to put some distance between myself and these mountains, too."

Teddy's expression grew solemn. "Desperado ruined it all for us."

Ray nodded. There was nothing to say. "Now we'll be wanted for murder, too."

"All we wanted was a little extra money for our old age. Never wanted to hurt no one." Teddy sighed and headed uphill from the mine entrance. "I saw some berries earlier, and I got me a need for a serious purge."

Ray laughed and called, "You're sleepin' outside, old man."

Teddy kept walking, though Ray saw his shoulders heaving with laughter. He'd miss Teddy and Luther, but it was best they part ways after this.

Damn Desperado.

There was nothing to be done about it all just now, so Ray turned his attention back to his mission. After grabbing the pail Teddy had indicated, he settled down near the creek and propped the small shard of broken mirror against a rock.

It was time for Ray to reveal himself to his hostage. Lady Elizabeth's reaction to seeing him without his beard could answer a whole passel of questions. He had to do it.

Because he *had* to know the truth. There was no doubt he'd slept with the woman, but that didn't mean the baby was his. Dirk had married her, after all. It could be his kid. Ray swallowed the lump in his throat. Still . . . he had to be absolutely certain.

After stropping the razor, Ray looked in the blue jar Teddy had in the bucket. Whatever the greasy substance was, it smelled like pure shit. *Probably bear grease.* Whatever it was, the rancid, lardlike substance was a necessary evil. Without proper shaving lather, this was the best he could do. Even lard of unknown origin would help keep him from taking a layer of hide off with his beard.

He used a huge pair of shears to cut his scraggly beard as close to the skin as possible, then spread some of the grease on his face. He shaved off everything but the mustache, then trimmed it as neatly as he could with the awkward shears. Only three small nicks marred his appearance, but he really didn't give a damn about that. He just wanted to give Lady Elizabeth a good look at his face so he could measure her reaction.

After all, she was the only person who knew who'd fathered her child.

After shaving, he went down to the creek and washed off the rancid grease, then sat in the sun until his hair dried. Luther was probably on the verge of murdering their hostage by now. Chuckling to himself, Ray stood near the hideout entrance and listened.

"I don't give a rat's ass who your daddy is," Luther said in a gravelly tone.

"I'm leaving," Lady Elizabeth announced. "I can't bear this . . . this hovel any longer."

"You ain't goin' nowhere 'til we gets our money."

"Oh, yes, I most certainly am."

With a sigh, Ray stepped into the dimly lit mine and folded his arms. "Where are you planning to go, Lady Elizabeth?" he asked.

She turned toward him very quickly, her mouth opened to deliver one of her tirades, but she froze instead. "What did you?" Tilting her head, she stared for several long moments, then walked slowly toward him.

"Whoeee, boss," Luther said, "but you sure do clean up good."

"Take a break, old man." Ray shot his other trusted partner a lopsided grin. "You've earned it."

"That's for gol-durned sure. And I ain't never heard a *lady* outcuss me before. My ma woulda washed her mouth out with lye more'n once." Luther performed an exaggerated bow before the lady in question, then plopped his hat on his balding head and beat a hasty retreat.

"You enjoy giving old men a hard time?" Ray asked, still waiting for her reaction to his altered appearance. It was too damned dark in the mine. "How about some fresh air?" He wanted her to have a clear look at him.

"Anything to get out of this hole for a while." Her voice was unnaturally quiet, her gaze focused on his freshly shaven face.

Ray held open the door for her, then followed her into the late afternoon sun. Long shadows stretched across the clearing beyond the overgrowth. She walked several paces, then whirled around and planted herself in his path.

"You shaved." She folded her arms across her bulging belly, her expression filled with confusion and questions. "Why?"

"It's not illegal for a man to shave." He stroked his naked jaw. "Don't you like it?"

She drew a deep breath and shook her head. "You can't be him." She bit her lower lip. "A common highwayman . . ."

"I can't be who?" He took a step closer. "Who do you think I am?" *God help me, but I know.* Her expression said it all.

"Why . . . why are you doing this? You can't be him." Her voice rose with each syllable. "You *can't* be!"

He flashed her a devilish smile—the same one he'd wielded the night of her father's ball. "Would you prefer me dressed all in black?"

She gasped and took a step back, bringing her fingertips to her trembling lips.

"A cape?"

Another step.

He kept smiling and used his fingers to create a mask

around his eyes. "Or would a leather mask be more to your liking?"

She shook her head furiously. "No, no, no." Her lower lip trembled and tears literally squirted from her eyes. She didn't caterwaul this time, though. For a change, her weeping was quiet and genuine. No dramatics. "No," she repeated in desperate denial, her voice barely more than a stifled whisper now. "My . . . baby."

"What about your baby?" He stood right in front of her, terrified he'd already guessed the truth, and praying he was mistaken. It was time for him to press harder. He gave her a short bow and held his arms toward her. "Lady Elizabeth—or should I say Marie Antoinette?—may I have this dance?"

"Oh. My. God." Lady Elizabeth's eyes rolled backward and she fell forward with all the grace of a buffalo.

Ray caught her, staggering beneath her extra weight. With a grunt, he swung her into his arms and carried her back into the mine. He placed her on the narrow bunk she'd been using since their arrival and pulled a stool over beside it. Then he sat there and waited.

Her eyes finally fluttered open, as he'd known they would, and she pushed herself against the wall—as far away from him as she could possibly get. Her face changed from deathly pale to blazing crimson within a heartbeat. "You."

"Yes, me." He leaned closer, keeping his expression devoid of emotion. "You and me . . . in my carriage. Remember?" He arched a brow and waited, bracing himself.

The slap came without warning, but he was ready for it. It stung his freshly shaved cheek, but he barely flinched. He did, however, grip her wrists to prevent her from clawing him. A slap was one thing, but he wouldn't allow her razor-like claws to rip his flesh to shreds. She bared her teeth and fought against his hold.

"Ah, I see you *do* remember," he whispered, leaning even closer. He covered her mouth with his for a fleeting moment, hoping she wouldn't decide to bite him, then eased back to study her eyes. "I thoroughly enjoyed myself that night, and I think you did, too."

She didn't answer, and her flashing brown eyes made it clear she had murder on her mind. "You . . . *you* are Dirk Ballinger?" she asked, her gaze locked on his face. "You said . . . you said you own a ranch. Why, you even told my father that—"

"I am *not* Dirk Ballinger." He released her wrists and stiffened, swallowing the bile that climbed up his throat.

"But you said—"

"I just borrowed his name for a spell." Ray grinned, though he felt more like kicking something. "His money and his name."

"I don't understand." She sat upright very slowly, holding her forehead. "If you aren't Dirk Ballinger, then who are you?"

"You know my name."

"Ray Lovejoy." Lady Elizabeth dropped her hands to her belly and stared at him. "A highwayman."

"An outlaw or road agent in these parts." He gritted his teeth and nodded. "And the very same man you romped with in that carriage back in England. My lady."

"A . . . highwayman," she repeated, a glazed look in her eyes. "Then why did . . . ." She bit her lower lip, her expression shifting from dazed to calculating. "I don't understand any of this."

"Let's start with the truth." Ray braced his hands on his thighs, digging his short nails through the heavy fabric. "When and where did you marry Dirk Ballinger?" He held his breath. Waiting.

"I . . ." Her cheeks flamed and she looked down, then she met his gaze again. "I thought you were him."

"Well, I reckon now you know I'm not." Wary, Ray rubbed his palms along the heavy fabric of his jeans. The churning in his gut told him he was dangerously close to the truth, and it scared the holy hell out of him. "Are you sayin' what I think you're sayin'?"

She pressed her lips into a thin line and shrugged. "I . . . I've—"

He reached out and grabbed her wrists again, standing as he hauled her to her feet. Ray glowered down at her, hating her for lying to him.

And hating himself.

"Are you married to Dirk?" The words hung between them; the seconds ticked by. "Answer me," he said through clenched teeth.

"No." Tears spurted from her eyes again. "No."

Ray stared down at her face, the tears leaving white trails against her flushed cheeks. "Then why in blazes did you say you were?" His tone was gentle now, his guilt tremendous. "Why?"

"Look at me." She pulled away and cupped her swollen belly in both hands. "Just *look* at me."

His heart thundered, and a cold sweat coated his skin. "You've never even met Dirk Ballinger. Have you?"

The tears continued, but she managed to shake her head. "Never." Her voice was wretched, her eyes accusing. "And I have no idea why he agreed to marry me."

"Holy shit. That means"—Ray made a choking sound as he struggled for breath and words—"the baby is . . ."

"Yours."

* * *

Molly ached all over. Yesterday had been bad, but nothing like this endless day. They hadn't even paused for a noon meal, eating cold jerky and drinking tepid water from their canteens while they rode. The messenger had returned to the ranch, leaving Dirk, Jeremiah Zane, and Molly to continue on to Serendipity alone.

Aye, they were going to Serendipity. A surge of anticipation swelled within Molly, but she quickly calmed it by remembering Lady Elizabeth. Once her mistress was safe, Molly could turn her full attention to her own future and to finding Niall Riordan.

Da, are you still there? Will you be happy to see me? She squeezed her eyes closed in a silent prayer, then blinked away her unshed tears and concentrated on staying in the saddle and following Jeremiah and the pack mule.

Clouds gathered over the nearest peak, growing and darkening with every passing moment. Molly had yet to see rain in Colorado, though Dirk had said afternoon thunderstorms were common. Yesterday it had merely threatened, but she had a feeling today would be different.

The wind picked up slightly, drying the perspiration from her skin. She shivered, amazed by how quickly the temperature had dropped. Would they stop soon? And, more importantly, was there any shelter nearby?

Lightning flashed across the sky and the wind blew harder. Ahead of them, Jeremiah brought his horse and the mule to a stop, then glanced back over his shoulder and pointed to their left. Molly stopped Sadie but resisted the urge to look behind her at Dirk. She hadn't seen his face for hours, and it was for the best.

Even without seeing, she knew when Dirk acknowledged Jeremiah's unspoken message, because the old Indian gave a silent nod and turned his horse in the direction where he had pointed, the mule following obediently.

Dirk brought his horse up alongside Molly. She held her breath in the rising wind. Thunder boomed overhead and lightning flashed again, followed by more thunder.

"We're in for it," he shouted through the din. "There's an abandoned prospector's cabin ahead."

Molly met his gaze and nodded, not trusting her voice just now. Lightning flashed again, brighter and closer. A second later, another blinding flash split a huge pine directly in front of them. She screamed and the ground trembled beneath them, and Sadie took several skittish sidesteps.

Molly's heart skipped a beat as she clung to the pommel with both hands, her knuckles turning white. Sadie danced around nervously, but she didn't buck or rear. *Thank you, Mother Mary.*

Dirk reached over and grabbed Sadie's reins, then led the frightened animal around the felled tree and up the trail. The acrid stench of smoldering green wood made her consider how dangerous a fire would be up here. Just then a spattering of raindrops fell, hissing as they struck the charred tree. At least that would prevent a serious fire from starting.

The sky suddenly opened and rain pelted them, soaking every layer of Molly's clothing within seconds. She could barely breathe, and she leaned forward to shield her face from the deluge. The brim of her borrowed hat provided little help, but it was better than nothing.

Dirk pulled his hat lower and looked back at her but didn't speak, then they turned into the forest, where

Jeremiah had gone moments earlier. Molly couldn't see anything but rain and Dirk, because he was close. Beyond him there was only blinding water pouring from the sky.

The sky had darkened until it seemed more like twilight than late afternoon. Another flash of lightning illuminated the clearing and she spotted the cabin. Shelter.

The leather of her saddle grew slippery, but she clung to the pommel with all her strength, grateful Dirk had seen the wisdom of taking Sadie's reins. Tiny white hailstones joined the rain, beating down on them and stinging their skin. Even with her head bowed, Molly's cheeks burned from the onslaught.

Dirk brought the horses to a stop before the cabin and leaped from his saddle, hauled Molly down beside him, then grabbed both their saddlebags. Their horses trotted beneath a rock ledge beside the house, where Jeremiah's horse and the pack mule had already sought refuge.

"They'll be fine there," Dirk yelled above the storm. He half dragged Molly through the front door, slamming it behind them. The sound of hail and rain striking the roof was almost peaceful compared to the deafening tempest outside.

Molly leaned against the closed door, shivering and gasping. The floor was made of rough wood, and cobwebs filled every corner of the one-room cabin. But it was dry—blessedly dry. She saw Jeremiah stooped before a stone hearth that took up one entire wall of the structure. He had a small blaze started and was carefully adding kindling and tinder.

"Thank the fathers there was dry wood here." Jeremiah pointed to the wood box beside the hearth and flashed Molly one of his rare grins. "And the chimney draws well."

"Whoever built this place chose the site well," Dirk said. He found another door at the rear and peered outside. "We can tend the horses without getting wet."

Molly approached him and looked over his shoulder. The door opened beneath the rock ledge where the four animals were huddled, alternating nose to flank. A gust of wind made her shiver again, so she moved back inside and stood before the growing fire while Dirk closed the door.

"That feels g-good."

"Remove your wet clothes," Jeremiah said without preamble. "I'll tend the horses." The old man left through the side door, closing it securely behind him.

Dirk retrieved a blanket from a trunk in the corner and shook it hard. At least nothing crawled out of it. Once the dust settled, he approached Molly and handed it to her. "Zane is right. You'll never get warm if you're wet." His gaze drifted downward, resting on her bosom.

Molly felt her breasts swell beneath his gaze, her nipples already hard from the cold and damp. She suspected he could see every detail through the soaked fabric, but she resisted the urge to cover herself or to turn away.

She saw his Adam's apple bob up and down. Then his intense green gaze returned to her face. Mesmerized, she couldn't break the spell he'd cast over her. Warmth sizzled through her, chasing away the chill.

Dirk tugged at his collar. "I'll go help Zane while you get undressed," he said in a voice thick with an unnatural hoarseness. Turning away, he broke the spell. "Wrap that blanket around you until your things dry."

The chill returned the moment he closed the door behind him. Molly shivered violently as she struggled with the buttons of her soaked shirtwaist and peeled off her thin chemise, then the remainder of her clothing. She spread her wet attire out on the stones before the hearth, watching steam rise from the fabric.

With the blanket clutched around her, she was completely covered, yet she felt thoroughly exposed. Merely knowing she was naked beneath the blanket was more than enough to make her insecure.

Vulnerable.

Dirk was gone only a few minutes. When he returned, he brought supplies from the pack mule. He hung a kettle over the fire and poured a can of beans into it, then prepared coffee and set the pot down in the coals to heat.

Wind rattled the rafters, but the rain had diminished considerably. She was very grateful they had shelter, but she would have felt better wearing clothes. Tugging the blanket more snugly about her throat, she watched Dirk's efficient culinary efforts.

He seemed less harried now, more relaxed. Whatever worries had made him withdraw this morning had eased, thank heavens. His dark mood had been almost frightening.

He finally rose, leaving their food and coffee to heat, and dusted off his hands. Drops of water clung tenaciously to his curls as he unbuttoned his damp shirt and shrugged out of it.

Molly's mouth went dry at the sight of his bare chest. Strong didn't begin to describe this man. He was breathtakingly beautiful. Like a sculpture. Aye, that was it.

He draped his shirt from a peg on the wall near the hearth, then unbuckled his holster and hung it from another one. After kicking off his boots and removing his damp socks, he reached for the buttons on his dungarees, but hesitated. With a sheepish grin, he left his damp dungarees in place and poked at the fire, adding another log.

Jesus, Mary, and Joseph. She was naked and he was half naked. And they were very, *very* alone.

Suddenly wary, she looked around the cabin and at both doors. Dirk had closed them firmly when he'd returned. "Where is . . . Jeremiah?" she asked, her voice small and quivery. Her throat tightened and her breath caught.

"Gone." Dirk stirred the beans, then straightened again, turning to face her. "His nephew has a claim near here, so he went to visit the minute the rain eased up."

"It is quieter now. Did the storm stop?" Molly's heart raced and she tried not to tremble.

"Yes, but I warned him it wasn't finished with us yet." He chuckled, shaking his head. "Old Zane said he knew, but he wasn't about to let a little rain stop him."

Another onslaught of rain and hail struck the cabin and Dirk shook his head. "A little rain. He never listens to me." He smiled. "Don't worry. Jeremiah Zane is the most self-sufficient man I've ever known. He'll be fine."

Aye, but will I be? Uneasiness swelled within Molly as Dirk approached her with deliberate steps. She looked up at him, trying unsuccessfully not to notice the way his glossy damp curls fell rakishly across his forehead. At least she resisted the compulsion to reach up and push them away from his beautiful eyes. "Will . . . will Jeremiah be back later for supper, then?"

Dirk shook his head. He seemed even larger without his shirt, towering over her and looking downright delicious. *Jesus, Mary, and Joseph.* Her heart slammed against her ribs and she took a step back.

Dirk took a step forward.

"When *will* Jeremiah return?" Molly asked nervously. "We'll need to keep some food warm for him, I'm sure."

"No need."

Dirk caressed her with his eyes, his voice husky. It crawled through her bones and straight to parts of her that were best ignored.

"No need?" She swallowed the lump in her throat. "And why would that be?"

"He'll be back in the morning."

The room swayed. She bit her lower lip and took another backward step, her legs coming up against the edge of the trunk where Dirk had found the blankets earlier. "M-morning?"

He nodded slowly. Then a devilish grin split his handsome face. "Tell me something."

"Aye?" *Am I in as much trouble here as I'm thinking, Gram?*

Gram didn't answer.

"Tell you what?" she repeated when all he did was stare in that devilish way of his.

"Are you naked under that prissy blanket, Molly Riordan?"

Thirteen

Though Molly didn't answer him, Dirk knew. He'd noticed her chemise and bloomers near the hearth, along with her jeans and shirtwaist. She was completely, totally naked beneath the rough wool blanket.

Did it chafe her tender skin? Was she pink and glowing?

Warm?

He suppressed a shudder. *I am insane.* There was no other explanation. This morning he'd tried to convince himself he couldn't trust this woman, yet he did. For some reason—instinct, perhaps—he trusted her implicitly.

Almost as much as he wanted her.

He had no right to want her. None at all. But his presumptuous body didn't give a damn about rights or wrongs.

Or sins.

Here she stood wearing nothing but a blanket and looking irresistible. And they were alone. So very alone. . . .

His blood thickened and warmed, pooling between his thighs. The cadence of his need echoed through his entire body, his brain, culminating right where it counted and could inflict the most damage on his pitiful excuse for self-restraint.

Right where it could prove the most inconvenient.

He wanted her with a sweet fierceness that frightened him, yet drove him to seek more. He'd never known such a heady need or demanding hunger.

"Molly . . ." Her name left his parted lips on a sigh. Firelight bathed her in a golden glow, illuminating the bright blue of her eyes in the pale oval of her face. Her lips were pink and shining, her hair loose in a riot of curls, cascading over her shoulders and down her back. "God, you're so beautiful."

Her cheeks bloomed with color and she looked away for a moment, then met his gaze with an intensity that stole his breath. He'd felt her response earlier, but now her eyes revealed that the urgency of her own desire mirrored his.

She wanted him.

He wanted her.

They were alone—traveling as husband and wife.

But she *wasn't* his wife. His conscience reared its insistent head, battling against desire. Dirk was a stubborn cuss—always had been. But somehow he doubted even his obstinate Ballinger blood could save him from the burning need rising within him.

The storm outside intensified, complementing the tempest raging within Dirk between logic and lust. His brain screamed logic. Sensibility. Honor. But his cock outshouted his brain.

The tiny cabin shuddered beneath the onslaught.

As did Dirk.

Swallowing the lump in his throat, he reached toward her, barely brushing the backs of his fingers against the softness of her cheek. "You're beautiful. So soft."

She chewed her lower lip, then the tip of her pink tongue swept out to moisten her lips. He could almost taste her. Memory filled in the details of how she'd molded against him, her softness countering his hardness in all the right places—all the most devastating ways.

He turned his hand to cradle her face in his palm. She leaned into the gesture, igniting a wildfire in his loins. Then she reached up and placed her cool hand against his, watching him with round, moist eyes.

"I don't understand this," she said so softly he almost didn't hear her. "What you do to me."

If only she knew what he *wanted* to do to her.

His heart slammed against the wall of his chest and his breath released in a whoosh. "The feeling is mutual, pretty lady." He tried to smile, but the tension between them made that impossible. He wanted her so desperately he couldn't bear it.

"I . . . I dreamed about you." She rubbed her cheek against his palm. "About this . . . *thing* between us."

Oh, God. He would never forget the agony of listening to her dream. She'd moaned and arched and twisted in her bedroll until he'd damned near exploded. "Tell me, Molly"—his voice was hoarse and low, his need a palpable force between them—"about your dream."

Her small gasp told him he'd shocked her, but her bright eyes darkened with naked longing.

Naked. Yes. She's naked.

Dirk brushed his thumb across her cheekbone and she turned, pressing her lips to his hand. Echoing the lightning, a jolt sizzled into his palm and arrowed straight through the rest of him with incredible precision. The woman was dangerous, and she didn't even know it.

"I . . . dreamed," she murmured against his palm, then looked right at him again, "that you . . ."

Dirk held his breath. "That I what?" he urged, dying a little inside with each thud of his heart.

"That you . . . you kissed me." Her cheeks reddened more, but a tremulous smile reached her parted lips and crawled into his heart.

"I did kiss you." *God, yes, and I want to again.* He took a step closer, his gaze dropping to where her free hand continued to clutch the blanket at her throat. "And you kissed me back."

"I remember." Her voice grew husky and her eyes darkened to cobalt. "Sweet Jesus, help me, but I . . ."

"You what?" He moved even closer, keeping his hand on the softness of her cheek. "Tell me, Molly. Tell me."

"I . . . I liked it," she confessed, lowering her lashes against her cheeks.

"Yes." He eased his thumb across her lower lip and she opened her eyes again. "I've never enjoyed kissing a woman more."

Shock displayed itself clearly in her eyes. She didn't speak, nor did she shy away from his caress. He saw her quiver, watched her pulse leap at the base of her throat, noticed the way her knuckles whitened around the knot of blanket she clutched so fervently.

"I want to understand this," she confessed, her expression so sincere it unmanned him.

"You're killing me, Molly Riordan." He smiled, gently stroking her lower lip and wanting to do so much more. "And if you don't finish telling me about your dream, I'm just going to keel over right here and now."

She flashed him a brilliant but fleeting smile, then her lip trembled beneath his thumb as her expression grew solemn again. "It . . . it's embarrassing."

"If what you feel for me is anything like I'm feeling

right now, embarrassment be damned." His words came out in a rush, straight from his heart.

Bypassing his brain entirely.

She blinked, her lips forming an open circle of surprise. Then she cleared her throat, her eyes softening as she held his gaze. Gently, she kissed the pad of his thumb.

And damned near killed him.

The gesture was like another bolt of lightning. A direct hit. Dirk shuddered from the tips of his toes to the top of his very confused head, felled as surely as that pine tree outside.

"Your dream," he urged, barely able to speak as he inched closer.

"Aye," she murmured against his thumb. "My dream."

"I'm listening." *I may not breathe for a while, but I am listening.*

"You kissed me and . . . I know it's silly, but in my dream I was wearing that scandalous blue robe again."

He arched his brows. "I like the way the silk molds against your skin."

Her cheeks flamed, though a smile curved her lips. "Aye, you liked it in my dream as well."

He couldn't suppress his smile. "What happened next?"

"I told you." She sighed. "You kissed me."

He eased his hand to the smooth line of her jaw. "Did I kiss you . . . like this?"

Lowering his lips closer, he brought his other hand up so he cupped her face. She tilted her chin upward, and at that point he knew no force on earth could have held him back. He would kiss this beautiful woman, and he would do so thoroughly.

Slowly, he pulled Molly close, then closer still. A

subtle stiffening overtook her body as his thighs pressed against hers through his jeans and her blanket.

She's naked.

No matter what, he couldn't forget that little detail. The urge to push away the folds of wool and reveal the bounty hidden from his gaze burned hotter and brighter with every beat of his heart.

"Did I hold you like this in your dream?" he whispered, so close he inhaled her essence with every breath. He tugged her closer, pressing his hips to hers. "Or like this?"

She gasped and nodded, her eyes huge, her pupils dilated. "Aye."

Slowly, he tailored his mouth to hers. The initial silken feel of her lips scorched him so brutally it was all he could do not to growl. The gravity of his longing staggered him.

Only a kiss, he promised himself, trying to remember that he had no right to this delectable woman who was *not* his wife. He nibbled her lower lip, savoring her compelling flavor, drinking in all that was Molly.

The hitch and sigh of her breath was as intoxicating as Edward Ballinger's finest brandy to Dirk's finely honed senses. His arms tightened more, drawing her closer to the eager outline of his body.

Molly shifted slightly in his embrace, the brush of her body against his feeding the flames of desire. He gently traced the shape of her exquisite lips with his tongue, eliciting a quiver and a moan from Molly that urged him to take more.

God, yes, more.

Dirk nibbled and licked her lower lip, starving for another intimate morsel. More. It would always be more with this woman. He couldn't get enough of her. She was intoxicating, thrilling, humbling.

Another sigh washed over him, and her parted lips summoned him inside—an invitation he'd rather have died than refuse. He caressed the smooth warmth of her mouth with a tenderness that made her moan, a husky, seductive sound that rumbled from deep inside her and into him.

Her response incited his passion, and he deepened the kiss. She softened in his embrace, her curves melding against him even further. Dangerously.

She gave as much as she took. More. Dirk shivered as her tongue parried his, stroked the inner recesses of his mouth, and demanded more and more. *Yes, more.* He felt her breasts pressed against his bare chest, the rough wool of the blanket abrading his flesh as he knew it did hers.

The desire to see her and touch her drove him wild. She moaned as he arched her backward against his arm to deepen their kiss, and her arms swept up to the back of his neck.

Leaving the blanket trapped between them.

He inched his mouth away from hers and down the curve of her jaw to her silken throat. Her pulse leaped beneath his lips as he journeyed lower. And lower.

As he found the firm softness of the uppermost curve of her breast against his lips, he damned near exploded. His cock gave a demanding throb against the buttons of his jeans, and the thunder of his blood drowned out the small and annoying voice of reason.

He inched his mouth away from her warmth and gazed at her. Her milky flesh curved enticingly above the edge of the blanket, where only his body kept it from falling away. "Molly?" he whispered, the sound ragged. Desperate.

"What?"

"Did I do this in your dream?" He held his breath, waiting for her answer.

"Aye."

Her eyes were glazed with passion. Drugged. He wanted her with a fierceness that frightened him even as it drove him. Slowly, he eased the wool from between them until it draped across the trunk he'd unknowingly backed Molly up against. As the fabric slid away to reveal her luscious curves, he eased her down to sit atop the trunk.

His arms trembled, but not from the task of bearing her weight. He trembled from the powerful onslaught of longing and the near reverence that flowed through him as he gazed upon her glorious nakedness.

"You're so beautiful." He could barely speak. Color crept from her breasts to her neck, blooming in her cheeks. She cast her eyes downward as he feasted upon her beauty. "So incredibly beautiful."

Filled with awe, he dropped to his knees before her and buried his face between her full breasts. Her hands rested on his shoulders, and he felt her tense as he nuzzled her soft flesh.

"Did I do this in your dream, Molly?" Testing the weight of her breasts with his hands, he gently teased the inner slopes with his tongue. He brushed her nipples with his thumbs, rewarded by her sharp indrawn breath. "Or this?"

"Aye." She twined her fingers through the hair at the back of his neck. "Oh, aye."

He watched her nipples tighten into hard buds as he worked his way closer, finally displacing his thumb with his mouth. *Ambrosia.* He'd never tasted anything sweeter.

She tightened her grip on the back of his neck,

clutching him against her. Dirk alternately teased and suckled until she moaned and squirmed.

Dying inside for every moment he couldn't bury himself inside her, he reached between her thighs and found her womanly folds. She gasped as he dipped his finger inside her hot center, rotating the nub above it with his thumb.

"Oh, what . . ." She clutched him to her breast as he drew her deeper into his mouth. "What are you doing to me?"

He didn't answer. He couldn't. As her passion mounted, she pressed herself against his hand, moaning and panting. Her breasts swelled in his mouth, and he knew she was near her peak. How he wished he could join her.

A violent spasm gripped her and she growled with pleasure, answering one of the questions that had plagued him since overhearing her dream.

Yes, Molly Riordan was as vocal awake as asleep. *Thank God.*

He slipped his arms around her waist again, devouring her breasts. She rained kisses over the top of his head, massaging the back of his neck. He reached down and wrapped her legs around his waist, pressing himself against her.

He groaned, unable to breathe for several moments. She rocked herself against him through the rough fabric of his jeans, and he groaned again. "Oh, God, Molly." He cupped her breasts in his hands, flicking his tongue across her sweet nipples.

She rocked against him again and he did what came naturally. His explosion pulsed through him, filling the front of his jeans with his scalding seed.

Sighing, he rested his forehead against her breast.

"Now you've done it," he murmured against her soft warmth as his breathing slowly returned to normal.

"Done what?" she asked guilelessly.

"Uh, trust me. You don't want to know." He looked up at her swollen mouth, her flushed cheeks, and the gleam of satisfaction glistening in her eyes. Her expression held the candor only an innocent could've mustered. Relief flooded him. Another few minutes and she would no longer have been innocent.

He eased himself away from her and looked at her. *Really* looked at her. Who could've blamed him for losing himself this way? She was incredible. Perfect. Her breasts were high and full, her nipples large and tempting. Her waist was so tiny he could almost encircle her with his hands, and the gentle flare of her hips was just enough to drive a man to distraction.

God knew he'd been distracted.

The dark triangle of hair between her legs beckoned him. His cock roared to life again, but Dirk forced himself to pull away this time. He drew the edges of the blanket around her shoulders and across her enticing breasts.

"It's a shame to cover such beauty," he whispered.

"I . . . I shouldn't have . . . have . . ."

"Shh." He pressed his fingertip to her lips. "You're still a virgin."

She pulled the blanket snugly in place. "I still shouldn't have."

"You had help."

She met his gaze and smiled. "That was . . ."

"Was what?" He returned her smile, though his body urged him to resume their activity. Her expression smoldered, stealing his breath. "Was what, Molly?" he repeated, struggling for control.

"More than I ever dreamed."

* * *

Ida Jensen worried her lower lip while she stood stirring the pot of stew she'd been simmering all day. Rosa had taken a few days off to visit family down in Pueblo, leaving Elena here to help Ida.

And flirt with Lance.

A smile curved Ida's lips as she considered her son's total lack of awareness concerning Elena's interest. Elena was a good girl, and she'd make a good daughter-in-law. And, truth be told, Ida had other reasons for wanting Lance married.

She wouldn't be here forever. He would always have a home here at the ranch, but she wanted something more for him. She wanted him to have love *and* security. His obvious fixation on Dirk's new wife would pass.

Ida knew what it felt like to be wildly, passionately in love. She'd had that kind of love once with Lance's father. Though she'd given her love openly, her husband had always held himself back. Eventually he'd shunned her and completely shut her out of his life.

Tears of remembrance gathered in the corners of her eyes, but she blinked them into submission. "What's past is past, Ida." She stirred the stew with more vigor. "And best forgotten."

But she would never forget the day her husband had turned his back on her and their newborn son. The hate in the man's eyes when he'd gazed upon their imperfect child was burned into her memory. It haunted her day and night.

Each morning when her son greeted her with his warm smile and a kiss to her cheek, she knew she'd done the right thing. Taking her infant son and turning

her back on her husband and the life they'd made had
been the right choice.

If only—

She heard the door open and turned to see Clyde
slipping through the back door as he removed his hat.
Since their walk the other evening, seeing him had
made her feel giddy and young again.

Foolishness, Ida. But true.

"Afternoon, ma'am." Clyde remained in the doorway. "Somethin' sure smells good. I hope I'm not in-
trudin'."

"No, not at all." She covered the pot and wiped her
hands on her apron, then patted the pesky strands of
white hair that had crept from her bun. Once upon a
time her hair had been the color of cornsilk, so her
husband had said. "I must be quite a sight after standing over this hot stove all day."

"The heat from the stove makes your cheeks rosy,
and I reckon these are near as pretty as you." He produced a bouquet of columbine from behind his back.
"Ma'am."

Ida froze, then found her breath and said, "Oh,
they're beautiful." She approached him and took the
delicate blossoms in her hand. Those pesky tears gathered again and her throat felt full and clogged. "Thank
you."

He shrugged and crimson stains appeared on his
cheeks beneath his leathery tan. "I seen 'em bloomin'
behind the barn and figgered they'd look better in one
of your pretty vases than trampled by horses and wranglers."

She couldn't speak. All she could do was nod, which
broke the dam holding back her tears. Several of them
dropped in rapid succession to the back of the hand
holding the flowers. She quickly wiped them away with

her other hand and sniffled, unable to meet Clyde's gaze.

Then, amazingly, she felt his hand on her chin, urging her to look up at him. She did, noting the clearness of his light eyes in his tanned complexion. Despite the wrinkles and cragginess of his features, he was a handsome man. The sun kept his skin a warm bronze, while his eyes and hair were like spun silver.

Listen to yourself, Ida.

Oh, but it was true. She sniffled again. "I'd best get some water for these." She hurried to the cupboard near the back door and retrieved a small vase, then reached for the handle on the pump, but Clyde's large hand covered hers.

"Let me," he said, standing so near she felt his warmth seep into her.

She nodded and allowed him to take the vase, then stepped aside. Mesmerized, she watched the way his muscles rippled in his long, lean body as he worked the handle until water filled the delicate vase and the wash pan beneath it.

"Thank you," she whispered, taking the vase and carrying it to the large table in the center of the kitchen. She arranged the blossoms in the vase. "They're perfect."

She hadn't realized he'd followed her from the sink until the warm, manly scent of him filled her nostrils. He stood right beside her, so close she could feel the heat of his breath. Her knees turned to cornmeal mush as she stood there smiling like a fool. The man was making her crazy. Frisky as a filly.

Silly old woman.

He took her hand, startling her. Ida found her gaze drawn to his by some invisible force. The expression in his eyes made her heart flutter in her chest; her insides turned all warm and soft like custard just before it set.

"I been doin' some thinkin'," he said. "And some rememberin'."

The warmth fled, replaced by a profound and penetrating chill. "Remembering?" Her heart didn't flutter now. It pounded out the rhythm of her greatest fear.

And her most cherished wish.

Yes, it was true. If they all knew the truth about Ida's past, she would be free in so many ways. Free to pursue a future with a man like Clyde.

Where had that thought come from?

But the truth could also rob her of something precious. She couldn't risk that. A shiver rippled through her.

He leaned around her and dropped his hat to the table, freeing both his hands to hold hers. "Rememberin'." He directed a half smile at her and shook his head. "I may just be loco, but I got me a feelin' we've met before. Maybe durin' the war?"

The war? That means he doesn't really remember. Disappointment and relief washed through her. "No . . . no, I was in Denver then." That was the truth. She and Lance had lived in Denver until she'd received word about . . . no, that was best forgotten, like her identity.

Forever.

She drew a shaky breath, trying to concentrate on the feel of his work-roughened fingers against her hands. He traced circles on the back of her hand with his thumb, sending rivulets of liquid fire pulsing up her arm and throughout her body.

"No, it must not have been the war then." He shook his head. "It's been tormetin' me, though—the rememberin'."

"Didn't you say you were in Texas then?" Her voice quivered and she prayed he hadn't noticed. The expression in his eyes seemed solemn. Sincere. No trace of suspicion flickered in the silvery depths.

"Yep, in Texas." His gaze never wavered. "I dreamed about you as a young woman."

Warmth flooded her cheeks. "You . . . you did?"

He nodded. "You had shiny golden hair and a smile that could've lit up the darkest night."

Ida smiled—how could she not? "My . . . my hair was the color of Lance's," she said, wondering if she dared give him even this much information.

Clyde nodded. "That's close to what I'm rememberin'." He grinned. "Or dreamin'."

Relieved, Ida laughed. "I think that's far more likely, because if we'd met I would surely remember you."

He chuckled. "Oh, I dunno," he said. "I look mighty different than I did as a young fella." His expression grew sober again. "Hard work, hard livin', and hard weather'll do that to a man."

Ida nodded. She remembered from the early days of her marriage how harsh the environment could be on a body. Folks lived much better now than they had then. "What did you look like, Clyde?"

The color heightened in his cheeks again. "My hair was the color of rust, ma'am." He grinned, fine white lines crinkling at the corners of his eyes and mouth. "Edward and the boys called me Rusty until the gray took over."

The room swayed. Ida felt his grip tighten on her hands, but she couldn't speak. Was it her imagination or was the floor coming toward her?

Clyde grabbed her waist and hauled her against him just in time. "Ma'am? Ida?" Worry gave his voice a gruff quality. "You all right?"

Ida drew several deep gulps of air and shook herself, commanding the wooziness to pass. "It's so warm in here," she said, her voice weak. "I shouldn't have picked such a hot day for stew and baking." She grew suddenly aware of the long hard length of his body pressed against her.

Then reality thrust itself to the forefront of her thoughts again. *Rusty.* A barrage of memories flew through her mind, image after image bringing it all back. Her chest tightened and her breath came in short, unsatisfying gasps.

"Ma'am, you ain't gonna swoon, are you?"

His voice broke through, dragging her back to the present, and she found the deep breath that had been eluding her. "No, of course I'm not going to swoon." She forced a smile and saw his expression shift from worried to enchanted.

"You called me Ida earlier," she continued. She had to forget about the past . . . and pray he would, too. Using her middle name could be the only thing to save her.

And the only thing to keep her imprisoned by her own lies.

Fourteen

The sound of Dirk opening the door jarred Molly awake. She'd slept on the only bunk, while he'd taken the floor. Fortunately they'd found enough dry blankets and wood to ensure their warmth through the long stormy night.

Sitting upright, she stretched and yawned. The feel of her bare breasts against the wool blanket reminded her of her continued nakedness.

And of all the ways and places Dirk had touched her.

Remembered heat poured through her again like warm syrup. Her hand fell to her breast, her nipple hardening against the wool. He'd touched and kissed her almost exactly as she'd dreamed. She'd never imagined reality could be even better than a dream.

Aye, but it is ever so much better. Molly sighed and swung her legs to the floor. The sound of Dirk talking to the horses outside told her he would be occupied for a while. She hurried across the room and grabbed her stiffly dried clothing. After she was dressed, she pulled on her shoes and tied the laces, then folded all the borrowed blankets and returned them to the trunk.

The sight of the trunk reminded her of how Dirk had lowered her down to sit atop it, then knelt before her.

Her knees grew weak and she had no choice but to sit there again. It was either that or fall to the floor.

Seated on the trunk, she contemplated how it had felt to have his silken mouth tugging at the tips of her breasts. They tingled and ached now, begging for more of the magic Dirk Ballinger had to offer. She glanced down, noticing the shape of her nipples outlined through her shirtwaist *and* the chemise beneath.

"Jesus, Mary, and Joseph," she muttered, lowering her face into her hands. She would never be the same now—not after having tasted that forbidden fruit Gram had so fervently warned her about.

Aye, and isn't Dirk the sweetest of fruits?

"Listen to yourself." Shaking her head, she pushed to her feet, then noticed the strange man standing in the doorway. She gasped, but forced herself to meet his gaze.

"Mornin', ma'am," he said, tipping his hat. Sunlight poured in from behind him, shading his face and features. "Or should I say . . . Mrs. Ballinger?"

Uneasiness crept through Molly, and her gaze darted to the other door, willing Dirk to return. "Who are you?" she asked, knowing she should recognize the man from somewhere. Was he one of the highwaymen?

He stepped farther into the cabin and the sun's angle shifted lower, allowing her to discern his identity. "Ah, the sheriff," she said, though more suspicious than relieved.

"Sheriff Kevin Templeton." He inclined his head, making his bright yellow hair seem even more unusual than it had before. "I came up to see if Dirk has made any progress in tracking down Lovejoy."

He arched an eyebrow and raked the length of Molly with a gaze that made her feel soiled. She hadn't done her hair yet. It hung loose in a riot of wild curls. Considering the direction her thoughts had taken just before the sheriff's arrival, she had the uncomfortable suspicion that the man knew exactly what had happened here last night.

Rather . . . *almost* happened.

Her face flooded with heat and shame and she looked toward the side door again and discovered it ajar. Dirk stood there now, looking from the sheriff to Molly and back again, his gaze narrowed, nostrils slightly flared.

"Ever heard of knocking, Templeton?" Dirk asked, approaching the fire to check the coffee.

"I did." The sheriff walked into the center of the room. "She must not have heard me."

Molly barely stopped herself from calling the man a liar. She didn't want to cause trouble for Dirk, and, for some reason, she didn't trust Sheriff Templeton. Shouldn't she be able to trust a man of the law? Aye, but this one made her flesh crawl and her throat constrict.

Dirk opened another can of beans for breakfast. He obviously had no intention of preparing a big meal this morning. Considering their present company, Molly wasn't in the mood for one, either.

"Aren't you a long way from Estes Park, Templeton?" Dirk asked, stirring the beans as they warmed. He glanced over his shoulder at Molly, a somewhat winsome expression in his eyes.

Aye, it would have been nice to have had Dirk all to herself a bit longer. Nice, but dangerous. She barely resisted the urge to sigh, then realized the sheriff hadn't answered Dirk's question. She looked at him and found him staring at her again—a knowing gleam in his amber eyes.

Faith. The man made her skin crawl and her stomach lurch.

"Templeton?" Dirk straightened and placed his fists on his hips. "I asked you a question."

"I heard you, Ballinger." Templeton sighed as if answering Dirk was beneath him. "Just checking to see if you've made any progress." The sheriff lifted one shoulder and a half smile curved one side of his mouth.

No, Molly didn't like him at all.

"Some." Dirk poured coffee into three cups.

Molly accepted a cup from him, wishing she had thick cream and lots of sugar for the bitter concoction, but life on the trail didn't provide such amenities. At least last night they hadn't been forced to hoist their supplies and clothing into a tree.

Though she'd still been quite naked.

A heated flush rose to her cheeks. Then she realized what Dirk hadn't told the sheriff. She studied Dirk's guarded expression and determined he didn't trust Sheriff Templeton any more than she did. For some reason, he obviously didn't want the sheriff to know about the ransom note.

And he definitely didn't want Sheriff Templeton to know Ray Lovejoy was Dirk's half brother.

The sheriff sipped the coffee and grimaced. "You make lousy coffee, Ballinger." He laughed at his own joke, but Dirk remained silent.

No, Dirk most definitely did not like or trust this man either. Concern ate at Molly's belly, the strong coffee roiling around and making her wish for one of Gram's warm scones dripping with butter. And tea. She'd have given almost anything for a cup of real tea. She closed her eyes for a moment and imagined she could almost smell the fragrant brew.

"You're about as far along the trail as my posse got."

The sheriff took another sip of coffee, then bent down to set the cup on the hearth. "I figured you'd hole up here when that storm hit."

"Yep." Dirk spooned beans onto a plate for himself and Molly, but didn't offer any to their uninvited guest.

Sheriff Templeton struck a challenging pose—his chin lifted, his eyes narrowed, his fists clenched at his sides. "So just what the devil makes you think you're gonna find 'em when we didn't?"

Dirk lifted a shoulder and spooned beans into his mouth. He chewed for several silent moments, then cleared his throat. "Call me motivated."

"For which I'm eternally grateful," Molly chimed in, finishing her beans and wondering how many more beans she'd be forced to eat during this journey.

Dirk smiled at her, then resumed his solemn expression as he faced the lawman again. "In case you've forgotten, there's a hostage involved. Sheriff." The last word sounded almost like an insult and hung on the air between them.

Molly sensed the tension crackling between the men. Why, she wouldn't have been a bit surprised to see them coming to blows at any moment.

"Oh, yeah," the sheriff turned his gaze on Molly again, "your wife's faithful servant."

That annoying gleam entered the man's eyes again, and Molly drew a shaky breath. Did he know she wasn't Lady Elizabeth? *Jesus, Mary, and Joseph.* It wasn't possible.

Even so, an insistent voice from the back of her mind believed it was so. Molly drew a deep breath to steady her nerves and busied herself with cleaning up their breakfast dishes and packing their supplies.

The flesh on the back of Molly's neck crawled, but she didn't look at the sheriff. She refused to meet his insulting gaze again. She stowed items in her saddle-bags and her hand brushed against something cool and metal.

A shiver raced through her as she recognized the object as Lance's small pistol. For the first time since leaving the ranch, she was glad to have it, though she wasn't entirely certain why that was so.

"Good morning," Jeremiah called from the doorway.

Molly spun around to greet the older man, relief washing through her. "Top o' the mornin' to you, Jeremiah," she returned in an exaggerated brogue that would've made any Irishman proud.

"Morning," Dirk said, then faced the sheriff again. "Don't you have something to do back in town, Templeton?" He punctuated his question with an arched brow, his true meaning clear.

He wanted Kevin Templeton gone.

Molly held her breath as the sheriff looked at each of them, then his gaze rested on her far longer than necessary. "I guess we really do learn new things every day." A nasty smile curved his lips. "I didn't know English ladies came complete with Irish accents." He donned his hat and left the cabin.

She swayed and Dirk gripped her elbow to steady her. "Easy, Molly," he whispered, gently massaging her arm. "The snake's gone now."

Jeremiah cleared his throat and said, "We don't need *that* white man's help."

"I completely agree," Dirk said, giving Molly's arm a squeeze before he banked the fire and gathered their belongings. "You've eaten, old man?"

Jeremiah patted his slim abdomen and flashed them a mischievous grin. "Enough for three very *young* men."

"Good, because we need to reach Serendipity before sundown."

Serendipity. She needed to stop thinking about Dirk Ballinger and remember the reason she'd accompanied Lady Elizabeth to America in the first place.

Da, I'll find you.

Ray watched Lady Elizabeth sort through a box of folded papers the miner who'd once worked this claim had left behind. She grew bored easily and made it clear she was willing to read anything she could find.

He'd been keeping a close eye on her for any sign that the child—*his* child—might come early. He didn't know much about breeding women or childbirth, but he'd heard somewhere that shock could bring on a baby early.

And he'd dealt the uppity lady one hell of a shock.

The last thing he wanted or needed was to be forced to deliver the baby himself. If that became anything more than a remote possibility, he figured Teddy and Luther would disappear almost immediately. Ray chuckled quietly and leaned back in his chair. He sure couldn't blame the ornery old farts for that.

"What's so funny?" Lady Elizabeth asked, looking up from the pile of papers she was reading.

"Oh, nothing important." Ray rose and approached the overturned crate he and the boys had used as a card table. Their hostage had commandeered it and showed no signs of relenting anytime soon. "You find anything interesting in that junk?"

A wrinkle marred her brow as she glanced up at him. "One thing." She turned her attention back to the papers.

"Well, what?"

"It wouldn't interest you," she said, not looking up from the papers as she spoke. "I know someone else who'll be *very* interested, though. I need to make sure my maid sees these." She gave him a sober look. "They'll mean a lot to her."

"If you say so." With a sigh of impatience, Ray snatched the document from her hand and skimmed it. "I don't see anything interesting here."

"You can read?"

"Yes, I can read," he said with a snarl.

"Good, then go read something." She looked up at him, her expression smug. "Now leave me alone so I can get all these facts straight."

"Fine, fine." He raked his fingers through his hair and paced the low-ceilinged cave. He was going stir-crazy himself in this hole. Maybe he should start digging and see if there was more silver in the played-out mine after all. Or gold. He could do with a nice fat vein of ore.

That's bullshit. The mine was played out, and digging would be a waste of time and energy. He glanced up at the timbers again. Besides, he didn't want to disturb the questionable steadiness of the support beams.

No matter how much he avoided the subject, he knew in his gut that his priorities had shifted. The minute he'd discovered Lady Elizabeth's child was his, everything had changed. He swallowed hard and stepped outside for some fresh air.

But one question tormented the holy hell out of him.

Why had Dirk agreed to marry a woman carrying Ray's child?

Unless Dirk didn't realize it. No, that couldn't be. Lady Elizabeth had finally admitted she'd never even met the real Dirk Ballinger. The child was Ray's.

And Dirk must have realized that when he'd agreed to marry the woman.

That still didn't explain *why*. Ray couldn't think of any man who would willingly marry a woman carrying another man's child, let alone pay a ransom to get the woman back. No one.

Then he remembered some of the things Dirk had said about family. Ray leaned against the mine opening and shook his head. Dirk had offered to give Ray the Ballinger name. Wouldn't he also be willing to give that name to an unborn child?

An unborn *Ballinger* child?

"Shit."

Dirk Ballinger was too damned honorable for his own good. He was willing to give up his freedom to give Ray's bastard a name. The reality of his half brother's unselfishness compounded Ray's guilt tenfold.

How could two such opposite men be of the same blood?

Dirk was a saint. Ray was a sinner.

He swallowed hard and raked his fingers through his hair, realizing he would soon be forced to face Dirk again. Ray should've tried to devise a scheme to make the exchange without having to see his half brother, but the truth was he *wanted* to see him one more time. God only knew why.

"I'm hungry," came the grating voice from inside the cave.

Ray released a long sigh and caught sight of Teddy and Luther shuffling toward the mine with a mess of fish. "I hope you caught a lot of fish."

Teddy and Luther paused to stare at each other. They appeared to have reached some unspoken agreement by the time they reached Ray and handed him the full stringer. They tipped their hats and headed back toward the trees.

"Hey, where are you going?"

"I'm hungry," their hostage called again.

"Fishin'," the old men called back without looking.

Ray looked down at the gaping eyes of the fish, their scales glistening silver in the sunlight.

"I'm hungry," the woman called again.

He poked his head inside. "We're having fish. Now hush."

"Fine."

She pursed her lips in a pout, and for a moment he remembered the beautiful woman he'd seduced the night of her father's masquerade ball. He'd been on fire with wanting her from the moment he'd first seen her floating down the stairs toward him. His gaze dropped to her distended belly, where her hand now rested.

Despite her puffy face and distorted body, she was still a beautiful woman. At least, she was when she was asleep. And silent. He swallowed the lump in his throat, remembering how he'd sat beside her and watched her sleep last night after learning the truth. He'd even touched her belly once and felt the baby kick against his hand. A peculiar sort of madness had shot through him then.

Half protective, half possessive.

His baby. This beautiful, infuriating woman was carrying his child.

And she was engaged to marry his half brother.

"Is that fish cooking yet?" she whined.

"Well, shit." Shaking himself to his senses—he hoped—he grabbed a sharp knife to clean the fish and headed back outside. "Just shit."

* * *

Dirk's uneasiness grew with every mile they traveled. By mid afternoon, they were close enough to Serendipity to practically hear and smell it.

The town of Serendipity meant something to Molly. What? She was from across an ocean and had never visited America before, let alone Colorado. More importantly, why hadn't she told him *why* Serendipity was important to her?

The answer smacked him between the eyes and made him blink. *Because I haven't asked her.*

"Fool," he muttered, ducking beneath a low branch. Molly hadn't given him any reason not to trust her. On the contrary, he knew in his gut she was completely trustworthy. He made a promise to himself to ask her about Serendipity as soon as they were settled in the hotel.

He'd never been to Serendipity before. It was one of several mining camps in the area that had grown into boom towns practically overnight. As cattle ranchers, neither he nor his father had ever had any reason to visit such places.

Zane paused and cocked his head at a listening angle, obviously hearing something only he could. And maybe the horses. The man was uncanny with his ability to see, hear, smell, and simply sense things ordinary men couldn't. Furthermore, Dirk had complete confidence in Jeremiah Zane's abilities. If he heard something, then, by damned, he heard something.

Molly stopped a few feet ahead of Dirk, and he eased Cloud in beside Sadie. "I think we're almost there," he said quietly.

She nodded and gave him a weak smile, but he sensed the sudden tension within her. Yes, as soon as they were settled, he would ask her why Serendipity was important to her. Then, once she answered, he would have no reason at all to distrust her—not even imaginary ones.

"Over this rise," Zane said, pointing ahead.

"Lead on, old man," Dirk returned with a grin, knowing Zane wouldn't even bother to look back at him. A moment later, the Indian and the pack mule continued their steady, uphill trek, with Molly and Dirk riding side by side where the trail widened enough to permit it.

He enjoyed being close to her. She was beautiful, soft, alluring, sexy, and *good*. Molly Riordan was everything he would have looked for in a wife if he'd ever considered searching.

His gut roiled and burned. Now he'd never have the opportunity to fall in love and marry the normal way. Fate had dictated his future—or, rather, his half brother's dishonor had.

Dirk Ballinger would marry the mother of his bastard half brother's child. If she was still alive.

He swallowed the bile rising to his throat and cast a sidelong glance at Molly. Another realization waylaid him and his breath came out in a whoosh.

No matter how many years he might be married to Lady Elizabeth Summersby, he would never forget Molly. Hell, he would never stop *wanting* her.

God help him.

He drew a long, slow breath and held it, watching a bead of perspiration trickle down the side of her neck and disappear inside her collar. He longed to follow the glittering droplet, to trail kisses along the side of her throat, to bare her lush breasts to his ravenous lips and hands, to part her virginal thighs and—

Oh, God.

A shudder rippled through him and he grew hard so fast it made him dizzy. Touching her last night had been a mistake. Having tasted her, touched her, and seen her naked beauty only made him want her more.

He shifted in the saddle to ease the pressure on his single-minded male anatomy, but no matter how he tried, he couldn't drag his gaze away from her. Cloud plodded along on the trail, keeping pace with Sadie.

At the moment, Dirk didn't have to think about the trail or anything but the woman at his side and how to deal with his desire for her. His gaze drifted lower, where her breasts strained against the blouse she'd borrowed from Lady Elizabeth's belongings.

He'd never seen or touched breasts quite like Molly's before—perfectly round and plump, their rose-colored tips velvety soft and infinitely sweet. Her breasts moved with the rocking motion of the horse, and his thoughts turned to another similar but far more pleasant rhythm.

He tugged on his collar, remembering the way she'd climaxed last night, rocking and thrusting herself against him. She'd had no idea, of course, about the consequences of her actions. Remembering the way he'd exploded in his jeans made Dirk's cock throb against his fly in search of an encore performance.

He glanced down with a wry grin. *There will be no more of that.* Nothing like that had happened to him since adolescence, when he'd had little control over such matters.

He flinched again, remembering, then glanced up to find Molly watching him. Her eyes practically smoldered, mirroring the same burning need that coursed through him.

Where Molly Riordan was concerned, he had no more control over his physical urges than a schoolboy. *Hell.*

Zane stopped at the summit and waited for them to

catch up with him. A vast high mountain meadow opened up before them. A creek snaked its way across it, and right in the middle sat the town of Serendipity, Colorado.

"Well, there it is," Dirk said on a sigh. He looked at Molly, who sat more erect in the saddle and leaned slightly forward. Soon, he promised himself, he would have the answer about her obvious interest in this town.

"Let's move out," Dirk said. "We need to find a hotel and the local bank."

"For the ransom?" Molly asked, breaking her silence.

Dirk met her gaze and nodded. "Twenty-five thousand dollars."

"I'm sorry." She reached over and covered his hand with hers.

He looked up to meet her gaze. Her blue eyes reflected sincerity and sadness—no trace of subterfuge. "Why are you sorry?" he asked. "This isn't your fault."

"No, but . . ." She worried her lower lip. "I mean about the money."

He shook his head, holding her gaze. "I don't care about the money, Molly."

Surprise flickered in her eyes. "You don't?"

"Well, no man wants to part with that much money, but you know what bothers me." His gaze never wavered from hers. "You remember?"

"Aye." Her smile was sad, her gaze filled with empathy. "Your brother."

Dirk didn't correct her about Ray's relationship to him, because he found it somehow comforting to know that she remembered why this quest was so important to him.

He heard Zane start down the trail toward Serendipity, but Dirk lingered behind with Molly, staring deeply into her eyes and into his own soul.

And his heart.

Realization slammed into him with all the finesse of a cattle stampede. This was nothing like the dawnings or glittering rainbows he'd read about in his college days.

No, his reckoning was fierce and sudden—downright thunderous.

And undeniable.

He was in love with Molly Riordan.

Fifteen

Molly rode along in silence as they entered the outskirts of Serendipity. The streets and boardwalks were filled with rough-looking men, probably miners. Some didn't look old enough to be away from their mothers, while others were probably grandfathers many times over. The men whose attention drew hers were those who fell somewhere in between.

Da, are you here? Could one of these grizzled men be Niall Riordan? Would he recognize her after all these years? Aye, she knew he would, for she was the image of her mother, but for having his eyes.

If he was here and still alive, he should recognize her. But would he care? She blinked back the insistent tears pricking her eyes and drew a shaky breath as Dirk grabbed Sadie's reins.

Molly looked up at the disturbance that had erupted in the street, where a pair of men swung punches at each other. She hadn't seen anything such as this since leaving Ireland more than a decade ago. Gram had often said that a true Irishman loved good horses, good whiskey, and a good brawl on occasion. Of course, Molly had no way of knowing if these men were Irish, nor did it matter.

Unless one of them was Niall Riordan.

She squinted as a meaty fist made contact with an

already swollen jaw. No, these men were far too young. Her da would be at least fifty by now.

Dirk guided Sadie around the melee and the cheering men who'd gathered to witness the excitement. She glanced up and found his curious gaze on her, which brought heat to her cheeks. The man confounded her . . . and so much more.

"The hotel." Jeremiah pointed to a building next to the saloon.

A muscle twitched in Dirk's jaw and he shook his head slowly. "Let's keep riding." He gave her a slow smile that warmed her heart and made it flutter. "There must be a quieter place."

As they neared the edge of town, the false storefronts and loud music were replaced by quiet homes and shady streets. Molly saw two children playing in a puddle near the road and smiled when they waved. Serendipity had families and homes and decent people.

So why hadn't her da sent for her?

A lump swelled in her throat and she swallowed convulsively. If he was here, she would find him.

And she would show Niall Riordan just how Irish his daughter's temper could be.

They finally came to a boarding house. A wooden sign swung in the breeze with the words "Beth Anne's Room and Board" carved into it.

"Here?" Jeremiah asked quietly, bringing his horse and the mule to a halt.

Dirk sighed. "This will have to do. The hotel is no place for a lady."

Jeremiah nodded and flashed Molly a toothless and endearing grin, then returned his attention to Dirk. "I will camp near the creek south of town until you need me."

"Suit yourself, old man." Dirk smiled. "I know the thought of sleeping under a roof makes you twitch."

Jeremiah chuckled. "Until the snow flies."

Dirk glanced upward. "Could be anytime now."

"But it's still August," Molly argued, shivering. Surely it couldn't snow so early.

Dirk's smile was indulgent and gentle. "At this altitude, it isn't unusual to see snow even in July, and the first snow will fall early in September at the latest."

"In Ireland we have our snow in April."

Dirk chuckled and winked at Jeremiah. "We call April snow our spring showers."

Molly obviously had much to learn about this beautiful country. She gazed toward the mountains ringing the small town. "It must be beautiful in winter."

The sound of a gunshot from the center of town split the silence, making Molly jerk. "Jesus, Mary, and Joseph, but I'll never get used to that."

"Quieter here than at the hotel, too," Jeremiah added.

"Most of the prospectors will winter at a lower altitude," Dirk explained.

That meant she had to find her da now, before the snows came.

Dirk dismounted and looped both their horses' reins over the hitching post, then assisted Molly's dismount. "Let's see if they have room for us."

The feel of Dirk's strong hands lingering at her waist sent a shiver of longing skittering through her. Molly's breath caught and she gazed up into his eyes. A wicked part of her would love to share a room with this handsome man. *Two rooms, Molly.* She drew a deep breath to steady herself.

The house was painted a sunny yellow, with blue shutters and frames around the windows. Ornate white trim adorned the corners where rails and posts came together, and the screen door was a work of art—an oval center surrounded by what looked like filigree. Molly had never seen so much detail in such a modest house. It was beautiful and welcoming at the same time.

Dirk lifted the knocker and let it fall against the wood. A woman's voice called through the door, then it opened a moment later. She was a tiny thing, with spectacles perched on her nose. Her dark hair was streaked with gray and pulled into a tight bun at her nape.

"Welcome to Beth Anne's," she said, her voice quiet and friendly. She held open the screen. "You must have seen the hotel and are now seeking refuge from the madness." Laughter edged her voice.

Dirk chuckled and removed his hat. "Good afternoon, ma'am." He placed a hand at the small of Molly's back. "I'm Dirk Ballinger, and this is my wife."

"I'm Beth Anne Nichols." She motioned for them to enter. "Pleased to meet you, Mr. Ballinger, Mrs. Ballinger."

Molly stiffened slightly, though she would rather be addressed as "Mrs. Ballinger" than as "Lady Elizabeth." The scent of lemon oil assailed her nostrils as they entered the house. As her eyes adjusted to the dim interior, she noticed dark gleaming wood and a massive piano in the center of the parlor. The parlor and foyer had been decorated with care and warmth. Molly immediately fell in love with it.

"It's beautiful," she said, noticing the way the older woman's eyes twinkled behind her spectacles. "Do you have room for us?"

"I have one room left." Mrs. Nichols tilted her head and smiled at Molly.

"Oh." *Only one room?*

"I'm not sure how long we'll be staying," Dirk said, redirecting them to practical matters. "I'll be needing the bank, and my wife needs a safe place to stay while I tend to business."

Tending to business without me? Molly frowned.

"Bank's right off Main Street, about half a block behind the saloon." Mrs. Nichols arched a brow. "I know you didn't miss that den of inequity on your way through town."

Dirk's lips twitched. "No, ma'am."

"Room and three meals a day are two dollars a week," the woman said. "That includes tea, if you've a notion."

Molly's mouth watered and her heart sang as she clapped her hands together. "Tea? *Real* tea?"

Mrs. Nichols laughed and took Molly's hand. "I just put the kettle on, dear."

"I'll get our gear," Dirk said, his eyes growing intense as he met Molly's gaze. "Then I'm going to the bank on my way to let Zane know we're staying."

"All right," Molly said quietly, finding it difficult to catch her breath or to reel in her wayward emotions. This man made her think and want crazy things.

Forbidden things.

"Room's at the top of the stairs, first door on your left," Mrs. Nichols called over her shoulder as she led Molly through a swinging door and into a spacious kitchen.

The ceiling was high, the walls covered with cabinets the likes of which Molly hadn't seen since leaving England. Even the kitchen at Dirk's ranch wasn't this well appointed. A woman could spend days in here and never leave.

"Milk?" Mrs. Nichols asked, setting the large table for tea. "You're Irish."

"Aye, and I'd love milk, please." Molly drew a deep appreciative sniff, relishing the aroma of real tea. "Ambrosia."

Mrs. Nichols chuckled. "I know you can't tell it from listening to me now, but I'm from Cornwall originally."

The woman didn't possess the distinctive accent. "How old were you when you came to this country?" Molly asked, slipping into the chair the older woman had indicated.

"Nine." Mrs. Nichols poured out, then took a seat across the table. "My father was a cobbler. He had a shop in Denver."

"However did you end up in Serendipity?" *And,* she added silently, *do you know my da?*

Mrs. Nichols heaved a sigh and took a sip of tea. Obviously fortified, she held Molly's gaze and said, "Married a miner, buried him, and now this house is all I've got."

Molly's breath caught and she met the woman's gaze. "I'm so sorry," she said, but something told her this woman didn't want sympathy. At least not now. "And a lovely house it is, too."

She took a sip of tea laced with sugar and milk, savoring the taste and feel of it in her mouth. "I've missed tea desperately."

Mrs. Nichols gave a knowing nod. "Mr. Nichols died almost eleven years ago," she said, looking beyond Molly, who sensed the woman didn't expect a response. "That's the way things are up here." The woman's voice quieted. "But knowing that didn't make it any easier on me when a cave-in took my only son last year."

Molly squeezed her eyes shut, trying not to wonder if a similar fate could have befallen her da, then she reached for the woman's hand. "A terrible loss for any woman."

Mrs. Nichols gave Molly's hand a squeeze, then cleared her throat. "Enough of that." She sniffled and sipped her tea. "You'll be wanting a bath and to change into a dress before supper, I expect."

"And wouldn't a bath be a slice of heaven?" Molly gave in to a wistful sigh and savored another sip of tea. "Thank you for making us feel welcome, Mrs. Nichols."

"Pshaw." The older woman dismissed the gratitude with a wave of her hand. "This big old house isn't good for anything else."

"It is a large one."

"That it is." Mrs. Nichols smiled and a distant expression entered her eyes. "My husband, God rest his soul, had a way with a hammer and saw. He and my son built this house for me." She bit her lower lip to still its trembling. "I'm sorry. I still miss them."

Molly reached out to pat the woman's hand. "I'm sure you do." She smiled and added, "And isn't it lovely to have this treasure of a house to remember them by?"

The older woman nodded and drew a shaky breath. "Enough about me," she said, obviously eager to change the subject. "I'll bet you and that handsome husband of yours are newlyweds. Hmm?"

Scalding heat flooded Molly's cheeks and she shrugged, unable to lie outright. It would be better to allow Mrs. Nichols to assume what she wished.

"A blushing new bride," Mrs. Nichols chided, patting Molly's hand. "How wonderful. Your room is the finest in the place."

"Oh, that isn't nece—"

"Yes, it is, and it's the only room available anyway."

Mrs. Nichols leaned closer. "Just wait until you see the bed," she whispered conspiratorially.

"The . . . bed?" One bed. Singular bed. *Jesus, Mary, and Joseph.*

Dirk made arrangements with the local banker to have the ransom money available. He had no idea when or how Ray would contact him, or how much time he'd be given to collect the funds. Throwing the Ballinger name around had its advantages, and this was one occasion when he didn't mind wielding it.

After visiting the bank, he found Zane's campsite and made plans to continue their search of the surrounding area at dawn. Ray was holed up somewhere near Serendipity, and if Dirk could find him before his half brother expected him, that would be all the better.

It was time for Ray Lovejoy to get what was coming to him, and Dirk sure as hell didn't mean the twenty-five thousand dollars the kidnapper had demanded. No, now it was time for justice.

And revenge.

Dirk visited the local sheriff, who had his hands full with drunks and claim jumping. The overworked lawman had never heard of Ray Lovejoy or the Lovejoy Gang.

For some reason, Dirk was relieved about that news. And he was also relieved only a few people knew of his relationship to Ray Lovejoy.

Next, Dirk dropped into the saloon for a single shot of whiskey, which he lingered over, hoping to overhear any useful information. A sign over the bar boasted hot baths in the back room, and he had the sudden urge to be clean before he saw Molly again.

In fact, the more he thought about it, the more eager

he was to see her again. He paid the premium price for fresh water and arranged to have new clothes delivered as well. A short time later, clean and freshly shaven, he left Cloud at the livery stable with Sadie, then stopped to buy Molly a dress and all the confusing undergarments women wore, except for a corset. He didn't want anything like that changing her already perfect appearance. He could only guess at her size, of course, though he figured his memory of how she'd filled his hands last night was pretty accurate.

Dangerously so.

Eager to see her, he turned toward Beth Anne's Boarding House. And Molly.

Molly. The woman had crawled under his skin and into his heart. He was one lovesick bastard, and there wasn't a damned thing he could do about it.

Every step he took closer to Beth Anne's Room and Board took him that much closer to Molly. His pulse quickened, his blood warmed, his body thrummed with the need to see her, to touch her.

To love her.

You're hopeless, Ballinger. At last, he stood before the boarding house with his hand on the gate, gripping the wood so tightly his knuckles turned white. A lump formed in his throat and he swallowed it with difficulty.

He was promised to Lady Elizabeth, the mother of his half brother's child. Resolve settled in Dirk's gut with all the gentleness of a stick of dynamite.

He would not allow another Ballinger child to be born a bastard. It was within his power to prevent it, and prevent it he would. Gnashing his teeth, he glanced heavenward, but realized he was looking in the wrong direction.

God damn your black soul, Edward Ballinger.

He drew a deep, cleansing breath, squared his shoulders, then opened the gate and proceeded up the walk to the front door. Before he could knock, the door opened and Mrs. Nichols hurried him inside.

"Afternoon, Mr. Ballinger," the woman said, smiling. "Molly's in your room."

Those words knocked the wind out of him and every blessed ounce of common sense he'd managed to muster. Barely able to speak, Dirk thanked the woman for the unsolicited information and glanced up the stairwell. He remembered the room where he'd put their belongings earlier as he removed his hat and ascended the stairs. The room had been feminine and airy, with frilly curtains and doilies all over the place.

But one part of the room had beckoned to him—the massive four-poster bed in the center of the room. His breath caught as he contemplated Molly's reaction to finding them not only sharing a room, but a room with only one bed.

A very large, very soft, very comfortable bed.

He'd never forget the way Molly had looked and tasted last night. His blood reached a slow burn by the time he took the top step and paused at the bedroom door. He lifted his hand to knock softly, but there was no answer. She was probably asleep. Her endurance on the trail had been remarkable, but even he had his limit. Undoubtedly, she had passed hers miles ago.

Quietly, he turned the handle and opened the door. Its well-oiled hinges didn't make a sound, nor did he as he closed the door behind him.

Sunlight streamed through the lace curtains at the window, casting a myriad pattern across the patchwork quilt on the bed and on the floor around it. There was no sign of Molly.

Then a gentle splashing sound made his mouth go dry. A door on the far side of the room stood slightly ajar. He'd missed that earlier, but it was obviously the water closet.

He couldn't breathe as he approached the bed and placed the carefully wrapped parcel on it. For several moments, he stood there, debating whether or not to let her know he'd returned. The splashing noises stopped, and his curiosity—and something far less innocent—overtook him. Had she dozed off in the tub?

The thought of Molly naked and wet and glistening made him shudder. He grew hard enough to break the local blacksmith's anvil and clenched his fists at his sides. A few moments later, he found himself at the half-closed door, reaching slowly toward the handle.

He wanted her. He loved her.

God help him.

Spying on her was contemptible, but his desire to see her nakedness again compelled him to give the door a tiny shove. It swung wide, the opening framing the vision before him.

Molly lay back in a huge tub, her eyes closed and her dark hair curling in damp tendrils. The expression on her face was one of pure contentment and utter innocence. Guilt made his heart press upward against his throat, and his breath caught.

She wasn't his to want, but want her he did. She was in his blood, under his skin, and in his heart. He wanted nothing more than to protect her, to touch her, to love her.

Get over it, Ballinger. He squeezed his eyes shut and drew a shaky breath. He had no right to Molly—no right to love her or want her. Lady Elizabeth Summersby would become his wife, and he would be the father of her child in the eyes of the law.

Nothing else mattered.

He reopened his eyes and swallowed hard. A trickle

of water sluiced along the side of Molly's neck. She moaned and drew a deep breath, the tips of her breasts rising above the water's surface.

Dirk froze. He couldn't move. He couldn't speak. Hell, he couldn't even breathe. But this was wrong. His desire, his need, his love for Molly Riordan were all wrong. Forbidden.

Tragic.

Isn't that a little overdramatic, Ballinger?

Even so, he couldn't rid himself of the thought. Yes, to have found a love he couldn't have was the true meaning of tragedy. He clenched a fist and willed himself to leave before she discovered his transgression.

Resolute, he took a backward step.

A floorboard squeaked.

Molly's eyes flew open, her mouth agape in obvious shock.

"Ah, hell," Dirk whispered.

Her mouth moved, but no sound escaped. A blush crept up from the water's surface to cover her throat and face. Even the tips of her ears turned bright pink as she lowered her nakedness deeper into the water.

"I take it you've never heard of knocking," she said, keeping her gaze fixed on his.

The only part of her above the water was her head. Even her neck was completely submerged. Dirk licked his lips and remembered the way she'd tasted, the sweetness of her nipples in his mouth. *Dear God.*

"I . . . I'm sorry," he muttered and took another backward step.

Her blue eyes darkened and she bit her lower lip. "I, well . . ."

"I'll leave now." Dirk reached for the edge of the door, intent on closing it behind him.

"No." Her blush deepened.

Dirk's breath froze. "No?" His voice was barely more than a croak.

"I . . . it isn't as if I've anything you haven't s-seen." The words erupted in a hurried whisper, her gaze darting from his face to the door, then back. "And I was remembering . . ." Her tongue swept out to moisten her lips, leaving behind a silken sheen.

"You're killing me, Molly Riordan," he said, unable to control the slight tremor of his voice or the thunder of his heart. "I can't stand not touching you."

A small cry escaped from between her parted lips and a tear made its way from the corner of her eye to trickle down to join the bath water. "I can't stand not touching you either," she breathed, her words belying her confusion. "You . . . you've awakened something inside me. Something that was sleeping." She pressed her hand to her heart, between her magnificent, gleaming breasts. "Here."

A dull roar commenced in his head and his heart swelled. Dirk took a step toward her. "Molly . . ."

He barely had time to catch his breath before she rose from the water to stand before him.

Naked.

Glistening.

She held her hands out toward him. "Some sane part of me knows this is wrong," she whispered, her eyes sparkling with unshed tears. "But, Mother Mary forgive me, I can't help myself from wanting you."

That was it. She'd killed him.

Sixteen

Molly held her breath. Waiting. The lump in her throat nearly strangled her, but she didn't move as his gaze drifted over her nakedness, lingering in places that made her burn in more ways than one. After what seemed like an eternity, his gaze returned to her face.

His expression seared her.

And honored her.

Until this moment, she'd never believed herself beautiful, but he made her feel that way without uttering a word. His expression assured her he liked what he saw.

Warmth pooled low in her belly as she stepped over the edge of the tub. He moved then, offering her a steadying hand. As always, the power of his touch startled her, igniting the flames of desire he had created within her and fed continuously with no apparent effort.

He made her want him simply by *being*.

She shivered as the air from the open door wafted across her damp flesh. The peaks of her breasts drew tight and tingled with longing. She wanted him to touch her again, to kiss her, to put his mouth on her.

A flash of liquid fire shot through her and she shivered again, though certainly not from cold this time.

She met his gaze and swallowed hard, licking her lips to combat the sudden dryness of her mouth.

"Molly," he whispered, though his eyes said much more.

She tightened her hold on his hand, knowing what she wanted. What she needed. What she had to do.

Though he was promised to Lady Elizabeth, Molly knew he wanted her. And, Mother Mary help her, she wanted him. And just this once, she would have him.

Caution and propriety paled to insignificance beneath the onslaught of raw need that swelled within her. She'd never known a feeling this powerful. Unfortunately, she was too inexperienced to pursue her desire without his help and cooperation.

Her hand trembled as she lifted it to cup his cheek. "You shaved." She brushed her thumb along his cheekbone to the corner of his mouth and took a step closer, the tips of her aching breasts brushing against the front of his shirt. She drew a deep breath. "And you smell nice."

He swallowed so hard she heard him. "I . . . I wanted to be clean," he said, his green eyes darkening to a smoky shade. "For you."

She glanced down at her own nakedness, forcing aside the rising panic. This brazen behavior was so unlike her, though her determination to follow through overruled any lingering reluctance. "As you can see, I wanted to be clean, too." She stroked his lower lip. "For you."

"Molly . . ." His jaw tightened and his voice carried a warning note. "You're playing a dangerous game."

Emboldened, she pressed herself against him, rewarded when he dropped his hand to encircle her waist. She leaned into him, her body drawn tight. Tension coiled through her, begging for release—release only Dirk could give. "Not a game. Definitely not a game."

A shudder rippled through him and he pulled her snugly against him, her softness melding against his hardness. The searing ridge below his belt reminded her of that gnawing emptiness within her. Heat spiraled through her, chasing away any trace of chill.

He gripped her wrist with his free hand and kissed the tips of her fingers, trailing his thumb along the pad of her thumb. "Molly, Molly, Molly."

He drew the tip of her finger into his mouth, reminding her how it had felt to have him suckle her breasts. "I want you to"—she faltered, dying a little inside for each moment's delay—"touch me." She drew a shaky breath and held his smoldering gaze with hers, willing him to understand. "Love me . . . this once."

His sharp intake of breath told her he'd gleaned her true meaning. "Oh, God." He rested his forehead against hers, wrapping both arms around her bare waist. "I want you so much I ache." He raised his head, pinning her with his gaze. "Love you, Molly?" One corner of his mouth curved upward. "I *do* love you."

A small cry escaped from between her parted lips and tears rolled unheeded down her cheeks. She stared into his eyes, assuring herself he spoke the truth. No man could look at a woman this way and be untruthful. Aye, he did love her.

"I love you, too." She bit her lower lip and forced her tears into submission. Her hand trembled as she pulled his from behind her waist and pressed the flat of his palm against her breast. "I . . . I want this, Dirk. I want *you*."

A low growl rumbled up from his chest and he covered her mouth with his. She whimpered and trembled with need as he devoured her, thrusting his tongue

deeply into her mouth to entwine with hers. His kiss
thoroughly claimed her and made his intentions known.

Her heart swelled with love, banishing any remaining doubts. She would give herself to the man she loved
this once, and she would have no regrets. Determination and love strengthened her resolve, and she linked
her hands behind his neck to deepen their kiss.

He suddenly broke away and swept her into his arms
as if she weighed nothing. A few moments later, he
lowered her to the soft featherbed, knocking a package
onto the floor. She shivered as he moved away, but his
gaze displaced the chill with heat and the promise of
more. Much more . . .

He never took his eyes off her as he unbuttoned his
shirt and dropped it to the floor. She stared at the broad
expanse of his chest and licked her lips. Dark hair
curled over hard muscles, tapering to a vee and disappearing below his belt.

Curiosity and desire tempted her to watch as he unbuckled his belt and opened the top two buttons of his
dungarees. She heard him kick his boots off, then he
released another button.

Her heart thundered in her ears as she stared, mesmerized. She'd never seen a full grown man undress,
and she was shocked to discover she liked watching
the process. Or perhaps it was because she knew *why*
he was disrobing.

He hesitated for a moment, holding her gaze, his
thumb and forefinger poised to release the rest of the
buttons. "Are you sure, Molly?" he whispered, his expression mirroring her desperation and need. *"Very
sure?"*

Momentary panic echoed through her, but she drew
a deep breath to quell it and rolled off the bed to stand
before him. With trembling fingers, she replaced his

hand with hers and unbuttoned his dungarees. The heat of him made itself known before the velvety hardness brushed against her hand. Naked longing soared through her and she pushed her hands inside the waistband, easing his clothing down his muscled hips and buttocks.

"Very sure," she murmured, trusting her instincts enough to grasp the hard length of him with both hands. Surprised by the size and heat of him, she looked down between them. "Oh, my. It's so . . . so big."

A good-natured chuckle erupted from him, and he kissed her again, pressing her back down to the mattress and hovering over her. She heard his dungarees fall to the floor, then he claimed her mouth with a thoroughness that stole her breath. She wrapped her arms around his waist, still aware of the hard heat of him pressed against her hip. Soon she would know everything about the differences between man and woman. Soon . . .

He cupped the weight of her breast in his hand and stroked her nipple with his thumb. Molly moaned and pressed her hips upward against him, seeking to appease the emptiness. And, innocent or not, she realized exactly *how* that emptiness would be filled. Knowing that made her crave it all the more, and she reached between them to cradle the heaviness of his impressive manhood in her hand.

He broke their kiss, gasping, then trailed kisses along the side of her throat. He tarried there, driving her mad with the wanting. Wishing to torture him as much as he was her, she stroked his hard length and was rewarded by his shudder and another feral growl from low in his throat.

Empowered and curious, she brought her thumb to his tip and stroked it. With a jerk, he slipped his manhood deftly from her grasp, shifting himself so he was just out of reach. She opened her mouth to complain, but the intended words died on a moan as his lips encircled the tip of her breast.

Biting her lower lip and holding her breath, she twined her fingers through the soft curls at his nape, holding him to her. With the heated silk of his mouth, he drew deeply against her, and he stroked her nipple with his tongue. He cupped both her breasts in his large hands and parted her legs with his knee.

Jesus, Mary, and Joseph. Molly Riordan was naked, with an equally naked man between her legs. That thought both shocked and thrilled her.

He consumed her, nipping and stroking and licking both nipples alternately. She tensed and arched against him, lost in the heat and the glory and the *need*.

"Dirk." She whimpered, but he showed her no mercy. Her breasts tingled and swelled, while other parts of her wept for him.

Then, suddenly, he eased himself lower, forsaking her breasts to trail his devilish tongue along her belly, lingering at her navel. She tensed, wondering what madness he had in mind for her now. He dipped his fingers between her legs, stroking her damp flesh until she pressed herself wantonly against the heel of his hand.

She remembered enough of what they'd shared in the cabin to want more of his touch. Instinctively, she opened to him, welcoming the feel of his fingers inside her, stretching her. Scalding heat whirled through her, culminating between her legs. The hunger clawed at her now, no longer passive and merely curious. Her need became a palpable entity.

And a demanding one.

Every stroke of his fingers, brush of his tongue, beat

of his heart against her was maddeningly exquisite. Molly's breath came in short, rapid bursts, and her mind dissolved into useless mush. She no longer contemplated his next move, for all she could do was savor every little miracle of his lovemaking.

She shuddered, feeling that wondrous pinnacle of completion approach again. This would be even better, she knew, because he would join her. He stroked her feminine folds and kissed his way lower, lingering where her triangle of dark hair began.

Just when she thought he couldn't shock her again, he eased himself lower and tasted her. Shock made her freeze and she thought to push him away, but the warmth of his tongue against her most sensitive place made her abandon all conscious thought. Instead of pushing him away, she wound her fingers through his hair and allowed him to have his way with her.

Aye, and she loved his way with her.

She grew vaguely aware of him draping her legs over his shoulders, and he cupped her buttocks with his large, warm hands. He angled her hips to avail himself of her womanly essence, driving her mad with such pleasure she thought surely she would die before he finished.

All her thoughts, all her energy concentrated on where his mouth claimed her. Nothing else existed. The heat flared brighter and hotter until the glory she'd found before exploded within her. But this time he showed no mercy. He continued to inflict her with mounting pleasure until she shattered again and again.

His fingers filled her and he kissed his way back up her belly, pausing to flick his tongue across her nipples. She drifted slowly back to reality, enough to notice that

every stroke of his tongue against her breast created
an answering spasm where his fingers filled her.

He suckled at her breasts again as his fingers moved
within her, stroking, stretching, giving. Molly moaned
as renewed longing possessed her. His fingers and his
mouth were so hot. So powerful.

Shamelessly, she rocked against his hand and pressed
her breast more fully into his mouth. "I want you," she
murmured, and he answered her by climbing up her body
to nuzzle the lobe of her ear.

He withdrew his fingers and she felt the hot velvet
heat of his manhood replace them. His breathing grew
louder and raspy against her ear, and she knew the time
had come for them to join completely.

Momentary panic filled her, but she forced it aside
with the memory of the pleasure he'd shown her. She
reached between them to wrap her hand around his shaft,
suddenly eager to experience this ultimate intimacy. She
wanted and needed him inside her, filling her.

Loving her.

She maneuvered his throbbing tip into her moist
folds, then held him against her. Sensing his hesitation,
she looked up and met his gaze, answering the question
in his eyes by wrapping her legs around his waist and
arching herself shamelessly against him.

The muscles inside her quivered with longing, seem-
ing to sense what was about to happen. He inched inward a bit farther, torturing her with his dallying.

"Love me, Dirk," she whispered, holding his gaze.
"Please?"

Dirk paused on the threshold of heaven.

Molly angled her hips to receive more of him and
he bit the inside of his cheek to distract him. This
woman was downright dangerous. She'd already made

him explode in his jeans once, and he'd be damned if he was going to lose control too early this time.

Love me . . . this once. Her earlier words echoed through his mind again and he drew a shaky breath to steady himself.

They were both beyond the point of no return. He eased himself deeper into her tight sheath, holding his breath as she convulsed around him. She was impossibly small, but he'd done everything to prepare her. There was only one way to do this, but he didn't want to cause her pain.

"This is going to hurt," he murmured, raising up to study her changing expression.

"What hurts is the waiting."

She managed a smile, but he saw fear in her eyes, too. Then a mischievous expression warned him he was in trouble just as she dug in her heels and pulled him deeper.

"Oh." He groaned, trying to hold himself back, but she pulled again. "Oh, God, Molly." Again, she urged him inward, wiggling her hips and driving him insane.

"Now," she said simply. Emphatically.

Knowing he couldn't hold out any longer, Dirk thrust himself inside her. She opened to him and he felt the hot trickle of virginal blood between them. He met her gaze and saw pain . . . and something more.

He saw love.

Tenderly, he pressed his lips to hers, willing himself not to ravage her as he so desperately wanted. *Slow and easy, Ballinger.* "I love you," he whispered, feeling her smile against his lips.

"And I you," she said, wiggling her hips again. "It doesn't hurt anymore."

"Speak for yourself."

She giggled at that and damned near killed him.

"Will you be still, woman?" But her laughter was infectious, and he found himself chuckling along with her. He couldn't remember ever laughing while buried to the hilt inside a beautiful woman before. "You're impossible, Molly Riordan."

Her expression grew solemn and her laughter ceased. "Show me the meaning of this, Dirk." Her eyes glistened in the dappled sunlight shining through the lace curtains. "Show me."

His duty was clear, and he resolved to make this a wonderful experience for them both. Exerting every iota of self-control he could muster, he moved within her.

Withdrawing almost completely, he stroked the length of her again and again, watching her face for any indication of discomfort. But all he saw on her beautiful face was love and pleasure. She moaned and moved with him, demanding every inch of him and giving back as much, or more, than she took.

Every stroke drove him higher. Assured she no longer felt any pain, he quickened his movements, thrusting himself harder and deeper with every stroke. The muscles inside her tightened around him with growing intensity until he could barely breathe. Sweat trickled down his forehead and into his eyes, and he noticed a fine sheen of perspiration coated his lover's face as well.

Joy surged through him as he neared completion. The veins in her neck showed through her pale flesh as she clung to him, thrusting her hips against him. He felt her explosion as her insides tightened around him in a relentless vise.

He drove himself into her and she welcomed him with a voraciousness that stole his breath. His seed burst forth, pulsing into her and imparting his most intimate gift.

As their passion ebbed and their breathing quieted, he gazed down into her eyes and said, "I *do* love you, Molly Riordan."

Momentary sadness filled her eyes, and he watched her deliberately banish it. "And I love you, Dirk Ballinger."

Their words of love were like a benediction. Vows. He sensed the power of truth and the glory of love. Humbled, he rolled onto his side and cradled her in his arms. And, as darkness fell, he loved her again until they were both sated.

Hours later, he stared at the play of moonlight across the quilt that covered them, aware of the warm body snuggled against him. Molly's breathing told him she slept, and he allowed himself to doze off, too.

But his father's face appeared in his dream, followed by another face—that of his father's illegitimate son. Dirk awoke with a start, drenched in sweat and trembling. As he realized where he was—and with whom— he lay still.

His nightmare had reminded Dirk of his damned mission. Bile rose in his throat and bitterness surrounded his soul. His father had sired a child out of wedlock. A bastard. Dirk had vowed to never allow another Ballinger to be born a bastard—not even Ray's child.

The only woman he had ever loved, or ever would love, had given herself to him. Yet . . . he was promised to another. His breath caught in his throat and he clenched his fist at his side, thankful Molly was asleep.

The memory of making love to this beautiful woman brought another realization home. A heated flush swept over him, his guilt powerful and unforgiving.

He had sown his seed deep.
The sins of the father . . .

"*Señora* Jensen?"

Rosa's conspiratorial whisper found Ida in the kitchen, pretending to read some recipes. "Yes, Rosa?" She rose from the table, relieved to have someone distract her from worrying about Dirk and his bride.

Rosa looked down, uncertainty clearly visible in her demeanor.

Concern washed through Ida and she approached the woman, taking her hand. "What's wrong?" Fear clutched at her. "Has there been word about—"

"No, no, *Señora*." Rosa smiled reassuringly and her eyes shifted toward the kitchen door. "Come see. Come."

Relieved, Ida followed Rosa to the kitchen door. The woman pressed her forefinger to her lips and pushed the door open partway. "Look."

Ida peered through the narrow opening at her son, who sat at a desk in the foyer with the large book about cattle Dirk had given him as a birthday gift. Lance's head was bowed over the pages as he pointed at the pictures, then looked up at his audience to explain each one.

Elena smiled and nodded as if the bovine discussion was the most interesting of topics. But when Lance looked down at the book again, the expression in the young woman's eyes softened, and she reached toward Lance's blond head once as if eager to touch him.

Joy tainted with sadness eased through Ida as Rosa let the door swing shut and turned to face her. The expression on Rosa's face made it clear she wanted

Ida's blessing for the possible developing relationship between their offspring.

Hadn't Ida wished for something like this? Lance needed to love and be loved even after Ida was gone. And Elena was a lovely girl. A mother couldn't wish for a better woman for her son.

Ida smiled and squeezed Rosa's hand. "I think it's fine," she said. "Just fine."

Rosa nodded and a grin split her face. "As do I, *Señora*." She breathed a sigh of relief. *"Gracias."*

"No." Ida smiled again. "Thank *you*."

Rosa nodded again, then turned her attention to the pan full of dirty dishes remaining from breakfast. Ida couldn't resist peeking at her son and Elena again. The girl bent closer now and rested her hand on Lance's shoulder. He looked up, an expression of surprise on his face, then he covered Elena's hand with his.

With a sigh, Ida let the door close again and returned to the recipes and a cup of now lukewarm tea. Lance wasn't the type of man most women would look at romantically. That a fine girl like Elena was interested was the best thing that could happen to him. Perhaps they would marry. Ida closed her eyes in a brief prayer for Lance's future happiness.

With a sigh, she rose and said, "I'm going down to the root cellar to see how many pie apples we have left."

Rosa bobbed her head, but kept her attention on her chores as Ida slipped out the back door and lifted the door to the cellar. This time of day, enough light shone through the open doors to enable her to see without a lamp. She climbed down the steps and waited for her eyes to adjust to the dimness, then proceeded toward the bin where they kept apples.

In another month there would be a new crop in the

orchard. She paused, remembering the summer shortly after her marriage when she and her new husband had planted a variety of fruit trees. She'd carried water to them every day, willing them to survive in spite of the harsh climate.

Circumstances had prevented her from harvesting a single apple from those young trees. She heaved a sigh, remembering the day Lance was born.

The day her life had changed forever.

Her husband had taken one look at the baby and had asked the midwife what was wrong with the child. The woman—a neighbor and well-meaning friend—had used the word "Mongol" to describe the beautiful, fair-haired baby.

From that moment on, her husband never looked at Lance. He took no interest in naming the child, and when the time came to have him baptized, the man announced to his wife that he'd made arrangements to institutionalize the boy.

A tiny baby in an institution? Ida argued, but her husband insisted. He presented her with legal papers ordering Lance be remanded to an asylum.

That had been the last night Ida and Lance spent under that man's roof.

With hard work, love, and determination, she had managed to raise Lance alone. He was a fine young man, albeit a bit slow. He always would be. Nothing would change that. But her husband had been mistaken about the boy's worth. Her golden-haired son was good and kind and generous. He could even read and cipher some.

And now a beautiful young woman was romantically interested in him. A smile curved Ida's lips again as she gathered apples in her apron and turned toward the ladder. A shadow darkened the entrance and she glanced up to see a long pair of jean-clad legs near the opening.

"You down there, Miss Ida?" Clyde called into the cellar.

Her heart skipped a beat and she peered up the ladder. "Yes, I'm on my way up." She clutched the apple-laden apron in one hand and held the side of the ladder with the other.

Clyde had occupied more and more of her thoughts lately, and his handsome, weathered face had even intruded on her dreams a time or two. Warmth flamed in her cheeks as she neared the top rung and he reached down to take her hand to assist her.

Standing before him with an apron bulging with fruit, she smiled shyly, feeling girlish and downright giddy. The man made her think foolish thoughts and feel things a woman her age shouldn't feel.

There she went again with that nonsense. *And why not?*

"You look mighty purty this mornin', Miss Ida." He kept her hand in his.

"You're too kind," she said, wondering why the man made her so flustered. She met his gaze and warmth stole through her again, followed quickly with concern as she envisioned him as a younger man with red hair.

A man she'd known as Rusty.

Don't think about that, Ida. Don't remember.

He didn't remember her, so she had nothing to worry about. Nothing at all.

He closed the cellar door for her, then removed his hat and held it out to her. "Here, let me take them apples."

She placed them carefully inside his hat, then he cradled it in one arm and offered her his other. With a smile, she tucked her hand into the crook of his elbow and allowed him to escort her up the back steps and into the kitchen.

Rosa glanced up with a knowing smile as she dried the last of the pots and hung it from a hook near the stove.

Embarrassment heated Ida's cheeks as she took the hat full of apples from Clyde and placed them in a bowl. "I'll get these peeled and we'll have pie for—"

"*Señora* Jensen, come quick!"

Elena's voice shattered the silence as the girl flew through the kitchen door. "It's Lance. He's hurt."

My little boy. Ida's heart stopped and she swayed. "What . . ."

But rather than waiting to explain, Elena headed back the way she'd come, with Ida, Clyde, and Rosa right behind. The book Lance had been showing the girl still lay open on the desk, but there was no sign of him.

"Where?" Ida looked around the great hall, but there was no sign of Lance. The front door stood ajar and Elena darted through it.

"*El toro.* Outside. Hurry," the girl said, not pausing to look back.

The bull? Icy shards of fear shot through Ida when she spotted several wranglers standing in a circle around something—or some*one*—in the paddock. Panic stole her breath. She knew without seeing that her son was in the center of that circle.

And he was hurt.

Clyde raced past her with his long stride, and the circle parted for the ranch foreman. A moment later, Clyde bent down, gathered Lance in his arms, and turned toward the house just as Ida reached him.

"He's bleedin'," the man said, concern edging his voice. "Gored."

"Oh, God." Ida wanted to examine Lance now, but common sense made her hurry alongside Clyde.

Lance's face was pale, his eyes closed. Blood almost covered the side of his shirt.

He had to be all right. He had to.

Clyde carried Lance to the kitchen, and Rosa grabbed the bowl of apples off the table just before the foreman placed his burden there. Many wounded men had been tended on this old table, and most of them had survived. So would Lance.

Dear Lord, let it be so.

Ida grabbed the poultry scissors and cut away her son's shirt, knowing the others all stood around watching. Elena went to the other side of the table and took Lance's hand in hers. Ida spared her a reassuring glance, then exposed the wound and swayed.

"Dear God . . ." She wadded up the shirt and pressed it to the bleeding, yawning hole in her son's side. "Rosa, send for Dr. Stein."

"Needs stitchin'," Clyde said matter-of-factly.

"Yes." Ida took the clean rags Clyde brought to her and replaced the torn shirt, pressing hard to stanch the flow of blood.

Live, Lance. Live.

The endless mantra filled her head as they waited for the doctor. "Elena, just in case the doctor isn't available, will you fetch my sewing basket, please?"

The girl bit her lower lip, then released Lance's hand and darted away. Clyde placed a hand on Ida's shoulder. "Let me do that a spell," he said, his voice quiet and reassuring.

Ida was reluctant to leave her son's side, but if she had to stitch his wound herself, she would need her strength for that. "All right." She stepped to the side as Clyde's large, capable hands took over the task of holding the cloth to Lance's wound.

Ida slumped into a chair, her legs suddenly weak and shaky. She watched her son's chest rise and fall, his breathing unlabored. His color even seemed a bit better, though his eyes were still closed. If he'd been awake, he would have felt the pain. His continued unconsciousness was a small blessing.

"I think he's gonna be all right," Clyde said, capturing her gaze. "He ain't lost a terrible lot of blood." He glanced back at Lance and a strange expression claimed his features.

"What's wrong?" Ida started to rise, but some invisible force stayed her.

Clyde pointed to a spot on the uninjured side of Lance's rib cage. "Interesting birthmark." His jaw twitched as he pinned her with a knowing gaze. "One I've seen before."

A dull roar commenced in Ida's ears. She'd forgotten the birthmark—an unusual diamond shape. A family trait. All the males in her husband's family had it somewhere on the torso.

All.

Seventeen

Molly opened her eyes, blinking several times as she remembered where she was. She stretched, and aching muscles made memories explode in her mind.

Anxiously, she looked to her side, noting the wrinkled pillow where Dirk had slept. Heat flooded her cheeks and she smiled, albeit a bit shakily.

Making love with Dirk had been even more amazing than she'd anticipated. She drew a deep breath, remembering the ways and places he'd touched her, the completeness with which he'd filled her. She'd never experienced anything as spectacular, nor even imagined it was possible.

Even more amazing . . . he loved her.

Joy swept through her as she sat up, clutching the sheet to her breasts. *He loves me.* Suddenly eager to see him, she leaped to her feet and completed her morning grooming in record time. A wrapped package on the dressing table drew her attention. Her name was printed neatly on it.

She unwrapped it and folded back the tissue paper to reveal two dresses and most of the undergarments propriety dictated a lady should wear. Her heart warmed as she donned the soft cotton bloomers and chemise, then pulled a simple blue muslin gown over her head. An endless row of buttons and intricate smocking adorned the front, and a bit of white lace trimmed the collar and cuffs.

It was a simple everyday dress, but to Molly it was the most beautiful one she'd ever owned. A gift from the man she loved.

She brushed her hair until it gleamed, then tied it loosely at her nape. Molly hurried down the stairs to find Mrs. Nichols frying thick slices of ham. A basket of eggs sat on the sideboard.

But there was no sign of Dirk.

"Good morning," Molly said hesitantly.

"There you are," Mrs. Nichols said, wiping her hands on her apron and motioning Molly toward the table. "I have tea waiting for you."

"Thank you." Molly would have sacrificed tea for the rest of her life to see Dirk walk through the door. "Have you seen . . ." She bit her lower lip, still uncomfortable with the word husband. If only it could be true. *Really* true.

"Your husband?" Mrs. Nichols finished for her. She shook her head as she poured dark, rich tea into a cup. "He left over an hour ago."

"Oh." Molly's shoulders slumped and even the fragrant steam wafting up from the cup couldn't lift her spirits.

"He left a message for you." Mrs. Nichols returned to her stove and turned the ham slices with a fork, then turned to face Molly again. She held up one finger and said, "He's gone to take care of business once and for all, whatever that means." She held up a second finger. "You're to stay here until he returns for you." She put up a third finger. "And he said he might be gone a few days." The woman seemed satisfied with the delivery of her message and turned her attention back to the stove.

Days? "Oh, I see. Thank you." Molly stirred milk and sugar into her cup, hoping the trembling in her hands wasn't too obvious. She forced herself to sip her tea, trying not to think about how impersonal Dirk's message had been. He could have left a note for her in their room.

But he hadn't.

With a sigh, she touched the buttons at the front of her dress. But he had left a gift—a thoughtful one. She swallowed the lump in her throat and decided this was for the best. Molly could concentrate on trying to find her da while Dirk searched for Ray Lovejoy and Lady Elizabeth.

Lady Elizabeth. The man Molly loved with all her heart and soul was promised to the woman who carried his child. A sense of dread pressed down on Molly. How could she have forgotten that even for a moment?

Aye, his absence was for the best. She'd asked Dirk to love her once. Heat crept up from her bodice to her cheeks. It had been more than once, but only for one night. She had no right to ask or to expect anything more. Besides, after he completed his mission successfully, he would fulfill his promise of marriage to another.

Tears gathered stubbornly in the corners of her eyes. Molly scrubbed them away with the back of her hand and drew a shaky breath. She had no rights where Dirk Ballinger was concerned. None at all.

She had to think of her own future and the father she'd hoped to find here in Serendipity. Aye, she would concentrate on finding Da. That would keep her mind off Dirk and the magic of his touch.

Enough of that nonsense, Molly. Vowing to focus on practicalities, she finished her tea, poured another cup, then ate a huge breakfast she barely tasted and certainly didn't want.

As Mrs. Nichols cleaned up the breakfast dishes, the sound of children playing made her look out the window. A moment later, she glanced over her shoulder at Molly. "Are you and Mr. Ballinger hoping for children soon?"

Molly choked on her tea, coughing until tears filled her eyes. "I, uh . . ."

The older woman chuckled and rinsed the last pot, then turned to face Molly. "Nature will take care of that. Nothing for you to worry about." She dried her hands and draped the towel over the edge of the basin. "You have a strong handsome husband who'll undoubtedly sire many babes." Mrs. Nichols stepped out to the back porch with her pan of dishwater.

Molly's heart leaped to her throat. She hadn't stopped to consider the possibility she could have conceived. Her cheeks burned as she recalled how thoroughly and beautifully they had made love. Dirk's child might very well be growing in her womb even now.

A peculiar sort of joy soared through her, and she dropped her hand to cover her flat belly. However, a heavy weight descended to blot out the joy almost instantly as she remembered how swollen Lady Elizabeth had been when she'd last seen her.

Aye, swollen. With Dirk's child.

Remembering that the man she loved had also been intimate with Lady Elizabeth made Molly's stomach protest the huge breakfast she'd just consumed. There was no reason for Molly to assume she had conceived.

Molly bit her lower lip, trying to deny herself that small ray of hope. Besides, Dirk would marry the woman who claimed the child she carried was his. After all, he was an honorable man and would do the honorable thing.

But what if Molly also carried his child? A child that could be no one else's?

Cease! She had to quell these thoughts. Her cycle wasn't due for almost two weeks. She would know after that. Dwelling on it wouldn't change things one way or another.

Da. Focus on finding Da.

Mrs. Nichols returned with her empty dishpan. "It's a beautiful day," she said, smiling. "I thought I'd wander down to the dry goods for some thread. Would you like to come along?"

"Aye." Molly's quick answer surprised even her. "I would like that, Mrs. Nichols."

"Oh, do call me Beth Anne, child." The woman shrugged. "Everybody does."

"Mrs.—Beth Anne?"

"Yes?"

"Would you be knowing where a body would ask about mining claims?"

"Mining claims?" Beth Anne's eyes widened. "At the assayers office, I suppose, but why would you—"

"I'm looking for my da." Molly squared her shoulders, deciding there was no reason not to tell Beth Anne the truth. "The last letter my gram received from him came from Serendipity."

The woman's curiosity was obvious as she slipped into a chair across the table from Molly. "I've lived here for fifteen years, child. What's your father's name?"

Molly's heart stuttered, then raced ahead. "Niall Riordan." She leaned closer. "Do you know him?"

Beth Anne leaned back in her chair, her brow furrowed as she contemplated the name. "Not right off-hand," she admitted, "though it does have a familiar ring."

Hope blossomed in Molly's heart. "May we stop at the assayer's office?"

Beth Anne smacked the table's surface with her open palm. "We'll go there first," she said, rising and untying her apron. "Grab your bonnet, girl."

Molly jumped up and raced to her room to gather the battered sunbonnet she'd worn on the trail. The sight of the rumpled bed drew her attention and she walked to it, smoothing the sheets and fluffing the pillows. She pulled the quilt over it until the bed appeared not to have been slept in at all.

Of course, she knew otherwise. She caressed the pillow where Dirk's head had rested, remembering.

Determination stole through her and she forcibly banished the memories. She knew they would return to haunt her later, but she would concentrate on the things she could control. For now.

Squaring her shoulders, she marched down the stairs to find Beth Anne waiting by the front door.

"Let's buy you a new bonnet while we're out." The older woman's eyes twinkled.

Molly touched the brim of her bonnet. "I . . . I don't have any money."

"Pshaw," Beth Anne said, dismissing the problem handily. "I'll add it to your husband's bill."

Molly's eyes widened in shock. "But . . ."

Beth Anne winked and grabbed Molly's hand. "You've got a thing or two to learn about men, child." She opened the door and led Molly out into the bright morning sunshine. "Besides, your handsome husband told me to do just that if you need anything while he's gone, and you *do* need a new bonnet. Now, just follow me."

Aye, Molly Riordan had a great many things to learn about men, and she did indeed need a new bonnet. Resigned, she followed Beth Anne toward the heart of town.

And, hopefully, closer to Molly's da.

Dirk rode slightly behind Zane, remaining silent while the old Indian did whatever it was that seemed to help him see, hear, and know things no ordinary man could. No matter what it cost him in ransom, this nightmare had to end.

But the price he would pay for the emotional loss would be endless.

He swallowed hard, remembering. He'd never dreamed that Molly would give herself to him so eagerly, so lovingly, or that he would fall so thoroughly in love.

Love me . . . this once.

Once? He would love her forever.

Molly Riordan was the best thing that had ever happened to him, but at the worst possible time. If only he could undo his decision to give Ray's illegitimate child the Ballinger name. If only there was another way.

His gut roiled in protest. And he still had to face the possibility Molly could have conceived last night. One thing was for certain—he couldn't marry Lady Elizabeth until he knew Molly wasn't with child.

With a sigh, he mopped perspiration from his forehead and adjusted the angle of his hat to block the sun. Zane paused and Dirk brought Cloud to a stop beside him.

"Near here," the old Indian said, looking down a slope to a clearing where a creek babbled through it.

"There's no cabin or camp."

Zane pressed his hand to his chest. "The man you seek is near."

Dirk gave a curt nod. Experience had taught him never to question Zane's wisdom. "If you say Lovejoy is near, then he's near." He stared at the wilderness spread out before them. "We'll find him."

Zane turned slightly to face Dirk. "Or you could wait for him to find you."

"About the ransom." Dirk gritted his teeth. "That's what he expects me to do."

"Which is why you will not."

Dirk grinned, though he hardly felt like smiling. "Exactly."

Zane looked at the sun overhead. "Darkness will come soon."

Dirk drew a deep breath. He'd love nothing better than to sleep beside Molly again tonight, but he didn't want to put her at risk. If she hadn't conceived last night, then he sure as hell shouldn't tempt fate by making love to her again.

No matter how desperately he wanted to do just that.

It wouldn't be fair to her . . . or to Lady Elizabeth.

"We'll camp here," he said, deciding as he spoke. "If the Lovejoy Gang is nearby, then someone will have to come or go eventually."

"Good." Zane dismounted, then froze. "Listen."

Dirk remained in the saddle, listening intently, but all he heard was the sound of a gentle breeze sifting through the aspens and pines. He shook his head, but didn't utter a sound.

Zane met his gaze, an expression of confusion in the old dark eyes. "I thought I heard something."

Dirk narrowed his eyes as he dismounted. "What?"

Zane shook his head. "Maybe my ears are getting too old for this."

Dirk chuckled quietly. "Your ears and eyes are as young as they've ever been."

Zane appeared thoughtful, then grunted quietly. "I will let you know if I hear it again."

Suspicion slithered through Dirk, followed by pinpricks across the back of his neck. "What did you hear, Jeremiah?"

The expression in the old man's eyes grew solemn. "A woman."

Dirk swallowed hard. "A woman?"

Zane nodded. "In pain."

"I hate you!" Lady Elizabeth thrashed about on the bunk, her belly gigantic, her verbal abuse boundless.

"You said that already," Ray muttered on a sigh. "Several times."

"I can't say it enough." The woman rolled onto her side, clutching her belly with both hands. Sweat rolled down her face, and her brown hair was plastered to her head. "Oh, it hurts. Please make it stop hurting."

Guilt pressed down on Ray. If he could have undone the night he'd planted his seed in this woman's womb, he would gladly have done so. At any price.

She was in pain and it was his fault. *His!*

He clenched his fists, willing Teddy and Luther to return from their fishing trip. Darkness came fast, as always in the mountains, so his aging partners should return anytime now. He lit the lamp near the bunk and rinsed out the cloth he'd been using to bathe Lady Elizabeth's face.

She relaxed as the pain subsided and licked her lips as he bathed her face with cool water. "Thank you," she whispered, her face etched with exhaustion. "That helps."

Her polite words came as no surprise, as she'd shifted back and forth between viciousness and sweetness almost continuously since that fateful day when he'd abducted her.

Second biggest mistake of my life. He sighed. *No, the third.*

The biggest mistake of his life had been to ever set foot on the Ballinger Ranch. If he hadn't met Dirk, he wouldn't have had the money for that trip to England.

And he never would have met—let alone seduced—Lady Elizabeth Summersby.

So the biggest mistake of his life had led directly to the second biggest mistake, which had prompted the woman to travel to America and led—albeit inadvertently—to Ray's third biggest mistake.

One big mess after another. That was Ray's life to date.

And now here he was with a woman in labor. Ray Lovejoy. A man who'd never even seen a baby born, let alone participated in its delivery.

Hell, and it was *his* baby.

"Shit."

"Ray, promise me something," she said, her voice weak.

He moved closer, barely able to hear her. "What?" he asked, swallowing hard. Part of him wished he could take her pain and endure it for her.

"Don't let our baby die." Desperation tinged her voice and hung on the air between them.

Ray didn't breathe, but he nodded.

The door opened, admitting Ray's missing partners.

"It's darker'n pitch out there," Luther said, stopping so suddenly his brother ran into the back of him. His eyes grew huge in his wrinkled face as he stared at Lady Elizabeth. "Is she doin' what I think she's doin'?"

"Damnation," Teddy muttered, imitating his brother's reaction. "I'm outta here."

"I'm with you," Luther agreed.

"Men are all pigs. Cowards!" Lady Elizabeth spat on the floor, spurring the men into faster action.

Helpless, Ray watched the two old codgers gather their meager belongings. "What about the ransom?" he asked, standing to stare, his fists clenched at his sides. "Your share?"

"It ain't worth this," Teddy said, shooting nervous glances at the laboring woman. "Ain't nothin' worth this."

"I've never . . ." Ray drew a deep breath. "I don't know how to do this."

"And you think we do?" Luther barked, shoving items into his saddlebags. "Ain't neither of us ever even been married, Ray. You know that."

Ray nodded, unable to think of anything he could do or say to make them stay. "I'll send your share to your sister's place," he promised.

"Thanks." Both men paused in front of Ray, guilt written plainly across their grizzled features. They shook hands, then left the mine and disappeared into the Rocky Mountain night.

"Shit," Ray repeated, looking upward at the beamed ceiling. "What the hell am I supposed to do now?"

"Help . . . me . . . you idiot." Lady Elizabeth was rolled into a ball, clutching her knees. She fell back a second later, panting from exhaustion. "I need my . . . bloomers off." Amazingly, she blushed.

Ray held his hands up. "Keep them on. Maybe they'll help stop—"

"*Nothing* is going to stop this baby from—" She

clutched her belly again and screamed. "It's coming. Help me."

"Shit. Damn. Shit." Ray threw the rag into the basin and lunged for the foot of the bunk. He lifted back the rough wool blanket and saw blood and dampness. The stench made his belly lurch, but he gulped several deep breaths to keep from vomiting all over the woman.

He reached up to grasp the drawstring of her soiled bloomers and pulled them down her legs. "Blood. Is there supposed to be blood?" he asked.

"How the devil should I know?" She kicked the undergarment away from her ankles and spread her legs apart. "What do you see?"

"You want me to *look?*" He stiffened. *"There?"*

She gave him a look that could have sent an entire army to its knees. "You did a lot more than look before."

Heat flooded his cheeks and he bobbed his head nervously. "All right." He looked and his jaw went slack. "You'd better keep your legs together."

She laughed hysterically. "That won't stop this baby from being born." She grew solemn. "As much as I've . . . dreaded this, I really do want the baby to be all right. God help me." She bit her lower lip, then asked, "What do you see?"

Ray looked again, then met her gaze over the mound of her belly. "Uh . . . hair?" He gulped. "I think it's a head." Her words about wanting the baby to be all right had touched him somewhere he didn't want to think about.

Lady Elizabeth seemed to relax somewhat. "That's good," she said, breathing slowly and deeply. "I've heard it's bad if the feet come first."

Ray nodded. Even he'd heard that a time or two, but maybe that was in reference to horses. He met her gaze again. Thank God he wasn't stupid enough to compare Lady Elizabeth to a horse aloud. A smile tugged at the corners of his mouth.

"What's so funny?"

Before he could answer, she rose up off the bed, clutching her knees again. "I . . . I need to push."

"Shit."

Her face turned red, then purple, as she strained, trying to push the baby from her body. Ray stood by helplessly, watching. Then he realized they would need something to wrap the baby in. He hurried around the cave, gathering every clean rag he could find, and the least soiled blanket. When he returned, he dared to look again.

"Yes, it's definitely the head," he said, his voice sounding odd even to him. He tried to remember what else they would need. *Scissors and twine.* He vaguely remembered one of the whores who'd worked with his mother in Denver giving birth once. The old midwife had demanded scissors to cut the cord. That was it. And the twine was to tie it off to stop the bleeding.

God, not more blood.

Ray had never been squeamish before, but watching this woman writhe and bleed as she delivered *his* child was a humbling experience.

His child.

"It's . . . coming." Lady Elizabeth bore down again.

Ray readied himself to catch the baby. The vision of the child emerging held him transfixed. He didn't breathe as the infant slid smoothly free of its mother. "My God," he whispered reverently.

"Take it," Lady Elizabeth whispered, falling back and closing her eyes. "Take it away."

Spurred into action, he utilized common sense to tie off the cord, then cut it beyond the tie. "It's a boy," he said, his heart hammering so loudly he could barely hear himself speak. "A son."

He used a clean rag to wipe mucous away from the child's nose, eyes, and mouth, which made the infant screw up his face and emit a loud cry. Several more followed, assuring Ray that the baby was alive and healthy.

The baby felt wobbly in Ray's grasp. Delicate. "I sure hope I don't break you," he said quietly, wrapping the child in clean rags. The baby calmed, staring up at Ray with a blank expression. Something in Ray's chest swelled, and an odd sensation filled him.

He was a father. He had a son.

"Shit."

The baby started screaming again and Ray looked anxiously at Lady Elizabeth, whose eyes were open now. "Is he all right?" she asked, her voice weak. "He's nearly a month early."

Ray nodded his head and tried to speak, but found his throat clogged and tight. "He seems perfect," he finally croaked. "Little mite, though."

"Something else came out of me," Lady Elizabeth said. "But I think that's good. I remember hearing something about that."

"I'll get you cleaned up." Ray stared at her, overcome with a mountain of strange feelings. "Will you hold him while I do that?"

She hesitated, then nodded slowly. He nestled the baby in her arms, and the child turned toward her as if seeking something.

"I . . ." Lady Elizabeth's voice faltered. "I suppose he's hungry." She sighed. "At home he would have a wet nurse."

Ray kept quiet as he pulled the soiled blankets from beneath her and bathed her as much as he dared. He wasn't sure how to care for a woman who'd just given birth.

When he looked up, he saw something astonishing. Lady Elizabeth had exposed her breast to the baby, who was eagerly suckling and kneading her ample flesh with his tiny fists.

Ray piled the soiled items near the door. He'd wash everything at the creek tomorrow. "I guess he *was* hungry."

"I guess." The woman's tone sounded more confused than resentful. "It hurts a little."

Ray tried not to look at the child nursing at her breast, but he couldn't help himself. He had to fight against the sudden urge to reach down and touch his son's downy head. "Is it supposed to hurt?" he asked instead.

"I don't know." She reached down to stroke the baby's soft, dark hair, and a small choking sound erupted from her throat. "He's just perfect, isn't he?"

Ray's vision blurred as he knelt beside the bunk and indulged his need to touch his son.

And the woman who'd borne him.

"You did a good job," he said quietly, resting his hand softly against the baby's back, and brushing Elizabeth's hair back from her face. "I'm sorry this has been so hard—"

"Sorry?" Her expression shifted from tenderness to resentment before she drew her next breath. "You're *sorry?*"

"I . . ." Ray shook his head, letting his hand fall away from her, but keeping the other one on his son. "I didn't know you were with child," he said.

"This isn't fair, you know."

"Fair?" Ray shook his head in total confusion.

"I had to carry and deliver it."

"Him. He's not an it."

Lady Elizabeth scowled, confusion flickering across her face as she glanced down at their son. "Yes, him."

"You did it well," Ray said again.

"But don't you see? Now I have to keep doing it." The expression in her eyes was filled with bitterness. "It isn't fair. There's no one to help me."

Except me. Maybe she was just in shock from everything. She would feel differently tomorrow. "I would gladly feed the baby, but I don't have the right . . . uh . . ."

"How convenient for you." Venom edged her voice.

Ray looked away from her and down at his son again. The child would need clothes and a decent home and . . .

A name. Resolve eased through Ray, and he suddenly understood why his half brother had offered to marry Lady Elizabeth. But no one was going to give Ray's son a name but Ray.

That meant he'd have to marry Lady Elizabeth himself.

Eighteen

Molly stared at the document spread out on Beth Anne's kitchen table. She hadn't permitted herself to look at it again since they'd returned from town three days ago. Beth Anne had understood the significance of Molly's discovery, and had left her alone this morning to contemplate it.

Da's mining claim.

This claim had kept him away from her all these years. Had it been worth it? Was he a wealthy man now? Would he welcome her into his life, or turn his back on her?

She had only vague memories of her da, but they were all good. He'd been a laughing man and generous to a fault. Hadn't Gram said so often enough? She'd said Niall would give away his last morsel rather than see another man go hungry.

Yet he'd abandoned his only child.

"Enough of that, Molly," she muttered, looking at the crudely drawn map that described the location of her da's silver mine. She would go today.

Beth Anne hadn't returned from her errands yet, so Molly left a note on the table, explaining where she was going. She tied her new sunbonnet under her chin, then left the boarding house and Serendipity behind.

According to the hand-drawn map, Niall Riordan's

mine was only a little more than a mile north of town. She could walk there easily, leaving Sadie safely at the livery. Of course, Dirk would be angry if he discovered Molly's absence, but he should have considered that before he'd left to search for Lady Elizabeth without her.

Three days ago.

After all, he had promised Molly she could be a part of the search. In truth, Molly admitted to herself as she balanced on stones to cross a narrow brook, she'd convinced herself to be angry with him rather than to miss him. She'd slept little since his departure, and her dreams had been filled with images of their lovemaking. Warmth stole through her and she sighed, ruthlessly forcing the memories aside. She would deal with them and with Dirk Ballinger when necessary. For now, she would concentrate on finding da.

The other man who had left her.

Girding her resolve, she paused and gazed across the clearing, then looked at the map again. The small brook she'd just crossed appeared as a squiggly line across the yellowed paper. The mine should be somewhere on the far edge of this high mountain meadow. Assuming she was reading the map correctly.

She drew a deep breath of the fresh mountain air, understanding how and why her da had fallen in love with these mountains. But that still didn't excuse his decision not to send for her.

The sun was farther across the sky than she'd realized, and she paused to weigh her options. Should she return to town and resume her search in the morning?

She was so close. No, she would search a little longer.

She squared her shoulders and walked in the direction she assumed to be north. Shading her eyes, she noted a sheer wall of bluffs ahead. The map showed something similar, though the crude drawing was unclear. There were numbers as well, though they were completely meaningless to her.

Searching along the bluff made sense. After all, mines were dug into the ground or the side of mountains. Weren't they? Without further delay, Molly walked purposefully across the grassy meadow sprinkled with wildflowers and into a grove of trees. The brook she'd crossed earlier snaked its way through these trees as well, disappearing into the dense forest.

She looked at the map again. The X marking her da's mine was near the brook. It made sense, she decided, as even miners required water. Following the winding stream, she climbed upward toward the base of the bluffs.

By the time she reached the granite wall, she was gasping for breath. Though she'd grown more accustomed to the thinner air in the mountains, she still felt it during physical exertion. She rested several minutes while studying the bluffs nearest the brook.

Brush grew up against the stone walls, but a path was worn from there to the water. Molly's heart lurched and her mouth went dry. Her palms perspired and she wiped them on her skirt, switching the map from hand to hand.

She was close.

Panic stole through her, but she drew several deep breaths to steady her nerves. She'd come too far to turn back now. Her long-lost da could be right in front of her.

Her legs felt heavy as she trudged the last few yards. Aye, the worn area was definitely a path, but it could have been made by animals as well as people. All living things needed water, after all.

Even so, hope and fear crowded each other for supremacy as she grew close enough to make out a door amid the foliage. *Jesus, Mary, and Joseph.* She swallowed hard and crossed herself. Her moment of truth had arrived.

Here I come, Da.

She paused at the door, listening. Should she knock or just pull the leather latchstring and open the door? How would Da react to seeing her?

No point in wondering that. She would just find out for herself. Squaring her shoulders, she lifted her hand and rapped her knuckles against the splintered wooden planks.

She heard no sound from inside, and she'd already noticed the openings on either side of the door, though they could hardly be called windows. If someone were inside, wouldn't she have heard them?

And didn't that also mean they would have heard her?

She knocked again and a muttered oath drifted through the window. A soft thud was followed by another curse, then another totally unexpected sound.

The cry of a wee babe.

Confusion filled her just as the door swung wide. A mess of a man with wild eyes and a few days' growth of beard stood there with a screeching baby in his arms.

Definitely not Da. She searched the man's face for any clue to his identity and it struck with a certainty that left her breathless for a few moments.

"Mother Mary," she whispered.

"She's not here," the man said, narrowing his eyes. "Who the hell are . . ." Then he shook his head in obvious bewilderment.

Recovering herself, Molly dealt with two urgent facts that needed confirmation. "You're Ray Lovejoy."

He sighed, resignation evident in his eyes. "Yep. Who are you?"

"Molly Riordan—Lady Elizabeth's maid." Her gaze dropped to the crying baby wrapped in rags. "And this . . . is her baby?"

The man nodded, a muscle clenching in his jaw.

Molly swallowed. "Where is she?" She should have feared the notorious outlaw, but she didn't. She only wanted to see Lady Elizabeth for herself, to make certain the woman was safe. There was no one else in the mine—at least not in the part near the entrance where there was light. "Where?"

Molly found a look of utter helplessness on his face. He held the baby out toward her. "Help me find a way to feed him," he said simply.

Desperately.

"Please?"

A newborn baby needed to nurse. "Where is Lady Elizabeth?" She waited, holding her breath.

"I wish like hell I knew." An expression of utter disgust crossed his face. "She left as soon as she could walk."

Horror spiraled through Molly. "No, she couldn't have left her baby." She reached out and took the child in her arms. "No woman could walk away from her own child."

"Maybe *you* couldn't, but she did." He raked his fingers through his hair. "She went out to . . . to . . . take care of private things and never came back."

"Why? I don't under—"

"Why?" He barked a derisive laugh and a look of utter disgust gripped his features. "Because I asked her to marry me. That's why."

"What?" Molly's breath rushed from her body and

she swayed. Why in heaven's name would Ray Lovejoy want to marry Lady Elizabeth?

"Never mind about her." He raked his fingers through his unkempt hair. "I've been trying to feed him thin mush with a spoon, but it isn't working." He looked at her with wide, pleading eyes. "Please help me."

Molly gazed into the infant's eyes. They were a nondescript blue now, but she suspected they would turn Ballinger green in a few months. A part of her suddenly wished this child were hers. Oh, to bear Dirk's child would be the greatest joy Molly could imagine. "Dirk's son," she whispered.

The man made a choking sound. "No. Not Dirk's. Not hardly."

Molly studied the man. He didn't look like a highwayman or a kidnapper. He also didn't look like a liar. He looked like a man in turmoil.

In pain.

"Not Dirk's?" she echoed, her heart hammering against her breastbone. "What do you mean?"

Ray Lovejoy shook his head and released a ragged sigh. "Doesn't matter. Why did you come here anyway?"

Oh, but it did matter. *Not Dirk's?*

"I asked you a question."

She cleared her throat, trying to concentrate. "I came here searching for my da."

"Your father?" Ray shook his head. "Why would he be in this dirty hole?"

She retrieved the assayer's report from her pocket and handed it to Ray.

He read it, then looked up at her. "This was your pa's mine?"

She nodded. "According to this." She looked down at the screaming infant. *Not Dirk's son.*

"That trunk was here when we first got here," he said. "Might belong to your pa."

Molly glanced at the trunk, her heart racing at an alarming rate. "I'd like to look through it."

"Sure." He lifted a shoulder. "The baby's hungry."

Not Dirk's son. Those words played over and over in her mind. She swayed, clutching the baby closer as she studied this man's features. Seeing him unmasked made her realize how easy it had been to mistake him for Dirk after the stage robbery.

He'd worn a mask another time. That realization knocked the wind out of her, and for a few terrifying moments she couldn't breathe at all. "Sweet Jesus," she finally gasped. "You . . ."

"Finally figured it out?" One corner of his mouth curved upward. "I remember seeing you now. You were there that night. At the ball," he said.

It all made sense in a sordid way. *"You.* You're . . ." She drew a deep breath, keeping her gaze locked on his face. "You're the one. You said you were Dirk. It was you all along."

"Guilty." His sarcasm had returned. "But right now nothing matters except finding a way to feed this kid. I don't have what it takes."

He looked pointedly at Molly's bosom and arched a questioning brow. "Do you?"

Molly recovered from her shock and shook her head. "We'll need to go to town and find a wet nurse."

Ray seemed to weigh his options. "If I go to town, I'll be arrested."

Molly set her lips in a stern line. "Aye, and justifiably so." She was pushing him, but he seemed willing to do anything to feed the baby. Any man who would sacrifice himself for his child couldn't be all bad. "Two men were killed. A woman kidnapped."

His nostrils flared and he straightened. "I've never killed anyone," he said with conviction. *"Never."*

Molly stared at him for several seconds, trying to ignore the child's increasing agitation. The infant seemed oblivious to her lack of maternal nourishment and tried futilely to root against her fully clothed breast.

She stared unwaveringly at Ray Lovejoy, watching for any sign that he could be lying. Finding nothing but sincerity in his eyes and his demeanor, she gave an emphatic nod. "I believe you."

"You were at the stage, too." He sighed. "You . . . saw what happened."

"Aye," she said. "Another man shot the driver, though I didn't see who killed the passenger."

His jaw twitched. "The same."

"There were four of you, as I recall, Mr. Lovejoy."

"Ray. Just Ray." He nodded. "Two older men, myself, and one killer who calls himself Desperado."

The baby let out a particularly shrill scream. "He needs milk."

"Where am I going to get milk up here?"

"Will you let me take the baby with me to town if I help you feed him now?"

Ray sighed and pressed his lips together, his gaze resting on his son. His Adam's apple worked up and down the length of his throat. "Yes, but it's too late to start down now. It's almost dark."

The tenderness and helplessness in Ray's eyes broke Molly's heart. Her throat clogged with tears and she knew without a doubt that this man was good inside. There was hope for him.

For Dirk's brother.

"All right, then." She cleared her throat, concentrating on the challenge ahead of her. "Let's see that mush for now, and I'll take him to Serendipity in the morning." Molly hated to feed the baby anything other than what nature had intended, but desperate situations called for desperate solutions. After several attempts, she finally managed to get enough watery mush down the child's throat to calm him, and he fell asleep.

"Thank God," Ray said, slumping down to the bunk.

Molly nodded, not wishing to disturb the baby. She remained perfectly still, watching the child sleep in her arms. At last her mind was free to consider the significance of everything.

Dirk was not the father of this child.

Ray was.

She drew a shaky breath and glanced at Ray, who hadn't even stirred. The man had dedicated himself to trying to feed his son. A smile curved Molly's lips.

Ray Lovejoy and Dirk Ballinger were more alike than either of them would ever have admitted.

Dirk had been willing to sacrifice his freedom for the sake of this baby. Ray would end up losing his freedom for the same reason. Two honorable men. Half brothers by blood, but raised apart.

She looked down at the baby again, and a wave of unconditional love and pride washed through her. She closed her eyes, forcing herself to remember Lady Elizabeth. The last time she'd seen the woman had been in the stagecoach, just before Mr. Slim had stopped for water.

She remembered the exact words they had exchanged just before . . .

"Molly, promise me . . ." A strange desperation entered Lady Elizabeth's voice.

"What?"

Lady Elizabeth gripped Molly's hand and whispered, "If anything happens to me, you'll raise my baby."

Molly wanted to dismiss the woman's plea as foolishness, but something in Lady Elizabeth's expression stayed her. "I . . . I promise."

Alarm settled in Molly's belly and she stiffened.

Had Lady Elizabeth planned to abandon her baby all along?

"We're going down there," Dirk said through gritted teeth. "Tonight."

Zane's expression was wise and calm. "Yes. Tonight." He cocked his head. "A baby cries."

Shock ricocheted through Dirk. "What?" Had Lady Elizabeth's baby been born? "Are you sure?"

Zane nodded. "I am sure of what I hear, but I am not sure of its origin."

Whatever the hell that meant.

"Sometimes I hear and see what is yet to come." Zane turned to gaze toward the bluffs again. "Sometimes I just know."

Uneasiness trickled through Dirk. "You trying to tell me something, old man?"

Zane looked at Dirk, a knowing smile crinkling his face. "I know what you must learn for yourself."

Dirk rolled his eyes and shook his head. "And you aren't going to tell me?"

"You will know soon."

Dirk faced the bluffs again, gripping the reins so tightly his hands trembled. He swallowed the lump in his throat and forced himself to concentrate on ending this nightmare. Tonight, he and Zane would apprehend Ray Lovejoy, free Lady Elizabeth . . . and the baby, if it had indeed been born.

If that proved true, then Dirk had failed to prevent another Ballinger child from being born a bastard. Bitterness flowed through him as he pictured his father's face, then Ray's. "Damn."

Dirk would still make certain the child had his name. The same name he'd offered to Ray not so very long ago.

"Let's position ourselves in those trees across the creek," he said, deciding to act rather than think.

"Good." Zane grunted and led Dirk along the edge of the meadow, circling back toward the area where the mine was located.

They remained hidden in the trees until the sun began to sink beyond the western-most ridge. Fingers of orange stretched across the sky, and Dirk gazed heavenward with a prayer in his thoughts.

Please . . . just let it be all right. No matter what.

He couldn't be more specific than that, because he was in the proverbial damned if he didn't and damned if he did situation. Hell, he wasn't sure what to pray for at this point.

If he followed his heart and what he *wanted* more than anything, he would pray he and Molly would be together. That was his heart's most fervent wish.

If he followed his sense of honor and duty, he would pray Lady Elizabeth's child remained unborn and that he would be able to fulfill his promise of marriage.

Ray's face flashed through his mind.

And if he listened to his lust for revenge and justice?

Ida was grateful Clyde didn't mention the birthmark again for the rest of the day. Dr. Stein had arrived and treated Lance's injury, saying how lucky the boy was that no vital organs had been damaged.

"Let's get some fresh air," Clyde said to Ida after Lance was comfortably in his own bed with Elena at his side.

"Oh, no," Ida protested. "I couldn't leave—"

"I will stay with Lance," Elena announced, her gaze never leaving the patient's face. "You go. I will not leave him."

The girl's eyes shone with love, and Ida thanked God someone besides her cared so much for her son. "Thank you." She patted the girl's shoulder, then squared her own and faced Clyde.

A steely glint flickered in the man's eyes, and she knew her moment of reckoning had arrived. With a sigh, she preceded him from the room, knowing what she had to do. Clyde Yeager would never settle for anything less than the truth.

The entire truth.

They went through the kitchen and out the back door. The sun was just beginning to sink beyond the mountains, and a cool breeze wafted down the pass. Ida hugged herself, but savored the invigorating chill.

Clyde stopped at her side and put both hands on her shoulders, turning her to face him. His face was a mixture of hard planes and angles in the waning twilight, his expression unreadable.

"Your name ain't Ida Jensen," he said matter-of-factly. "Is it?"

A tremor washed through her and she swallowed hard. "Ida is my middle name. Jensen is my maiden name."

He tightened his grip. "Why did you lie?" He shook his head. "You've been here for years. Why didn't you tell the truth?"

"I . . . I was afraid."

"Edward's dead." Clyde's words were clipped and

sounded harsh against the silence of evening. "You afraid of dead men?"

She bit her lower lip and shook her head, tears welling over the rims of her eyes and sliding down her cheeks. "I . . . I came back after he'd lost his sight, but I always wondered if he knew me anyway."

Clyde nodded. "I remember when you came to work here." His grip on her shoulders eased and he slid his hands down to massage her upper arms. "Go on. I'm listenin'."

His voice had gentled along with his touch. Ida drew a shaky breath. "He . . . Dirk . . ."

"Thought you was dead." Clyde bowed his head. "We all did."

She shook her head slowly. "Not all."

"Edward?"

"I was careful to disguise my voice around him," she said, reliving the fear. "But he knew I didn't die, though he told you all I had."

"Dirk has a right to know the truth."

Tears streamed down her face and she tried to pull away from Clyde, but he tightened his grip. "I . . . I . . ."

"You're gonna tell the truth now." Clyde's voice softened again. "No more lies. Hell, I don't even know what to call you. Are you Prudence . . . or Ida?"

Resignation swelled within her and she drew a shaky breath, banishing her tears. "Oh, I'm Ida now. Prudence died a long time ago—in almost every way." She mopped the tears from her cheeks. "The truth. I'm too old and too tired for more lies."

"You can start with me."

"Can we sit down before I fall down?" she asked, trying to smile.

He took her arm and led her to a bench near the

well. She shivered as she lowered herself to it, and he sat close, placing his arm across her shoulders.

"You're cold," he said, pulling her against his body.

"I'm all right." She savored his warmth, wondering if he would ever so much as look at her again after he heard everything.

"You left durin' the war," he said. "While I was gone."

She nodded, staring toward the house. "The Ballinger Ranch was nothing but a cabin and a sod stable then." She looked up at Clyde and smiled through the darkness. "Rusty was the one and only wrangler."

"Didn't need more'n one then." He rubbed her arm, his gaze holding hers through the darkness. "What happened?"

Her breath stuttered as she struggled against a renewed onslaught of tears. Resolutely, she cleared her throat and said, "Lance."

"I still don't understand."

"Dirk was only three when Lance was born." She smiled, remembering Dirk as a baby. "His father . . . Edward . . . wanted to send . . ."

Clyde's breath came out in a rush, warm against her cheek. "He wanted to send Lance away?" The man tightened his arm around her shoulders. "Because he's slow?"

Ida nodded rapidly, struggling against the need to cry. Years of frustration welled within her. "From the moment Lance was born, we knew something wasn't . . . normal." She bit the inside of her cheek to keep herself focused on the present, despite her journey to the past. "I . . . I loved him anyway."

" 'Course, you did." Clyde bowed his head for a moment, then faced her. "You left to protect Lance."

"Yes. Edward had papers from a judge, ordering . . ."

A sob escaped from deep in her soul, and it took her several moments to regain control. "I'm sorry."

"You left your husband to protect your baby," Clyde said, tilting his head to one side as he studied her through the darkness. "But you left another baby behind."

She found herself in Clyde's arms, sobbing uncontrollably. All the years of torment flowed forth in a torrent of grief and regrets and the knowledge that she would do it all again if she had to.

Some time later, her tears spent, she looked up at Clyde's kind face and cleared her throat. "I left Dirk for two reasons," she said, forcing her voice to remain calm. "He was strong."

"And the second reason?" Clyde asked when she fell silent.

She sighed and said, "Because I loved Edward Ballinger too much to take the only son he cared about." She laughed nervously. "It sounds foolish now, but I was also being practical. I figured I stood a better chance of raising one boy alone than two."

Clyde remained silent for several moments. "And he would have gone after you if you'd taken Dirk."

"Yes! You *do* understand." The tears burst free again. "I knew that in my heart. I also knew he'd never bother to come after Lance, and that he'd let me go easily enough." She sobbed and bit her knuckle. "And, God help me, I was right."

"Dirk turned out fine. He's a good man." Clyde continued to rub her shoulder. "And he knows what a mean old cuss his daddy was, too."

She nodded. "He's paying the price for that now."

"Lovejoy." Clyde sighed.

"Yes." She squared her shoulders. "I'll tell Dirk the truth when he returns."

"Yep, you will." Clyde slid his other arm around her, turning her to face him. "But you and me is gettin' hitched before then."

"What?" A dull roar commenced in Ida's head. "You're spouting nonsense, Clyde Yeager."

"No, I ain't." He drew a deep breath. "I been plannin' to ask you anyway, but now I'm inclined to hurry it up a mite." He dropped to one knee before her and took both her hands in his.

She frowned, shaking her head. "I don't understand why you would—"

"First reason and most important is that I love you, no matter what you call yourself." His warm breath fanned her hands, still clutched in his. "Second reason—now don't you get mad—is that if you're hitched to me before you tell Dirk, it'll . . ."

"Offer me some protection?" She laughed nervously. "He isn't like his father, Clyde. He'll be angry, of course, but I think he'll understand." Warmth and a small dollop of confidence eased through her. "And I think he'll be happy to hear Lance is his brother."

Clyde chuckled low. "You're a sly one."

She nodded. "I've had to learn."

He sobered, then lowered his head to kiss her hand.

"Yes," she whispered. "I'll marry you, but only on one condition."

"Anythin' you ask."

"Get up off your knee this instant."

Chuckling, he obeyed and slid beside her on the bench. He gathered her in his arms and covered her lips with his. She leaned into his kiss, savoring his strength, his goodness, his love.

As he broke the kiss, he kept her pulled close and said, "There might be one more reason to hurry this weddin' up."

"Why?" Breathless, Ida waited.

"Because if I don't get you in my bed real durned quick, I'm gonna be loonier than a rabid coon."

She gasped, then cleared her throat, heat spiraling through her at the thought of lying in Clyde's arms tonight. And every night. "Let me check on Lance first," she whispered, dizzy with the realization that Clyde knew the truth and still loved her.

"You'll do it?" He rose, pulling her up with him, holding her snugly against his long, lanky frame. "Tonight?"

She laughed nervously, amazing herself. "Tonight."

Nineteen

Lady Elizabeth Summersby had gone to hell.

She'd been kidnapped by the man who'd seduced her and left her with child while using another's name, she'd given birth in a *cave,* she'd been forced to allow the child to suckle at her breasts in lieu of a wet nurse.

Pinpricks swarmed over both her engorged breasts at the thought of her baby, and milk soaked the front of her dress. Again. Right now she would gladly nurse the child.

Her child.

Who could have guessed her heart would swell with love for the tiny being who had complicated her life? The moment Ray had placed him in her arms, she had known nothing was as important as her son. *Nothing.*

My baby. A tear trickled down her cheek to dampen the already saturated gag even further. Who would feed her baby now? Would he starve? Would Ray risk his freedom to find a wet nurse for their son?

And had he meant it when he'd asked her to marry him?

His proposal had shocked her, but she couldn't deny the modicum of warmth that had stolen through her as well. The man had looked at their child—and at her, amazingly enough—with tenderness. True caring.

And, even more amazing, she cared for him, too.

Lady Elizabeth Summersby had fallen in love with a common highwayman. No, there was nothing common about Ray. She should know. Though she'd pretended to be a virgin that night in the carriage, he'd known. She'd had other men, but none of them had . . . had . . .

A heated flush crept to her cheeks at the memory, which made more milk seep from her breasts. She was a mess. A mother without her baby. A woman in love without her lover.

And now—*now*—she was suffering the ultimate insult.

She'd been kidnapped again.

However, this abductor was far more ill-mannered and dangerous. She remembered having seen him at the stage robbery. This same yellow-haired devil had slain two innocent men right before her eyes.

He called himself Desperado.

And she was terrified.

She glowered at the man standing over her, wishing the gag were gone so she could follow her instinct to spit in his face.

"Pity you've been spoilt," the man said, smirking at her. "We could've had us some fun before you popped that kid." His expression darkened. "Too damned messy for my tastes now."

The gag prevented her hot retort, which was probably just as well. Maybe the inability to share her thoughts with this creature would save her. Maybe . . .

"We'll give old Ray one more day to get the ransom, then we'll collect." His laugh was evil. Menacing. "I've had enough of these mountains *and* the high and mighty Ballingers to last me ten lifetimes."

Curiosity edged through Elizabeth and she sat very still, willing her breath to quiet enough to enable her to hear the villain's every utterance.

"First, old Edward lorded himself around, making my life miserable." Desperado snorted and shook his head as he cleaned his fingernails with a wicked-looking blade. "Fixed him, I did."

Since she couldn't speak, she tilted her head and widened her eyes, hoping the demented man would realize she was encouraging him. Maybe if she understood Desperado's motives, she could expedite her freedom.

And stay alive in the process.

"Spooked his horse when he was on his way back to the ranch one night." Desperado cackled, obviously quite pleased with himself. " 'Course, he was supposed to die, but spending the rest of his life blind was even better, really."

"Hmm?" Elizabeth managed through the gag, forcing a curious and interested expression.

"Bastard tried to tell me how to run my town one too many times." Desperado flung the blade to the ground, where the point stuck in the earth near his hostage's feet. "His son is just as bad. Estes Park is *mine*. Was. I won't be going back now. They'll all know, and it's all Ballinger's fault."

Elizabeth had recognized only one name—Ballinger. She shook her head and shrugged, wondering if the Edward in question was a Ballinger. If so, then it stood to reason that the son to which this vile highwayman had referred was Dirk Ballinger.

Her husband-to-be.

Rather, her former husband-to-be.

A wicked gleam entered Desperado's amber eyes as he stared beyond her at something she suspected only he could see. "Yessir," he muttered, hatred dripping from every syllable, "once I get my money, Dirk Ballinger is a dead man."

* * *

After placing the sleeping baby beside Ray, who curled his arm instinctively around his son, Molly lit another lantern and sat beside an overturned crate where several papers lay strewn. An open trunk sat nearby, drawing her attention.

She wasn't tired enough to sleep, but she wanted to remain quiet so she wouldn't disturb the exhausted baby or his father. A smile curved her lips as she looked at Ray, who had snuggled his son closer. At least the child was content for the time being. Tomorrow, she would take the baby to town and ask Beth Anne to help her find a suitable wet nurse.

Molly had no choice but to remain here until morning. She couldn't have found her way back to Serendipity in the dark, and she couldn't risk the child.

Dirk would be angry with her, but once she explained she'd been in search of her da, he would understand. Remembering what had brought her here in the first place, Molly wondered what had become of Niall Riordan. This had been his mining claim, yet an outlaw now used it as a hideout.

Bewildered, she furrowed her brow and resigned herself to continuing her search for information once she returned to town. Perhaps Da had sold his claim to Ray. She made a mental note to ask Ray after he woke.

Meanwhile, she needed to keep herself from going stir crazy. She picked up a parchment from the pile before her and scanned the information. A name leaped off the page and stabbed through her.

Niall Riordan.

Swallowing the lump in her throat, she rose and walked around the crate to the trunk, where she lowered the lid enough to allow her to see the initials carved into the scarred wood.

N.K.R.

"Da?" she breathed, turning her attention back to the papers on the crate.

Several moments later, she determined this had indeed been her da's mining claim. There was no evidence he had sold it. In fact, every indication was that he had left suddenly.

Or died?

That possibility had lingered in the back of her mind for years. Gram had insisted that only death would've kept her son from sending for Molly.

Either way, Molly needed to know once and for all. She'd spent too many years wondering to leave the question of her da's fate unanswered now.

She looked upward at the beams on the ceiling, warmed by the knowledge that her da—her own flesh and blood—had lived and worked here.

A slight squeaking noise from the rear of the cave made her shiver, and she turned the lantern's flame higher. The light, she prayed, would keep bats and other nocturnal creatures at bay.

Da had been here. Now *she* was here. She would find her answers.

She moved the lantern to the opposite side of the crate to illuminate the contents of the trunk, then bent over it and pulled out a stack of papers and a leather pouch. Setting the papers aside, she opened the pouch and slid its contents into her hand.

A carved wooden frame surrounded a miniature oil painting of a woman and child. The dark hair, the blue eyes, the soft features . . ."Mama," Molly whispered, then permitted her gaze to drift to the child—her own image in years gone by.

She'd been a babe in arms then. A tear eased from the corner of her eye and she gently touched her mother's face.

Da had kept this. All this time . . .

He still cares.

Molly resisted the urge to sniffle, and she bit back the sob that threatened to erupt from deep in her heart. If her da was still alive, he still cared. And she would find him.

She propped the frame up with its easel back where she could glance at it often, then turned her attention to the papers. She slid a letter from an envelope. It was a letter offering Niall Riordan a position as a driver. The letter didn't say what sort of driver. Did this have anything to do with silver mining?

Confused, Molly reread the letter, then noted the date was May of 1886, more than two years earlier. Had her da walked away from this mine to become a driver of some sort?

I don't understand any of this. And none of it answered her most desperate question. *Is Da still alive?*

Besides, he must have meant to return, for he'd left his personal belongings behind. Her gaze slid to the portrait again and a tight fist of trepidation clutched her heart.

She tilted the lantern to illuminate the recesses of the trunk and spotted a bundle of envelopes tied with a piece of string. A sense of foreboding washed through her as she placed the stack in her lap and eased the lantern into a position that would allow her to read.

She untied the ribbon and turned each envelope over, stunned to find them all sealed with wax. Bewildered, she read the faded script on the front of each one.

Faith. They were addressed to her.

He had written his thoughts down, but had never

shared them with his daughter. Molly's throat convulsed and she pulled the envelope from the bottom of the stack, deciding to read them in order. She had no qualms about opening them, as they were addressed to her.

Tears blurred her vision, but she angrily scrubbed them away, then drew a steadying breath before immersing herself in the task at hand. Letter after letter was more of the same. Each one read like a catharsis for a man who considered himself a failure. She had the feeling many of these letters had been written for himself as much as for her.

Niall Riordan had apologized in every letter for not sending for her. He'd explained to her that the conditions he lived in weren't suitable for a lass. Molly paused and looked around the cave.

They aren't suitable for a man either, Da.

Or a babe. She looked over at the still-sleeping child.

As there was no source of heat in the mine, her da couldn't have remained here through the winter months. How had he survived in this brutal wilderness?

One letter spoke of his life here, how hard it was for the miners and their families. He wrote about cave-ins and explosions and disease.

Molly remembered Beth Anne's expression when she'd spoken of losing her husband and son. "Oh, Da."

The last letter freed her tears. Da had given up hope of ever making a life for himself or his child. After learning of his wife's death from Gram, he'd accepted a position driving a stage.

A stage?

Later in that same letter, he'd written that the other miners never called him Niall or Riordan. They'd all teased him about being so tall and lanky, and had always called him "Slim." The name stuck, and after a while they all but forgot his real name.

NO PLACE FOR A LADY

Slim? Molly remembered Mr. Slim dying in her arms and her heart lurched. Her blood pounded through her head.

Pain exploded behind her eyes and she doubled over, clutching her belly as silent sobs racked her. She bit down on her knuckle to silence her keening.

Da. Mr. Slim. Both Irishmen. Both stage drivers. Both dead.

No, not both. One man. The same man.

Her da was dead. And she had watched him die. Why hadn't Mr. Slim—Da—told her the truth?

She remembered the expression in his eyes after she'd told him her name and her da's. He'd known immediately. An invisible force squeezed her heart, and she struggled to breathe.

As he'd lain dying in her arms, his life's blood pouring out to cover them both, he'd pleaded with her to tell him about herself and how she'd come to be in America. He'd cared. He'd wanted to know about his daughter before his death.

And he'd told a great lie about her identity.

Confusion shocked her tears away and she straightened. Why had he told Dirk and the others she was Lady Elizabeth?

Why?

She glanced down at the pile of letters, remembering his pain, his shame, his sense of failure. Suddenly, she understood.

Niall Riordan had seized the opportunity in death to redeem himself. And to provide for his only child, after a fashion.

Gulping great breaths of air, Molly shoved aside her grief for now and wiped her blurry eyes, then commanded herself to continue with her discoveries. Da had written of his plans to return to his mine one day, at least to send his daughter the letters he'd never mailed and his most cherished belonging.

The portrait of his love and their child.

A knifelike pain stabbed through her, but the baby whimpered just in time to stave off the monsters. Molly welcomed the respite from pain and truth as she hurried to the bunk. Gathering the infant into her arms, she held him close to her cheek and allowed her tears to flow.

Oh, Da.

Under cover of total darkness, Dirk and Zane closed in on the hideout. Dirk stood outside the shuttered window, peering between the cracks in the weathered wood.

His breath froze as he caught sight of Molly with a baby in her arms. She pressed the child's cheek to hers and tears trickled down her cheeks.

Molly Riordan, what the devil are you doing here?

Had Ray harmed her? Dirk's fists clenched and he clamped his teeth together. His plan had been to take Ray to the law, but if his half brother had so much as insulted Molly . . .

But, somehow, Dirk managed to remember his initial impression of his half brother. Ray Lovejoy didn't seem like the sort who would stoop to harming women.

Of course, those limitations didn't include seducing a woman under another man's name or kidnapping the same woman while she carried his child.

The entire situation was almost laughable. Absurd at the very least. And Molly seemed fine, despite her tears.

Maybe Ray had delivered the ransom note. That could easily explain Molly's presence, for she was too stubborn to have waited for Dirk. Yes, that was the most plausible explanation.

Then his gaze rested on the child, swaddled in rags. Ray's child. A Ballinger in every way except in name.

Dirk didn't see any sign of Ray or Lady Elizabeth. In fact, Molly appeared to be alone with the child. Perplexed, he took a step back and looked at Zane through the darkness.

"Lovejoy is there," Zane whispered. "The woman is gone."

Gone? Dirk shook his head, deciding he'd get his answers soon enough. His half brother must be asleep. He eased himself toward the entrance, and Zane imitated his moves. Positioned on either side of the portal, guns drawn, Dirk nodded.

In unison, they crashed through the door, turning in opposite directions. Ray started awake and fell off the bunk. Molly screamed. The baby wailed.

"Helluvan entrance," Ray muttered, brushing himself off as he rose.

Dirk kept his gun aimed at his half brother as he glanced over at Molly. "You all right?" She nodded, her eyes wide.

He turned his attention back to Ray, taking in the man's soiled clothing, unshaven face, and obvious exhaustion.

"You look like hell."

"Thanks, Dirk." One corner of Ray's mouth curved upward. "Same to you."

Ignoring his half brother's sarcasm, Dirk motioned for Zane to cover Ray, then went to Molly, placing a protective arm across her shoulders. He looked at the baby, now crying in earnest. The child appeared healthy, though very small.

He turned his gaze to Ray again. "Where's Lady Elizabeth?" His voice fell to a menacing pitch. "Have you harmed her?"

"You might say I insulted her," Ray said on a sigh. "I asked her to marry me."

All the air rushed out of Dirk, and the baby let loose an amazing howl for such a tiny thing. "You did *what?*"

"Look, you don't need the guns," Ray said, his tone weary. "I'm too dang tired to run away, and there's the kid to think about."

Dirk gave Molly's arm a squeeze; the baby continued to wail. "Is there anything here to feed the baby?" he asked.

"No milk," she said, her voice quivering. "But there's some mush we can thin and warm." She glanced at Ray. "How do you cook?"

"Outside."

Zane grunted and motioned for Ray to accompany him outside. Ray grabbed a covered pan, and they left to warm the baby's food.

Molly turned to face Dirk, and he saw clear evidence of the tears he'd noticed from the window. Without speaking, he gathered her into his arms with the crying infant still cradled against her shoulder. She clung to him as if her life depended on it, and he showered her face and head with kisses.

"I was terrified when I saw you."

"I'm sorry," she muttered. "I . . . I . . ." She pulled back to gaze up at him, her expression filled with pain. "I came looking for my da."

"Your father?" He shook his head. "Why?"

More tears spilled from her eyes and she pulled a document from her pocket and passed it to him. It was a mining claim under the name Niall Riordan. Molly's father. The map at the bottom of the sheet explained exactly how she'd come here.

She reached for a letter on the table and held it out to him with trembling hands. "The last letter Gram received from Da came from Serendipity," she said quietly. "I thought . . . I thought . . ."

"You thought you could find him here." Now Dirk understood the woman's anxiety about reaching Serendipity. He reached for her, but she shook her head.

"Read this." Her lower lip quivered. "Please?"

Nodding, he took the letter still clutched in her hands and scanned the faded scrawl. "Stage driver?" He looked up at her and shook his head. "He left his mine to drive a stage?"

Obviously struggling to maintain her composure, she cleared her throat and patted the screaming baby on the back. "He mentioned that the people here called him . . . Slim." Her face crumpled and she bit her lower lip.

Dirk pulled her into his arms again, allowing the letter to flutter to the table. His gaze fell to the portrait of a woman and a child propped beside the lantern. Tentatively, he reached past Molly and picked it up to examine more closely.

The woman was the image of Molly, though her eyes were a paler blue. The little girl in the woman's lap was obviously Molly. Dirk's heart ached for her. Learning her father had left all his memories of his wife and child behind must have broken Molly's heart.

"My da is dead," she whimpered against his shoulder.

"Why do you think that?" he asked, placing the portrait on the table again. "Just because he left doesn't mean he's—"

"Dirk." She pulled back to stare into his eyes. "He said they called him Slim. The driver of the stage Lady Elizabeth and I were on was called Slim, and he was an Irishman."

Realization punched Dirk in the gut. "So that's why . . ."

"He lied about my identity."

"He wanted you to have a better life than he could give you." Dirk sighed and pulled Molly close again. "I'm so sorry," he murmured against her hair, trying to ignore the hungry baby's wails. "To come so far to find your father only to lose him."

"He . . . he died in my arms." Molly wailed along with the baby, clinging to Dirk. "He lied for me." She looked up at him, blinking. "He died for me."

Dirk nodded. "He must have loved you very much," he said, holding her gaze. "As do I."

A sad smile curved her lips. "I love you, too," she whispered. "No matter what happens." She looked meaningfully at the baby who was now thrashing in frustration. She patted his back and he hiccuped.

Dirk suddenly realized he didn't even know if the child was male or female. "A boy?" he asked.

She nodded. "He seems healthy." She drew a shaky breath. "Now we need to find his mother."

"Do you . . ." Dirk heaved a sigh. "Do you really think Lady Elizabeth is capable of abandoning her own child?" The words sounded almost as bad as the deed itself, but he had to ask.

Molly contemplated the question for several moments. "I . . . I'm not sure. I don't want to believe it." She squeezed her eyes shut, then reopened them to meet his gaze, her expression sober. "But . . ."

He nodded in response just as the door opened. Ray walked in holding the pan with a rag wrapped around its handle. Zane followed with his weapon now holstered.

"Soup's on," Ray said with a cockeyed grin.

Dirk gritted his teeth, remembering not to fall for his half brother's false charm again. He'd done that last time—a huge error in judgment.

Molly sat with the squirming baby in her lap and Ray placed the pan on the crate. "Is that you?" he asked, pointing to the woman in the portrait.

Molly's lower lip trembled as she took the spoon Ray handed to her. "My mother." She cleared her throat and uncovered the mush, spooning a bit of it onto the inside of her wrist, then wiping it off on her skirt. "The babe is me."

"Oh." Ray straightened, appearing chagrined. "Was . . . Slim your father?"

Her gaze darted up to meet Ray's. "You knew him?"

"Only by name." Ray shrugged. "Desperado ran him off last time he tried to come back to this claim. Told him he could have it back when he was through with it."

"And you helped him, no doubt." Dirk waited while his half brother turned to face him. "And did you know who he was when you killed him?"

A muscle twitched in Ray's jaw. "I've never killed anyone." He drew a deep breath. "Desperado did all the killing."

"Convenient to blame someone who isn't here to defend himself," Dirk said, folding his arms. "Isn't it?"

"I believe him." Molly's voice drifted up from where she sat trying to spoon thin mush into the baby's mouth. Most of it ran down the sides of the child's face and even into his ears, but it appeared that some of it was making it into his empty belly. "We're talking about my da's murderer, and I believe Ray is innocent," she repeated, pinning Dirk with her gaze.

Dirk saw resolve and determination in Molly's eyes. "Fair enough," he said, turning his attention back to Ray as Molly resumed trying to feed the baby. "Who's Desperado?"

"Wish I knew."

"So you're claiming someone named Desperado killed both those men, but you don't know who he is?"

"That's right." Ray hooked his thumb through his belt and waited.

"And you don't know where Lady Elizabeth went or if she'll be back?"

An expression of loss crossed Ray's face and Dirk wondered. Did his half brother care for the mother of his child? Had her abandonment wounded him?

Don't, Dirk. Don't care.

"I have no idea where she went or if she'll ever come back." Ray sighed and walked across the room, raking his fingers through his hair in much the same manner as Dirk often did, and like their father before them had.

"Damn." Dirk didn't want to notice family resemblance. But here it was, staring him in the face. Even Ray's voice reminded Dirk of his own. No wonder it had been so easy for him to pretend to be Dirk.

Zane sat in the corner, his arms folded, a knowing smile curving his mouth.

"What are you laughing at, old man?" Dirk asked, practically snarling.

Zane's grin widened. "The future."

Dirk shook his head and turned his attention back to Ray. "We're at an impasse on the killings and kidnapping then, but you'll go to jail for stage robbery anyway."

Ray nodded. "I reckon that's so."

Regret settled in Dirk's gut and burned like the fires of perdition. "Damn," he repeated.

"But you're forgetting something." The sound of Ray's voice barged into Dirk's thoughts.

"What?"

"I know more about Desperado than you do," Ray

said, a malicious smile spreading across his face. "And I know the devil will be back."

Molly gasped, and Dirk spared her a glance before he pinned his half brother with a look that would have intimidated most men. However, Ray Lovejoy wasn't most men. He stood his ground and his gaze never wavered.

"How do you know he'll be back?" Dirk finally asked, knowing that Molly waited for an answer.

"He'll be back for his share of the ransom."

"Ah." Dirk rubbed his chin with his thumb and forefinger. "And when is this event supposed to occur?"

"Well, we didn't settle on a time exactly." Ray shook his head. "Me and Desperado didn't part on good terms last time we talked."

"Oh?"

"Well . . ." Ray shot a sidelong glance at Molly. "I didn't take kindly to him killing those men."

Dirk saw more tears trailing down Molly's cheeks. "Damn."

"All we wanted—me and two old codgers—was enough money to go away." Ray sighed and shook his head. "They wanted to go somewhere warm for the winter." He choked a bitter laugh. "And I wanted a fresh start somewhere far away from here." He met Dirk's gaze, his expression sober.

"Yeah?" Dirk waited, swallowing the lump in his throat.

"Yeah." Ray looked away and added, "Away from here." He met Dirk's gaze again. "And you."

Twenty

Molly was torn. She didn't want to leave Dirk, yet she understood his reasoning. Someone had to take the baby to town where he could get proper nourishment. Dirk and Ray would wait here for Desperado to return for his share of the ransom, assuming the evil man didn't know Lady Elizabeth was gone.

Jeremiah fashioned a carrier for the child from a clean skirt she'd found in the satchel the highwaymen had believed was Lady Elizabeth's. The child was literally tied in front of Molly.

Dirk took her in his arms and kissed her soundly, and Molly returned his kiss without reluctance, though the baby made it difficult to get close enough. One positive development had come from all this. Now she saw a possible future for her and Dirk.

Together.

She melted into his kiss, careful not to crush the baby. Dirk's tongue mated with hers, making her ache for another, far more intimate contact. That one night they'd shared had fueled her dreams for days. And nights. She was beyond ready to experience Dirk's lovemaking again.

And again.

"You'd better go before I ravish you right here on

the ground," he murmured against her lips. "I want you so bad I can taste it."

"Mmm, let me see." She kissed him again, wishing she could meld her hips against his. Frustrated, she shifted slightly to the side, rewarded by the hard, throbbing length of him pressing against her hip. Now that she knew how wonderful being loved by Dirk could be, the yearning was even stronger. Breathlessly, she said, "Aye, I can taste it, too. And feel it."

"And you were planning to marry another woman?" Ray mumbled from his position near the mine entrance. "My, my, my."

Dirk eased himself away from Molly and cast his half brother a scathing glance. "Things change," he said with admirable self-control. "As *you* damned well know."

Ray nodded in agreement, and Dirk turned to face Molly again. "I'll come for you within three days."

"If you don't, I'll come after you." Molly lifted her chin a notch. "And don't you be thinking I won't, Dirk Ballinger."

He held his hands up in mock surrender. "I will *never* underestimate you again. Never." His expression grew solemn. "If Desperado doesn't show up by then, I don't reckon he ever will."

"He'll show." Ray's tone was ominous.

Dirk kept his hand on Molly's elbow as he turned to face his half brother. "You never said what this Desperado character looks like. I'd like to know so I can see him coming."

Molly was proud of Dirk for changing the subject, rather than arguing with his brother. More and more often, she had to remind herself that they were *half* brothers. They had no idea how much alike they really were.

"Easy to spot. I'd say he likes it that way," Ray said, folding his arms across his abdomen and leaning nonchalantly against the stone wall. "Bright gold hair and eyes."

Molly's breath caught and she felt Dirk stiffen at her side. "Jesus, Mary, and Joseph," she muttered, crossing herself. "It can't be."

"I've always had a bad feeling about that man," Dirk said. "So did my—our—father."

Frowning, Ray approached them, obviously deciding not to react to Dirk's mention of *their* father. "What man? Do you think you might know who Desperado is?"

Dirk drew a deep breath. "Maybe." He raked his fingers through his hair.

So did Ray.

Molly shook her head in amazement, then turned her attention back to more urgent matters. She forced herself to think back to the day of the stage robbery. The day of her da's murder and Lady Elizabeth's kidnapping.

"I can't remember what the killer looked like," she said, her voice sounding strange even to her own ears. "He was masked and wore a hat pulled low. But I keep thinking there's something else I should remember."

"His horse," Ray supplied, stepping away from his son, though his gaze rested on the sleeping infant with tenderness and, perhaps, regret. "It's as conspicuous as he is."

"His horse?" Dirk echoed, drawing his half brother's gaze. "What about his horse?"

"Same color as his ha—"

"Well, now. Isn't this a pretty picture?" a menacing voice said from the trees.

Dirk and Jeremiah both whirled toward the intruder,

reaching for their guns, but they froze when they saw the woman perched atop the golden horse, her mouth gagged, her hands bound. Her brown hair was matted to her head, her face streaked with dirt, her eyes round as saucers.

Molly gasped, her fists clenched at her sides. "Lady Elizabeth."

"Shit," Ray swore.

"You." Dirk shook his head, pointing at the man who stood holding the reins of the golden horse in one hand and a pistol in the other.

The pistol that killed Da.

"Desperado," Sheriff Templeton provided, his amber eyes glittering in the sunlight.

Ray held Lady Elizabeth's gaze, and Molly saw something pass between the two of them that gave her hope.

She suddenly remembered the small gun Lance had given her and wished fervently she had it in her pocket now. She rested her hand on the baby's back. Then again, she couldn't endanger the child.

"Are . . . are you all right?" Ray asked, his voice quiet but intense.

Lady Elizabeth's expression softened and she nodded, her eyes glittering with unshed tears.

Molly's heart broke, and she swallowed the tears clogging her own throat.

Templeton's gaze shifted to Ray. "Where's Luther and Teddy?"

"Gone." Ray's body quivered with tension.

Molly's heart went out to him. Dirk had to recognize the goodness in his brother, but right now they had to save Lady Elizabeth.

And themselves.

"The old coots took off as soon as that one started

howling," Ray said, pointing toward Lady Elizabeth, whose gaze now darted daggers at him. "Can't say I blame 'em."

Templeton snorted. "That's for sure. Leaves more of that ransom for us." He tilted his head backward toward his hostage. "She'd better not turn out to have been more trouble than she's worth." He swung his gaze back to Dirk. "If you get my meaning."

Dirk remained still, never taking his gaze off the man. Finally, he said, "I should've known."

Templeton wheezed a menacing chuckle. "Yeah, you should've." He took a few steps and the horse obediently followed. "Your old man never saw me coming." His eyes narrowed. "And neither did you."

"What the hell are you talking about?" Dirk's lips barely moved as he bit off the words.

"Your daddy's accident weren't no accident, cowboy," Templeton taunted. "Can't believe he never figured out how his horse got spooked that night."

"You?" Dirk shook his head. "Why?"

Templeton shrugged. "Revenge."

"Or jealousy, because he was a bigger man than you?"

Molly watched Templeton's expression darken, and fear pulsed through her. She couldn't—wouldn't—lose another man because of this evil, twisted sheriff.

She had to do something, but with the baby tied to her, there was nothing she *could* do without endangering the child.

"You didn't have to take the woman," Ray said, stepping toward the sheriff. "I would've given you your share, just like I said."

"I like to be in control, Lovejoy." Templeton chuckled low. "You're too much of a sissy."

Ray took another step and stopped again. "Because I don't believe in killing?" He lifted a shoulder as if he didn't have a care in the world. "If that makes me a sissy, then I'd rather be a sissy than a killer." His casual air belied his words.

Hear him, Dirk. Hear your brother.

Molly kept her gaze fixed on Lady Elizabeth, turning slightly so the woman could see her baby's face. As she'd hoped, Lady Elizabeth immediately reacted to the sight of her baby. Her eyes widened and her lips trembled. She reached toward Molly and the baby, a desperate expression in her eyes.

No, Lady Elizabeth couldn't possibly have abandoned her child.

There was more goodness in Ray than Dirk knew, and obviously there was more goodness in Lady Elizabeth than Molly had ever recognized. Or perhaps all this had both softened and hardened the woman after a lifetime of being waited on hand and foot.

Molly noticed Jeremiah creeping slowly away from the group, and she suspected he planned to circle back behind the sheriff and his hostage. She prayed Templeton wouldn't notice the quiet old Indian.

Keep his attention on us. Molly stepped to the side, toward Ray. Away from Jeremiah.

"One of the men you . . . you killed . . ." she began, her voice faltering. She cleared her throat and met the supportive gaze Dirk aimed her way. Did he realize what she was doing? "One of the men you killed was my da."

"Da?" Templeton frowned. "Father?"

Lady Elizabeth's eyes widened, then filled with sympathy.

"Aye, my father." She lifted her chin and took another small step toward Ray and the mine. From the corner of her eye, she noticed Dirk did as well.

Good. He understands.

"You killed my da." Anger crept into her tone, though she'd intended to remain calm. However, looking at the very man who'd snuffed out her da's life just when she'd found him infuriated her beyond reason. "You filthy murderer."

The child chose that moment to emit a blood-curdling wail. Templeton started at the sound, waving his pistol around as if trying to discern its source. "What the hell?"

From a tree Molly hadn't even seen Jeremiah climb, she watched him fly like a bird. He knocked Templeton to the ground and Ray bolted for Lady Elizabeth. Dirk rushed forward and slammed his boot heel down on Templeton's wrist. With his other foot, Dirk kicked the pistol out of his reach.

"You're going to hang, Templeton," Dirk said, his voice filled with hate. "In Estes Park, in front of the people you *pretended* to serve."

Templeton sputtered and swore, but he made no effort to move. Ray had Lady Elizabeth off the horse and was untying her hands. He eased the gag from her mouth and shocked them all—mostly Lady Elizabeth—by kissing her soundly on the lips.

"I'll be damned," Dirk muttered, bending down to haul Templeton to his feet.

Molly retrieved the pistol and held its weight with both hands while Jeremiah bound Templeton's wrists behind his back. For a few terrifying moments, she wanted to pull the trigger. Mother Mary help her, but she wanted to take his miserable life. She burned to do it—to kill this man as he had killed her da.

Tears stung her eyes and she blinked, then looked up and met Dirk's gaze. His expression said he understood. After all, this horrible devil had blinded his da and murdered hers. Aye, of course he understood.

But his gaze also promised Molly that justice would be served. She didn't have to take a human life with her own hands to prove anything. Not now. Not ever.

For she couldn't have lived with herself if she did. Aye, she could kill to protect another, but not merely for revenge.

Once Jeremiah had bound not only Templeton's wrists, but his ankles as well, Dirk released him to the old Indian's capable hands and went to Molly's side. He reached tentatively for the pistol still clutched in her trembling hands, and she relinquished it to him gratefully, then found herself enclosed in the protective circle of his embrace.

"I want my baby," Lady Elizabeth said, her voice weak and anxious. "Let me hold my baby."

Ray held her elbow and guided her to Molly, where he released the ties that held the infant safely in place. He carefully lifted the baby from the carrier and held him out to his mother's waiting arms.

"He's all right." Tears flowed freely down her face. "He's all right."

"He's *hungry,*" Ray said.

Dirk chuckled, as did Molly. The baby seemed to sense Lady Elizabeth was his mother and that she had the nourishment his tiny body craved.

"Well. Then I shall feed him," Lady Elizabeth said, walking into the mine with Ray at her side.

"I'll be damned," Dirk repeated.

Molly brushed her tears aside and said, "I do believe Lady Elizabeth Summersby has met her match."

Dirk left Molly and Lady Elizabeth at Beth Anne's Room and Board, then proceeded to the center of town with Zane, Ray, and the now gagged and bound Kevin

Templeton. Between the three of them, they had enough witnesses to ensure the crooked sheriff hanged.

Molly's testimony regarding the stage holdup and killings would clinch it, but Dirk wanted to spare her if at all possible. She'd suffered enough by losing her father.

He cast a side glance at his half brother. What the hell was he going to do about Ray? Part of Dirk still demanded vengeance. Another part—a growing part—wanted to forgive and forget.

He sighed as they brought their horses to a stop before the Serendipity Jail. Zane dismounted and went inside, leaving Dirk and Ray alone with their prisoner.

"Can I ask you a favor, Dirk?" Ray said, breaking the silence.

The man had a lot of nerve asking for any favors after all the trouble he'd caused, but Dirk found himself nodding instead of saying so.

"I know I've done you wrong, and I'm sorry for that." Ray shoved his hat back from his face, and the sun glinted off his bright green eyes.

His Ballinger eyes.

"Go on," Dirk said, more confused than he'd ever been.

"I'm going to jail. We both know that."

"Probably."

"I know this is a lot to ask—a helluva lot more than I have a right." Ray sighed and leaned closer, his expression intense. "Will you . . . let me marry Lady Elizabeth before I go to jail, and will you give her and our son a place to live until I can come for them?"

Dirk studied his half brother for several moments, remembering the agony of betrayal. And, much to his dismay, he also remembered the joy he'd felt last year upon believing he had found a brother who would stay and become part of the family.

"*Will* you come back for them?" Dirk asked, though the answer would not affect his decision. He asked to help him gauge Ray's motives. He needed to know for himself.

"I promise," he said. "Elizabeth is the most confounding female I've ever known, but . . ."

A smile tugged at Dirk's lips, but he held it in check. "I understand." He nodded. "They can stay permanently, if need be."

"Thanks." Ray exhaled a long, slow breath, as if he'd been holding it forever. "I appreciate it."

"You know something, Ray?"

"What?"

"If you'd never gone to England pretending to be me, Lady Elizabeth and Molly would never have come to Colorado."

"I reckon that's so." A knowing smile curved Ray's lips. "I saw the way you kissed her. Looked serious to me."

"Very serious. I plan to marry the woman." Dirk shoved his hat back, wondering how to approach the matter of the baby's name. "Do you understand why I offered to marry Lady Elizabeth?"

"I didn't at first." Ray cleared his throat. "Then I remembered . . ."

Templeton grunted from where he was slung over his palomino's saddle. "Shut up, Desperado, before I do what I'm just aching to do." Dirk said, turning his attention back to his half brother. "You remembered what I offered you last year."

Ray's face reddened and he looked down, then met Dirk's gaze with an intensity that made Dirk hold his breath.

"You offered me a dream. A name." Ray shook his head. "It's what I always wanted, and turning it down was the biggest mistake I've ever made." He looked away again. "I'm sorry for that now." He looked back and sighed. "I'm sorry for a lot of things."

Dirk's heart pressed upward against his throat and he drew a deep breath, knowing what he had to do. "The offer stands," he said, smiling when Ray appeared shocked. "On one condition."

Ray mopped perspiration off his forehead, then pinned Dirk with his gaze. "Name it."

"You give that boy his rightful name."

Ray's eyes glittered and he rubbed them with his thumbs, then cleared his throat. "That's more'n I deserve, but I thank you." He smiled and looked toward the jailhouse. "I guess the wedding will be have to be here." He released a resigned sigh.

"We'll see." Dirk was afraid to think too far ahead. Right now he just wanted to trust his instincts, and every one he had insisted he was doing the right thing. "Just let me do all the talking to the sheriff. Deal?"

Ray lifted one shoulder. "What do I have to lose?"

Dirk flashed him a grin. "Good point."

The jailhouse door opened and Zane walked out with a stoop-shouldered sheriff. "So this here's the notorious Desperado?"

"I'm afraid so," Dirk said, sorting through it all as he spoke. "Also known as Sheriff Kevin Templeton of Estes Park, Colorado."

The sheriff released a low whistle. "You don't say?" He grabbed a handful of Templeton's hair and tilted his head up to look at his face. "This town was overdue some excitement, but I reckon the folks down in Estes Park'll wanna host your hangin'." The aging lawman straightened and rubbed his lower back. "Now if I can impose on you younguns to haul his sorry ass into a cell, we'll untie him and wire the circuit judge."

"My pleasure," Dirk and Ray said in unison.

They dragged Desperado off his golden horse and delivered him to the dank cell inside. After the cell door closed and the sheriff turned the key, he asked them all to sign statements for the judge.

Dirk's mind churned through a sketchy plan as they made their statements for the lawman. Only a few people knew Ray Lovejoy was Dirk Ballinger's half brother. Therefore, no one would suspect Ray Ballinger was anyone other than Dirk's long, lost brother. A sense of closure and certainty washed through Dirk as he met his half brother's gaze.

Dirk smiled at Ray and said, "We'll be back to sign those statements before we head home."

"Home?" Ray echoed, swallowing hard.

"Don't ask questions," Zane whispered, winking.

"First . . ." Dirk met his half brother's gaze and knew he was doing the right thing.

The only thing.

"We have a wedding to attend."

The sheriff grinned, displaying a shiny gold tooth. "You don't say?" He nodded approvingly. "Just leave me your names and where you're stayin' in case anythin' comes up."

"We'll be at Beth Anne's Room and Board on the edge of town." Dirk met Ray's gaze as he spoke. "Just ask for Dirk or Ray . . . Ballinger."

Dirk paused at the summit to gaze down into the valley that cradled most of the Ballinger Ranch. Molly brought Sadie near and reached over to cover his hand with hers.

"Are you nervous?" she asked.

He didn't answer, but a voice from behind them did.
"I am," Ray said.

Dirk twisted around and gave his half brother a nod.
"No need." A smile tugged at his mouth. "Just let me
do all the talking."

"Is this a habit of yours, Dirk?" Ray chuckled.
"Seems I've heard that before."

"Worked, didn't it?" Dirk grinned openly, then
turned to look at his ranch again. No, it wasn't only
his ranch now. He would make arrangements to share
it with his brother.

Some niggling doubts remained in the back of Dirk's
mind, but as long as Ray remained at the ranch and
behaved like a Ballinger, no one need ever learn he
was once known as the notorious Ray Lovejoy. As far
as Dirk was concerned, that was past, and only Ray
could decide whether to reveal his secret to anyone.
Dirk had a pretty good hunch that would never happen.

He sighed and turned his palm toward Molly's, giving her hand a squeeze. "Are you ready to face them?"

"Aye." She lifted her chin, her eyes sparkling. "I
know in my heart they'll understand why we deceived
them."

Dirk gave a nod and glanced back at Lady Elizabeth.
He'd had serious reservations about her riding so soon
after giving birth, but she had insisted, and even the
doctor in Serendipity had announced that both she and
her son were in perfect health.

Amazingly, she had complained very little during
their journey and had carried her son in the pack Zane
designed. Even the baby seemed content now that he
had his mother back.

"Let's go home," Dirk said, then led the group down
the pass toward the ranch house.

By the time they reached the circular drive in front of the house, several people had gathered on the porch to meet them. He recognized Clyde first, and a pang of guilt hit him like a fist. How could he have ever doubted that man? Hell, he had doubted them all for a while. Even Molly.

Fool. But Dirk was over all that doubt now. At last.

His gaze drifted to Ida, standing beside Clyde. She appeared nervous and had her hands clasped in front of her. Lance sat in a chair. His arm was in a sling and his shirt merely draped over his shoulders, revealing bandages wrapped around his torso.

"What happened to you, Lance?" he called as he dismounted, then assisted Molly.

"Got gored," Lance said, trying to rise, but Elena appeared behind his chair and placed a restraining hand on his shoulder.

The young woman whispered something in Lance's ear, and Lance blushed clear to his ears. "So it's like that," Dirk muttered.

Molly whispered, "Thank you, Mother Mary."

He shot her a questioning glance, but she merely smiled. "Women." He wisely smiled as he spoke.

"Gored?" Dirk turned his attention back to Lance. "How?"

"He was showin' off for Elena." Clyde came down the steps and extended his hand toward Dirk. "Welcome home, boss."

Dirk shook the man's hand, reminded how fortunate he was to have such a foreman. "Thanks for keeping things under control."

"I hope you still feel that way after I tell you everythin'." Clyde grinned at Dirk's arched brow, then inclined his head toward the others and whispered, "Lovejoy?"

Dirk shook his head, his expression solemn. He'd learn what all had transpired at the ranch during his absence later. "Ray, come on over here and meet everybody."

Ray left Lady Elizabeth with Molly and joined Dirk at the base of the steps. He removed his hat and Dirk heard him swallow hard.

"I'd like you all to meet my half—my brother, Raymond Ballinger."

Ida gasped and gripped the arm of Lance's chair for support.

"He's a Ballinger now . . . in every way." Dirk expected someone to comment, but they all waited silently. "Ray and the real Lady Elizabeth got married in Serendipity."

Lady Elizabeth came forward to stand beside her husband, her son in her arms.

"A baby." Ida came down the steps, gushing and making much of the tiny infant.

That was easy enough. Dirk smiled to himself. "The woman you thought was Lady Elizabeth is really Molly Riordan." He reached behind him and took Molly's hand, drawing her to his side. "I've asked her to be my wife, and she's agreed."

"You did?" Molly gaped at him. "I didn't hear any asking, Dirk Ballinger."

"I didn't?" He blinked, watching her eyes shoot sparks. A sinking sensation swept through him. "I didn't. Oh."

She shook her head.

"I'm going to," he said, smiling, but her expression remained stern. "No?"

She lifted a shoulder and looked away. He would have to remedy his oversight very soon. He swallowed hard, trying to remember where he'd left off with all the introductions.

"Molly is the woman I *want* to become my bride," he corrected, not looking at her as he spoke. "If she's willing."

"We won't know until you do the asking," she said. "Will we?"

He cast her a sidelong glance, and the impish expression in her eyes nearly unmanned him. The woman was too alluring—dangerously so. Damnation, but he loved her.

"I guess we won't," he said, his voice low and filled with promise. He hoped.

"A wedding?" Ida reached for Dirk as if she would hug him, but she stopped short. "I'm so happy for you both."

"We had a wedding," Lance said from his chair on the porch.

Dirk patted Ida's shoulder, confused by her sudden display of emotion. "Did you now?" He looked at Lance and winked. "Did one of our wranglers get caught by one of those town girls?"

"Weren't nothin' like that," Clyde said, moving closer to Ida and taking her hand. "Me'n Ida got hitched."

Stunned, Dirk looked from one to the other, then released a long, slow breath. "I'll be damned." He laughed quietly and shook Clyde's hand again, then kissed Ida's cheek. "I had no idea, but congratulations to the both of you." Another thought dampened his joy for them. "As long as you're planning to stay on here, that is."

"As long as we're welcome," Ida said, drawing a deep breath. "There's a lot more I have to tell you." Her gaze darted between Dirk and Ray. "Inside?"

Suspicion slithered through Dirk, and he stiffened. What did they have to tell him that couldn't be said here and now? However, he respected both Clyde and Ida too much to question their motives in front of the others. Resolve settled in his gut and he nodded.

Ida drew a deep breath and held it, then gave him a quivery smile. "All of you, come," she said.

Twenty-one

Dirk was considerably relieved when Ray announced he wanted to help his exhausted wife and baby get settled. Whatever Ida had to tell him must be significant, and he didn't want anything to rattle Ray's already precarious sense of belonging.

Dirk had gone from having no family to a brother, a sister-in-law, a nephew, and—he prayed—a bride-to-be. He glanced at Molly after they all gathered in the parlor. She accepted a glass of sherry from Clyde, though Dirk had never seen her partake of spirits before. She perched on the edge of the davenport, her spine rigid and her lips set in a thin line. Her hand trembled slightly as she lifted the small glass to her lips. The first sip made her cough and gasp, but she took another one a moment later.

He really had intended to propose—so much so, he thought he had. *Really stupid, Ballinger.* But so much had happened in such a short time. His throat tightened as he remembered the loss of her father. He would make this all up to Molly. Very soon.

Clyde helped Lance get settled in a chair, then poured himself and Dirk each three fingers of bourbon. He shot a questioning glance at Ida. At her nod, he poured a much smaller portion for Lance, splashing water into the glass as well.

Dirk took a sip of bourbon and savored the slow burn it ignited in his throat and gut. "Thanks, Clyde," he said, turning his attention to Ida. "Now, why don't you tell me what's on your mind?"

Ida fidgeted with her glass and took a huge swallow, then set the glass on the table. She pinned Dirk with her gaze. "My name isn't Ida Jensen." She shook her head. "No, it is my name, but not my entire name."

"All right." Dirk had no idea what this was leading to, but he had a feeling it would take a while. With a weary sigh, he sat beside Molly on the davenport. "I'm listening." He slid closer to her and felt her stiffen.

"My name is—was—Prudence," Ida continued.

Dirk looked up and met Ida's gaze again. Her eyes glistened and several tears spilled over the rims to trail down her face. She removed her spectacles and wiped them on her apron, then she replaced them and looked right at him. "I'm your mother."

He clamped his jaw tightly and shook his head. "My mother died in childbirth when I was three." His blood roared through his veins as he watched this woman he'd trusted for years lie to him. "What kind of sick game are you playing?"

Clyde stepped behind Ida's chair and rested his hand on her shoulder. "It ain't a game, Dirk," he said, drawing Dirk's gaze to his craggy face. "Your ma didn't die. Your pa drove her away."

Molly reached over and rested her hand on Dirk's thigh. He wanted to grab her and run from this room, but he didn't. He had to see this through.

Your pa drove her away.

Was this another of Edward Ballinger's legacies?

Dirk drew a deep breath and gripped Molly's hand in his. No matter what happened here with Ida and Clyde, Dirk wasn't letting Molly go. The feel of her hand in his anchored him, and he faced Ida and Clyde again.

"All right," Dirk said. "Tell me how, why, and when my father drove my mother away." Sarcasm edged his voice, but he didn't care. They were the ones who had something to prove. Not him.

"You're my brother, too," Lance said, smiling. He took a sip of the watered down bourbon and made a face, then set the glass aside. "Ma told me so."

Dirk shook his head. They'd dragged Lance into this deceit, too? No, he didn't believe that. He'd known Clyde and Ida most of his life. They wouldn't knowingly hurt Lance. Hell, they wouldn't knowingly hurt anyone.

That meant . . .

"It's true?" He drained his glass and set it down with surprising reserve. What he really wanted was to smash it. Instead, he clung to Molly's hand and faced Clyde and Ida.

No, not Ida.

"Mother?" His voice had an odd catch, and he cleared his throat. "Lance is the baby I . . ."

She nodded and rose, tears streaming down her face as she dropped to her knees in front of Dirk. She took his free hand in both of hers and gazed up at him.

"I . . . I used to sing to you, and you helped me carry water to the apple trees," she said, a distant expression in her voice. "I loved you more than anything." Her voice broke and she bit her lower lip. "I'm so sorry, Dirk."

It all started to make sense. Dirk remembered something he'd found in his father's safe after his death, and he rose, pulling Molly up with him. He looked down at the woman who claimed to be his mother and offered her his hand. She rose and Dirk stood holding both women's hands.

He met Clyde's patient gaze, then looked at Lance. His brother.

My God. Dirk had found Ray and now his mother and younger brother, as well. Could it be true?

Again, his thoughts turned to the document in his father's safe. "Come to Father's study," he said. "I have something to show you."

A few moments later, they all stood by while Dirk opened the wall safe and withdrew a leather folder. He sifted through the contents until he found the strange document, then withdrew it. Holding his breath, he unfolded it and handed it to Ida.

"I found this after Pa died," he said. "I didn't understand it then." Dirk drew a deep breath and released it slowly. "But if you're telling me the truth . . ."

"I am." Ida's hands trembled as she read the document, then her face crumpled and she doubled over. Clyde caught her before she collapsed.

"You've seen this before." It was a statement rather than a question, for Dirk suddenly saw the truth with a certainty that stunned him. "Edward Ballinger was a bigger bastard than I knew."

Dirk also knew the contents of that document would not be read aloud. His gaze settled on Lance—his brother. The baby his father had wanted to lock away from society. Dirk's gut burned as if the devil himself had crawled down his throat.

He reached for his mother's hands and Clyde released her. A moment later, his mother was in his arms, clinging to him and weeping.

Vague memories of planting trees and singing and baking cookies filled his mind. His mother had been a golden-haired woman then, and now he could see her clearly in Ida. Why hadn't he realized that day she'd shown up looking for work after Edward's accident?

"Ma," Dirk croaked, his own eyes filling with tears. "Welcome home. Welcome home."

Clyde cleared his throat and wiped tears from his eyes, helping Lance get close enough to hug his brother, too.

Dirk gazed down into this face he knew so well—the face of his brother. He had two brothers now. *Two*. He embraced Lance and handed the vile document his father'd had drawn up decades ago to Clyde. Lance would never know how evil their father had been. Never.

"Burn this," Dirk said quietly, then turned to Molly and took both her hands in his. He dropped to one knee, gazing up into her eyes. "Forgive me for not doing this sooner, but I've been sorely distracted."

She smiled through her tears and laughed gently. "Aye, you have at that." Her eyes glowed with love.

Dirk's heart stuttered. Her smile always had that effect on him. "I love you. Right here, right now, in front of all these witnesses," he said, "I'm asking you to be my bride, Molly Riordan."

"In front of his own mother," Clyde muttered. "Now *that's* love."

Molly visited Da's new grave in the Ballinger cemetery immediately following the wedding. Dirk stood at her side, never uttering a single complaint about her odd request.

"Da, I married Dirk Ballinger today," she said, beaming a smile at her husband, then she looked down at the headstone. "Thank you for looking after me, Da."

Her voice broke and she felt Dirk's hand rest at the

small of her back, giving her strength." You and Ma be happy in heaven," she said, then turned into her husband's embrace.

A few moments later, they returned to the house while the reception was still in full swing. Several neighbors had gathered for the big event, bestowing gifts on both newly married couples. Dirk whirled Molly around the dance floor. She felt like a princess in the dress Ida had made for her. Everything was just perfect.

After the waltz, Dirk grabbed two plates filled with cake and dragged Molly up the stairs to the room they would share as husband and wife. She didn't have to ask his motives.

He placed the cake on the bedside table, then kicked the door shut and turned the key in the lock. She licked her lips in anticipation.

"Ray and Elizabeth were arguing again," Dirk said as he turned to face her, leaning casually against the closed door.

"Aye, but I finally understand those two," she said, walking slowly toward her husband. "They *enjoy* the arguing. Even when they're insulting each other, there are sparks in their eyes that have nothing to do with anger."

Dirk chuckled. "I think you may be right." With a hooded gaze, he crooked a finger at Molly. "Come here, Mrs. Ballinger."

Before she drew her next breath, Molly found herself being thoroughly kissed. She had never considered herself a woman capable of swooning, but in this man's arms she just might. Breathless, she pulled back. "I've missed you."

He reached behind her and released the buttons and hooks holding her gown in place. A moment later, it

lay in a pool of white lace at their feet. "Oh, dear," she said, pushing his jacket from his broad shoulders. "Our clothes are mussed."

He let his jacket fall to the floor to join her dress, then reached for the straps of her chemise and eased them slowly downward. He stopped with the fabric dangling precariously from the tips of her taut nipples. Molly's breath caught as she watched him watch her.

He flashed her a devilish grin and his gaze drifted down the length of her. He reached out and released the ribbon holding her petticoat in place.

It landed with a swoosh and she stepped out of it, unashamed. Toward him. "What took you so long, Mr. Ballinger?" Her voice sounded strange. Huskier. Swallowing hard, she loosened the studs of his shirt and eased her fingers inside against his taut, muscular chest. "Mmm."

"Mmm?" he echoed, sliding her bloomers down her hips. "What have we here?"

She unbuckled his belt and made short order of his trouser buttons. "Aye, what indeed?" she breathed, moving closer as she slipped her hands into his waistband and cupped him. "You're so hot."

"On fire." He scooped her into his arms, and within moments they were both naked on the bed in a patch of silver moonlight that streamed through the curtains. "I love you so much," he murmured.

"And I'm the luckiest woman alive for that," she said. "I love you."

Dirk reached for the plates of wedding cake he'd brought upstairs with them and scooped up a glob of frosting. Wickedness danced in his eyes as he decorated her with the fluffy confection.

"What—"

Her question died on a gasp as he proceeded to lick

and kiss the sticky substance away. "Oh, my," she whispered, melting beneath the warmth of his mouth.

Later—much later—Molly stared out the window, loving the feel of Dirk's naked body stretched out beside her. A star arced across the heavens and she bolted upright, pointing.

"Did you see it, Dirk?" she asked, her voice filled with wonder. "A shooting star. Gram always said to make a wish on a shooting star." She squeezed her eyes shut and thought her most fervent wish.

"Did you make a wish?" he asked, love and laughter in his voice as he pulled her down beside him again.

A strange and wondrous sensation washed over her and she took his hand, pressing it to her lower abdomen. "Aye," she said. "But I think you granted it a bit earlier."

He pulled her close for a lingering kiss, then traced the line of her jaw with the tip of his finger. "I can't think of anything I want more than babies with you, Molly Riordan."

"Ah, and what about the making of those babies, Mr. Ballinger?" she asked in a thick Irish brogue.

He kissed her again, then rested on his elbow to hold her gaze in the moonlight. "You are, and always will be, the very best part of the rest of my life."

She knew exactly what he meant, for she felt the same way about him. "I thought you said this was no place for a lady, Mr. Ballinger."

His low chuckle vibrated through her. "So I believed," he whispered.

"Aye, but it's the perfect place for *this* lady."

Embrace the Romances of
Shannon Drake

ABOUT THE AUTHOR

Since publication of her first novel in 1995, Deb Stover has received the 1999 and 1997 Pikes Peak Romance Writers' Author of the Year Award, the 1999 Dorothy Parker Award of Excellence, a 1998 Heart of Romance Readers' Choice Award, six *Romantic Times* nominations and the Reviewer's Choice Award for Best Innovative Historical of 1999, and more than a dozen *Affaire de Coeur* Readers' Choice Awards. Five of her first eight books received the *Romantic Times* "Top Pick" rating, and *Publishers Weekly* called her "clever, original, and quick-witted." For more information, visit www.debstover.com. You can write to Deb at P.O. Box 274, Maryhurst, OR 97036-0274.